MURDER AT KENSINGTON PALACE

Books by Andrea Penrose

Murder on Black Swan Lane 2017

Murder at Half Moon Gate 2018

Murder at Kensington Palace 2019

MURDER AT KENSINGTON PALACE

Andrea Penrose

KENSINGTON BOOKS
www.kensingtonbooks.com

KENSINGTON BOOKS are published by

Kensington Publishing Corp.
119 West 40th Street
New York, NY 10018

All Kensington titles, imprints, and distributed lines are available at special quantity discounts for bulk purchases for sales promotion, premiums, fund-raising, educational, or institutional use. Special book excerpts or customized printings can also be created to fit specific needs. For details, write or phone the office of the Kensington Special Sales Manager: Attn. Special Sales Department. Kensington Publishing Corp, 119 West 40th Street, New York, NY 10018. Phone: 1-800-221-2647.

Library of Congress Card Catalogue Number: 2019940166

ISBN-13: 978-1-4967-2281-2
ISBN-10: 1-4967-2281-7
First Kensington Hardcover Edition: October 2019

ISBN-13: 978-1-4967-2283-6 (ebook)
ISBN-10: 1-4967-2283-3 (ebook)

10 9 8 7 6 5 4 3 2 1

Printed in the United States of America

To Ellen M. Iseman

The best of friends.
Thanks for always being ready with laughter and a bon mot
when The Muse is misbehaving.

PROLOGUE

A graceful melody wafted through the air, the low, sonorous sounds of the violoncello deepened by the curling plumes of spice-scented cheroot smoke. The musicians were playing Haydn's String Quartet Op. 20, No. 4, a great favorite of the host, and the violin's sinuous notes danced above the background noise of gentlemanly bonhomie. *The clink of crystal. The fizz of champagne. The deep-throated buzz of masculine conversation, punctuated by well-mannered laughter.*

"Amidst all the turmoil of war and man's savagery toward his fellow man, it's edifying to see some pockets of civilized splendor still exist to celebrate intellectual achievement," observed Count Rumford to the half dozen gentlemen gathered around him. High overhead, the classical deities of the frescoed ceiling beamed down upon them with lordly benevolence. "Our royal duke's soirees always provide an enjoyable evening of cerebral conversation for our society of scholars." A smile. "Along with very fine wine."

"Unlike his reprobate brother, the Prince Regent, Sussex does have some redeeming qualities," replied Sir Joseph Banks, the elderly president of the Royal Society, as he surveyed the aristocratic crowd from the confines of his wheeled Bath chair. "His interest in science and art harkens back to the enlightened court of his great-grandmother, Caroline of Ansbach," he added somewhat querulously. "Now, *those* were the days."

"Come, come, you can't claim to be speaking from experience," chided Rumford dryly. "You're not *quite* as old as Methuselah, Sir Joseph."

The comment drew a grudging laugh. "No. And yet, as my gout and the other unpleasant accompaniments of encroaching old age worsen, I often feel over nine hundred years old." Banks drew in a mouthful of brandy, which sparked a reproving look from his personal physician. "As the Reaper's blade swings ever closer, I find myself thinking of how I shall miss seeing all the new scientific discoveries that are looming on the horizon."

"As shall I," replied Rumford regretfully. "Our ships will soon be furling their sails and sinking beneath the waves, leaving the exploration and adventuring to the young."

"A lament that all of us mere mortals make sooner or later." Justinian DeVere, a courtly gentleman whose thick mane of hair was liberally threaded with silver, paused in passing and lifted his drink in salute to the group. "The thrill of discovery is seductive for those of us who belong to scientific societies, such as this one. We don't wish to give it over to Death's grasp."

"And yet we must." Banks gave a wry snort. "We live, we die." He paused for a moment to watch one of the duke's beloved pet birds fly into the room and perch atop a marble bust of Sir Robert Boyle. "It's the natural order of the world, from the tiniest organisms we see in our microscopes to us supreme beings."

"So it seems," agreed DeVere. "And yet, all of us would agree there is much we don't know about the workings of the universe. Perhaps the secret of Life is out there, waiting to be discovered by one of our young luminaries."

"Hear, hear," murmured Banks. "Ideas that many considered no better than lunatic ramblings a century ago are now at the forefront of science."

"Yes, as Humboldt so eloquently says, Reason and Imagination lead us to new ways of seeing the cosmos," replied DeVere. "There are those who believe Nature will be stripped of its magic if we learn all its secrets. But I think that knowledge will never kill the creative force of imagination. Rather, it inspires excitement, astonishment—and a sense of wonder."

Banks nodded thoughtfully. "An interesting point."

"Only consider the new discoveries of Volta, and his voltaic battery. The possibilities are exciting. If—" began DeVere, only to be interrupted by Rumford, who abruptly hailed two young men who had just entered the main room from one of the side salons.

"Ah, speaking of our young luminaries—here are the Golden Geminis, our bright flames for the future! Come here, my dear fellows, and allow me to introduce you to Sir Joseph," he called in a booming voice. To Banks, he added, "Enough prosing from us old men. Lord Chittenden and his younger brother represent the new generation of our country's intellectuals."

Seeing that his own observations had been nipped in the bud, DeVere narrowed his eyes in irritation and then moved away to join another group of scholars.

The young men squeezed past the crowd at the refreshment table and hurried to acknowledge the count's summons.

"It's a great honor to meet such a legendary man of science, Sir Joseph," said Cedric, Lord Chittenden, giving a deferential bow to Banks after greeting the others. "Though Count Rumford is being way too kind. My brother and I are merely callow dabblers—"

"On the contrary, Chittenden. True, you have much to learn, but the two of you embody the future," said Rumford. "Your contributions to our weekly discussions at the Royal Institution show great imagination and curiosity. I sense great potential in your abilities. Indeed, I'm sure you will make meaningful contributions to the betterment of society."

"That is high praise indeed, milord." With a flush of pleasure darkening his cheekbones, Cedric acknowledged the compliment with a self-deprecating smile. "But—"

"But be assured my brother and I will do our best to live up to your expectations," interjected his younger sibling with an air of confidence.

"Yes, of course. My sentiments exactly." Another smile, though his eyes seemed to flick a warning at his companion. "As you see, Nicholas and I tend to think alike."

The clever remark drew appreciative chuckles from the older gentlemen. The brothers were twins, so close in appearance that acquaintances often had trouble telling them apart. Tall, golden-haired, and gifted with faces that mirrored the fine-boned masculine beauty of a Botticelli painting, they were fast becoming the darlings of the Royal Institution for both their boyish charm and scientific acumen since arriving from the North to take up residence in London several months ago.

"Let us toast to great thoughts and great expectations," said Rumford, and then gave a small cluck of concern on seeing their glasses were empty. "Ah, but you're both in need of more champagne." He moved away before the young men could demur, and returned a few moments later with two tapered flutes filled with sparkling wine.

"The first lesson that you young jackanapes must learn is that one *never* allows one's glass to be empty at gatherings like this," drawled Rumford. "Liquid refreshments keep the conversations well lubricated."

"Ah, well if you insist." Nicolas flashed a crooked grin and accepted the drinks. "Cedric and I certainly don't wish to disappoint," he said, turning to his brother with an exaggerated flourish.

Cedric hesitated, then dutifully took one of the glasses.

"To exploring beyond the current boundaries of science," said Nicholas with effervescent enthusiasm.

"Nicky," murmured Cedric softly, looking a little embarrassed at his brother's cocky outburst in front of London's leading men of science.

"That's the spirit!" applauded the count.

"Yes, to exploration," said Banks, staring meditatively at the last bit of brandy in his goblet before he raised it in salute. "And the never-ending discovery of new knowledge."

"The hour is late, Sir Joseph," said Banks's physician, discreetly taking hold of the Bath chair's handles as soon as the toasts were downed. "It's time to take you home."

"It's a cursed nuisance to grow old," grumbled the elderly scholar, surrendering his empty goblet with a scowl. "It appears I must bid you adieu," he added, giving a curt wave to the group as he was wheeled away.

After darting a look at the tall case clock in the corner of the room, Cedric gave an apologetic shrug. "My brother and I must be going as well."

"I daresay the prospect of more pleasurable company than a gaggle of aging intellectuals lies ahead," said Rumford with a wink.

"For Nicholas, perhaps, but not for me," answered Cedric politely. "Unfortunately, I have some pressing estate matters to review for the morrow, so I will be heading back to my town house."

"Poor Cedric—I shall take it upon myself to drown your sorrows." Looking a little unsteady on his feet, Nicholas allowed a laugh at his own witticism and clapped an arm around his brother's shoulder. "As we younger sons have no official duties, we must find other ways to keep boredom at bay." Another shaky laugh. "Come, we had better take our leave from the duke and be off."

After exchanging the requisite polite pleasantries, the pair hurried off to thank the Duke of Sussex and make their way out into the night.

The air had taken on a chill, the dampness forming serpentine swirls of mist. Stirred by the breeze, the ghostly pale vapor floated through the leafy shadows of the topiary trees lining the graveled walkways.

They paused, both taking a moment to look up at the stars playing hide-and-seek among the scudding clouds.

"Nicky," murmured Cedric. "If I may be allowed a word of counsel, I fear you're becoming a trifle too fond of brandy and wine. It does you no credit, especially among such a learned circle of gentlemen. A reputation for unsteadiness—"

"Ye gods, what a stiff-rumped prig you've become," interrupted Nicholas. "Since Father died and you inherited the title, your pompous prosing has become a dreadful bore." His eyes darkened. "Or perhaps it's *you* who are stirring the malicious whispers of my unsteadiness in order to distract attention from your own."

Cedric stared for a moment in mute shock. "T-That's a damnably unfair accusation—"

"Ha! You, of all people, aren't entitled to talk about fairness," jeered his younger brother. "Pray tell, where is the fairness in you getting everything simply by virtue of popping out of the womb a mere three minutes before I did?" Nicholas sucked in a harsh breath and wagged a warning finger. "As for unsteadiness, have a care, dear twin. I think you are treading on far more dangerous ground than I am."

Clenching his teeth, Cedric remained silent. There was no point in trying to reason with Nicholas when he was in the grip of such unreasonable anger. And besides, his own blood was now up. He had shared everything—*everything*—that could be shared. If the title could be sliced in two, he would have shared that, too! His brother had no cause for complaint.

As for his own activities here in London . . .

"Nothing to say?" Nicholas flashed a rude gesture and turned away. "Then you may take your lordly lecture and shove it back down your gullet."

"Arse," muttered Cedric as he watched his brother stalk away. Nicky's drinking was becoming worrisome, sparking volatile mood swings. A gentle chiding—the duty of an older brother, he told himself—was no reason for such caustic comments about acting the high-and-mighty lord. The mantle of responsibility, along with the title of Baron Chittenden, had only recently come to rest on his shoulders. And if truth be told, it was still an uneasy burden.

The devil take it—Nicky has no idea of its weight!

Granted, he may have strayed into making some unwise decisions recently, but he was taking steps to correct the lapse . . .

Cedric winced and pressed his palms to his throbbing temples. As for alcohol, he had drunk more than he was used to, and was feeling a little light-headed. Drawing a deep breath, he wandered deeper into the Palace gardens, trying to gather his wits. Perhaps a short stroll through the famous wiggly walks would help to clear his head before he headed out to the street to hail a hackney.

He dimly recalled that Queen Anne's Alcove, an architectural gem designed by Christopher Wren, was located nearby. Praised as a sanctuary of peace and beauty, it held a lovely covered seating area for quiet reflection . . .

On impulse, he cut across to one of the curling side pathways.

Crunch-crunch. It took a moment for his befuddled brain to realize that he was not the only one treading over the well-raked stones.

Is Nicky coming back to apologize?

Cedric slowly turned. Clouds covered the moon, and though the upper windows of the Palace were ablaze with light, the gardens were shrouded in shadows, the flitting black-on-black shapes blurring together with the dark silhouettes of the shrubbery. He squinted, trying to make out any sign of life within the amorphous gloom.

Nothing.

A figment of his cup-shot imagination, he decided. The champagne had begun to stir a bilious churning in his gut and it was now bubbling up to pound against his temples.

He continued on, though his steps were growing more erratic.

Crunch-crunch. Up ahead, Cedric spotted a marble structure of exquisite beauty rising out of the mist-swirled darkness. Classical columns flanked an arched opening in its center. Set beneath the vaulted ceiling of the semicircular space was a curved wooden bench built into the decorative dark oak paneling.

"Wren understood the exquisite beauty of symmetry," he murmured, taking a moment to gaze up in admiration before stumbling up the steps and taking a seat.

Stretching out his legs, Cedric released a pent-up breath and watched the moonlight flitter over the tips of his boots. Ivy ruffled against stone. Crickets chirped. From within the dark silhouette of the nearby boxwood hedge, a bird twittered a low, languid night song.

The cosmos was a wondrous place, alive with infinite possibilities and interconnections, he reminded himself, feeling his earlier agitation mellow into a pleasant fugue of wine and the ideas stirred by the scientific soiree.

It was heady stuff—to hear such learned men expound on the idea that scientific discovery involved passion, as well as the mere recording of information. That it demanded poetry, as well as facts . . .

Reason and imagination. Closing his eyes, Cedric felt a

warmth pulse through him as he mulled over such thoughts. This was why he had come to London. To be inspired by the great minds of the country's leading men of science, to be part of new discoveries . . .

A sudden bump, wool against wool, jarred him from his reveries as someone sat down beside him.

"Nicky?" he mumbled, shaking off his lethargy.

In answer, a gloved hand clamped down over his mouth. Cedric tried to pull away, but found himself caught in a viselike grip. Eyes widening in disbelief, he tried to scream, only to have the breath crushed from his lungs as his assailant slammed him back against the oak paneling.

No, no, no! It couldn't be!

He kicked out—an instant too late, as the steel-sharp knife blade slid between his ribs and pierced his vital organ.

The cloaked figure held his victim tenderly, letting the warm weight of the senseless body slump against his shoulder as he envisioned the heart shuddering to a stop, the blood ceasing to pulse through the veins.

"Rest easy, my dear Cedric. You won't have died in vain. This will all be for the greater good, I swear it."

He waited another long moment, inhaling the mist-chilled fragrances of the night. The clouds had blown off, leaving the black velvet of the heavens alive with a sparkling of diamond-bright stars.

A good omen, if one believes in such signs.

Taking out a large black silk handkerchief from his coat pocket, the assailant calmly wrapped it around the sleeve of his coat, then slowly withdrew the blade from Cedric's chest. Starlight skittered along the razor-sharp blade as it cut again through the night.

Swoosh, swoosh. The slashes were lightning quick, cutting through fabric and flesh. With a dancer's grace, he twisted away from the spill of wine-dark blood.

After unknotting the protective silk from his sleeve and carefully wrapping his prize in it, he took another few moments to appreciate the night's beauty, then rose and walked off, whistling softly.

Crunch-crunch. As the darkness deepened with impending rain, the nightingale's song quickly swallowed the receding notes of Beethoven's Third Symphony.

Sinfonia Eroica—the Heroic Symphony.

For tonight was a night for epic heroes.

CHAPTER 1

"M'lady, m'lady!"

Charlotte Sloane looked up from her drawing as two mud-encrusted boys peltered up the stairs and burst into her workroom.

"There's been another Bloody Butcher murder!" announced the one called Raven in a breathless rush.

"Oiy, and this time the victim's a titled toff!" piped up his younger brother, who was known as Hawk. "And—"

"And it's disgusting," cut in Raven. "Lilly the flower girl said—"

"Said it were so 'orrible the Bow Street Runner puked all over 'is boots," exclaimed Hawk, tripping over his tongue to be first in revealing the gory details. "Because—"

"Because the Butcher cut off one of the gent's bollocks!" finished Raven.

Holy hell. Though rarely shocked by man's viciousness toward his fellow man, Charlotte felt the blood drain from her face. Putting down her pen, she leaned back in her chair, for the moment too taken aback by the gruesome news to chide the boys about their filthy faces and less-than-perfect English.

These mutilation murders seemed to be taking a terribly sinister turn. The first two victims had been nameless vagrants, followed by a respectable tradesman.

And now an aristocrat.

What madman was on the loose?

"Who was the victim?" she asked, forcing herself to focus on the grim practicalities of the news.

Her livelihood as London's most popular satirical artist depended on feeding the public's insatiable appetite for scandal and depravity. And they looked to A. J. Quill to be the first to trumpet all the juicy details of the evils that man did to his fellow man—though the fact that a woman penned such scathing commentary was a well-kept secret. She would need to do a drawing of the crime by evening so the engravers could have it ready for sale in Fores's print shop for tomorrow morning.

"Lilly didn't know," answered Hawk. "She heard the news from one of the gardeners who found the toff."

"Where?" demanded Charlotte.

"Kensington Gardens," replied Raven. "The Duke of Sussex had a fancy party for some visiting men of science from Prussia last night at the Palace."

Science. The word stirred a pricking at the back of her neck.

"Word is," continued the boy, "the victim looks to be one of the guests. But Lilly said Bow Street's being tighter than a flea's ars—" He stopped and flashed an apologetic grin. "That is, the Runners are being closemouthed about any further details."

Her brows drawing together in a frown, Charlotte took a moment to think over what she had just heard. Augustus Frederick, the Duke of Sussex and sixth son of King George III, had a keen interest in scholarly subjects and was a member of the Royal Society, which, along with the Royal Institution, was the leading bastion of London's scientific minds. He often held lavish receptions for its members and guests in his apartments at Kensington Palace.

Given that such soirees usually included those who moved within the highest circles of Society, she couldn't help but wonder . . .

"If Lord Wrexford was there, he might know more about it," Charlotte mused aloud.

"You want for us to run along to Berkeley Square and ask?" volunteered Hawk, his pronunciation quickly improving. The earl's cook was very generous with sweets.

Charlotte hesitated. But pragmatism quickly overruled emotion. She needed information, and if Bow Street was keeping tight-lipped about the crime because the victim was an aristocrat, her usual sources wouldn't be of help.

"Yes," she answered, and quickly penned a short note. "If he hasn't risen from his lordly slumber . . ." A glance at the mantel clock showed it was well before noon. "Ask if you may wait for a reply."

Both boys bobbed a quick nod and clattered off with undisguised enthusiasm.

Her own feelings were a bit more ambiguous. *Wrexford.* A man of maddening complexities and contradictions. Though, conceded Charlotte, she was just as difficult.

A sigh. She and the Earl of Wrexford had first been drawn together when he was the main suspect in a gruesome murder. Through her network of informants, she had reason to believe him innocent and so they had grudgingly agreed to work together to find the real killer. A wary friendship had developed . . . though that was a far too simplistic description of their relationship.

They had recently collaborated on solving another complex murder, which had caused Wrexford to come within a hairsbreadth of death. She had helped to rescue him, and in the heat of the moment, both of them had revealed personal secrets and expressed certain emotions . . .

Which perhaps they were both regretting.

It had been a fortnight since his last visit, and she couldn't help but wonder whether he, like herself, felt a little rattled at having spoken—however obliquely—from the heart.

"What a pair we are," she muttered. "Prickly, guarded, afraid of making ourselves vulnerable."

Taking up her pen, Charlotte carefully cleaned the dried ink from its nib with a damp rag. As a rule, she tried not to brood over a decision once it was made. *Noli respicere*—don't look back. But much as she tried to return her thoughts to her unfinished sketch of the Prince Regent's latest peccadillo, she couldn't keep from asking herself whether it was wise to get involved in another murder with the earl.

A shiver, sharp as daggerpoints, danced down her spine as Charlotte recalled how the thought of losing Wrexford had shaken her to the core. The depth of her sentiment had frightened her. Weakness of any kind was dangerous. Only the strong survived.

"I *am* strong. I always have been," she whispered, trying to give some force to her breath.

Or am I?

Of late, so many of her defenses felt under siege. Caring too deeply made one vulnerable. Raven and Hawk, the two homeless, half-wild urchins she had found sheltering in her previous house, had taken hold of her heart in ways she had never expected. Charlotte couldn't say exactly how it had happened. They had started running errands to her network of informants in return for scraps of food, and . . .

And now, they had a snug little aerie in her attic, respectable clothing, and an Oxford-educated tutor giving them lessons several times a week. Ye gods, they even had fancy new names to go along with their avian monikers! *Thomas Ravenwood Sloane and Alexander Hawksley Sloane.* A smile touched her lips. However unconventional, they had become a family, tied together not by blood but by love.

Love. In that word lay the heart of her dilemma. It set off a tangle of conflicted emotions, and Charlotte wasn't quite sure how to go about unknotting them. Over the years, adversity had shaped her to think that in order to survive, one's core inner strength had to come from within. One couldn't count on others.

Now she wasn't so sure. And that was frightening.

Which brought her full circle back to Wrexford.

"Hell's bells, I'm simply asking him for some information," she muttered. "Neither of us is in any danger of being drawn into this murder." Forcing aside further thoughts on the earl, Charlotte dipped her now-pristine pen into the inkwell. Finishing the drawing of the Prince Regent was something she could control.

And besides, it was her art that paid for her independence. Despite all fears and uncertainties preying on her mind, that wasn't something she ever intended to give up.

Focused on her work, Charlotte lost all track of the time. It was the loud thump of the front door falling shut and a tandem shout from the boys announcing their return that drew her back to the present.

"Excellent," she murmured, anxious to learn what Wrexford had told them about the scientific soiree. However, that sentiment was quickly revised when the Raven added, "His Nibs has come along with us."

Repressing an oath, Charlotte glanced down at her paint-smudged cuffs before quickly tucking a few strangling strands of hair behind her ear.

"I thought I might as well come along and subject myself to your interrogation in person," drawled the Earl of Wrexford as she entered the downstairs parlor. "Knowing your infernal attention to detail, it seemed likely you would have so many questions, the Weasels would wear out their boots running back and forth between our residences."

"Weasels" was what Wrexford had dubbed the boys, much to their hilarity. They knew he had long ago forgiven Raven for sticking a knife in his leg during their first encounter.

"How *very* thoughtful of you, milord," replied Charlotte, matching his note of dry humor. "Would you care for—"

"Tea?" said the plain-faced, middle-aged woman, who had hurried out from the kitchen. "I've just set the kettle on the hob, Mrs. Sloane. And a pan of ginger biscuits are about to come out of the oven."

Ignoring the hungry looks from the boys, Charlotte raised an inquiring brow at the earl. As McClellan was still technically in his employ, she left the decision to him.

"Halloo, McClellan," said Wrexford with an amused smile. "I trust Mrs. Sloane isn't proving too terrible a taskmaster." He had dispatched the woman—whose arsenal of skills apparently included being a crack shot with a pistol—to stay with Charlotte after an intruder had broken into the house during their investigation of Elihu Ashton's murder. The arrangement had proved to have a number of practical advantages, and so she had remained as member of the unconventional household. Her somewhat nebulous duties included serving as a lady's maid on the rare occasions when Charlotte was required to venture into Polite Society, but most importantly, her presence allowed the earl to call at the house without violating the rules of propriety.

"I've no cause for complaint, milord," answered McClellan dryly. "No one has tried to kill us lately." A pause. "Though the lads do their best to slay any semblance of cleanliness to the floors and their clothing."

"Tsk, tsk," clucked the earl. "I would say no biscuits for the wicked—"

Hawk's grimy face pinched in horror.

"Except I happen to be famished," he finished.

"Now that we've performed all the necessary social graces," said Charlotte to McClellan, "might you kindly fetch the refreshments, so His Lordship and I can get down to business."

Assuming an air of innocence, Raven and Hawk fell in step behind the woman as she headed off for the kitchen.

The earl settled himself on the sofa, all well-tailored broad shoulders and long-legged elegance. The room suddenly felt much smaller as Charlotte took a seat in the facing armchair. He seemed to crowd out all else.

"This is a very pleasant room," he remarked, looking around with an approving glance at the simple but tasteful furnishings. "You were wise to make the decision to leave your old residence." A tiny, tumbledown sliver of a house, it had been located in a far less savory part of London. "I trust you have no regrets?"

"No," she replied a little testily, impatient to get to work. In her profession, time was money. She needed to have a finished drawing of the murder to Mr. Fores as quickly as possible in order to best the competition. "Now, might we put aside household matters and turn to what you know about the Bloody Butcher's latest victim?"

His mouth quirked in amusement. "Likely not enough to satisfy your artistic sensibility, but I shall try." He shifted and recrossed his booted legs. "To answer the question in your note, yes, I was present at the duke's gathering. However, I left early as Tyler and I were conducting a complex chemical experiment that required precise timing."

The earl was one of the country's leading experts in chemistry, though his devil-may-care behavior and hair-trigger temper often overshadowed his intellectual accomplishments. Tyler, his nominal valet, had advanced scientific training and served as his laboratory assistant.

Charlotte blew out her breath. "Damnation, I was hoping you could confirm the ghoulish details. Raven and Hawk heard that the victim's—"

"They heard right," interrupted Wrexford. "Mr. Griffin had the same idea as you did. He came to see me early this morning to see if I had attended the soiree, and whether I had seen anything suspicious."

Griffin, regarded to be the best of the Bow Street Runners,

had been involved in investigating the earl when he had been a prime suspect in a murder. Despite a less than auspicious start, they had developed a grudging respect for each other.

"And did you?" she pressed.

"Alas, no. But I managed to squeeze some of the more intimate details of the crime out of him." A wry smile. "If he knew I was passing them on to the infamous A. J. Quill, he'd likely slice off one of *my* bollocks."

Charlotte winced. "So it's really true." She waited as McClellan entered and set the tea tray on the side table and discreetly withdrew. "Just, er, one is missing?"

The earl nodded in confirmation.

Taking a small notebook and pencil from the pocket sewn into her work gown, she looked up expectantly. "Did Mr. Griffin describe how the victim was situated when he was found, and what the state of his clothing looked like?"

"I thought you might inquire about that. The poor fellow was seated slumped, but still upright, on the bench in the Queen's Alcove. Death was caused by a single knife thrust to the heart. The blade then sliced the fastenings on the left side of the trousers . . ." Wrexford gave a short, succinct summary of the corpse's condition.

For all the ghoulishness of the killer's mutilation, it sounded as if he had performed the task with a certain civility, removing the trophy with surgical precision. No other damage or disfiguration had occurred.

From what Charlotte had heard about the previous deaths, it was the same modus operandi. Though, she reminded herself as she finished jotting her notes, that didn't necessarily mean it was the same killer. Over the years, she had learned that criminals could be diabolically cunning. Someone might be mimicking the Bloody Butcher to cover his own personal reasons for wanting the victim dead.

Whatever the motive—assuming a madman could be said to

have rational thoughts—Charlotte had a feeling this was going to be a horribly difficult murder to solve.

That the victim was from the highest circle of Society could soon have the investigators caught up in a vortex of secrets and lies. Beneath their gilded smiles and polished manners, the wealthy hid a multitude of sins.

"What a coil," muttered Charlotte as she rose and went to pour tea for him before it turned cold.

"Indeed," agreed Wrexford. "Though you will likely make a fortune, given the rather sensational nature of his injuries." He pulled a face. "Thank God I can't be accused of having any connection to the fellow. I hadn't yet made his acquaintance."

She began adding sugar to his cup. "Is the identity of the victim known?"

"Yes. He's a young gentleman from the North by the name of Lord Chittenden."

The spoon slipped, sloshing hot tea over her fingers.

"A baron from the Lake District," the earl went on. "Apparently, he had only recently come into the title . . ."

A strange buzzing rose in Charlotte's ears, drowning out the rest of his words.

And then suddenly the room began to spin.

CHAPTER 2

"Allow me to congratulate you, Mrs. Sloane," drawled the earl as Charlotte's eyes fluttered open. "For the first time in our acquaintance, you've finally reacted like a normal, flighty female who swoons into a dead faint at the mention of an indelicate subject."

She tried to sit up, only to choke back a retch and sink back down against the sofa pillows. Her ghostly pale face was now shaded with a faint tinge of bilious green.

Wrexford realized with a start that he had never seen her look so shaken. Refraining from any further jesting, he rose and fetched the bottle of brandy that he knew was kept in one of the cabinets.

"Drink," he commanded, splashing a measure into the empty teacup and bringing it to her lips.

Charlotte gagged at the first sip, but managed to down a weak swallow.

"Oh, dear God," she whispered, so softly that he barely could make out the words. "This changes everything."

A cryptic announcement, which could mean any number of

things. Given the secrets within secrets in which she had swathed her true self, it wasn't surprising.

She had recently revealed her real identity to him. It had come as a bit of a shock to learn the fiercely independent young widow, who through hard work and unshakable strength had created a profitable business for herself, was, in fact, an aristocrat. The daughter of an earl, who had tossed away a life of privilege and comfort to elope with her drawing master . . .

Shaking off his momentary musing, Wrexford asked, "Would you care to elucidate on that statement?"

But before Charlotte could reply, McClellan hurried in with the reviving compress he had called for.

"Permit me to be of assistance, Mrs. Sloane." With her usual show of brisk efficiency, McClellan took a seat on the edge of the sofa and applied a wet cloth to Charlotte's brow.

"A whiff of vinaigrette might also be advisable," murmured the earl. Charlotte was still looking as pale as death.

Both women reacted with a very unladylike reply.

"Nor do we need to burn a feather under my nose," added Charlotte. "Or any other of the damnably stupid remedies you men deem essential for the weaker sex."

Wrexford was somewhat reassured by her show of sarcasm. "Yes, I can see that you're well on the way to recovery."

She chuffed a snort.

"M-M'lady's not . . . going to die, is she?"

He turned to see the two boys hovering in the shadows of the doorway, their faces clouded with uncertainty. Growing up in the stews of London, they had no illusions about how swiftly the Grim Reaper's scythe could strike.

"No, lads," he answered quietly. "It was just a passing megrim. These things happen."

"Not to m'lady." Fists clenched, Raven edged into the room, belligerence not quite covering the flicker of fear in his eyes. The boy had assumed the role of protector to his younger brother and Charlotte—a heavy weight for such young shoulders. "Ye must have done something to upset her."

"Not intentionally. But if you feel compelled to bloody my beak, we can step out to the garden and settle the matter like gentlemen."

"Good God, let's not add any further violence to the morning," rasped Charlotte. To Raven, she added, "Be assured, His Lordship was no more annoying than usual."

A grudging grin tugged at the boy's mouth. "Oiy, well, in that case, I won't have to thrash him to a pulp."

"If you wish to be truly useful with your fives," interjected McClellan, "you and your brother could fly to the greengrocer and fetch me more gingerroot for an herbal tisane."

As their steps peltered down in the corridor, Charlotte pushed herself into a sitting position. Her gaze, noted Wrexford, avoided meeting his.

"I fear I must have eaten something that disagreed with me," she muttered. "I'm still feeling rather nauseous."

She looked ill, but the earl was sure it was not on account of any tainted food.

"Milord, if you would excuse us, I think it best for Mrs. Sloane to retire to her bedchamber," suggested McClellan.

Charlotte's eyes remained averted. No question she was hiding something.

"Of course." He rose without argument. "I'll see myself out."

On reaching the street, he climbed into his carriage and leaned back against the squabs as the coachman cracked the whip.

Questions, questions.

Closing his eyes, Wrexford pondered the strange scene that had just taken place. No one—*no one!*—of his acquaintance possessed the same core of unshakable strength as Charlotte Sophia Anna Mallory Sloane. Not only had she calmly faced terrible revelations about her late husband, which would have crushed a lesser woman, she had also endured death threats to her beloved urchins . . . and charged into danger, time and time again, with no thought to her own safety. Not to speak of her profession, where she had not let the harsh realities of life corrupt her idealism or her commitment to justice and social reform.

Her courage, both moral and physical, was frightening—which made her reaction to the Kensington Palace murder all the more disturbing.

There seemed to be only one logical answer. Lord Chittenden was not a stranger.

A past lover, perhaps?

The idea was more unsettling than he cared to admit. Granted, as a widow, she was allowed more freedom in her personal life than other women. Or ladies, he corrected himself. Charlotte *was* a highborn lady, which allowed her even more leeway . . .

Pushing such thoughts aside, Wrexford concentrated on the practical question—what was her connection to the murdered baron? For the rest of the ride home, he pondered the possibilities.

"Tyler!" he barked, striding into his workroom without pausing to hand over his topcoat and high-crown beaver hat to the trailing footman.

"Milord?" His valet looked up from the various cauldrons suspended over several flaming spirit lamps. Steam had plastered his red-gold hair to his angular brow. In the glow of the fires, his eyes had a demon-like glow, giving him the look of Vulcan's apprentice.

"Might I finish adjusting the temperatures before you go on?" added Tyler with an aggrieved sniff. "The process, as you well know, requires precise concentration."

Wrexford perched a hip on his desk and folded his arms.

After several minutes, Tyler straightened, and wiped his hands on his shirtfront, leaving a gunpowder grey streak on the white linen. "I shall need to cool the liquids in a quarter hour. In the meantime, is there some other task you wish done?"

"I'll take charge of the chemicals." The earl quickly scribbled out a few lines on a piece of paper. "I want you to gather all the information you can on this gentleman. I've suggested a few lines of inquiry to pursue." Likely, he would think of more.

As his valet read over the note, a frown tugged at the corners of his mouth. "I thought you said the Bloody Butcher murders had had nothing to do with you."

Wrexford set aside the pen. "I've changed my mind."

The sweet-sharp scent of ginger tickled at her nostrils as a gossamer plume of steam floated up from the mug. "Thank you," murmured Charlotte, accepting the fresh-brewed tisane.

McClellan smoothed a crease from the coverlet. "Is there anything else I can get you?"

"No. A bit of sleep is all I need to put me right." She forced a smile. "My apologies. My digestion is not usually so delicate."

McClellan fixed her with an unblinking stare. "No, I don't imagine it is." A flick of her fingers banished another wrinkle. "Do you wish to talk about it?"

"About what I ate?" asked Charlotte. "In all honesty, I've no idea what it could have been."

The reply earned a tiny frown and a stony silence as McClellan reordered her tray and prepared to leave.

It deserved worse, thought Charlotte guiltily. She disliked being less than forthright with her friends, but she needed to think.

Think.

If only my thoughts would stop spinning and screaming like wild whirling dervishes inside my skull.

"The lads went out to get you flowers from Covent Garden. I'll make sure they wait until you've woken before presenting them."

"Thank you," repeated Charlotte, hating the prim hollowness of her words. She despised the everyday deceptions and manipulations that passed for politeness in the beau monde. The self-serving little lies, the puffed-up conceit.

She took pride in being unflinchingly honest, and yet, like Achilles, she had one elemental vulnerability. Whether it would prove mortal to her present existence remained to be seen.

Aside from Wrexford, she hadn't revealed her true identity to anyone else yet. She had told him she needed time to consider all the ramifications of such a momentous decision.

One that would irrevocably change her life.

Throwing off the covers, Charlotte rose and moved to the mullioned window overlooking the tiny back garden. A chill prickled against her skin as she pressed her forehead against one of the panes. Her breath fogged the glass, and in the blink of an eye, the familiar tree was blurred beyond recognition.

Vita et praebebit spem fallacem—life is but an illusion.

She had always known, deep down inside, that this day would come. Even before Wrexford had known the truth, he had been challenging, cajoling . . .

Daring her to confront the life she had so painstakingly constructed out of smoke and sleight of hand.

Charlotte stepped back and pressed her palms to her eyes, feeling the hot sting of tears.

"Cedric," she whispered, finally allowing her grief to well up in a shuddering sob. Cedric was dead. Never again would she see the golden glint of his hair dancing in the wind as they rode neck and leather through the rolling fields. Never again would they help each other translate a particularly difficult passage of Ovid from Latin into English. Never again would they steal apple tarts and gorge themselves out by the lake.

They had been little fiends. *Cedric, Nicky, Charley*—a trio bent on devil-may-care mischief in those long-ago carefree summers.

Her throat tightened. Dear God—what of Nicky? Did he

know yet? The two of them had been the closest of friends—
twins in spirit, as well as looks. He would be devastated by the
news.

Murder, as she had come to know all too well, always had
more than one victim.

Pushing aside raw emotion, Charlotte forced herself to re-
gather her wits and think rationally. *Chittenden, Chittenden...*
She paid little heed to the social gossip of the beau monde, but
she seemed to recall reading that Lord Chittenden had recently
taken up residence in London. She had assumed it was Cedric's
father and had thought nothing more of it.

She had long ago made the decision to cut off any contact
with people from her previous life. But if Nicky was in Town,
the instinct for self-preservation must yield to the bonds of
love. She couldn't—she wouldn't—remain aloof from the two
stalwart friends of her youth.

Murder...

"Murder," she rasped, suddenly recalling that duty demanded
she make a drawing of the Bloody Butcher's latest victim.

For an instant, every fiber of her being rebelled against it.
But she quickly silenced the protest. Rather than a betrayal, her
art could be a powerful force in provoking the public to demand that the murderous madman be apprehended before he
struck again.

After splashing some water on her face and pinching a bit of
color back to her cheeks, Charlotte drew a deep breath and
headed for her workroom.

Cedric had always been willing to think outside the boundaries of conventional wisdom. She felt sure he would applaud
her decision.

Wrexford looked up from his laboratory ledger at the sound
of fast-approaching footsteps in the corridor.

"Back so soon?" he remarked as his valet flung open the

door and entered the workroom. "Your efficiency is always impressive, but in this case it seems unusually so."

"The plot thickens," said Tyler, punctuating the announcement by removing his hat and shaking off the raindrops. "I thought you would want to know right away."

"Then kindly stubble the theatrics." His valet had a penchant for drama. "What have your learned?"

"That Chittenden's younger brother—younger by naught but a few minutes—has been taken into custody by the Runners and charged with the murder. Apparently, a bloody knife was found hidden in his quarters at the Albany Hotel, along with a silk handkerchief containing a gristly scrap of flesh."

Good God. A depraved twist to an ugly crime. Wrexford pursed his lips, wondering how Charlotte would take the news.

"You are sure of this?" he demanded.

Tyler nodded. "Aye. On hearing whispers of it at the Royal Institution—where, by the by, both men had frequently been attending scientific lectures and discussions—I made a visit to Bow Street. Griffin had just returned from taking the prisoner to Newgate and confirmed all the details. It's not yet been released to the public, but the Honorable Nicholas Locke stands accused of fratricide."

"When is the trial?" asked the earl.

"A date has not yet been set," answered Tyler. "But I imagine the hangman is already preparing a noose."

Mr. Locke's guilt certainly seemed assured. The evidence was glaringly clear. And yet . . .

Wrexford tapped his fingertips together. In his experience, crimes were rarely quite so tidy.

"Do you wish for me to continue investigating Lord Chittenden's background, milord?" A pause. "That is, the *late* Lord Chittenden."

"Yes." The answers he was seeking lay hidden in the past.

And now, more than ever, it was imperative to find them. "And with even greater urgency, if you please."

Tyler, to his credit, retrieved his sodden hat and, after snapping a quick salute, hurried off.

The earl rose and began to pace. On passing the assortment of beakers and canisters arrayed on the work counter for the next phase of his experiment, he exhaled a harried breath. The demands of chemistry—precise timing and measurement, objective observation, results based on facts, not theory—appealed to his sense of logic. There was an order to science. Rules applied.

He liked the cerebral challenge of figuring them out.

Emotions were messy. Unpredictable.

Though there was a certain commonality, he admitted wryly. Both were capable of exploding in one's face.

"Bloody hell." Much as he wished to putter away with his powdered ores and acids, he couldn't in good conscience keep what he had learned from Charlotte. She needed to know.

Though he doubted she would thank him for it.

"Ah, well, no good deed goes unpunished." After fetching his hat and coat, he extinguished the Argand lamp on his desk and quit the room.

Through sheer force of will, Charlotte managed to ink in a detailed picture of the scene—the graceful symmetry of the marble structure, the ominous shadow, the slumped body. It was a strong piece of art, compellingly moody and menacing without showing the horrible details. After the addition of crimson highlights and a suitably scandalous headline, she knew it would sell well.

Mr. Fores would have no cause for complaint.

As for her own feelings, she felt she had danced along a razor's edge, somehow maintaining her balance in spite of how much it hurt. She could only pray some good would come of it.

A flutter of cheery color caught her eye, drawing her out of her musing. Earlier, the boys had come to her workroom and presented her with a bouquet of flowers to brighten her spirits. Charlotte knew she had frightened them with her momentary swoon. Opening one's heart to another did not come without perils.

A glance back at her drawing hammered that point home.

Grief cut like a knife, but Charlotte was determined to counter it with a more positive force. She had enlisted Raven and Hawk to make inquiries on whether any of the denizens of the streets around Kensington Palace had noticed anything odd on the night of the murder. Urchins, kitchen maids, street sweepers, night soil men—those who toiled in anonymity were never noticed by the upper classes, but they missed very little of what went on around them.

Charlotte depended on their sharp eyes and ears for her work. She was often better informed than Bow Street on everything that went on in both the high and low neighborhoods of London. She prayed it would prove the same in this particular case.

After adding the splashes of color to her drawing, she carefully rolled the finished art in a length of oilcloth and set it aside for the boys to take to the engravers when they returned home.

Turning her thoughts from Cedric to his brother, Charlotte considered how best to contact him. It wouldn't be difficult to learn his address if he was living in London. But then—

"Mrs. Sloane?" McClellan gave a tentative knock on the door. "His Lordship has returned, and wishes to have a word with you." A pause. "He says it's important."

Charlotte felt her insides clench. The pain still felt too raw to share. But to refuse to see him seemed lily-livered. Whatever the complexities of their relationship, neither of them had ever taken the coward's way out of a confrontation.

"I shall be down in a moment," she replied. Drawing several deep breaths, she sought to steel her spine.

He was standing by the bank of windows, his back to the

doorway. Charlotte hesitated before entering the parlor, trying to discern his mood from the chiseled angles of his silhouette. His dark hair, always too long and too wind-snarled to be fashionable, fell over the collar of his coat. The expensive fabric and exquisite tailoring of clothing accentuated the broad stretch of his shoulders and the long, lithe lines of his legs.

He had a careless grace that fit him like a second skin. And yet, he appeared tense.

"To what do I owe the honor of a second visit, milord?" she asked, hoping to sound calmer than she felt.

He turned slowly, and though his face was wreathed in shadows, his eyes seemed to hold a strange uncertainty.

"Please have a seat, Mrs. Sloane. I'd prefer not to have to save you from smashing your skull against the floor for a second time today."

A frisson of alarm shot down her spine, but she hid her reaction beneath a sardonic smile. "I daresay you'll take great amusement for the next little while in needling me over that little display of weakness." The *swoosh, swoosh* of her skirts whispered over the carpet as she moved to the sofa. "Now that you've had your fun, might we get down to the real reason for your visit? Unlike you, I must work for my bread."

His expression remained solemn.

Charlotte's uneasiness ratcheted up another notch. The earl rarely sheathed his sharp sense of humor.

"Be assured, it gives me no pleasure to bring you further news on the murder." He settled himself rather stiffly in the facing armchair. "But I decided you wouldn't thank me for it if I held back new information."

Her hands fisted together in her lap. "Go on."

The earl took a moment to recross his legs. "Griffin has made an arrest. A bloody knife and . . . other incriminating evidence was found in the man's rooms, leaving precious little doubt as to his guilt."

"Who?" Her voice sounded strangely disembodied to her ears.

Again he responded with a very un-Wrexford-like hesitation. His gaze seemed to ripple with sympathy before he answered. "The Honorable Nicholas Locke."

A fresh wave of nausea washed over her.

"Locke is the younger brother of the victim," added Wrexford softly. "But I daresay you know that."

Charlotte swallowed hard, trying to banish the acid burn of bile in her throat. "Griffin's wrong," she rasped.

He remained tactfully silent.

"Nicky would never harm Cedric." Her hands, though clenched, were shaking. "*Never.*"

"A porter at the Palace overheard a rather violent argument between the two brothers as they were leaving the soiree," responded Wrexford. "One in which Mr. Locke railed at the unfairness of Lord Chittenden inheriting everything, simply because he had the good fortune to pop out of the womb first."

"The porter could very well have misunderstood," she insisted. "Or is making it up to appear important."

"Perhaps," agreed the earl. "Though Griffin, as you know, is very careful and methodical about his investigations. And damning evidence was found in Mr. Locke's rooms at the Albany Hotel."

Her heart lurched. The boys she remembered were bright, generous-spirited souls, full of laughter and kindness. But people changed. Saints became sinners. Goodness turned to greed.

Hugging her arms to her chest, Charlotte wrenched her thoughts back to the present. "Has Griffin taken Nicky to Bow Street?"

Wrexford shook his head. "Newgate."

"Newgate!" A surge of outrage lifted Charlotte to her feet. "That putrid, pestilent bastion of depravity! He's from a well-born family—"

"And accused of murdering his brother," he pointed out, "in a shockingly foul way."

"Nicky didn't do it!" She was shouting, and didn't care. "Be damned with Griffin and his evidence. I tell you, he's made a dreadful mistake."

The earl drew in a measured breath and released it without making a sound. His air of stoic calm was infuriating.

"I must see Nicky." She started for the door. "Now."

Wrexford's reaction was panther-quick. He was out of his chair in a blur of black and caught hold of her arm.

"Let go of me," demanded Charlotte, trying to pull free.

His grip tightened. "Mrs. Sloane, you aren't thinking with your usual clarity. What do you think the chances are of an un-accompanied woman arriving unannounced and being let through the iron-banded portal of London's most formidable prison?"

Nil, she mentally conceded.

"Exactly," he murmured when she said nothing. "Even if I were to come with you, it would be a waste of time without ar-ranging for the proper permissions—and the requisite bribes."

Charlotte knew he was right, and at that instant hated him for it.

"You needn't bother with all that. I shall ask Jeremy to help me." Her childhood friend, now Baron Sterling, was a better choice—not simply out of spite, but because he, too, had been a playmate with the two brothers.

Wrexford's brows notched up in sardonic reaction. "It's un-derstandable that you would prefer Sterling." The two gentle-men had come to know each other during the investigation of Elihu Ashton's murder. But to call them friends would be exag-gerating the connection. "However, if you recall, he's away in Yorkshire, helping to work out the ramifications of the last murder we investigated." Jeremy had been very good friends with the victim and his two assistants. "Even if you send an urgent summons, it will take a number of days for him to return. And time is of the essence."

He was right—she wasn't thinking straight. Even if Jeremy could arrive quickly, it would be wrong of her to call him away from those who needed his expertise.

"I'll go see Griffin now and work out all the arrangements to visit the prisoner tomorrow," he went on. "I'll send around a carriage, if that is acceptable to you."

Her blood still at a boil, Charlotte was tempted to throw his well-reasoned offer back in his face. But sanity quickly re-asserted itself.

"Thank you." Suddenly ashamed of her earlier outburst, Charlotte lifted her gaze to meet his. "Forgive me, Wrexford. It's not you. I'm simply angry at . . ."

At what? The fickleness of Fate?

"I'm simply angry at the whole bloody cosmos, I suppose."

"I'm aware of that, Mrs. Sloane," he said softly.

"Damnation." She felt the skin tighten over the bones of her face. "I thought you said the universe ran on orderly, scientific rules—the Earth circles the Sun, the tides rise and fall, the seasons come and go in an unchangeable pattern."

"The laws of Nature do have a natural cycle for our life and death," Wrexford replied. "It's we ourselves who muck it up with our unholy attraction to the Seven Deadly Sins."

Nodding absently, Charlotte shifted her stance, suddenly desperate to be alone. She knew he was trying to help, but her emotions were too jumbled for rational conversation. She needed to think.

The earl waited another few moments, and when she still didn't reply, he moved to the doorway. "Tomorrow, then. I'll send word once I've arranged the final timing."

She waited until he left the house before returning to her workroom. Time seemed skewed—it felt like it took forever to climb the stairs and take a seat at her desk. The colors on her palette looked all wrong. Her mind felt numb, a deadweight detached from her body, floating within an impenetrable black cloud.

One swift slice of steel, and her carefully constructed world had been knocked to flinders.

A minute ticked by, and then another. "And I can either cry while every drop of hope spills out," she whispered, "or find a way to salvage what's left."

The thought of Nicky in prison roused her from the stranglehold of despair. He would likely swing from the gallows unless she could find a way to prove him innocent.

Charlotte sat unblinking, unmoving. To do so might require her to sacrifice her own hard-won life in order to save his.

Which, of course, she would do in a heartbeat.

CHAPTER 3

It was late, a spitting rain deepening the night shadows to an impenetrable gloom by the time Wrexford tracked Griffin to a seedy tavern near Covent Garden.

"Milord." The Runner looked up from a plate of pickle and cheddar. "What brings you to these humble environs—other than the magnanimous urge to gift me with a joint of roast beef and an apple tart for the rest of my supper."

The earl took a seat at the rough-planked table. "A favor." He signaled for the barmaid to bring two tankards of ale. "Given your prodigious capacity for consuming food when I'm paying for it, I daresay you're getting the best of the bargain."

"Indeed?" Griffin took a small bite of cheese and chewed meditatively. "To what do I owe such good fortune?"

"The misery of others," shot back Wrexford. He leaned forward and lowered his voice. "I'd like you to arrange for me to meet with Nicholas Locke."

The Runner's heavily lidded gaze suddenly sharpened. A big, chunky man, Griffin's slow movements and taciturn manner fooled many people into thinking he was a beef-witted slug-gard. They quickly learned their mistake.

"You told me earlier that you didn't know the fellow from Adam. Why the sudden interest?"

"Call it scientific curiosity."

Griffin snorted a low sound that sounded suspiciously rude. "There's nothing scientific about murder, milord. It's all about pure primal passions." He paused as the barmaid set down the drinks, then took up one of the tankards and quaffed a long swallow. "But since we're talking about curiosity, I can't help wondering why you're so interested in Mr. Locke."

Wrexford took a swallow of his ale and quickly set it down. "You have execrable taste in taverns. This is horse piss—if not something worse."

A chuckle rumbled in the Runner's throat. "Flossie brought you the cheapest brew, to save your purse."

"I'd rather save my gullet."

The quips didn't distract Griffin from his original question. Like a mastiff with a bone between his teeth, he never let go of any evidence that might affect his investigation of a crime.

"Swallow your sarcasm, milord." He took another bite of cheese. "Have you reason to believe Locke is innocent?"

"I'm not sure," answered the earl. "Let's just say I've had a conversation which indicates the possibility exists."

Griffin set his elbows on the table. "What sort of conversation?"

"A private one." The earl held up his hand to forestall the Runner's retort. "That's all I can say right now. I've no evidence to indicate that you've arrested the wrong man, merely the as-sertion from a friend of Locke that he couldn't be guilty of such a heinous crime. The brothers have apparently always been close."

"Greed and envy have a way of poisoning brotherly love," observed Griffin. "Chittenden had only recently inherited the title. That could have changed everything."

"True," agreed the earl. "It seems the most logical explanation. And I'm a great believer in logic . . ." He leaned back and watched Griffin dig into the just-delivered platter of beef and boiled potatoes.

"And yet?" said the Runner after swallowing a bite.

"And yet, I don't see the harm in my having a talk with the young man. He might be more forthcoming with me than an officer of the law."

Griffin took several long, drawn-out moments to consider the earl's suggestion.

He was, thought Wrexford wryly, far quicker with his fork than with his words.

"Very well." Finally a muffled murmur came as the Runner finished with the beef and turned his attention to the wedge of apple tart. "I'll make the arrangements. But it goes without saying that in return, you'll inform me of any facts I ought to know."

"Agreed." The earl rose, hiding a smile. Clever as Griffin was, he had left his demand wide open to interpretation. "Thank you. And now, I'll leave you to finish your supper in uninterrupted bliss."

The Runner wiped a bit of custard from his chin. "Doing business with you is always a pleasure, milord."

Wrexford made his way out to the narrow street, and wound his way down through the byways to the Strand, where he managed to flag down a passing hackney. Even though the rain had turned to a fine mizzle, he was chilled to the bone when he arrived home. Tossing his damp overcoat and hat aside, he moved to the sideboard of his workroom and, ignoring the rumbled protests of his empty stomach, poured himself a whisky instead of ringing for a late supper.

After stirring the coals to life in the hearth, he took a seat by the fire and sipped at the dark amber malt, feeling its heat slowly seep through his body. Still, much as he tried to relax, the muscles in his shoulders refused to unknot.

Secrets tangling with conundrums. Whatever the ties that bound Charlotte to the two brothers, the murder had shaken her to the core.

"Bloody hell." An exasperated sigh fogged the glass as he held it up to the flames. Damn her for not having enough faith in their friendship to confide in him as to why. They had tested each other's mettle in ways that should have forged a stronger bond of trust. And there had been that brief interlude when both of them had lowered their defenses enough to say . . .

But perhaps the words and the brief, ethereal kiss had been sparked by the impulsive elation of having dodged death.

Lapsing into a dark mood, he swallowed the rest of the whisky in one quick gulp and then rose to pour himself another.

As he set the decanter back on its silver tray, the door flung open and Tyler hurried in. From the look of his dripping garments, it appeared the rain had come back with a vengeance.

"I trust you'll offer me a dram as well." After stripping off his coat and hat, his valet moved to warm his hands by the fire. "In fact, you ought to hand over the key to the wine cellar for the coming week," he added a little smugly. "I richly deserve it."

Wrexford wordlessly poured a healthy measure of whisky and handed it over.

Tyler took an appreciative gulp and held it in his mouth for a moment before swallowing. "Ah, lovely. The nuanced flavors of a Speyside malt always warm the cockles."

"When you've finished your theatrics," muttered the earl impatiently, "might you consent to share with me what you've discovered?"

With a martyred sigh, the valet carefully pulled a sheaf of papers from inside his jacket. "I think I've found the answers you're looking for."

Wrexford stared at the notes, watching the red-gold firelight flit across the creases and curling corners.

"It seems that Mrs. Sloane—" Seeing the earl's brusque wave, Tyler fell silent.

"Just hand them over, if you please," he muttered.

Sensing the earl's unsettled mood, the valet refrained from further comment and did as he was asked.

The notes gave a whispery crackle, the night-chilled smoothness of the paper setting off sparks against his palms. Strangely enough, with Charlotte's secrets now at his mercy, Wrexford found himself hesitating.

Tyler tactfully turned away and began to fuss with hanging up their wet overcoats.

Tit for tat, he told himself. Charlotte would have no right to complain of his methods, given how she made her living. Uncovering the intimate foibles of others was fair game . . .

Turning abruptly, the papers still unfolded, Wrexford crossed to the hearth and dropped them atop the burning coals.

Flames shot up.

Perhaps I'm a bloody fool, he thought, watching the papers blacken and then dissolve to ghostly white ash. But friendship, however exasperating, was friendship. It seemed elementally wrong to steal Charlotte's personal secrets through subterfuge. When she was ready to tell him, she would.

And if she decided he couldn't be trusted, then bloody hell, they weren't really worth knowing.

Charlotte awoke from a fitful sleep and lay still as the grey, watery dawn light seeped in through her bedchamber window and spread over her coverlet. Her body ached from tossing and turning all night. If only the previous day had been just a bad dream.

"Yes, and if wishes were unicorns, then I could fly to the moon in a spun-sugar carriage," she whispered.

The thought was absurdly appealing.

Throwing off such longings, along with the bedcovers, she

rose and padded down to the kitchen to riddle the stove and put on the kettle. Perhaps tea—pip, pip, the English panacea for any ailment—would help settle the queasy churning in her stomach.

The boys had learned nothing from their inquiries. None of their usual sources reported seeing any suspicious activity around the Palace on the night of the murder.

Which begged the question . . .

Is Nicky guilty or innocent? Charlotte was dreading the coming meeting. It was, in a sense, a two-edged sword. Either way it swung would cut her to the bone.

The hiss of the water coming to boil echoed her own conflicted feelings.

"You're up early." McClellan entered the kitchen and quietly set to measuring out tea from the canister and preparing the pot.

Charlotte shifted in her chair.

"Do you wish to talk about whatever is plaguing your thoughts?" murmured the maid as she carried the tea tray to the table and poured a cup for each of them.

The swirl of fragrant steam seemed to release some of the tension from her overwrought nerves. "Not really." A hesitation. "I simply fear I'm going to have to make a very difficult decision. One that will leave me no choice as to what I must do."

"One always has a choice, Mrs. Sloane." McClellan put a pan on the hob and began slicing bread to fry with the fat-streaked strips of gammon. "You're simply too principled to choose your own self-interests over aiding those in need."

How much the other woman guessed about her dilemma was impossible to know. McClellan, too, kept her thoughts to herself, but there was no missing the glint of lively intelligence and steely sharpness in her eyes.

"*Principled?*" Cradling the warm cup in her hands, Charlotte took a sip. "More likely buffle-headed." She blew away a wisp of steam. "Both the victim of the recent murder and the man accused of the crime are very dear to me. If I am to find the real killer and see that justice is done, there's a good chance that I must step out of the shadows. Which means I will have to tell the boys, and you, and all my friends—about my past."

"That includes Wrexford, I imagine," murmured McClellan.

Charlotte drew in a deep breath. "Wrexford already knows."

The other woman's expression didn't change.

"I asked him to keep it a secret until I felt ready to take the momentous step."

"And you don't really wish to?"

"Let's just say it will change everything," Charlotte replied carefully.

Grease sizzled as the meat slapped against hot cast iron. "How so?"

"I . . . I suppose secrets are like a comfortable cloak. They hide all the warts and imperfections that we prefer for our friends not to see." Charlotte gave a wry grimace. "Or perhaps it's merely the illusion of having our vulnerabilities covered that provides the comfort."

"It seems to me that Wrexford doesn't look at you any differently." Taking up a fork, McClellan shifted the fried meat to a plate and added eggs to the frying pan. She didn't elaborate on the statement.

The smell of food was unexpectedly welcome. Charlotte hadn't expected to feel hungry.

"I'm not so sure," she replied. "The earl can be mercurial." And unpredictable. "His moods make him—"

A sudden rapping of the front door knocker interrupted her words. Charlotte tensed. The early hour meant it wasn't a social call.

"I'll go see who it is." McClellan wiped her hands on her apron and hurried down the corridor—though not before slipping a kitchen knife into one of the pockets.

She returned shortly with a missive bearing the earl's crest.

Charlotte quickly broke the wax wafer and scanned the contents. Wrexford had somehow worked magic overnight. "It seems the earl has arranged permission to visit Newgate, but it must be done before the night guards go off duty. He'll be here shortly." Which meant the moment of reckoning was coming even sooner than she expected. "I must hurry and dress."

The wide brim of Charlotte's oversized hat curled down to hide her eyes, making impossible for Wrexford to read her face. Dark on dark, shadows dipped and darted beneath the drab brown wool. She had smudged dirt on her face, making her expression even more impenetrable.

In his note, he had suggested that she dress as a street urchin, a disguise she wore like a second skin. A lady seeking entrance to Newgate would draw too much attention, something they wished to avoid.

"Mrs. Sloane," he said, reluctantly interrupting whatever thoughts were swirling in her head. "I must remind you to let me do all the talking with the officials. Once we are in the cell, I shall defer to you."

"Yes, yes. I'm not a complete widgeon, milord," she replied.

"No, but your nerves are on edge, and we can't afford to have you make a careless slip. Newgate runs by its own rules. A wrong move will cut off any access to Locke, even with Griffin calling in favors."

She nodded, but made no reply. Another sign that Charlotte wasn't herself.

He leaned back against the squabs, content to let the rest of the journey pass in silence. She would need all of her strength for the ordeal ahead.

After a last jolting turn, wheels clattering over the uneven cobblestones, the carriage finally rolled to a halt. The grey day felt even darker with the oppressive stone bulk of the prison looming over them. Wrexford didn't dare shoot a glance at

Charlotte to catch her reaction. He passed through the main portal with quick, confident strides and demanded of the first gaoler he spotted to be taken to the warden on duty.

"Stay right behind me, lad," he barked at Charlotte.

"Oiy, there's many in here who wud snatch up a pretty cully like ye," said the man with a nasty leer before turning to lead the way into a dark corridor reeking of urine. "And even iffen His Nibs found ye, he wouldn't want what wuz left of ye."

The stench grew even more overpowering as they made their way deeper into the bowels of the prison. The gloom grew thicker, and from some unseen block of cells, a cacophony of screams and demented laughter reverberated against the un-yielding stones. Wrexford had known what to expect. He wondered if Charlotte fully understood the horrors that lurked within these walls.

Another turn brought them to a small windowed office overlooking one of the inner courtyards. The warden, a greasy-haired fellow with a beaky nose and reptilian eyes, read over the papers from Bow Street that the earl thrust into his hands.

"Locke, eh?" He looked up with a sniff.

Smelling the scent of money, no doubt.

"Now," snapped Wrexford, curling a hand around the purse in his pocket.

"Doesn't say anything here about two visitors. Why's the lad with you?"

In answer, the earl slowly lifted up the soft chamois bag. The weight of gold guineas made a very distinctive ring. "Take me to Locke."

The warden smiled, revealing two missing teeth, and plucked the purse from Wrexford's palm. "Burley," he bellowed, "escort these gentlemen to the Golden Beauty's cell."

More darkness, more filth, more screams.

At last, the gaoler stopped in front of a heavy iron door and shoved a massive key into the lock. Metal scraped against metal, and the mechanism released with a groan.

"I'll be back in a quarter hour," warned the gaoler as he pushed the door open with his boot. "Be ready te move yer pegs quick-like. Ye can't linger." Once the two of them entered the cell, he slammed it shut and relocked it.

Charlotte waited until the footsteps were swallowed by the other prison noises before taking a step toward the narrow cot, where a figure lay curled like a hedgehog, a threadbare blanket pulled up over his head and shoulders.

"Nicky?" she said softly.

A pitiful moan shivered through the ragged wool. "Be damned with you, Lucifer—stop plaguing me with such devil-cursed dreams!"

"Nicky." Charlotte crouched down and pulled the blanket down, revealing a tangle of pale gold hair. "Come, rouse your-self. It's no dream. I need to talk with you and we haven't much time."

Wrexford watched as a pair of muck-encrusted boots scrab-bled free of the blanket. After slowly twisting up to a sitting position, Nicholas Locke slumped back against the stone wall and blinked in confusion. "C-C-Charley? Oh my God, i-is it really you?"

She gripped his shoulders and gave him a shake. "Yes!" Leaning closer, she spoke with a rapid-fire urgency, punctuat-ing her words with a light slap to his cheek.

The earl kept his distance, allowing her a private exchange with the prisoner before they began their questioning. Char-lotte hadn't yet clarified her relationship to Locke, and much as he was curious, he wasn't going to ask.

He didn't hear what she said, but Locke seemed to shake off his lethargy. His gaze became more alert.

"Come join us, sir." Her brusque wave indicated the lone stool set near the sliver of window.

As Wrexford shoved it closer to the cot and took a seat, Charlotte added, "I assume I have you to thank for the amenities. Be assured I shall pay you back."

Ah, so she did know the sordid details of Newgate. Prisoners had to pay through the nose for even the barest necessities, otherwise they slept on the cold stone, half-starved and surrounded by their own filth. For those without money, incarceration could be a death sentence in itself.

"The wheels of graft move slowly at first." Wrexford gave a sardonic smile. "By evening, Mr. Locke will have better furnishings, along with decent food and drink." A pause. "We shall settle up accounts after he's released, but for now, let's not waste our breath on such trivialities."

Charlotte nodded. Steeling her features, she looked back at Locke. "We can't afford to shilly-shally, Nicky, and in order to help you, I must know the truth, however grim. So I must ask you straightaway—did you kill Cedric?"

"God in heaven, no!" His face crumpled in anguish. "As if I could ever do such a horrific thing! C-C-Cedric was my best friend."

And yet, in a moment of mad rage, thought Wrexford, love could turn to murderous hate. Life was littered with the ugly proof of it. Charlotte knew that as well as he did. Whether she could put aside her emotions remained to be seen. Whatever her connection to Locke, it was clearly a close one.

"How do you explain the bloody knife and bits of flesh found in your rooms?" he demanded, assuming the role of the devil's advocate to spare Charlotte from having to ask such painful questions.

"I can't," replied Nicholas helplessly. "I've no idea how they got there."

"You'll need a better answer than that if you wish to save your neck," he shot back. "The evidence is damning. And you have a compelling motive. With your brother dead, a title and fortune are suddenly yours."

Nicholas's face, already ashen, turned bloodless. "I've all the money I need! Cedric is—was—exceedingly generous. As for the title, it means nothing to me. It's more trouble than it's worth." He sucked in a shallow breath. "The fact is, Cedric had the better temperament for all the responsibilities, and we both knew it."

Charlotte placed a hand on his thigh. "That may be, Nicky, but the Runner investigating the murder has statements from several members of the Royal Institution saying some very emotional arguments had taken place between you and Cedric recently. And one of the porters at Kensington Palace over-heard a very ugly exchange as you were leaving the Duke's soiree."

"Yes, Cedric and I had the occasional disagreement," exclaimed Nicholas. "What brothers don't?"

"This one went far beyond a brotherly brangle. You were heard ranting about the unfairness of Cedric getting everything, simply by virtue of being born a few minutes before you were," said Wrexford. "Fate played a cruel jest on you. The question is whether you sought to repay the favor."

"We *never* quarreled over the inheritance," insisted Nicholas. "I was drunk, and in a foul mood about . . . other things. Cedric was generous, and kind, and . . ." Taking his head in his hands, he choked back a sob. "And I—I c-can't believe he's gone."

"Alcohol and anger are a volatile mix," pointed out the earl. "Perhaps you simply lost control—"

"I didn't kill him!" Nicholas's whole body began to tremble uncontrollably. He looked at Charlotte, tears running down his cheeks. "I swear by all that is holy, I'm innocent, Charley."

"Then we must prove it," she replied softly.

By now, Charlotte's hell-bent idealism shouldn't surprise him, reflected Wrexford. When roused by injustice, she would charge headlong into hellhole conundrums, where even the most avenging of angels should fear to tread. No matter what demons lay in wait.

He must have made an exasperated sound, for she turned to spear him with a scowl.

Thinning his lips, Wrexford held his doubts in check.

Charlotte looked back to Nicholas. "But to do so, Nicky, you must be entirely forthcoming with me." Her voice hardening, she went on, "I need to know everything—*everything*— that might give a clue on who might have had a motive to murder Cedric. Do you understand? Holding anything back, no matter how embarrassing or unpleasant, puts your own life in jeopardy."

"I . . . I'm not sure w-what to say," rasped Nicholas. "We all know how innocent exchanges can be twisted to look incriminating." He suddenly looked ill. "Oh, Lord, I suppose I'll be painted a ravening monster by A. J. Quill's satirical pen."

"Never mind Quill," said Charlotte. "Satire may cut at your pride, but it's hard evidence that will send you to the gallows. Right now, the authorities have items that incriminate you in Cedric's murder. Unless I can find the real culprit, you will hang."

"But how can *you* possibly find—" began Nicholas.

"Leave that to us," snapped Wrexford. "You heard Mrs. Sloane. You had better start focusing what wits you possess on coming up with some possible suspects or motives, no matter how unlikely."

Nicholas nodded, looking miserable and frightened. "I-I will try to wrack my brain."

"You had damn well better," said Wrexford. Their time was nearly up, and he doubted the warden was the sort of fellow who gave away anything for free. "Think! There must be something you can give us now," he pressed. "No one is a saint. Cedric must have had some enemies."

Shoulders slumping, Nicholas shifted uncomfortably.

"Nicky!" Charlotte grabbed hold of his open shirtfront and gave him a hard shake.

"Come, let's not waste any more of our time," snarled Wrexford in disgust. "Clearly, Mr. Locke would rather keep his delicate sensibilities intact instead of his neck."

"It's probably nothing," mumbled Nicholas as the earl rose, "but a few weeks after Cedric and I arrived in London, we were invited to join the Eos Society."

CHAPTER 4

*E*os. The name hung for a moment in the foul-scented air.

Rosy-fingered Dawn, a favorite deity of Homer, thought Charlotte, recalling *The Iliad* and *The Odyssey*. The mother of the Morning Star, Eos opened the gates of heaven to allow the Sun to rise.

Would that she could bring a sliver of light to this pit of darkness.

"The Greek goddess of Dawn," mused Wrexford, echoing her thoughts. "I take it that the name implies that it is a group dedicated to seeing the world in a grand new light."

"Yes," answered Nicholas. "The members are all interested in stimulating an interchange of new ideas for the new world taking shape around us." He sounded somewhat defensive. "We talk about a wide range of subjects—science, social reform, and how radical thinking is necessary to effect change."

Ah, youthful hubris. Fledgling men spouting pompous platitudes, their intellectual assumptions untempered by actual experience. Charlotte didn't bother looking at the earl, knowing the mocking cynicism she would see curled on the corners of his mouth.

"Go on," she encouraged.

Nicholas looked confused. "I—I don't really know what to add. Granted, we disagreed among ourselves over scientific method or abstract ideas on the nature of government, but that's not the sort of thing to spark a heinous murder."

"There were no personal animosities?" asked Wrexford.

Nicholas looked about to shake his head, then hesitated. "A few small sparks, but nothing that mattered."

Charlotte itched to slap some sense into him. "Nicky, for God's sake, your bloody life hangs in the balance! *Everything* matters."

"Very well . . ." Staring down at his hands, he knotted his fingers together. "If you must know, Cedric and Sir Kelvin Hollister were vying for the attention of the same young lady. A mutual animosity seemed to be developing between them, and they exchanged some heated barbs at the last few meetings, but . . ."

"But it's definitely a thread worth following," said Charlotte decisively. She drew a small notebook and pencil from her pocket and wrote down Hollister's name. "And the young lady?"

"Lady Julianna Aldrich."

The name meant nothing to her. But she paid little attention to the flock of dewy-eyed young chits who came onto the marriage mart each season. "A casual flirtation may have sparked—"

"There was nothing casual about it for Cedric." For an instant, a ripple of emotion darkened Nicholas's eyes. "He found her . . . mesmerizing."

"Anyone else?" asked Wrexford before she could follow up on the statement.

Nicolas ran a hand through his tangled hair. "There was some friction with Benjamin Westmorly." He drew in a ragged breath. "It had to do with gaming debts. Cedric mentioned Westmorly owed him a hefty sum of money and was being difficult over its repayment."

"So we have two leads," said Charlotte, making herself sound more hopeful than she felt. In truth, it all seemed nothing more than the usual friction between young men who thought themselves wise in the ways of the world. Hardly cause for a macabre murder.

"And motives for both of them," pointed out Wrexford. "Love and money have been the cause of countless murders since time immemorial."

"So has jealousy and lust for power." Nicholas shot them an anguished look. "Which means I'll probably swing for Cedric's murder."

"Not if we can help it," said Charlotte, gazing around the filthy, crypt-dark cell. But he was right—at the moment, things didn't look overly bright.

The minutes were slipping away. She made herself think. "We've looked at Cedric, but what about you, Nicky? The Runner said you had no alibi for the night of the murder," said Charlotte. "Is there really no one who saw you, even for a fleeting moment?"

Nicholas averted his eyes. "I was walking the streets for several hours after leaving the Palace. It wasn't until much later in the night that I have someone who could attest to my whereabouts. So it doesn't matter."

"We don't know that," replied Charlotte. "Who was it?"

"I . . ." He scrubbed a hand over his unshaven jaw, setting off a flickering of golden sparks. "I was with a woman." A half-hysterical laugh slipped from his lips. "But I didn't bother mentioning it because Bow Street won't consider her a credible witness."

"I take it you were at a brothel?" said Wrexford.

After darting a baleful look at Charlotte, Nicholas didn't answer.

"Bloody hell, answer him," she muttered in exasperation.

"I'm not a dewy-eyed virgin who'll fall into a faint at the mention of sex."

That brought the blood back to Nicholas's face. His cheeks turned scarlet as he gave a small nod.

"Give me the name of the establishment," demanded the earl. "And that of the girl."

Nicholas hesitated, then mumbled an answer.

Charlotte added the information to the other names in her notebook.

The metallic clang of the lock releasing and the gaoler's growled order to hurry forestalled any further questions.

It was precious little to go on. Assuming, of course, that Nicky wasn't lying through his teeth. She rose quickly and darted one last look at his shadowed profile before hurrying to quit the cell. Whether it would lead them anywhere but in a roundabout circle back to the gallows remained to be seen.

"Yer Nibs!"

Charlotte had already climbed into the carriage. Turning around, Wrexford paused, his foot on the iron rung, as a sentry hurried over and passed him a note.

"The devil take it," he muttered, crumpling the paper and stuffing it in his pocket after giving it a quick glance. "The warden is demanding that I meet him at one of the nearby taverns to work out the terms of future visits to your friend. If we are to have any hope of proving Locke innocent, we'll need access to him. So I'd better go."

She slid over the seat and caught hold of the door latch. "I'm sorry to have drawn you into this damnable coil. If Jeremy were here—"

"He isn't, and you can't very well handle things on your own. So whether you like it or not, you need my help."

Charlotte looked up through her lashes, the jagged shadows making it impossible to read her eyes. "That wasn't what I meant."

He blew out his breath. This wasn't the time or place to delve into the tangled complexities of their relationship. She had enough worries preying on her mind.

"However," he went on, using sarcasm to hide his uncertainties, "I do hope your friend is innocent. It would pain me deeply—not as deeply as poor Cedric, of course—to be throwing away a fortune on the sort of miscreant who would slice off his brother's bollock."

"That's *not* amusing," she muttered.

"It wasn't meant to be."

"I mean to reimburse you for your expenses," she said haltingly.

"Don't be daft. I shall send the bill to the prisoner's bankers. The new Lord Chittenden can well afford to pay for his own upkeep."

Charlotte repressed a shiver, but not quite quickly enough to escape his notice.

With all the emotions roiling around inside her head, Wrexford imagined the practical ramifications of Cedric's death had not yet fully penetrated her consciousness. When he spoke again, he softened the edge of his words. "Forgive me. As you know, my sardonic view of life is often offensive."

"I'm used to it," she murmured.

A faint smile tugged at his lips. "We are, I suppose, well-acquainted with each other's eccentricities and have learned to put up with them."

"True." She shifted closer to the carriage door. "Which is why you won't bother brangling when I take my leave and make my way home on foot."

Damnation. He had let down his guard for an instant, only to find himself hoisted on his own petard. A reminder that Charlotte's steel was just as sharp as his own.

Not many people had the mettle to match his thrusts and parries.

Narrowing his eyes, Wrexford replied, "Allow me to point out that this isn't the most salubrious of neighborhoods."

"All the more reason that a lordly peer would keep his carriage, and the bantling with him would hare off on his own."

She was right, a fact that only exacerbated his darkening mood. The meeting with Locke had unsettled him. He wasn't sure whether the prisoner's evasiveness was due to fear and shock, or whether the cause had a more sinister root. Regardless, the fellow seemed an unworthy cause for Charlotte. Involving herself in a scandalous murder investigation would be dangerous in any number of ways. Secrets had a way of slipping free.

He didn't like to think of her being forced to make elemental decisions about her own life before she was ready to do so, all because . . .

Because Locke had some emotional hold on her.

"Keep your head down and move quickly," he muttered in grudging reply. "You heard the gaoler—a sweet young morsel like you would be devoured by the ravening beasts around here."

"I'm no stranger to the stews, sir. I can take care of myself."

"Pride goeth before a fall."

Her mouth quirked. "You must truly be in a hellish temper to quote the Scriptures at me."

Before he could react, Charlotte added, "I'm going to take a roundabout route home and make some inquiries as to whether my sources near Kensington Palace have heard anything suspicious about the night of the murder. As for the brothel—"

"Leave the brothel to me. I'll visit there this evening," he growled.

She raised a brow, the clouded look in her eyes giving way to a momentary flash of amusement. "A late-night assignation coupled with this early-morning meeting? I fear the demands of this investigation will exhaust your . . . patience."

"It's *you* who must be tired," shot back Wrexford. "Your wit is usually capable of cleverer sarcasm than that." Their gazes locked, and he found himself adding, "If I were looking for fleshly pleasure, I would seek it in a more inviting setting."

"Is Boudicca's Bosom not a pleasant place? I've heard it caters to an exclusive clientele."

Wrexford didn't rise to the bait. "If I learn anything worthwhile, I'll send word to you in the morning. I trust you'll do the same."

A brusque nod. "Of course. Now kindly step down and let me be off."

He did so, silently cursing her devil-benighted sense of stubborn independence.

"My thanks for your help, Wrexford. I'm aware this is not your fight." Her words were almost lost in the whisper of wool as she brushed past him.

Steel and silk. Hard and soft. Charlotte had the infuriating ability to keep him off balance.

A frown momentarily formed between his brows as he watched her dart across the cobbled square and disappear into the maze of narrow alleyways. Like a cat. Or rather, a lioness. All feline grace, ferocious courage, and a hunter's instinct for tracking down its prey.

Turning away, he slammed the carriage door shut and headed off in the opposite direction. The question, he asked himself, was how many of her nine lives did she have left?

Charlotte wove a sure-footed path through the slanting shadows, keeping alert to all the little sounds around her. She didn't need the earl's warning to know that the scum of humanity was drawn to the environs of Newgate and Old Bailey. Misery loves company—or perhaps it was more that depravity begets depravity. The prison housed some of the most deranged and dangerous of London's criminals.

Including the new Lord Chittenden.

A sudden *crunch-crunch* sounded behind her. She shot a nervous glance over her shoulder, but saw nothing within the dark-as-Hades gloom beneath the overhanging roofs. Feeling the hairs at the back of her neck stand on end, Charlotte quickened her pace. She was feeling jumpy as a cat on a griddle. Cedric's murder had cut like a knife to the heart, reminding her of how cruelly and casually a loved one could be ripped from the here and now.

Raven and Hawk . . . the irascible Basil Henning and devil-may-care Kit Sheffield . . . the mysterious McClellan.

And the enigmatic Earl of Wrexford.

She had somehow gathered a mismatched circle of friends around her during the past few years. They had become very dear to her.

Once again, she was aware of how frighteningly vulnerable she felt because of it.

A solitary existence was far safer, uncomplicated by the complexities of emotions. Danger now held more consequences than the question of her own measly survival. The boys depended on her . . .

Charlotte shook off her brooding. She couldn't afford such distractions when she was on the hunt.

After weaving her way through the putrid maze of passageways, she skirted around Lincoln's Inn Fields and made her way up to High Holborn, where she joined the flow of traffic heading west onto Oxford Street. No one paid the least attention to yet another ragged urchin as she cut into Hyde Park and hurried on into the neighborhood surrounding Kensington Palace. The boys had their sources for information—the urchins who swept the dung from the streets, the flower girls, the night soil men. But she had her own set of contacts. Men and women whose shady dealings depended on knowing everything that went on within their little world.

Her first stop was a curio shop on Church Lane, just several streets away from the main entrance to Kensington Palace. A dreary-looking front room stuffed with nondescript flotsam and jetsam masked a hidden basement filled with purloined treasures from Mayfair. Broad Billy had the reputation for running the best flash house in London.

Charlotte squeezed through one of the narrow aisles and approached the bored-looking clerk at the back counter. Fisting a hand, she waggled a quick signal.

A jerk of his head indicated she should pass through a closed door set halfway down a short corridor. It led into a tiny chamber where the rug had been thrown back, revealing a trapdoor that now stood open. A flicker of weak light wavered within the murky depths below."

"Billy," hissed Charlotte, careful to disguise her voice.

She heard the shuffling of boots and the sonorous chiming of crystal. A chandelier by the sound of it. Quite an expensive one.

"That you, Magpie?" A pudgy face appeared an instant later, the eyes two beady black dots nearly swallowed by the doughy folds of flesh.

Woe to anyone who assumed they didn't see much. Charlotte was of the opinion that Billy could count the hairs on a flea's arse from ten paces away.

A lamp, held aloft by a meaty hand, shifted slightly, illuminating the figure's near-bald pate streaked with a few greasy strands of black hair.

"Aye," answered Charlotte, quickly pulling a purse from her pocket. She had come prepared.

Broad Billy's hearing was just as acute as his vision. He must have heard the faint chink of gold against gold for he quickly humped his massive bulk closer to the ladder. "Whacha need?"

"Whatever you might know about the murder that happened in the Palace gardens several nights ago."

"Nasty business, that," remarked Billy, though a low chuckle punctuated his words. "Say what they will, but the highborn swells are far more savage than us unwashed."

Her ears pricked up. "You have reason to think it was a swell who did it, and not the madman they call the Bloody Butcher?"

A leer slowly stretched across his broad face. "Who's saying the Butcher ain't an aristocrat?"

Charlotte shook the purse. "Tell me what you know."

Billy eyed the chamois bag, as if judging just how much information it would buy.

"Only that my ears and eyes on the street saw naught but the fancy gennelmun coming outta the gardens that night. The Duke o' Sussex wuz having one of his parties. But I daresay you know that."

Fear drove a spike through Charlotte's chest, but she kept her reaction well hidden. "Were any of those ears and eyes close enough to Queen Anne's Alcove to see what happened?"

"Alas, no." Another leer. "Otherwise I'd likely have the victim's gold pocket watch and assorted fobs and rings te add te my wares." Billy gave a mournful exhale and shook his head. "A pity to think all those valuables were jest sitting there fer the taking."

Scavenging was fair game in the underworld, but the thought of Cedric's corpse being stripped of its valuables made her skin crawl.

She dropped the purse into the waiting upturned palm. "Ask around again. If you hear anything different, tell Lilly, the flower girl, and she'll get word to me. There'll be another purse for the efforts."

Billy patted his protruding belly. "Oiy will. But my gut tells me ye should be looking high, not low, fer the Butcher."

Is Nicky lying? Charlotte wondered as she quit the shop and headed north, to a tiny hole in the wall near the Kensington gravel pits. She hated to consider it, but the alternative was equally unsettling.

The Bloody Butcher an aristocrat? It seemed unthinkable. However, her work had exposed her to the underbelly of Polite Society. *Scandal and betrayal. Greed and jealousy.* She had good reason to know that Billy's assessment was right. Beneath the thin veneer of civility, there lurked dark-hearted Blue Bloods whose depravity would put wild savages to blush.

O'Malley, a rag-and-bone picker who worked out of a cramped stable on Blackman Lane, often wheeled his barrow through Kensington Gardens late at night. At this hour, he would likely be sleeping. But for a few extra shillings he would gladly have it interrupted.

As she had hoped, the man was curled up on a pile of dirty straw, snoring with a shuddering volume that belied his scrawny body. The jingle of coins brought him instantly awake.

He blinked and rubbed a hand over his bristly jaw. "What sins be ye looking fer today, me fine feathered friend?"

"The sin of murder."

O'Malley grunted. "The Palace gardens?"

"Aye. Did you see anything?"

He let out a regretful sigh, knowing "yes" would earn him more than "no." But Charlotte never did business again with anyone who told her lies, and her informants knew it.

"Wish I could help ye, Magpie. But when I rolled me way home that night, I saw nuffink save fer a solitary mort sitting in the Alcove. Thought he was sleeping or foxed, so didn't think anything of it."

"When was that?" She didn't expect the exact hour, but knew O'Malley would have a natural sense of the night, and whether it was closer to midnight or dawn.

"Business was good down by the river, so I didn't return until mebbe an hour before the sun rose."

So, just a short while before the gardener had found Cedric and sent word to Bow Street. It wasn't any help, but still, she placed a generous payment in his lap.

"My thanks."

O'Malley smiled in answer, revealing several missing teeth, and sank back down into the straw, clutching the coins to his breast.

Feeling dispirited, Charlotte turned away. Her inquiries had raised more questions than they had answered.

All of them uncomfortable.

Because they seemed to suggest that Nicky, for all his tearful denials, was guilty. She could only pray that Wrexford's visit to the exclusive fleshpot would uncover more than a shapely derriere.

Once back on the street, she hesitated. The quickest route home was via Tyburn Turnpike, rather than cutting through the Palace gardens. But some impulse drew her to a pathway leading into the leafy greenery. Was it horribly macabre to feel compelled to view the murder site? Griffin and his men were very competent. There would be no lingering clues.

Still, Charlotte found her pulse quickening as her steps crunched over the graveled footpaths. As an artist, she often saw things differently than others. Her eyes—and her intuition—had proved invaluable in previous investigations. However fragile a thread it was, she clung to the thought that something at the scene might spark an idea.

Another turn brought her to a wider walkway lined with stately plane trees. The leaves whispered softly in the gentle breeze, setting off a fluttering of dark and light greens, deep forest shades dancing with pale lime hues. The cacophony of city sounds didn't intrude upon the sylvan setting. It was aching peaceful.

Up ahead, a dappling of sun caught on the pale stone pediment peeking out from the trees. Charlotte paused as a twist in the path brought Queen Anne's Alcove into full view.

Its beauty squeezed the air from her lungs. A graceful arched opening was centered beneath the triangular top, flanked on each side by double Corinthian columns and matching wall niches sculpted of creamy marble. The symmetry was sublime. Inside the center arch was a curved bench and high paneling made of dark, carved wood.

It looked inviting. An oasis of tranquility.

Oh, how looks could be deceiving. She, of all people, knew that elemental truth.

Forcing herself forward, Charlotte slowly approached and mounted the shallow steps. The interior was cool, with velvety shadows softening the lines of the carved oak. She took a seat on the center of the bench and looked up at the high-vaulted ceiling. A profound sadness took hold of her as she thought of Cedric's last moments, sitting here surrounded by such loveliness.

And then by death.

She closed her eyes for an instant, and then made herself focus on why she was here. Emotion must not be allowed to cloud her gaze.

Looking left and then right, Charlotte studied the curve of the bench and the grain of the wood. She rose, and, starting at one end, slowly ran her hands over the smooth surface, looking for . . .

Anything.

However, the oak yielded no hidden secrets.

After finishing her search, she got down on hands and knees and once again began to follow the curve of the bench, looking for any clues beneath it.

Had the sun not broken through the scudding clouds and speared a blade of light within the flitting shadows, she would have missed the flakes of tobacco blown up in a tiny pile against the wooden stanchion. Her heart thumped against her ribs. *A clue?* However unlikely, Charlotte quickly withdrew her handkerchief for the second time and gently gathered the bits with the tip of her finger. A sweet, spicy scent tickled at her nostrils as she deposited them into a separate fold of the cloth.

Snuff.

Repressing a sneeze, Charlotte tucked away the evidence and continued her search. On finding nothing more, she quickly rose and retraced her steps back to the street.

Reason warned her that her findings likely had nothing to do with Cedric.

And yet, Reason was not always right. There were times when one had to trust Imagination.

CHAPTER 5

After a glance at the mantel clock, Wrexford dipped his pen in the inkwell and returned to the notes he was writing. It was not quite time to leave.

"Your cravat is askew," said Tyler with a critical squint as he entered the workroom.

"To the devil with my cravat," muttered the earl. He stared down at the list, trying to put his thoughts in order.

"And I must say, your claret-colored coat would be a more appropriate choice." The valet made a pained face. "All that unrelenting black makes you look like a walking storm cloud."

The earl chuffed a sarcastic laugh. "I daresay the denizens of Boudicca's Bosom don't give a toss about the color of my clothing. It's the glitter of my purse that concerns them. Assuming, of course, that I had any interest in paying for anything other than information."

"That doesn't mean you can't dress with a little more flair when you visit such an establishment." A sniff. "As your valet, I have a reputation to maintain."

"God forbid I blacken your name." The earl frowned in

thought as he read over the page. "Now, kindly stubble the chatter. I'm trying to concentrate."

"On what?"

Scowling, Wrexford put down his pen. "On why I don't terminate your employment and send you packing without a reference."

"*That* requires precious little mental effort, milord," quipped Tyler. "Who else would tolerate your ill humor? Not to speak of knowing the secret of shining your boots, no matter what disgusting substances you traipse through."

"Be grateful my boots are exceedingly comfortable. Unlike you, I would find it a cursed nuisance to have to replace them."

Ignoring the comment, Tyler moved to the earl's desk and craned his neck to read what the earl was writing.

"Those appear to be notes on the recent murder." The valet's voice had lost its note of needling.

Wrexford grunted in affirmation.

Tyler's expression turned serious. "I take it you've had a talk with Mrs. Sloane."

He remembered with a start that his valet knew all of Charlotte's secrets from his recent research.

"Yes. And it goes without saying, of course, that her real identity is a secret we both must respect. As of yet, she isn't ready to share it with others."

"Of course, milord," answered Tyler quietly.

"As to the murder, Mrs. Sloane has not yet confided in me what her connection is to the victim and the accused," he answered. "But it's plain as a pikestaff that they are both very dear to her. She's intent on proving Locke innocent, regardless of the damning evidence."

His mouth thinned to a grim line. "I'm not quite as convinced as she is about the unbreakable bond between the brothers. Locke struck me as evasive during our brief interview. But as she's hell-bent to plunge into yet another dangerous undertaking, I can't very well let her do it alone."

"Indeed not." Perching a hip on the edge of the desk, Tyler leaned in for a closer look. "How can I help?"

"I'm not yet sure." Wrexford shot another look at the clock and swore under his breath. He needed to leave shortly. "Locke mentioned two gentlemen who may have had a grudge against his brother." He tapped a finger to the names underlined on the top sheet of paper.

"A grudge serious enough to provoke cold-blooded murder?" questioned the valet.

"Love and money have been sparking primal passions throughout the course of human history."

"What—" began Tyler, only to be interrupted by a discreet knock on the workroom door.

"Excuse me, milord," intoned the earl's butler as he opened it a crack. "Mr. Sheffield wishes to see you."

In no mood for his friend's usual theatrics, Wrexford expelled an impatient breath, but knew it was pointless to say no. "Show him in, Riche. Otherwise he'll go raise holy hell in the kitchens by pestering Cook to him serve him a late supper."

Christopher Sheffield, however, entered without his usual flair for the dramatic. Even more surprising, he took a seat in one of the armchairs by the hearth without helping himself to one of the expensive brandies and whiskies sitting on the sideboard.

"Please tell me you're working on something interesting." Sheffield stretched out his legs and stared moodily at his boot tips. "I need something to . . ." On looking up, he seemed to sense the tension in the room. "Dear me, has there been another murder?"

Sheffield, despite his outward show of careless insouciance, had actually been of great help in the previous investigations. Wrexford knew that boredom lay at the heart of his friend's frequent reckless behavior. He was not nearly the charming but feckless fribble he pretended to be.

"It's London, Kit—there is always another murder," replied Wrexford.

"Yes, but very few of them would interest you." Sheffield's gaze suddenly widened. "Sussex . . . the scientific soiree . . . Ye gods, the young lord found stabbed to death in the Palace gardens! What a sordid business. Word is, his younger brother committed the unspeakable act." His brow furrowed. "But how the devil does that involve you? Did you know the fellow?"

Wrexford drew a breath. *Secrets tangling with secrets.* His friend was well acquainted with Charlotte, and he was one of the few people who knew she was the notorious A. J. Quill. Of course he could be trusted with the current conundrum.

"No," he replied. "But apparently Mrs. Sloane did. Quite well, it would seem."

A spasm of surprise crossed Sheffield's face. *"How?"*

"She's not yet confided that to me." Out of the corner of his eye, he saw Tyler's expression turn unreadable. "But she's convinced that the brother didn't do it, and is determined to prove it."

"Bloody hell!" His friend straightened from his slouch. "We're going to help her, aren't we?"

"Of course we are," muttered Wrexford. "Though for now, the evidence is quite damning." He went on to give his friend a succinct summary of the murder's grisly details—they had not appeared in the newspapers—and the interview with Locke.

Sheffield winced at the mention of the mutilation, and remained silent for a long moment after the earl had finished. "We've faced daunting challenges before," he finally said, though there was a hollowness to the bravado. "We'll prove him innocent and catch the real culprit."

"*If* he's innocent," murmured Wrexford. He hoped against hope that Locke wasn't guilty. His gut tightened. Charlotte would be devastated. She had already suffered enough disillusionment about the people she loved—

"Where do we start?" Sheffield rose and began to pace. Tyler, too, fixed the earl with an expectant look.

The earl glanced down at his notes and explained about the two gentlemen mentioned by Locke. "We have a specific reason for there being bad blood between them and the murdered man—assuming Locke isn't simply whistling into the wind."

"You don't like the fellow," observed Tyler.

"Let's just say I don't trust him," replied Wrexford. And if Locke's lies hurt Charlotte, he would be tempted to throttle him with his bare hands, rather than leave it to the hangman.

"I can look into the gambling matter and find out more about Westmorly," volunteered Sheffield.

Wrexford nodded. His friend spent more time in the gaming hells of London than was good for him, but there were times when such habits came in useful. "Excellent. I will think of how to probe into the romantic conflict—" He broke off with a grimace as the clock began to chime the hour. "But for now, I must head off to the brothel."

Sheffield gave a strangled cough. "Given that we don't have much time to unravel all this, can't pleasure wait?"

"Stubble the witticisms, Kit," he muttered, then added a terse explanation.

"I could accompany you, if you like, before I head to the gaming hells."

Wrexford was about to demur, then reconsidered. Sheffield was clever and sharply observant, though he took pains to seem otherwise. "Very well, come along then. Let us hope that between your charm and my purse, we can coax the truth out of Locke's Bird of Paradise."

Charlotte added a slash of shadowing to her drawing, the bruise-purple hue accentuating the black depths surrounding the caricature of Nicholas hunched in his prison cell, a mangy blanket draped over his head. She hadn't had the heart to sketch his features.

The caption was carefully composed to stir a hint of doubt as to his guilt. A. J. Quill had earned a reputation with the public for having an unholy ability to know the truth before the authorities did. That she could shape popular opinion was a sobering power to possess, and she was very careful not to abuse it.

A clench of guilt squeezed at her heart. Was she doing so now? Much as she yearned to believe Nicholas's claim of innocence, she wasn't sure . . .

And there was no question as to Wrexford's view. Though he had refrained from outright sarcasm, she knew him well enough to read the cynicism in his eyes.

And yet, he was still willing to help her.

Charlotte wasn't sure whether that made her feel better, or worse. Though he would deny it, the earl had an unbending sense of honor. She hated the thought that he might be compromising it out of . . . friendship.

"All the more reason I must find proof that Nicky is telling the truth," she whispered.

Truth. Charlotte added a flourish to the bold-lettered caption before setting aside her pen. Like quicksilver, it could be maddening elusive—a gleam here, a flash there, only to slip through one's fingers when one tried to grasp it.

As she leaned back and waited for the ink to dry, she found herself thinking back on her afternoon journey to the Kensington Palace neighborhood. The tobacco flakes offered its own challenge. She had some ideas on how to confront it, and would discuss them with Wrexford on the morrow . . .

But at the moment, something was bothering her about her talks with Billy and O'Malley, though she couldn't quite identify what it was. She didn't think they had lied to her, but her intuition told her something was missing from their answers.

Her brows drew together. Perhaps she hadn't asked the right questions.

Think! What was she overlooking?

After a moment or two, Charlotte pulled a piece of writing paper to the center of her blotter. Wrexford would apply logic, not emotion, to the question. She stared at the blank page, aware of the earl's recent warning echoing against the back of her skull.

"Mrs. Sloane, you aren't thinking with your usual clarity."

Charlotte blinked, willing herself to focus. As she shifted slightly in her chair, her eye caught the pooling of bloodred paint on her palette.

Blood. She was suddenly reminded that Cedric was not the first shocking murder involving mutilation. But neither she nor the earl had given much thought as to whether he was merely another random victim of the madman.

Picking up her pen, Charlotte slowly wrote down the names of the other victims. After consulting the reference notes she kept on all her drawings, she added the dates and locations. Would a more careful look at these crimes reveal a telling clue?

It was, perhaps, grasping at straws. But she didn't dare turn her back on any possibility, preposterous though it might be.

And she had an idea on how to begin.

After quickly rolling up her finished drawing in a length of protective oilcloth, Charlotte made her way up the stairs to the attic aerie. Raven was sprawled on his bed, reading a book on mathematics, while Hawk was on the rug, sorting through an odd collection of bits and bobs that he had just pulled from his pockets.

Good heavens, was that a mouse's skull?

"My goodness, what have you there?" she asked, momentarily putting aside her own mission.

"Look, this is a very unusual piece of rock. I think it may be quartz." Hawk held up a pebble that he had plucked from a tangle of string, bits of paper, and the stub of a pencil. "And I found this seed"—he pointed to a wrinkled, misshapen bean— "near Covent Garden Markets."

His eyes widened in delight. "And this feather is from the tail of a barn owl. It's not easy to find them in the city."

"Mr. Linsley is teaching us all about Alexander von Humboldt," explained Raven. "He—"

"He is a very famous man of science, and an expert in how the world of Nature all fits together!" interrupted Hawk excitedly. "He traveled to faraway exotic places and collected all sorts of rock, animal, and plant specimens."

Wrexford had arranged a tutor for the boys. She had been leery at first—both boys had a natural intelligence, but they had grown up wild in the slums and had a wary streak of independence that didn't bode well for the discipline of formal lessons. However, the experiment was proving a great success. The young man had sparked an enthusiasm for learning. More than that, he had sensed their particular interests and encouraged them.

"Daft, if you ask me, finding bits of stone and weed interesting," piped up Raven. However, a quick smile at his brother took the sting out of his words.

"No more daft than thinking a tangle of numbers is fun to unravel," retorted Hawk.

Charlotte crouched down to take a closer look at the collection. "Fascinating," she murmured, fingering through the various things that had caught the boy's eye. "These things intrigue you?"

Hawk nodded. "Mr. Linsley makes the study of the natural world very interesting." A pause. "He thinks I'm very observant and would make a good explorer."

"I think he's quite right." She ruffled his hair, then reached for one of the scraps of folded paper jumbled among the other objects and smoothed it out. It was a pencil sketch of a leaf from the rowan tree growing in the back garden.

"Why, this is lovely!" Hawk's drawings had always shown a natural exuberance, but this attention to detail was a surprise.

He smiled shyly. "You think so?"

"Indeed, I do."

"Show her your notebook," urged Raven. A snicker. "Though it's filled with bugs and worms, as well as flowers."

The boy dutifully fetched it from his desk drawer.

Charlotte felt a clench of guilt as she turned through the pages. How had she missed this? The move to the new house, and her worries over the changes it wrought to life, both for her and the boys, had weighed heavily on her thoughts of late. As had the demands of her own work. But that was no excuse. Hawk had a budding talent, and she had failed to see it.

Another fault—and yet another reason to be questioning her own judgment of late.

"You have a real gift for art."

Hawk's narrow face lit up at her praise. Which made her feel even more guilty.

"And a sharp eye for Nature," she said. "We must take a trip to Kew Gardens, where there are all sorts of exotic plants that have been brought back by English explorers."

Hawk's eyes widened. "Mr. Linsley says Kew Gardens is a very magical place."

"We will go there soon, I promise," Charlotte said decisively. Death must not be allowed to override Life. She turned to Raven. "Would you like to come, too?"

He raised his nose from the book, his expression turning oddly tentative. Unlike those of his younger brother, his inner feelings weren't always easy to discern. "Not really." The bed creaked as he shifted against the pillows. "Mr. Tyler has asked if I want to assist him in Lord Wrexford's laboratory on the days I don't have lessons. He said I could be of help in calculating some of the equations they need for their chemical experiments."

It was said casually, but Charlotte sensed it meant more to

him than he was letting on. His innate talent for mathematics had recently become apparent. "That sounds like a very exciting project." She hesitated. The earl was careless about a great many things, but science was not one of them. He was very serious and disciplined about his experiments. "And Wrexford is aware of the arrangement?" she asked gently.

"Aye," answered Raven. "Mr. Tyler said he suggested it."

Another surprise. Though after a moment's thought, she realized it shouldn't be. For all his mercurial moods and snappish sarcasm, Wrexford had always been very tolerant of the boys.

"Well, then, by all means, you must take advantage of such a splendid opportunity."

Raven gave a small shrug. Unlike his younger brother he was guarded about showing his emotions. But she saw through the fringe of his dark lashes a glimmer of happiness at her approval. "I s'pose it may be halfway interesting. Mr. Tyler says I can help him polish the instruments, and perhaps learn how to work the microscope as well."

"Excellent," murmured Charlotte, uncomfortably aware that another debt of thanks must be added to the earl's side of the ledger. The tally was growing dangerously unbalanced.

Seeing her shift the rolled drawing from hand to hand, Raven quickly set his book aside. "You need for us to deliver that?"

"What?" She had nearly forgotten why she had come. "Oh, yes. I'd be grateful if you would. Mr. Fores is expecting it."

Both boys were up in a flash.

"And then, after that," she added slowly, "if you are willing, I could use your help in another task." Charlotte didn't like to ask it, but with Nicky's life hanging in the balance, she set aside her reluctance. The boys were the only ones who could do the task.

"As if you need to ask, m'lady," replied Raven, fixing her with a reproachful look. His gaze then turned probing. "Does it have to do with the toff who was knifed in the Palace gardens?"

"Oiy, what can we do to help?" chimed in Hawk.

They were frighteningly quick to sense trouble—a skill that had likely kept them alive in the dog-eat-dog world of the stews.

"Yes, it concerns the gentleman who was killed on the night of the scientific soiree." Charlotte took out her notes on the Bloody Butcher murders. "I have reason to believe that the person arrested for the crime is innocent," she explained.

"They say his brother did it," said Hawk, his expression turning troubled.

"Yes, and I think they're wrong," assured Charlotte. The boys had survived a grim childhood with only each other to depend on. The idea of such an ultimate betrayal must seem like an unimaginable evil. "But I must try to gather the proof of it."

"Go on," said Raven, in unconscious imitation of the earl's coolly detached drawl.

A ghost of a smile passed over her lips, before her expression quickly tightened. "I need to dig deeper and learn more about the Bloody Butcher's first three murders. Someone must have seen something. A detail, no matter how small, might help me figure out the identity of the real killer."

The people who lived in the shadows of the city's alleyways and hellholes had not offered any help to the authorities. But with the right coaxing, they would speak freely to the boys and their ragged band of urchin friends.

"I'm looking for anything," continued Charlotte. "The description of any stranger spotted in the neighborhood, the sound of a voice, a footprint—every detail, no matter if it seems unimportant, is key to gather."

She rechecked her notes and gave them the locations, along with a reminder of the dates and time of day. The denizens of the streets didn't gauge time by clock or calendar, but they would remember the murders on account of the mutilations.

Raven nodded in understanding. "We've friends in those areas. If anyone saw something, we'll winkle it out of them."

"Thank you." Charlotte thought for a moment. "I know

you've done it once, but please ask again around Kensington Gardens. Your contacts said they saw naught but gentlemen leaving the grounds around midnight . . ." Including Nicholas. "But if possible, I'd like a more complete description of them." It might only be grasping at air, but she couldn't afford to overlook any chance of finding a telltale clue.

The boys quickly fetched their jackets. She passed over the print and followed them down the stairs to the front door.

"One last thing—both you and your friends must be very careful in how you go about the questioning," cautioned Charlotte, keeping hold of the latch for a moment. "Whoever is responsible for these crimes is a ruthless killer. He won't hesitate to strike again."

CHAPTER 6

"This way, gentlemen."

A Nubian porter, swathed in a scanty crimson toga that displayed a goodly amount of oil-sheened ebony muscles, opened the portal wider and beckoned Wrexford and Sheffield to follow him through a curtain made of jewel-tone glass beads. The whispery chatter as it fell closed behind them seemed redolent with the promise of more exotic experiences to come.

Illusion was often just as seductive as reality, thought the earl as he watched the light of the wall sconces flicker over the erotic murals of the corridor.

"Welcome to our Bosom." The proprietress rose and gave a graceful curtsey as they entered the fancy salon—a gesture clearly designed to display her impressive cleavage. Age had added hints of silver to her upswept blond tresses and a bit more voluptuousness to her curves. But Madame Boudicca was still a beauty.

"I'm honored." A gleam of crafty intelligence lit her kohl-rimmed eyes as she ran a quick assessing gaze over them. "We've not yet had the pleasure of your patronage here, Lord Wrexford. Or yours, Mr. Sheffield."

The earl wasn't surprised that she recognized them. It was her business to know her potential clientele.

"What enticements might we offer you? I'm sure we can cater to your every desire."

"Just the pleasure of a private conversation with Jeannette, if you please." He took a purse from his pocket. "For which, naturally, I expect to pay."

She hesitated. "We have earned a reputation for discretion here, milord. It's worth a great deal to an establishment such as mine."

"I, too, have a reputation for discretion," he countered. "You have my promise that what I hear tonight won't come back and bite you on your lovely derriere."

A twitch of amusement pulled at her carmine lips. "*Discretion* is not the first word that comes to mind concerning your reputation, sir." She considered the request a moment longer before adding, "Nonetheless, my sense is, your word as a gentleman can be trusted." With a deft quickness, she plucked the purse from his palm. "And besides, I have always had a weakness for handsome rogues who possess clever tongues."

Sheffield stifled a snort.

A gesture indicated they should take a seat on one of the velvet sofas. "Wait here. A servant will come shortly and take you to Jeannette."

After sinking down into the soft pillows, his friend looked around at the ornate furnishings and gilt-framed paintings of satyrs cavorting with nubile young maidens. "A pleasant place," he murmured.

"Feel free to return another time," said Wrexford. "And enjoy it with your own guineas, not mine."

Sheffield contrived to look injured. "It was simply an observation. I'm not in the habit of having to pay for my pleasure."

Wrexford didn't doubt it. The younger son of a nobleman wasn't seen as an attractive commodity on the marriage mart.

But Sheffield's charm and golden good looks made him a welcome partner in the boudoirs of the beau monde, despite his lack of title or fortune.

"What about you, Wrex?" murmured his friend. "Word is, you haven't chosen a new mistress to replace the divine Diana Fairfax."

True. The earl watched the candlelight dip and dance over the erotic pictures of coupling flesh. But he had no intention of explaining why.

Sheffield was wise enough not to press. They waited in silence, for several more minutes, before an older woman swathed in plum-colored silk entered the salon.

One of the matrons who supervised the girls, decided Wrexford, noting her basilisk eyes and hard-set mouth. Business was business—Madame Boudicca and her staff would keep careful watch that nothing havey-cavey was going on within the intimate pleasure chambers of the establishment.

"Please follow me, gentlemen."

Matron Plum led the way through a paneled portal set at the far end room. The lighting in the corridor was softer and more subdued than that of the reception room. Musky perfume—roses scented with an earthier undertone of spice—hung heavy in the warm air, while underfoot a tufted Turkey carpet muffled their steps, giving the illusion that they were walking on some strange multicolored cloud.

Swoosh, swoosh. The only sounds were the sinuous murmurs of voices tangling with the silky swoosh of fabric and flesh.

There were four doors lining each side of the way, each painted a pastel shade of pink and marked with an ornate brass numeral. Matron Plum stopped in front of Number 6. A quick touch to the latch and it released with a whispered *snick.*

"Please enter. When you are done, give a tug to the bellpull by the bed and I will come escort you out." A pause. "The house rules forbid gentlemen to move around outside the reception area on their own." Her eyes tightened in warning. "I trust you will respect them."

Or the hulking brute in the toga will break a few bones, thought the earl as he acknowledged the warning. "But of course."

After a grim nod, Matron Plum retreated.

More pink. As Wrexford followed Sheffield into the chamber, he felt as if he had stepped inside a spun-sugar confection of rose-colored hues. *Pink light, pink frills, pink flesh . . .* The hanging oil lamp flickered silently inside a ruby-hued glass globe, casting a soft glow over the lovely young woman lying amidst a tangle of cerise linen sheets.

A plate of ripe strawberries sat on the side table, along with three flutes filled with blush-colored champagne.

"You wish to speak with me?" Her voice was low and lush. "What a pity," she added with a husky laugh after looking them over. "Conversation ain't my strongest skill."

"I'm sure you'll prove quite satisfactory." Wrexford drew one of the delicate gilt chairs closer to the bedside and took a seat. Sheffield chose to stand in a shadowed spot behind the table.

Jeannette tittered and batted her fire-gold lashes. "Would ye care te wet yer whistle before we start?"

"Thank you, but I'm here for business, not pleasure." He held up a fist and slowly opened it to reveal half a dozen gold guineas nestled in his palm.

Her gaze became wary. "About what?"

"Nicholas Locke."

She sighed and then shivered. "Oiy, te think I might o' had the hands of a murderer still tainted with blood tickling my cockles that night."

"Locke was with you the night of the murder?"

"Aye," confirmed Jeannette as she reached for the coins and quickly tucked them beneath the sheets.

"At what time," demanded Wrexford. "And please be as precise as possible."

She gestured at the gilt clock on the dressing table. "Time is money, milord. So I can tell ye exactly when Nick was here. He arrived at one in the morning, and didn't leave until sunrise—that is, around half past six."

That confirmed what Locke had told him. But it was no help in proving his innocence. The argument between the brothers had occurred a little before midnight.

Leaving plenty of time for the gruesome deed to have been done before the accused showed up at Boudicca's Bosom.

"How did Locke appear? Agitated? Upset?" he asked. "Any signs of a physical struggle?"

Jeannette thought for a long moment. "He seemed unhappy, but that wasn't unusual. He'd told me he was worried about Cedric—"

"In what way?" interrupted the earl.

"He didn't say exactly. But . . ." She slowly curled a strand of her golden hair around her forefinger. "In my line o' work, ye learn te sense a man's primal nature. Nick's a very sweet and generous gent. I can't believe he wudda hurt his brother."

"You're not alone in holding that sentiment," he replied. Women apparently found Locke charming, though he had yet to see the allure. "Which is why I'm here. If you know anything else that might help prove his innocence, I'd like to hear it."

"I wish I could help ye, but all I can say is, Nick never said an unkind word about his brother." Her expression turned sad. "I hope ye find the bloke what killed Cedric."

Something about the way she said the murdered man's name stirred a prickling at the back of his neck. "Were you acquainted with Lord Chittenden, too?"

A sad smile tugged at her rosebud lips as she nodded. "But please don't tell Nick."

Wrexford glanced at Sheffield, who merely raised his eyebrows. "Are you saying you were intimate with the baron, as well as his brother?" he asked.

"Aye, two peas in a pod, they were."

That was one way of putting it, thought the earl.

"Cedric was a sweetheart, just like Nick. Very kind and generous—a perfect gentleman in every way." Jeannette smoothed at the ruffles on her boudoir wrapper.

"Which made," she mused softly, "those strange marks on his body even odder."

CHAPTER 7

Wrexford leaned forward in his chair. "*What* marks?"

Jeannette bit at her lip and looked away. "I dunno—mebbe it's best te leave the dead te rest in peace."

Wrexford bit back a sardonic comment. His views on the Hereafter were admittedly heretical.

It was Sheffield who quickly responded, "It may help us find his killer and bring him to justice."

"Well, seeing as ye put it that way ..." She blew out her breath. "There were some strange sores and a series of small cuts—made by a knife is my guess—on his breast and around his rib cage." Her mouth puckered in puzzlement. "Along with a few small spots of blackened flesh. They looked like burns, though God only knows how a gentry mort would get 'em."

God—or the devil. That was the trouble with murder, thought Wrexford. All too often, the moment of Death wasn't the end of Evil, it was merely the beginning. Like a stone hitting water, its impact could ripple out, bringing secrets to the surface that were best left submerged. And suddenly there were more victims.

Wrexford felt his gut tighten. He feared that Charlotte's sense of honor and loyalty might hurt her in ways she hadn't imagined.

"Did you ask Chittenden about the marks?" inquired Sheffield.

The earl shook off his brooding and forced himself to focus on Jeannette's answer.

She lifted her bare shoulders in a shrug. "Aye, but he mumbled some humble-bumble that made no sense te me. Don't see how hurtin' yerself can bring ye te some higher plane o' knowledge." A wry grimace. "But then, I ain't got a fancy brainbox like you educated gentlemen."

Pain. For some, it was a way of exploring the dark side of one's nature.

The earl rose abruptly. "Thank you." He gave a tug to the silken bellpull, then placed a few more coins on the bedcovering. "Don't tell anyone else about what we've discussed. If there's a dangerous killer on the loose, he won't hesitate to strike again."

Her eyes widened. Lifting a hand to her mouth, she made a quick pantomime of turning a key. "Oiy, me lips are locked right and tight, milord."

Matron Plum appeared a moment later. She led them through a side corridor and down a dark stairwell to an iron-studded door that opened into an unlit alleyway next to the mews.

Wrexford and his friend stepped out into the fog-misted night. Without a word, the woman drew it shut, and through the thick oak, the earl heard the rasp of the bolts being thrown back in place.

The air felt cold as ice against his face after the warmth of the brothel. He started walking.

"I can think of several establishments where Chittenden might have acquired such marks," murmured Sheffield after they had traversed a connecting passageway and emerged on the adjoining street.

"As can I," growled Wrexford. London catered to all manner of vices and obsessions. "None of them are pretty."

They walked on in silence for several strides. "I can make some inquiries, if you like," added his friend. "Not that I'm familiar with the world of pleasure and pain, but I know of one or two people who would be willing to talk."

Already the ripples were spreading, churning up waves in an ever-widening circle.

"My thanks, Kit. We can't afford to overlook that possibility," he replied. "But there's also Westmorly and the gambling debts. We need to know more about those, too." As for his own next steps . . . a sudden thought came to mind, spurring Wrexford to quicken his pace.

"I'll set both inquiries into motion tonight," promised Sheffield as he hurried to catch up. "Where are you racing off to?"

"I want to pay a visit to the morgue. But first, I need to rouse Henning. If anyone can make a corpse talk, it's him."

"Bloody, *bloody* hell." Slapping down her pen in frustration, Charlotte gave up trying to sketch a satire on the Prince Regent and his latest peccadillo. Lust and gluttony seemed such paltry sins compared to murder.

She rose and began to pace the perimeter of her workroom. Shadows stirred, their dark shapes dancing just out of reach of the flickering lamplight. The draperies were closed, but still she could sense the black-fingered gloom of the moonless night pressing against the windowpanes.

Pausing, Charlotte peeked through the folds of fabric, trying to spot any sign of movement in the street. Yet another sign her wits were out of kilter. It was far too early for the boys to be returning. As for dawn, it seemed an eternity away.

She resumed her pacing, suddenly aware of how impatient she was to show Wrexford the tobacco flakes. In the meantime, there *must* be some other lead to follow. But another turn around the small space only exacerbated the sense that she was spinning in circles.

As she came to an abrupt halt and stared at the fast-dying coals of the banked fire, Charlotte fisted her hands and felt a clench of impotent fury take hold of her. She *hated* feeling so helpless. A passive bystander, while the earl and the boys were out searching for clues.

In her previous home, a ramshackle structure squeezed up against the stews, she had been a nameless nobody, free to come and go as she pleased. The move to a nicer neighborhood had not come without consequences.

There were times when she questioned whether she had made the right decision.

Charlotte repressed a grimace, reminding herself of the aphorisms learned in long-ago schoolroom lessons. *Virtus tentamine gaudet*—strength rejoices in the challenge. At the time, such pompous platitudes had made three unruly adolescents snicker behind the tutor's back. Strange how they had stuck with her over the years, providing unexpected steel for the spirit in times of doubt.

She wondered if Nicky was lying on his miserable cot, using them as a talisman to keep the blackness at bay.

A gust of wind rattled the glass. The shadows shivered and slipped deeper into the dark corners of the room.

"I'll go mad if I stay in here any longer," whispered Charlotte. She drew in a ragged breath—and then spun around to blow out the desk lamp's flame.

Within minutes, she had stripped off her skirts and donned her urchin's garb. After penciling a quick note so McClellan and the boys wouldn't worry if they discovered her absence, Charlotte tucked her boots under her arm and tiptoed for the stairs.

*   *   *

"Auch, you had better be prepared to buy me a very ample breakfast—and a bottle of whisky to fortify my coffee." Henning's irascible grumble echoed within the slivered alleyway.

"Why is it all my friends think my purse is ripe for the plucking?" retorted Wrexford, pausing to peer through the swirls of silvery mist floating up from the muck beneath their boots.

"Because it is," replied the surgeon. He shifted his leather satchel from hand to hand, setting off a *snick-snick* of metal.

"Sssshhh," warned the earl.

"And be advised, I'll expect a generous donation to the clinic in return for rousing me out of bed at this ungodly hour." Henning ran a hand over his unshaven jaw. "Is there a reason we're slithering through the night like a pair of feral rats?"

"At this hour, the morgue's guard is likely slumbering off his midnight gin. I'd prefer he remain in the Land of Nod while we make our little visit."

A raspy chuckle stirred the air. "Tsk, tsk. You mean to say we don't have official permission?"

Wrexford ignored the sarcasm. Henning was happiest when he could thumb his nose at Society's rules. "This way," he whispered, leading the way across a narrow rutted cart track to the back of the stone building. Double doors, wide enough to allow the mortuary wagons' entrance, were set in the center of the grimy brick.

The earl drew a thin-bladed knife from his boot and made quick work of the lock.

Once inside, they moved quickly over the stone-flagged unloading bay and slipped into an unlit corridor. Up ahead, a lone candle was framed in an open doorway, its flame fluttering wildly in the gasp-and-wheeze rhythm of rattling snores.

Henning tapped his shoulder and silently signaled for them to turn down a connecting passageway. The sickly-sweet stench of decay grew more pronounced as they came to a weighty door of iron-banded oak. Setting his shoulder to the rough planks, the surgeon gave a hard shove.

It swung half open with a mournful groan.

Wrexford reeled back a step as a fresh wave of smells assaulted his nostrils.

"The perfume of death takes some getting used to," murmured Henning as he slipped inside the morgue.

Shallowing his breathing, the earl followed.

"Close the door."

He heard the surgeon fumbling around inside his satchel. A moment later, sparks flew as flint struck steel and the wick of a small metal lantern flared to life. Henning opened the shutter and handed it over before lighting a second one.

The beams illuminated a row of stone slabs, each draped with a length of stained canvas. Light and shadow slid over the heavy cloth, accentuating the macabre contours beneath the shroud.

Seemingly oblivious to the clammy cold, Henning removed his coat—the earl wasn't sure why, seeing as it was already spotted with a number of noxious-looking substances.

"Thank God we know what we're looking for," quipped the surgeon as he rolled up his shirtsleeves. "Faces can bloat and twist out of recognition, but I daresay there will only be one poor sod with a cod cut off."

After a quick look under the first covering, Henning moved on to the next slab. "Keep up with me, laddie. I'll need the extra light when we find our man."

Wrexford shuffled closer.

"Seeing as you wish to keep our visit a secret, it would be best not to spill your guts."

"You needn't worry. I've a strong stomach," shot back the earl, though the mingled fumes of putrefaction and carbolic acid were enough to turn a cast-iron pot upside down.

"Hell's bells, I hope you guessed right and they brought the body here," muttered Henning after checking under another shroud.

"So do I," said Wrexford, taking care to breathe through his mouth. The stench was appalling.

The surgeon's shuffling steps sounded unnaturally loud in the cryptlike silence. Somewhere close by, the steady drip of liquid splashed against stone.

"Ah. Eureka." Henning peeled back the canvas and let it slip from his fingers. It slithered to the floor with a flaccid sigh. "Bring your lantern closer. Let's not linger here any longer than necessary."

Death was not a pretty picture, mused Wrexford as the beam fell on Chittenden's face. It robbed a man not only of his soul, but also of his dignity. The young man's once-handsome features were distorted, and decay was already ravaging the flesh. If Locke were the murderer, he ought to be made to confront the ghastly portrait of what he, too, would look like when the Grim Reaper came for him.

A reminder that we are, for all our hubris, ultimately food for the flies and maggots.

"Shift the light," ordered Henning, indicating a spot on the baron's chest. Crouching down, he pulled a magnifying lens from his satchel and carefully examined the flesh.

"Hmmph." The surgeon moved methodically over the corpse's torso, pausing here and there to palpate a spot, though Wrexford was finding it hard to discern any injuries from the overall mottling.

Sliding a hand over the left side of the rib cage, Henning let out another grunt and reached for a pair of tweezers. "Well, well, what have we here?" he muttered, withdrawing a tiny fragment from a small incision between the bones.

"What is it?" demanded Wrexford.

"I've not a clue," replied Henning as he dropped it into a tiny glass vial from his bag and replaced the cork. "I'll need to look at it more closely at my surgery."

After another few pokes and prods at the discolored flesh,

Henning shifted his attention down to where the baron's scrotum had been severed.

The earl gave a pained wince. "Must you?" he muttered, averting his gaze as a primordial shudder snaked down his spine.

"Since when have you developed such delicate sensibilities?" Angling his head, Henning leaned in even closer. "It's not out of ghoulish interest. I'm looking at how the cut was made." Lamplight winked off the magnifying lens. "Hmmph. It was done with precision, and the blade was razor-sharp . . ." He finally looked up. "I'm wondering whether the Bloody Butcher's other victims showed the same style. It's a question worth asking."

"Very clever," conceded Wrexford.

"Which means I shall feel free to order a beefsteak to go along with broiled kidneys at breakfast," came Henning's cheerful reply. Looking satisfied, he set aside the lenses and rose.

"Help me turn him over."

Together, they managed to reverse Chittenden's deadweight.

A muffled sound caught Wrexford's ear. He spun around and listened for a moment. "We better hurry," he murmured. "I think I hear the sound of a cart entering the back courtyard."

"Hold your water, laddie. We won't have another chance with His Lordship, and I imagine you'd prefer that I don't miss anything."

Wrexford shuffled his feet in impatience, but kept his mouth shut.

Finally, after several long moments had slid by, a rough growl rumbled against the stone. "There's nothing else of interest. Let's put everything back in order."

Thump-thud. The body rolled back in place—and not a moment too soon. There were voices coming from somewhere in the building, and they were getting louder.

Wrexford snatched up the canvas. "Damnation, stop fiddling with his privates and snuff out your light."

"We need to leave him as we found him," retorted the surgeon. He finished arranging the body parts, then signaled for the earl to throw on the shroud. As Wrexford extinguished his lantern, Henning grabbed up his satchel and they both hurried through the darkness for the door.

Too late. Just as the earl caught hold of the latch, the clatter of hobnailed boots came to a halt on the other side of the age-dark oak. In another instant . . .

Grabbing Henning's arm, he bolted to his left, praying that the jog in the wall he had noticed earlier would afford enough of a hiding place.

Leaning back against the warehouse wall, Charlotte closed her eyes and tilted her face to the clouded sky. The rough bricks dug into her shoulder blades, but the pain felt good. Perhaps it would rouse her from the strange somnambulant fugue that was holding her in thrall. Her rush of restlessness had worn itself out in aimless wandering, leaving her aware that she couldn't keep running and hiding from her demons.

She must face her fears. Cowardice was crippling. It would slowly grind her into dust.

Fortes fortuna adiuvat—fortune favors the bold.

Ah, those aphorisms again. This one tugged a wry quirk to her lips.

"For better or for worse, I seem to have spent my life spitting in the eye of caution." A few fat drops of rain splashed against her cheeks and ran in chill rivulets down the line of her jaw.

Charlotte started walking again. Still too unsettled to return home, she wove her way through the maze of alleyways toward Lincoln's Inn Fields, hoping to intercept the boys. Their regular route should bring them along the northern side of the square.

A short while later, from her vantage point within a small copse of trees behind the iron fence, she spotted them, flitting dark-on-dark shapes that would have eluded her eye if she hadn't known what to be looking for.

Two quick hoots—the tremulous call of a tawny owl—alerted the boys to her presence. In an instant, they appeared from out of the shrubbery, stirring naught but a whisper of the leaves.

Raven's features were drawn taut. "What's wrong?" he demanded, his hand sliding down to his boot, where he carried a deadly-looking knife given to him by the earl.

"Nothing," she assured him. "I—I simply felt the need for a breath of fresh air."

"It's dangerous to be wandering the streets at this hour," chided Hawk.

Out of the mouths of babes, she thought wryly.

"Without us," he added hastily, realizing that path of argument might quickly trip him up.

"I'm always careful," she responded. "But never mind that now—how did your inquiries go?"

"We've spread the word to our friends," replied Raven slowly. He was still watching her with a wariness beyond his years. "If a rat so much as scratched his arse near the murder scenes, we'll soon know of it."

"Don't be vulgar," murmured Charlotte.

Hawk snickered, earning a swift cuff from his brother.

"We did hear something interesting tonight," continued Raven. "Dunno if it means anything, but . . ."

Charlotte heard the note of suppressed excitement in his voice.

"But you can decide for yourself."

"I'm all ears," said Charlotte, coming instantly alert.

A grin flashed across his face. "You're going to need your peepers as well," he began, only to spin around at the rustling of leaves from somewhere in the shadows behind them.

"Though we should return home first," added Raven in a low whisper. "And then Hawk is going to show you his drawing."

CHAPTER 8

Wrexford flattened himself against the clammy stone just as the door swung open with a rusty groan. More scuffling and scraping sounded as a wobbly beam of light pierced the darkness.

"Bloody hell, yer tipping yer end—iffen his guts slide out, it ain't me who's wiping 'em up."

"The sodding cove weighs more 'n an ox," came the grunted reply as a burly man, clad in a bloodstained smock and squashed Regent hat, took a step into the morgue. "Damnation—stop wigglin' the light, Willy! I can't see where I'm going."

The beam steadied somewhat.

Out of the corner of his eye, Wrexford watched Regent Hat stagger forward, his meaty hands clasping the handles of a stretcher bearing a misshapen mound topped with a greasy oil-cloth. A beefy leg had escaped from beneath the folds and was dancing a macabre jig through the foul air.

"Which way?" demanded the bear-sized fellow holding up the rear of the stretcher.

"Straight ahead." The lantern-bearer, a short man with long, ratty hair framing his narrow face, squeezed through the door and hurried to light the way. The scent of cheap gin wafted in to join the fugue of other smells. "There be an empty slab at the end of this row."

The *clack-clack* of the hobnails punctuated the bumps and curses as the three made their way deeper into the morgue. Then suddenly the lamp flickered and went out.

"Ye gin-soaked booby! Strike a flame, or your poxy carcass will be joining this one on its slab."

Wrexford made a split-second decision. Nudging Henning, he whispered, "Follow me!" and darted for the doorway. The surgeon, though no paragon of manly muscle, showed himself to be surprisingly agile in hurrying down the corridor and making the turn for the back door. It wasn't until they were two streets away from the mortuary that Wrexford allowed them to pause for breath.

"Auch, I've grown too old for skulduggery," wheezed Henning, bending over and bracing his hands on his knees. "If my poor, thumping heart gives up the ghost and I shuffle off this mortal coil, it's your bloody fault."

"Oh, come—you're cobbled together from granite and flint, with naught but Highland malt running through your veins," quipped the earl. "And you've said on numerous occasions that you don't have a heart." A pause. "You'll survive."

Henning's mouth twitched, but he covered it with a scowl. "Not if I don't get my breakfast." Dawn was just beginning to tinge the horizon. "There's a tavern near Covent Garden that serves a decent meal at this hour."

Wrexford flagged down a passing hackney. "What about the fragment you found?"

"Unlike me, it isn't going to expire of hunger if it's not fed in the next half hour," retorted Henning as he slouched back against the squabs. "I'll need to do a careful examination in my surgery, so stubble your nattering. I'll have an answer for you later today."

Tamping down his impatience—no mean feat as his temper was frayed and his clothes were reeking of death—Wrexford refrained from further comment. In any case, he needed some time to gather his thoughts and grab a few hours of sleep before facing Charlotte.

God only knew what reaction she would have to these new developments. A barrage of questions, to begin with.

For which he, as yet, had precious few answers.

"What's your guess as to what the late Lord Chittenden was involved in?"

"I prefer not to guess, laddie. We are, after all, men of science, who ought to adhere to fact and evidence, not conjecture." Henning closed his eyes. "But whatever it is, I have a suspicion that none of us are going to like it."

Charlotte followed the boys up the stairs, unsure whether the clench in her chest was dread or elation. No matter which way it cut, knowledge was better than having her emotions trapped in a netherworld of doubts and suspicions.

Imagination could often be worse than the truth.

Or so she told herself. And yet, with each thud of her steps on the wooden treads, her heart kicked harder against her rib cage. The pain seemed to seep into her bones.

McClellan cracked open her door as they trooped by her bedchamber. "Do you wish for some tea and sustenance?" she asked, unruffled by the ungodly hour.

"No," answered Charlotte, unable to contemplate any distraction. She quickly softened her curtness with a forced smile. "But thank you."

To her credit, the maid simply nodded and drew the latch shut.

Raven had already lit the Argand lamp on her work desk. Hawk was beside his brother, both hands jammed in his jacket pockets.

Crackle, crackle. The whispery sound of paper twisting between his fingers sent another spurt of fear bubbling up in her chest.

"Please explain yourselves," said Charlotte, after expelling a carefully controlled breath. Hoping against hope to hide from them how rattled she was by this crime, she added a light note. "Before I explode from curiosity."

Raven's dark lashes dipped to shadow his eyes.

Damnation—he didn't look in the least fooled.

Hawk responded by brandishing a smudged piece of folded paper. "It's all about the—"

His brother caught his hand and forced it down to the desktop. "Oiy, put a cork in it for now—we need to start from the beginning."

The boy bit his lip in frustration, but remained silent.

"Don't look so Friday-faced. You'll soon get your chance to show how clever you are," counseled Raven before turning to Charlotte. "We followed the order of the murders you wrote down for us and started in Seven Dials."

Charlotte nodded. The first of the Bloody Butcher's victims had been a shiftless vagrant known as Greybeard, who begged for coins at the monument—a stone pillar adorned with the circle of sundials—which had given the now-infamous slum area its name.

"Greybeard didn't have a regular lair. He slept in whatever hidey-hole he could find at night, which is likely why nobody witnessed the crime," continued Raven. "But on that night, some of the locals did recall seeing a few fancy coves pass through the alleyways near where the body was found."

"Gentlemen who are cup-shot or feeling daring occasionally pass through the slums on their way home from the gaming hells," mused Charlotte. "It doesn't necessarily mean anything." And yet she felt a prickling of gooseflesh rise at the nape of her neck.

"Aye, m'lady, I know that. Still, it seemed a useful bit of information to report back to you. But it turns out I had it arglebargled." Raven allowed a bemused grimace. "Much as I hate to admit it, Hawk's fiddling around with all those disgusting bugs and bits of rock isn't as daft as I thought."

His brother grinned.

"It's him who remembered to look for the little details, and . . ." Raven lifted his shoulders. "You go ahead and tell her."

"It's you and your drawings I learned from, m'lady," said Hawk in a rush. "Y'know, look for the little details—you're always saying it's the small bits and bobs that help piece together the truth."

Charlotte sucked in a breath. She had used the aphorism to explain to the boys why gathering so much seemingly meaningless information was important for her work. Apparently, Hawk had taken her words to heart.

She stared down at the grubby piece of paper, which was still clutched in his hand. "And you've found one of those bits and bobs?"

Hawk tugged at the front of his jacket—she didn't care to identify what foul-looking substance was streaked over the notched collar—and cleared his throat.

"Mebbe," came the tentative answer. "I arsked—asked— each person we questioned to think hard and describe what the coves were wearing. The first few didn't remember nuffink— nothing—save for a dark coat and hat."

When Hawk became excited, his English tended to lapse back into the patter of the stews.

"But then, Fat Mary said she recalled that one of the gentlemen wuz wearing a hat with the brim curled up at the sides, and that there seemed to be a flash of something bright, like a bit of metal, on the band."

"So Hawk thought to draw a sketch," interjected Raven. "And Mary gabbled 'nay' and 'yea' until he got the shape right."

"We talked to another cully," went on Hawk, "who remembered something about a hat—"

"Said he noticed what looked to be a silver ornament in the

ribbon band because he was thinking of following the gentleman and pinching it," cut in Raven. "But then decided against it
because the fellow looked too alert."

"Oiy," agreed Hawk. "And when we showed him the finished sketch, he said it was bang on the mark."

Charlotte realized her heart had started to thump against her
ribs. "May I see it?"

Hawk solemnly unfolded the paper and slid it across the
desktop.

Though smudged and rife with creases that trapped a flickering of tiny shadows, it seemed unnaturally light against the
dark-grained wood.

Unclenching her fingers, she drew it closer and took a long
moment to study the penciled image. The boy had a real knack
for drawing. The lines were quick and simple, yet he had captured the curl of the sides and the jaunty dip of the brim at the
back and front. Charlotte recognized the style—it had a name,
though she couldn't recall it—as being popular, but not at the
pinnacle of fashion with the Tulips of the *ton*.

Distinctive, but not too distinctive.

"We planned on going to Bermondsey tonight, and then on
to the Puddle Dock," said Raven, mentioning the two other
murder locations. "If anyone mentions a hat, we'll show them
the drawing."

"You think it might help?" asked Hawk.

"Yes," replied Charlotte, still staring at the image. "I think it
might help a great deal." She took a sheet of drawing paper
from her desk drawer and quickly copied the sketch.

Dare I hope the villain is a gentleman? The answer was still
tauntingly unclear. Finding a madman among the vast multi-
tudes of the city seemed an impossible task, especially as the
morning papers had hinted that the authorities planned to
move quickly in bringing Nicholas to trial.

Horrific crimes called for swift retribution.

If the miscreant were a member of the beau monde, that would narrow the choice of possible suspects. Which might also tighten the noose around Nicholas's neck.

Charlotte gave the sketch back to Hawk. "That was very good thinking on your part."

The praise brought a tinge of pink to his cheeks. His smile seemed to lighten the darkness squeezing in around them.

"Indeed, I'm grateful to both of you for your help. But now, I must insist that you head up to your aerie and get some sleep." As the boys turned to go, she added, "And another thing—I won't permit the investigation to interfere with your lessons. You'll attend your regular sessions with Mr. Linsley and finish all your reading and writing assignments before taking on any other tasks."

Raven's expression turned mulish. "Are you saying reading and writing is more important than saving your friend's life?"

The question was like a punch in the gut, but Charlotte managed an unflinching reply. "Yes, for the two of you, it is."

Guilt over involving them in such a sordid brother-against-brother crime was already pricking at her conscience. She was determined that Cedric's death not undo all her efforts to give them a life where depravity and death weren't everyday companions.

Evil was like acid—it could all too quickly and silently corrode one's soul.

"But . . ." Shoulders stiffening in defiance, Raven lifted his gaze to meet hers. Their eyes met and locked for several heartbeats.

Thump. Thump.

Thankfully, he looked away without further protest.

Charlotte waited until the sound of their steps died away on the stairs before expelling a shuddering exhale. Taking the key to the locked compartment in her desk from its hiding place, she added the sketch to the folded paper packet containing the snuff. Her mind was too muzzy to think of anything but stumbling to her bedchamber and sinking into the blessed oblivion of sleep.

A sip of scalding coffee—dark as the devil's temptations—helped burn away the lingering sour taste of death's degradations. Wrexford grimaced. How quickly all of man's grand illusions of his supreme importance in the universe was reduced to a carapace of rotting flesh and putrid ooze.

He took another swallow, ignoring the plate of freshly made toast by his elbow. Thank god Charlotte had not witnessed the gruesome scene. This crime was testing her strength in ways he had never seen before. She was, he feared, perilously close to snapping.

He wished he knew why.

"Ah!" An appreciative sniff punctuated the exclamation. "I see breakfast is still being served."

"Why is it that all my acquaintances seem to think of nothing but their stomachs?" groused the earl as he poured himself more coffee. The sight of Henning wolfing down broiled kidney and slices of blood-rare beefsteak earlier that morning had left his stomach feeling a little queasy.

"Because your chef is superb," replied Sheffield as he went to help himself to a plateful of delicacies from the silver chafing dishes.

"He ought to be, considering the obscene amount of money I pay him."

"Speaking of obscene . . ." Sheffield forked up a bite of shirred eggs and mushrooms. "Did you learn anything of interest at the mortuary?"

Wrexford could think of several sarcastic replies, but held them back as the sunlight caught on the lines of fatigue etched around his friend's eyes. He, too, had been digging for dirt in the less salubrious parts of London in order to help Charlotte.

"Henning and I were able to examine the corpse, though we only evaded being caught by the skin of our teeth," he replied quietly. "There were, as Jeannette said, strange bruises and cuts on Chittenden's body. Henning extracted a small fragment from one of them."

Sheffield stopped chewing. "A fragment of what?"

"I hope to learn that later today, once Henning has had a chance to examine it in his surgery."

"Are you going to tell Mrs. Sloane about this discovery?"

A good question. One tangled in complexities and conundrums.

Outside the mullioned windows, the well-tended shrubbery swayed in the gentle breeze, setting off a subtle flickering of sun-kissed greens. Charlotte would know all the names of the hues. The depth of her perceptions never ceased to surprise him. She saw things that most people missed.

He shifted in his chair, forcing his thoughts back to the moment. "She would never forgive me if I didn't."

No frivolous quip, just a solemn nod came in answer.

The muted clink of silver against silver sounded as a footman discreetly removed the empty coffeepot and replaced it with a fresh one. A plume of steam wafted up from the spout, filling the room with the smoky spice of dark-roasted beans.

Sheffield set aside his plate and took a moment to refill his cup. "I don't envy you the task," he murmured. A pause as he added a small splash of cream. "Alas, I have some other unpleasant news to add. In making the rounds of gaming hells, I met Benjamin Westmorly. We had a discussion concerning his gambling debts to Chittenden."

Wrexford waited for the penny to drop.

"It turns out the amount wasn't quite as large as Locke seemed to imply. And it was paid off several days before Chittenden's murder."

"You know this for sure?"

"I do," answered Sheffield. "First of all, I threatened to cut off *both* of Westmorly's bollocks if he didn't tell me the truth." A muscle twitched on his jaw, the stubbling of unshaven whiskers sparking in the light. "Having a devil-be-damned reputation puts the fear of God into those who don't know the truth about what a lazy fribble I am."

He flicked a mote of dust from his sleeve. "More importantly, Debenham, whose word I trust, confirmed that he was with the pair when the vowels changed hands. According to him, the two appeared cordial."

"It seems Westmorly must move off our list of possible suspects."

"I'm afraid so—but that's not the worst of it. Very few bank-notes actually changed hands, because in lieu of money, Chittenden accepted certain promissory notes from a third party that Westmorly possessed. I imagine you can guess who owed him money."

"Bloody hell," muttered Wrexford. "Locke?"

"Yes. And apparently he plays as badly as I do at the gaming tables," answered Sheffield with a wry grimace.

Yet again, the earl wondered what hold the fellow had on Charlotte. Pushing the thought aside, he pursed his lips. "On second thought, it's still worth having a chat with Westmorly and delving deeper into how the three of them were connected."

"On a cheerier note," went on Sheffield. "It seems Locke wasn't lying about there being bad blood between Chittenden and Sir Kelvin Hollister. They were indeed vying for the attention of the same young lady, and their exchanges were becoming increasingly acrimonious." A sigh. " 'O, beware, my lord, of jealousy; It is the green-eyed monster . . .' "

"Ye gods, you've actually read Shakespeare."

"Only the parts that make a mockery of human foibles."

Wrexford chuffed a humorless laugh. "So it seems Sir Kelvin is still on the list." Along with the Honorable Nicholas Locke.

"If you like, I can try to learn a little more about Hollister," offered Sheffield. "As well as keep probing for information about Westmorly."

"I'd be grateful for that, Kit." He reluctantly rose. Loath as he was to tell Charlotte what he had learned, he ought not delay. Locke's life seemed to be dangling by an ever-fraying thread. If they were to have any hope of proving his innocence before it snapped, they couldn't afford to waste a moment.

"We need to gather all the facts we can."

Though he was beginning to fear that facts would do them little good. What they really needed was a damn miracle.

CHAPTER 9

The change was subtle, but the air in the parlor suddenly felt charged with the same sort of thrumming current that presaged a summer thunderstorm. Charlotte didn't need to look up from her notebook when in the next instant a long shadow fell across the sofa.

She knew who it was.

The earl seemed to suck all the oxygen from the room as he crossed the carpet, compressing the space around her and making it hard to breathe.

"Did you learn anything at the brothel?" she asked, after finishing what she was writing and setting down her pencil.

"Yes." He moved to one of the armchairs, but didn't sit. The planes of his face, always sharp to begin with, seemed chiseled to a harsher edge. Fatigue dulled the green of his eyes to a slate-dark hue. "However, you're not going to like it."

As if anything about this dreadful nightmare doesn't send a shiver of dread down my spine.

"Be that as it may, I need to hear it."

Wrexford hesitated for an instant. "How well did you know Chittenden?" he countered.

Fear squeezed at her lungs. What horror had he uncovered? The earl was not in the habit of pulling his punches.

"I should think it's obvious I knew him *very* well," she replied.

"But not, perhaps, as well as you might think." He ran a hand through his wind-snarled hair. It needed trimming, she noted.

"Let's stop playing cat and mouse, sir. Our previous investigations were hardly all sweetness and light. Haven't I proved myself capable of hearing grim news?"

"Actually, no," replied the earl softly. "You fell into a dead faint at learning of Chittenden's death. That begs the question of . . ."

Charlotte shifted uncomfortably under his hooded stare. "Sit down, Wrexford. I'm getting a crick in my neck staring up at you."

He didn't smile.

A stab of guilt cut through her conscience. She didn't blame him. Were she in his boots, she would take the lack of trust as a slap in the face.

"Sit down, Wrexford," she repeated.

The words were barely more than a breath of air, but the earl must have sensed the change in her tone, for he did so.

Swoosh, swoosh. With a well-tailored whisper of wool, his broad shoulders settled against the upholstered back of the armchair. Muscles rippled beneath the soft charcoal-colored superfine, reminding her of a stalking panther. A coiled tension radiated from every pore.

"You deserve an explanation," said Charlotte softly. "I know that."

His expression was inscrutable. They both were good at keeping parts of themselves well hidden.

"That you've respected my privacy on this matter is . . ." Charlotte was unsure of how to go on.

A moment ticked by, and then a tiny twitch pulled at the corners of his mouth. "Actually, I haven't. I asked Tyler to dig around for Locke's connection to you. It didn't take him long to unearth the answer."

She waited.

He shrugged. "I took his copious notes—you know what a stickler Tyler is for research—and . . ." Again he hesitated.

"The devil take it," she muttered, after he let the silence stretch out for an interminable moment. "You're worse than Sheffield at drawing out a dramatic moment."

"God forbid." His rumbled laugh seemed to dispel the tension in the air. "I took Tyler's notes and consigned them to the fire. Without reading them, I might add."

Conundrums within conundrums. "Why?"

"Because it was an act unworthy of our friendship."

Charlotte made a wry face. "Thank you—for making me feel smaller than a gnat on a flea's arse."

His eyes lit with a fleeting smile.

"Oh, Wrexford . . ." She looked away. "I'm so sorry. Cedric's death was a terrible shock. And that Nicky may have . . ." A pause. "It's confusing. I've been struggling to sort it all out."

He rose and came closer. She closed her eyes as his palm pressed lightly against her cheek. "Then let me help."

His touch seemed to still all the churning in her gut. "Thank you."

The earl let his hand linger a moment longer, then returned to his chair.

"Cedric and Nicky are my cousins, and were my closest childhood companions. Of all my family, they seemed to understand me and how confined I felt by the gilded cage of my existence. They encouraged me to read, to explore ideas thought unfit for a girl." Charlotte paused to steady her voice. "When I confided my plans to elope, they gave me their pocket money and said to spread my wings and fly."

"I see," murmured Wrexford.

"They wished to keep in touch, but I soon stopped writing to them. I didn't . . . I didn't wish for them to worry about me."

"I understand."

"I shouldn't have pushed away their friendship. But . . ."

"The past is the past," he said brusquely.

She huffed a low laugh in spite of herself. "How unlike you to utter mundane platitudes."

"Well, as you know, I have a great many faults."

And a great many strengths.

"As do I. However, I suggest we put them all aside for now." She shifted in her chair. "Please tell me what you've learned about Cedric."

Wrexford hesitated. "Where are the Weasels?" he asked abruptly. "Their ears are better than those of a bloody bat, and while the details would likely not come as a shock to them, I know your sentiments about discussing man's baser depravities in front of children."

"They are at their lessons with Mr. Linsley," replied Charlotte. "By the by, both of them are thriving under his tutelage. I'm grateful to you for suggesting him."

He shrugged off the thanks. "Perhaps a rigorous regime of studies will help keep the little beasts out of trouble."

She held back a smile. Despite his sarcastic needling, she knew he was very fond of the boys. "We have the house to ourselves as McClellan is out doing some errands. So, please, no more prevaricating."

"Very well. According to Locke's doxy, your late cousin was also sharing her favors," began Wrexford.

An oath slipped from her lips.

"However, it seems neither of them knew it, so Chittenden can't be accused of sordid depravity." A pause. "However, my interview with the young woman revealed a different cause for concern."

Charlotte listened with a sinking heart as the earl described the doxy's mention of the strange marks on Chittenden's body and the visit he and Henning had made to the morgue. By the time he finished explaining about Westmorly and Nicholas's misleading statement about the gambling debts, she could no longer deny what was staring her in the face.

"Much as I hate to admit it, brotherly jealousy may very well be the motive for murder," she murmured. "Given Nicky's rant about Cedric getting everything by virtue of his being the older by several minutes, it might have triggered a fit of uncontrollable rage." Her hands knotted together in her lap. "The mutilation certainly fits in with such a scenario."

"Let's not jump to conclusions. I've asked Sheffield to look further into Chittenden's friction with Sir Kelvin Hollister, in case there is more to it than a romantic rivalry," Wrexford counseled. "But, yes, there are a great many more questions that Locke needs to answer."

His gaze turned searching. She could feel it poking and prodding into every tiny chink in her armor.

"I was able to arrange with the warden for a visit with him later this afternoon. But there's no reason you need to come along. I'm perfectly capable of questioning him on my own," continued Wrexford.

It was tempting. But giving in to self-serving weakness was merely another name for hypocrisy. Let that happen and she might as well toss her pen into the River Thames. She would be no better than any other of the silk-swathed scoundrels and liars in Town.

"Since when," asked Charlotte, "have you known me to take the coward's way out?"

"There is a first time for everything." He was gentlemanly enough not to mention her swoon again.

"Hypothetically speaking, yes. But I'm not about to dance stark naked down Piccadilly Street or crown myself Queen of England, either, so we can set aside absurdities that aren't going to happen."

"There's nothing absurd about feeling emotionally involved with a loved one," he said quietly.

Charlotte sighed. It was true. Love addled the wits. It made one behave irrationally. "Be that as it may, if we try very hard, I think it's possible to make ourselves overcome emotions."

The earl's eyes hadn't left her face. "But at what cost?"

Damn him for asking a question I don't dare contemplate.

Unclenching her hands, she looked down and started smoothing a crease from her skirts. As she did so, her fingers brushed up against paper. Hawk's drawing, along with the packet containing the snuff, had slipped from the cushions to become tangled in the folds of sprigged muslin.

Lud, the earl's revelations had chased all thoughts of her own discoveries from her mind.

"What have you there?" asked Wrexford as she carefully cupped the two items in her upturned palms.

"You were not the only one out looking for clues yesterday." Charlotte quickly told him about her foray to Kensington Gardens, and the inquiries made by the boys.

With his usual scientific detachment, the earl studied the crinkles and smudges for a long moment before taking up the sketch and subjecting it to a more thorough scrutiny.

"Wellington," he murmured.

Her eyes widened. "The *duke*?"

"No, the hat." He refolded the sketch. "It's called a Wellington."

"I don't suppose that helps."

"Not particularly. Any number of hatters make the style."

Charlotte now felt even more foolish offering the grains of snuff. "You needn't bother looking at this." She closed her hand around the clue. "It won't be of any use."

"The scientific method is to *not* make assumptions, even if common sense seems to indicate that you are right." The earl held out his hand. "The workings of the world don't always conform to expectations."

She reluctantly gave him the pouched paper.

After a cursory peek at the snuff, he leaned closer.

Sniff, sniff.

Hope—irrational, though it was—flared to life. "The scent seems distinctive."

Wrexford looked down his long nose at her. "Have you any idea how many variations of snuff mixtures there are in London?"

"I'm not a mathematician—large numbers befuddle my brain," she shot back. Her shoulders slumped. "I know, I know. It's ridiculous. I was simply grasping at straws."

"If you'll allow me to take the evidence with me, I'll have Tyler examine it under the microscope and see if he spots anything useful. But I wouldn't have high hopes about it."

"The poor man will be cursing me from here to Hades for adding yet more work to his list of duties," said Charlotte.

"He's not paid to curse, but to perform whatever sartorial or scientific tasks need to be done," replied Wrexford dryly, pocketing the items. "And be assured, it's a princely amount. He has no cause for complaint."

Given the earl's mercurial moods, she thought, the valet likely earned every farthing.

His sardonic smile had already disappeared, replaced by a tight-lipped grimness. Rising, he began to pace the perimeter of the room. "You had better change into your urchin's garb if you intend to come along to Newgate. We need to be leaving shortly."

As Charlotte moved to the door, she heard a faint scuff.

Wrexford must have caught it, too, because he spun around, his eyes narrowing to a slitted stare.

Silence. But neither of them was fooled. The boys possessed the light-footed quickness of their namesake weasels to go along with their batlike hearing.

"As you are so fond of saying, Mrs. Sloane," he muttered softly, "no matter how much discretion one uses to keep them well-guarded, no secret is ever safe."

* * *

The stench, the screams, the ooze of utter despair bleeding from flesh and stone—a second visit only seemed to amplify Newgate's horrors. Wrexford followed the gaoler through the endless turns of the grimy corridor, their thudding steps lost in the cacophony of curses and howls.

Head down, Charlotte kept pace. Whatever she was feeling, she kept it well hidden.

Thank God. He didn't dare contemplate the consequences if she were to lose her nerve.

Nicholas's cell was marginally less revolting. There was a small table and several straight-back chairs... decent bedding... a hamper of food and drink... extra clothing brought from his lodging. All of which had not come cheap.

The earl hoped the fellow was worth it.

A look at him sitting on his bed, shoulders slouched against the wall, didn't inspire much confidence. His hair was matted, his jaw unshaved, his gaze dulled with apathy.

Or was it guilt?

"Nicky."

Charlotte's sharp voice roused naught but a momentary flicker of awareness.

"Go away," he mumbled. "Don't waste your time with me."

During the carriage ride to the prison, Wrexford had counseled her that a show of sympathy might salve her own spirits, but it wouldn't save Locke's neck. To have any chance of proving him innocent, they had to rattle the truth out of him.

"Feeling sorry for yourself, are you?" Charlotte crossed the small cell in several swift strides. "Fine. You have two choices— curl up like a muckworm and wait for the hangman to put you out of your misery." A kick to the bedstead punctuated her words.

Nicholas was suddenly sitting up straighter.

"Or pull your bloody wits together and help us figure out who murdered Cedric!"

"And then there's a third option," murmured the earl into the momentary silence. "You can confess your guilt here and now, and save us all a great deal of aggravation."

A flash of fire lit in Nicholas's eyes. An angry flush rushed to his cheeks. "I didn't kill my brother!"

Perhaps there is a spark of hope, thought Wrexford.

"Then stop throwing sand in our eyes, Nicky." Grabbing a chair from the table, Charlotte turned it to face him and took a seat. "No more half-truths and prevarications."

"I didn't—" began Nicholas.

"Westmorly," cut in Wrexford. "You neglected to tell us you owed gambling debts to Westmorly."

"Because it had nothing to do with Cedric!"

"You really think the fact that your brother paid off your vowels is irrelevant?" demanded Charlotte.

The color drained from Locke's face. "Cedric paid them? I—I had no idea!"

Unless he was a consummate actor, Locke's surprise appeared unfeigned. But then, a cold-blooded killer would be skilled at hiding his true self.

"Why?" added Locke, looking truly puzzled. "Why would he do that? I have a generous allowance."

"You tell me," she countered. "Word is, when Westmorly paid off his debt, Cedric asked to take your vowels as partial payment, and Westmorly was happy to comply."

Locke did naught but lift his shoulders in reply.

"You implied there was friction between them, and yet witnesses said the two of them were quite cordial," said Wrexford.

"I wasn't lying," said Locke hotly. "I don't care what the gamesters might have seen. There was some sort of bad blood between Westmorly and Cedric."

Charlotte leaned forward. "Just how much did *you* owe Westmorly, Nicky?" she asked abruptly.

Locke's gaze slid away to a clump of dirty straw on the floor.

Her expression hardened.

Wrexford shrugged as she darted a quick look at him. "Never mind that right now. The more pressing concern is the Eos Society and their activities."

Every muscle in Locke's body seemed to tense. Save for a tiny tic at the right corner of his mouth.

"Your little group does more than just talk, don't it?" went on the earl. "Given your inquisitive scientific minds, I would imagine you engage in experiments."

"Sometimes," came the wary reply.

Charlotte rose, setting the rancid shadows pooled on the floor to rippling across the rough stone. Locke's breathing turned shallow, as if he were panting for air.

A step brought her closer to him.

Twitch, twitch. The quivering grew more pronounced.

"You're no better now than you were as a child at keeping your face from giving you away, Nicky," she observed.

A deeply feral sound—it reminded Wrexford of a wounded animal—stuck in Locke's throat.

Her fingers spasmed. For an instant, the earl thought she might strike her cousin.

"I had a look at your brother's body," said the earl. "What dark games was he playing?"

It took a moment for Locke to master his emotions enough to speak "That's just it." His anguish was sharp as the shattering of glass. "I don't know!"

He looked up at Charlotte. "Some things about us don't change from childhood, Charley. But others do. Everyone, including you, saw Cedric as the paragon of a perfect gentleman— all glittering, golden sunshine against a celestial blue sky. But a change came over him when we came to London. He became more . . ."

"What?" prompted Charlotte.

"Secretive. Obsessive." Locke closed his eyes for an instant.

"God knows, I've let myself be seduced by London's enticements, and my behavior has been less than exemplary. But for him to rake me over the coals for partaking in normal pleasures, when his own passions were taking a dangerous turn."

"You knew about the marks on his body?" she asked.

Locke released a shuddering exhale. "I came into his room one morning as he was dressing and caught sight of his chest. He . . . He refused to tell me anything. Said I wouldn't understand."

"Can you hazard a guess as to what caused them?" asked Wrexford.

The question hung suspended for a moment in the sour fugue of smells before Locke gave a grim nod.

"A voltaic pile."

CHAPTER 10

"*A voltaic pile,*" repeated Charlotte. It sounded vaguely sinister. She had heard the term, but had no notion of what it was.

"It's a scientific apparatus that creates an electrical current through chemistry," explained Wrexford. "It consists of alternating metal discs of copper and zinc, separated by cloth or pasteboard soaked in a weak acid. One can adjust the strength of the current through the number of discs used."

"What's it used for?" she asked. Aside from unspeakable acts on the human body.

"It's proved invaluable in scientific experiments. Humphry Davy, working in his laboratory at the Royal Institution, made a number of important chemical discoveries using one—he isolated sodium, potassium, calcium, boron, and magnesium, just to name a few."

"Nicholson and Carlisle isolated oxygen and hydrogen at the turn of the century, right after the voltaic pile was invented by Alexander Volta," added Locke, his eyes coming alight. "A momentous discovery. And who knows what other ones lie ahead in the future?"

It was the first real show of life from him, she noted.

"You have only to look at the phenomenon of lightning to comprehend what awe-inspiring powers are waiting to be un-leashed when we learn more about electricity."

"Lightning may be an impressive display of pyrotechnics," pointed out the earl. "But it's also illustrative of power run amok. When uncontrolled, electricity can be a force for terrible destruction."

Locke winced and held clasped his arms tighter to his chest. "That's what Mr. DeVere says. One must be careful, rational. Restrained."

Wrexford nodded. "DeVere worked with Davy on several of his chemical experiments, though his main interest now lies with living organisms. He studies plant reproduction and has a reputation for disciplined thinking, as well as an orderly approach to empirical research."

High praise, indeed, coming from the earl, thought Charlotte. He considered most of his fellow men of science bloody idiots.

"Which is why," went on Wrexford, "I would find it hard to believe he had any knowledge of what Chittenden was doing."

"No, I don't believe he did." Locke shifted uncomfortably. "Must we drag Cedric's name through the mud over this? I'm not saying he was right to be so driven to make a name for himself in the world of science. But surely he deserves some dignity in death. The public will seize on the tawdry details to turn him into a gruesome joke—urged on by that damnable scribbler. A. J. Quill." There was a tiny catch in his voice as he added, "I will gladly go to the gallows if it means he can rest in peace."

"Murder strips away all dignity," said Charlotte softly. "Secrets are bared, truths are twisted. And your sacrifice would only throw oil on the fires of ugly gossip. The best way to honor Cedric is to give him some measure of justice by finding his killer."

"The answer doesn't lie in the Eos Society—"

"Cut wind, Locke," interrupted Wrexford. "You claim to be a man of science, so you know that only a bacon-brained fool assumes to have the answer to an inquiry before it's made."

A sudden banging in the corridor set off a chorus of howls and catcalls.

"Tell us who else shared your brother's fascination with electricity," pressed the earl.

Locke bit his lip. Charlotte saw the clash of conflicting emotions twist his features and knew all too well what inner demons he was fighting. It wasn't simply out of loyalty that he was loath to speak, it was out of fear.

Fear of what awful truths he might discover about his brother. *How well do we know our loved ones?* Not well enough, reflected Charlotte. Her late husband had . . .

She blinked as a blade of sunlight momentarily cut through the narrow window. Then it was gone and the murky gloom felt even darker. Yes, it was tempting to cower in the shadows. But uncertainty was ultimately more terrible than truth. It slowly ate away at one's soul.

"*Errare humanum est, in errore perservare stultum,* Nicky," she murmured, hoping he remembered their childhood Latin lessons.

His head jerked up.

"It's human to make a mistake—it's stupid to persist in it," he whispered, a question rippling in his eyes.

"You're trying to protect Cedric—and yourself—from his human flaws and frailty. It can't be done, and you'll end up destroying all that you value in yourself if you persist in it."

Charlotte could feel Wrexford's lidded gaze fix on her. Strangely enough, it helped steady her own jumpy nerves. It was he who had helped her summon the strength to unravel the tangled lies and deceptions around her husband's death. The truth had liberated her from the ghosts of the past.

"Listen to her, Locke," counseled the earl, breaking the tense silence among the three of them.

Locke took his head in his hands. His shoulders were trembling. "Dear God," he mumbled.

She waited.

"Sir Kelvin Hollister." The words rasped through his clenched teeth. "And Westmorly. Somehow the three of them were drawn into . . . the devil's own fire."

"Go on," said Wrexford, when nothing more followed.

Palms still pressed to his temples, Locke slowly shook his head from side to side. "I can't tell you more than that. Truly, I can't. Cedric wouldn't confide in me." He forced himself to look at Charlotte. "You remember, don't you, Charley, that we studied the Greeks, as well as the Romans? Well, I fear that they dared to open Pandora's box."

"A dramatic young man," murmured Wrexford, once they were back inside his carriage. "I take it the plays of Sophocles and Aeschylus—thundering with the fire bolts of Fate raining down from Mount Olympus—were also on your curriculum of study."

"That's not humorous," snapped Charlotte.

"It wasn't meant to be." He leaned back against the squabs and crossed his legs. "You believe him?"

"Yes," she answered without hesitation. A wry grimace tugged at her mouth. "When faced with a difficult dilemma, Nicky has always needed to go through several acts of wrestling with his demons. His position is a complicated one—jealousy is, after all, a primal human passion. But his good nature always triumphs."

"People do change," he replied. However obvious, he felt compelled to say it.

"I know that." Over the clatter of the iron-rimmed wheels, he heard her draw in a shaky breath. "And not always for the better. But let's just say, intuition tells me Nicky is finally telling the truth." *Clack-clack.* "As far as he knows it."

The earl slanted a sidelong look at her face through the flitting shadows. "I daresay we'll need to dig through a great deal more muck before we uncover the truth."

"If you're asking me whether I'm prepared to get my hands dirty, the answer is yes." Charlotte straightened the placket of her jacket. "The truth, however black, is better than the gilded glitter of self-deception."

The answer was what he expected. And yet, judging by what he had already seen, the truth was going to drag her emotions through the flames of hell.

"At the risk of having my words crammed back down my throat, allow me to remind you that the human heart isn't sculpted out of cold steel." Charlotte's fierce sense of independence demanded that she never allow herself a whit of weakness.

"I won't flinch from the answers we find, Wrexford," she replied. "No matter what they are."

"Fine. Then we need to move quickly. The government will be anxious to have a trial date set as quickly as possible. An aristocrat accused of murder is an acute embarrassment, especially during this time of social unrest. The sooner a sentence is meted out, the better."

"No matter whether the accused is guilty."

"But of course, Mrs. Sloane," he shot back. "You, of all people, know that pragmatism takes precedence over such sentimental notions as innocence or guilt."

She looked on the verge of replying, then merely turned to stare out the window. A thick covering of storm clouds had blown in to block the sunlight, dulling the already-drab streets around the prison to a muddle of gloomy grey hues.

"As it happens, I should be able to speak with both Hollister and Westmorly tonight." Tyler, with his usual show of efficiency, had learned that there was a meeting of the Eos Society scheduled at the Royal Institution, right before a lecture by a noted chemist visiting from Prussia. "They won't want to miss the talk on hydrogen by von Krementz."

"Given what Nicky said about a possible romantic conflict between Cedric and Sir Kelvin, it also seems imperative to speak to Lady Julianna Aldrich," mused Charlotte. "Women see things differently. Her observations could be invaluable."

"Perhaps. But I doubt a dewy-eyed young innocent is going to open up to a dark-as-the-devil rogue like me." A pause. "Assuming I would be allowed within twenty paces of her before her chaperone summoned a regiment of Hussars to chop me into mincemeat. So, I'm afraid we'll have to forgo that line of inquiry."·

Her mouth tightened, and Wrexford understood her frustration. The highest circle of London society was the one place where all her considerable skills—including the art of disguise—were of no use to her. The beau monde was a closed world. A small world, where everyone knew everyone. A stranger could not simply waltz in with a charming smile and well-practiced lies.

However . . .

Charlotte suddenly slid forward on the seat. Fisting a hand, she rapped on the trap, signaling the driver to halt.

"I'll get out here."

"Where—" began the earl.

But she was already out the door and moving with quicksilver stealth to disappear in the sooty shadows of the narrow streets.

"Damnation," he muttered at the fast-disappearing blur. Whatever she was up to, he wasn't going to like it. When one danced on a razor's edge, disaster was never more than a hairsbreadth away. And sure-footed though she was, the smallest slip . . .

Wrexford wrenched himself back from such brooding. *Logic, logic*—while she chased after the specters of her intuition, he must turn his own mind to piecing together the puzzle of tangible clues.

* * *

"Milord," said Tyler as the earl threw open the door to his workroom. "Mr. Henning has sent a note regarding his examination of the . . ." He paused to cough and dart a quick glance at the far end of the counter, where Raven sat polishing the microscope.

"The, er, object he retrieved last night," finished the valet. "It's on your desk, along with an accompanying packet."

Wrexford shrugged out of his coat and wordlessly took up the items from the leather blotter. After skimming over Henning's message, he carefully tore open the packet. A wink of red-gold flashed in the lamplight as he shook a small sliver of metal onto his palm. Now cleaned of all gore, it was revealed as a slender bit of copper wire.

The earl reread the surgeon's note, then set it aside. "Have the Weasel polish something else," he said gruffly. "We need to have a closer look at this under our lenses." The surgeon's instruments were not as sophisticated as his own.

Raven slipped off his seat and quickly cleared away the rags and rubbing compound. The boy was quick, but very careful, noted Wrexford. The fact that Tyler, who was as possessive about his instruments as a gentleman was about his mistress, didn't flinch spoke volumes about how well Raven was fitting in.

"You want me to fetch the slides, Mr. Tyler?"

"Bring one of the shallow glass dishes instead," replied the valet. "Use the felt cloths, as I showed you. We don't want finger smudges."

Wrexford notched up his brows.

"The lad seems eager to learn, and has proved himself a quick study," murmured Tyler. "I trust you have no objections."

"None at all." He watched Raven sort through the dishes. "Though if we need to order a new shipment of laboratory glass from Switzerland, I shall take it out of your salary."

"I'm not going drop it," said Raven without looking up from the task.

He had forgotten about the boy's batlike hearing—and received an even more compelling reminder a moment later.

"Is that what you pulled from the murdered toff's corpse last night at the morgue?" Raven went on.

"I ought to birch your bum for eavesdropping on your elders."

The boy made a rude sound. "First you would have to catch me."

"Ye gods, you're a mouthy little beast this afternoon." To Tyler, he said, "After we finish here, put him to work scrubbing out the chemical buckets. That should take some of the wind out of his sails."

The valet grimaced.

"Now stop shilly-shallying and step lively, lad," barked the earl. "We have work to do." The banter ceased as he sat down in front of the microscope and began fiddling with the levers. "We need the highest level of magnification. Henning thinks the wire shows a bit of melting at its tip, but given he used a quizzing glass for his examination, he can't be sure."

Tyler nodded thoughtfully. "Let me angle the reflectors to catch the light . . ." They worked together for the next few moments in preoccupied silence, making a few more minute adjustments.

"Hand me the dish, lad," said Tyler. Using a pair of tweezers, he placed the copper wire in it and set it under the lens.

Raven edged closer, his gaze intent on what they were doing. "Why would the wire be melted?"

Wrexford slowly spun a dial, trying to decide how to reply. Would Charlotte rake him over the coals for answering honestly, no matter that it would expose a dark facet of human nature? He mulled over the question for a moment and then made up his mind.

"A strong enough jolt of electrical current would generate sufficient heat to soften the metal."

"How—"

"From a scientific apparatus called a voltaic pile," answered Tyler. "I'll explain it later, but it creates a current."

Raven's face screwed up in thought. He plucked at his sleeve. "But if the wire was stuck in the toff's flesh, and it was hot enough to melt metal, wouldn't that hurt?"

"Yes," said the earl brusquely.

The boy took heed of the warning note and bit back any further questions.

"Shift the reflector to the right," ordered Wrexford. The shadow over the wire disappeared, allowing the copper fragment to snap into sharp focus. "Hmmph."

Shifting his position on the eyepiece, he studied the metal for a few moments longer before chuffing another grunt and looking up at Tyler. "Have a look for yourself. You've more experience with voltaic piles than I do, but it looks to me as if a strong current has been run through the wire."

The valet took his place and recalibrated the dials. "I agree." Another oiled whisper of brass turning brass. "Heat has flattened the oval shape. My guess is, it was indeed a strong current."

That would explain the ugly, half-healed burns on Chittenden's body. Wrexford had thought as much, but the evidence now confirmed his suspicion. As to what led a titled lord to practice self-torture and mutilation raised a whole new set of questions.

None of which, he suspected, were going to have pleasant answers.

Raven was holding himself very still and watching them intently. His dark eyes were guarded—far too guarded for a boy his age. No doubt he had seen and heard far worse horrors in his short, savage life. But that didn't dispel the niggling of guilt Wrexford felt at exposing the boy to such depravity.

Ye gods, I must be getting soft in my old age. A conscience was a cursed encumbrance. He couldn't recall having one until he had begun to butt heads with Charlotte.

Tyler, on the other hand, seemed to have no compunction over involving Raven in the investigation. "Here, would you like to have a look, lad?"

Raven jumped at the offer, and as the valet began to explain the fine points of metallurgy and electricity, the earl paced back to his desk.

"By the by, don't forget about the snuff that Mrs. Sloane found at the scene of the crime," he muttered.

Tyler nodded. "I'll get to that. But to be honest, milord, I wouldn't be too sanguine about it yielding any useful information."

Answers—they needed some answers. Wrexford frowned. In death, Chittenden had told him as much as he could. To learn more about the late baron's secrets, he would have to find a way to make Hollister and Westmorly talk.

Charlotte's nose told her she had found her quarry, though there were still a half dozen steps left before the narrow passage opened onto the street.

"Eel pasties!" bellowed the beanstalk-thin girl tending the barrow on the corner.

It was hard to believe such a skinny mite could emit such a prodigiously loud sound.

"Hot 'n' tasty as a lightskirt's kiss. C'mon 'n' gettum!"

"Halloo, Alice." Charlotte dug out a few coins from her breeches. "I'll take one for me, and one for you. Selling your wares is hard work."

Raven and Hawk's friend—known to their little band as Alice-the-Eel-Girl—gave a grateful grin. "Oiy, but 's been a gud day. Been so busy I ain't had time te fill me breadbox." She handed Charlotte her pasty, and then hurriedly gobbled down a big bite from her own.

"Mmmm..." Juice dribbled down her pointy little chin as the girl let out a blissful sound. "Thank'ee kindly, Magpie."

"Come, let's sit for a minute and enjoy them." Charlotte indicated the low wall flanking the well-worn steps leading down to one of the many landings that dotted this part of the river. In a lower voice, she added, "I have a few questions to ask you."

The more she had thought about it, the more it seemed her comment about women seeing things differently was important. Grasping at straws, perhaps. But right now, she had naught but a fistful of thin air.

Alice's gaze sharpened. She was a clever, observant girl, and had proved very helpful during their previous investigations. There was little that happened around her that went unnoticed.

And she knew that Charlotte paid generously for accurate information.

They found a spot where the shadows cast by the adjacent warehouse allowed them to blend in with the sooty stone.

"By the by, these are very good," murmured Charlotte, licking the greasy crumbs from her fingers. She had been too preoccupied to eat anything since breaking her fast at first light.

"Peg, the wife of Shoo-fly, who sweeps the horse droppings from Chancery Lane, makes 'um. She's a werry good cook."

"Indeed, she is." Though mention of her husband's profession gave Charlotte momentary pause for thought. After wiping her hands on her breeches, Charlotte looked around to check that they were alone. "As I said, I'm looking for information. I know Raven and Hawk have already asked you about the night of the murder in the Kensington Palace Gardens."

Alice sheltered at night with several other urchins in a spot close to one of the entrances to the gardens. Between her and her friends, very few movements in and out of the royal grounds escaped them.

"However, they were looking for the description of a stranger—someone who looked like he didn't belong."

Alice nodded thoughtfully.

"I'm now more interested in the fancy toffs you saw that night."

"Oiy, there was more of 'um than usual," volunteered the girl. "That's because there was a party at the Palace. It was all lit up, brighter than the sun."

Ah, but all that glitters is not gold. If Nicky could be believed, there was devilish darkness lurking beneath the polished charm and scintillating smiles.

"Yes, I imagine it was quite a sight," said Charlotte. "There were a great many guests invited, and I imagine some of them left the grounds on foot rather than by carriage."

"Oiy." The girl's attention was on full alert.

"I want you to think very carefully about the gentlemen you saw leaving the gardens." She took out Hawk's sketch. "Do you recall anyone wearing a hat like this one?"

Alice took the sketch.

"Take your time. It's important that you're sure of your answer."

Eyes narrowing in concentration, the girl studied it intently. Charlotte held herself still and remained silent.

"Oiy." Alice finally looked up. "A cully came out early, before the crush o' carriages. And his hat . . ." Her grubby finger tapped the paper. "His hat was jes' like this one."

"You are sure?" pressed Charlotte, careful to keep her voice neutral despite the quickening of her pulse.

"I remember becuz o' the brim. It's got a funny little dip in the front and back." Alice noticed the little details. "An' becuz there was a wink o' something shiny in the band. Ye see, when the cully passed unner the tree, a branch hit his hat and almost knocked it off. He reached te set it back, like dis . . ."

Alice mimed a motion of resetting a hat on her head. "That's why the liddle flash caught my eye."

Excitement was now fizzing through her blood. Even Wrexford, who bent over backward to explain things through logic, would have to admit that the presence of the same hat at two different murder scenes couldn't be dismissed as mere coincidence.

"Can you remember anything about the gent?"

Alice thought hard, then shook her head. "Only that I'd remember iffen he'd been real tall or real short."

"What about the shiny object in the hat—could you tell what it was?"

"Naw, 'fraid not. It looked like mebbe it was silver, but udder than that, I can't say."

"No matter." Charlotte quickly dug out some more coins from her pocket and put them in Alice's lap. "Thank you."

Alice hesitated at taking them. "Wuz it helpful?"

"Oh, very. More than you know."

A smile lit up the girl's plain-as-pudding face as the coins disappeared into her tattered skirts. "Ye think the Runners snatched up the wrong man fer the murder?"

"Yes, I do," answered Charlotte.

Now she just had to prove it.

CHAPTER 11

There was an electricity in the air. Though the lecture wasn't scheduled to begin for another hour, a crowd was already beginning to gather. Wrexford crossed the entrance hall of the Royal Institution, his boot heels clicking an impatient tattoo over the checkered marble tiles, and mounted the grand double staircase. Turning left at the first landing, he hurried past a pair of elderly gentlemen and made his way into the cavernous library.

Rising from floor to ceiling, carved wood bookshelves filled the walls, the row after row of leather-bound spines muting the buzz of scholarly conversation. The earl paused, scanning the faces of his fellow members . . .

"Wrexford, I'm surprised you're here tonight, given your opinions of von Krementz's scientific method."

The earl turned. "I try to keep an open mind, Children. I'm willing to listen—and perhaps learn."

John Children allowed a tiny smile to flit across his broad, bluntly chiseled face. A good friend of the famous chemist Humphry Davy, he had won acclaim for his own scientific studies—including the construction of the largest voltaic pile ever built while performing experiments with electricity. "I have a feeling our guest will find it a difficult challenge to impress your intellect."

Wrexford shrugged. "I don't suffer fools gladly."

"Science," replied Children, "has no place for fools."

"True. But that doesn't stop them from filling our journals and lecture halls with utter drivel."

Another smile. "Which again makes me wonder why you have come."

Wrexford suddenly realized how fortuitous this chance encounter was. "Because one does occasionally manage to strike up an interesting conversation at gatherings such as these."

"I would hope so, seeing as many of the leading thinkers in the country make up our membership."

"Speaking of fools," continued the earl, "are some of our young jackanapes taking their interest in electricity beyond the boundaries of serious scientific experiments?"

Children frowned. "What have you heard?"

"Nothing specific. Just a few things here and there that made me wonder. And as you're earning accolades for your work in the field of electrical currents, I thought you would know if anyone is making mischief."

"Not that I'm aware of. But then, my research keeps me busy in my own laboratory. I don't participate in the meetings of our young members or offer guidance. So perhaps your question is better directed to . . ." Children paused to give a small wave at the library entrance. "Ah, here's DeVere now. I hear he's been generous in sharing his knowledge with them."

The earl watched as a tall, silver-haired gentleman acknowledged Children's gesture and made his way to join them.

"Wrexford," murmured DeVere, after greeting Children. "What a surprise to see you here tonight. You've become a rare sight at our evening lectures. Indeed, I was beginning to think you had abandoned chemistry for biology."

It was, conceded the earl, a mildly amusing quip, given his

involvement in the investigations of several lurid murders. But not quite deserving of DeVere's self-satisfied smirk. The man tended to have a lofty concept of his own cleverness—and a fondness for the sound of his own voice.

However, his scientific work was first rate, so Wrexford held back a biting retort.

"I do hope you haven't stumbled over another dead body recently," added DeVere.

"I'm making every effort to tread more carefully these days," he replied. "My valet dislikes it when I get bloodstains on my boots."

"Forgive me," said DeVere, his expression turning more sober. "I didn't mean to jest about Ashton. He was a fine fellow and a brilliant man of science. He shall be sorely missed."

"Yes." The earl paused. "And it seems our august Institution has recently suffered the loss of another member."

"Ah, yes." A mournful sigh. "Lord Chittenden was a young man of remarkable potential. It was a terrible shock to hear of his demise."

"Children was just telling me you served as a mentor to him and his friends."

"You must mean the Eos Society," replied DeVere. "A very interesting group of young men. So full of enthusiasm and curiosity."

"Wrexford was wondering whether some of the fellows are a bit *too* curious," murmured Children as he signaled one of the waiters to bring over a tray of champagne. "He was asking whether they are playing with fire within our august walls."

DeVere's brows notched up. "In what way?"

"In playing dangerous games with the electricity generated by a voltaic pile," answered Wrexford.

"I suppose we all do silly things in our youth, and take reckless chances. It's the nature of life." DeVere took a small sip of his champagne. "But we learn from our mistakes and quickly become wiser."

"Assuming we survive them," said the earl softly.

"True," conceded DeVere, lifting his glass in salute. "However, having spent a good amount of time discussing science with the Eos Society and answering their questions, I'm happy to say I've seen no cause for alarm. They're passionate about their interests, open-minded and eager to explore—all excellent attributes for those who are looking to engage in serious scientific inquiry."

"Let us hope they don't waste their time exploring the works of Aldini and Galvani in regard to electricity." Children made a face. "Twitching frogs, vital forces of life—their concept of Vitalism was nothing but circus stunts and charlatanism!"

"True," mused DeVere. "But I've always believed there are good lessons to be learned from the wrong turns in science."

Wrexford didn't disagree. But what he had seen on Chittenden's corpse raised unsettling questions.

DeVere remained preoccupied with the point he had raised. Pursing his lips in thought, he went on. "When you think on it, a great many learned men were fascinated with Vitalism. Alexander von Humboldt wrote about experimenting with electricity on his own body when he was a young man."

"Out of sheer boredom, and frustration, if I recall," pointed out Wrexford. "To please his mother, who demanded that her sons be useful to society, he was working as a mining inspector for the government, but hated feeling confined to one narrow discipline. What he really yearned to do was travel and explore the wonders of the world."

"The allure of such electrical experiments passed," agreed DeVere. "As well it should have. There was nothing to be learned from following that path." His brow suddenly furrowed. "Are you implying the members of the Eos Society are doing more than just testing their curiosity with such stuff?"

The earl gave a small shrug. "You would know better than I."

"Good God." Frowning, DeVere quaffed a long swallow of wine. "I think you're wrong. But be assured I'll keep a watchful eye on the group and see that they don't stray too far from the path of rational inquiry."

That, of course, all depended on how one defined the word *rational.* Wrexford was cynical enough to have little faith that most people agreed on the definition. Given that DeVere had lived in India, well outside the cocoon of aristocratic privilege, he ought not be so naïve about man's capacity for illogic.

Another quick glance around the fast-filling room showed that Sir Kelvin Hollister had finally made an appearance, though there was no sign of Westmorly.

"Better you than me, DeVere" he responded. "But then, I'm not known for my patience." With that, Wrexford inclined a tiny nod and took his leave.

Forcing herself to concentrate was proving harder than herding a pack of feral cats. But reminding herself that Mr. Fores deserved more than a mediocre effort, Charlotte managed to compose a pithy satirical drawing on the Duchess of York and her ever-expanding menagerie of animals at Oatlands.

Eccentricity among the aristocracy was a popular subject. The public loved to laugh at their betters.

Once the last lines were inked in on the drawing, and the wash of colors added, she sat back and slowly began to clean her brushes.

Choices, choices. Since taking her abrupt leave from Wrexford, her thoughts had been agitated, her head at war with her heart. Cold logic demanded she take one course of action, while raw emotion spoke in far different terms. She could either choose to stay on her current path in life—one of hard-won independence, cobbled together on her own terms—or commit herself to saving Nicholas.

She didn't see how she could do both.

A soft knock on her workroom door roused her from such mordant musings. The boys had gone out to make the inquiries she had requested. Which meant it could only be the maid.

She hesitated, in no mood for conversation.

McClellan clicked open the latch on hearing no response. "Would you care for a cup of tea and perhaps a cold collation of meat and cheese?" she asked. "You ate nothing at supper."

"I wasn't particularly hungry."

"That doesn't mean you don't need to fill your breadbox. In my experience, an empty stomach can affect one's judgment. And not for the better."

Charlotte huffed a humorless laugh. "I'm not sure a bite of roast beef or cheddar is going to gift me with great wisdom."

"Perhaps not. But I daresay you'll feel better without a painful gnawing in your belly."

"I'm not sure food is going to do away with that."

Leaning a bony shoulder against the molding, McClellan cocked her head. "Still wrestling with your better nature?"

An unseen finger of air seemed to tug at the candle in the maid's hand. The flame shimmied, setting off jumpy flickers of red-gold light. They were gone in an instant, leaving behind a darkness that looked even more impenetrable than before.

"You've make it clear which combatant you think should win," said Charlotte softly.

"Nay, it would be the ultimate hubris to counsel another on what choices are best. God knows, I've made enough mistakes to fill my own lifetime twice over."

"*Sub omni lapide scorpio dormit,*" muttered Charlotte.

"Under every stone sleeps a scorpion?" A low laugh rumbled in the maid's throat. "Ain't that the truth." Her mouth twitched. "Though I rather prefer a more pungent saying— *semper in excretia sumus solim profundum variat.*"

In spite of her tangled emotions, Charlotte couldn't hold back a chuckle. "We are always in manure, it's only the depth that varies," she translated. "I wasn't aware that you knew Latin, McClellan."

"Only bawdy jokes or unladylike aphorisms." A shrug. "Tyler is a bad influence on me."

"Unladylike aphorisms—along with every other unladylike behavior known to man—are quite at home here."

Their gazes met and held for a moment.

"Trust your heart, Mrs. Sloane. It's a good one." Outside, the wind swirled and shivered against the windowpanes. "Trust the earl as well. I don't think you'll regret it."

McClellan straightened and tucked a lock of hair behind her ear. "Now I'll go fetch you some tea."

A warmth was already spreading in Charlotte's belly, slowly dispelling the lump of ice.

Choices, choices.

She drew in a deep breath, aware that the *thump-thump* of her heart had suddenly turned steadier. And then she reached for her pen and began to compose the letter that would more than likely seal her fate.

"Sir Kelvin." Wrexford caught up with Hollister as he turned into the arched foyer leading to one of the side salons.

The young man looked around, surprise widening his brown eyes. His face was undeniably attractive, the aquiline nose, well-shaped mouth, and square-cut jaw topped by a profusion of artfully tousled auburn curls. But no match for Chittenden's gilded beauty.

"Sir?" he said with a tentative smile.

"Might I have a word with you?"

A furrow formed between Hollister's brows, but he quickly smoothed it away with a polite nod. "Yes. Of course."

Wrexford indicated the doorway leading to the corridor. "Perhaps somewhere more private," he murmured. "I have some questions to ask you about Lord Chittenden."

The light beneath the vaulted ceiling was muddled, grey on grey shadows dimming the glow of wall sconces. Still, it seemed that Hollister's face paled at the mention of the baron's name.

"I—I don't know what I can tell you, other than I'm devastated by the news of his death. I wasn't at the Duke's soiree, so know nothing about the night of his demise."

"I'm more interested in his life than his death."

Hollister was now white as a ghost.

"Come, I won't keep you long." Taking the man's arm, the earl led him to one of the study rooms at the end of the corridor.

A long mahogany table set with straight-back chairs was on one side of the room. The two large oil lamps on the sideboard were lit and turned down low, the flames glowing gold within the glass globes. A pair of leather armchairs was set by the large hearth. Fresh coal chunks were in the grate, but they lay cold and dark.

Wrexford struck a flint to the brace of candles by the door and carried it to the marble mantel.

"Have a seat," he said.

Hollister hesitated. "Sir, the lecture—"

"The lecture won't begin for another half hour." The earl perched a hip on one of the chair's padded arms. "You won't miss a word. Not that it would be a great loss to your understanding of hydrogen's properties."

A weak smile twitched in response as the young man reluctantly moved to the facing chair and took a seat. "I take it you don't hold von Krementz in high regard, milord?"

"I have a reputation for being an overly harsh judge of my scientific peers," replied the earl. "But, then, I imagine you know that."

Hollister's jaw tightened. His spine was rigid, his hands clasped together awkwardly in his lap.

"Relax, Sir Kelvin. I'm not going to quiz you on your studies. I merely wish to chat about what sort of interests Lord Chittenden shared with you and your fellow members of the Eos Society."

"Like all of us, Chittenden was interested in a wide range of scientific subjects." A hesitation. "We all felt there was so much to explore before deciding to focus on any one area."

"Did your explorations perchance include experiments with a voltaic pile?"

The young man wet his lips. "Yes, we did some rudimentary work on generating electricity. After all, it's considered a revolutionary discovery whose potential has yet to be unlocked. However, the majority of our members decided to move on and sample other areas of study." An audible inhale. "As I said, we are still naught but dilettantes."

A very carefully worded answer, which did not escape the earl's notice.

"But not all of you decided to abandon the experiments with the voltaic pile," pressed Wrexford. "Chittenden found it fascinating—and word is, so did you and Benjamin Westmorly."

"I don't know who told you that, but our interest appears to have been much exaggerated, sir," replied the young man after chuffing an unconvincing laugh. "We were interested, but I would hardly call us *fascinated.* We performed a few extra tests on our own, purely out of curiosity."

Wrexford wondered why the fellow was taking such pains to prevaricate. He decided to cut to the chase. "And did that curiosity extend to applying the current to your own bodies?"

"Good God, what an odd question!"

"One that you didn't answer," observed the earl after several long moments of silence had slid by.

Wool whispered against leather as the young man shifted uncomfortably. "It makes no sense that Chittenden would do such a thing."

"Perhaps you should take up the study of law, not science, Sir Kelvin," he said dryly. "You excel at tying your tongue in knots without really saying anything."

The blood rushed back to Hollister's face, turning his cheekbones a telltale scarlet. "I'm not sure what you want me to tell you!"

"The truth would be helpful."

The young man's gaze dropped to the patterned carpet beneath his evening shoes. "To my knowledge, neither Chittenden nor Westmorly used a voltaic pile for the purposes you stated. And I certainly haven't." He shifted his feet. "M-Might I inquire why you're asking such strange questions?"

"Because I find myself curious about rumors swirling around his life," answered Wrexford. "And even more curious about why he's now dead."

"His brother—" rasped Hollister.

"Has been arrested, yes," cut in the earl. "I simply wish to feel certain that justice is being served." A pause. "I'm sure we all do."

"Yes, of course," replied Hollister. "I wish I could tell you more, but I can't think of anything to add."

"Thank you, Sir Kelvin." Wrexford slowly got to his feet. "I appreciate your time."

Hollister bolted up from his chair. "Then if you'll excuse me, I'm supposed to meet Mr. DeVere and several friends by the lecture hall entrance so we can all sit together."

"But of course." Smiling, he reached out and touched the other man's sleeve. "Come, let us shake hands. I shouldn't like for us to leave on less than a cordial note."

"Of course, sir."

Wrexford grasped the outstretched palm. A quick tug pulled Hollister close and at the same time he jabbed the heel of his other hand hard against the side of the young man's rib cage.

The breath came out of him in a gasp of pain.

"I saw Chittenden's body," he murmured close to Hollister's ear. "What devil's mischief were you playing at?"

Fear twisted the young man's face. "By God, if I knew anything about Chittenden's death, I swear I would tell it to you."

"Then you'll have no objection to answering some questions about what the two of you were doing with voltaic piles."

Hollister looked like he was about to be ill. The muscles in his throat jumped as he swallowed hard. "It . . . It was naught but stupid games. One of our friends in the Eos Society had read about von Humboldt's self-experiments with electricity—"

"Who?" interrupted the earl.

"Westmorly," came the reluctant answer.

So, Locke had been telling the truth about Westmorly being involved. "Go on," he said.

"We were curious—ye gods, that's not a crime, is it?" The young man exhaled a shuddering breath. "So one evening after DeVere's weekly talk on the history of science, we decided to see for ourselves what the current felt like."

"Just the three of you?" asked Wrexford.

"Yes." A nervous pause. "But after several sessions, Westmorly lost interest and stopped joining us—"

"Why?" he interrupted.

"He didn't say. He just stopped coming."

The earl frowned. "Then perhaps I ought to have a word with him, too."

"I doubt he can tell you anything—he really wasn't very involved." Hollister hesitated. "Look, I, too, found the allure fading. But Chittenden mocked Westmorly as a fellow of limited imagination, and, well, I suppose I took that as a challenge."

"Because of your rivalry over Lady Julianna?"

"H-How did you know—" Hollister bit his lip. "The truth is, there *was* no rivalry. By the time we began toying around with electricity, Lady Julianna had made it clear she preferred me over him."

Wrexford raised a skeptical brow. "Even though Chittenden had a more lofty title and a far fatter purse?" He let the words hover in the air before adding, "Not to speak of golden looks."

"Lady Julianna didn't care for any of that," insisted Hollister. "She wished to marry for . . . a joining of two kindred souls. And she chose me over Chittenden."

"That may be so," responded the earl dryly. "But I doubt her father gives a fig for girlish flutters of the heart. The girl is an heiress."

The young man's breathing quickened and turned shallow. "Her parents are deceased, and she's confident that her guardian will allow her to choose from the heart. I tell you, she informed Chittenden that she had made up her mind and his suit was unwelcome."

Wrexford regarded him for a long moment. "So you say." As Hollister's gaze slid down to the tabletop, the earl continued his questioning. "Getting back to your duel by fire with Chittenden, how did it end?"

"After our last session in the laboratory, just a few days before his demise, I told him I wasn't going to come anymore. His . . ." Hollister drew in a breath. "His fascination was growing . . . unnerving."

"What the devil does that mean?" pressed Wrexford. "The sooner you loosen your tongue, the sooner our little tête-à-tête will be over."

"I found his passion alarming, that's all," answered Hollister. "I just didn't have any interest in being part of it."

More evasions. The earl was fast losing his temper.

"What is it you're not telling me, Sir Kelvin?" Wrexford flattened his hands on the table and leaned forward. "Surely, you've heard that I'm not a man who possesses great patience. Nor am I a man you would wish to have as an enemy."

"If you must know, I was scared. Chittenden was making the voltaic piles more powerful . . ." The young man drew in a shaky breath. "And now, with the lurid nature of his death . . ." Another hesitation. "Murder stirs nasty gossip, and I fear if any talk gets out that associates me with Chittenden's experiments, it will ruin my chances with Lady Julianna. Mr. DeVere is a very open-minded guardian, but no man will allow scandal to taint a young lady's good name."

"DeVere is her guardian?" he demanded in surprise.

"Yes, he was close friends with her family in India. Her father and mother were killed in an attack during the Second Maratha War, and their will appointed him to oversee her upbringing." A pause. "DeVere dotes on her, but I'm sure there are limits as to how far his tolerance will stretch."

At last, thought the earl. He sensed he was finally getting a truthful answer. Though it only raised more questions.

"So, please, milord, I beg you to stop showing interest in me. You're known for uncovering sordid truths. People will notice and start asking why."

That all made sense. And yet, something in Hollister's eyes . . .

Their gazes locked for an instant, and then the young man flinched.

"Wrexford? Might I have a word . . ." Children hesitated in the doorway. "However, if I'm interrupting, it can wait—"

"No, no, I was just leaving," exclaimed Hollister. "Mr. DeVere is waiting."

The earl released his grip on Hollister's coat and stepped back without a word. The young man quickly refastened the buttons and smoothed the lapels back into place.

But not before Wrexford saw the tiny spot of blood on his shirt.

Children stepped aside to let the young man hurry past him, then came to join Wrexford by the hearth.

"Our earlier conversation on electrical current suddenly caused me to recall an exchange I happened to catch between Chittenden and Lord Thornton."

Wrexford frowned. The Marquess of Thornton's interest was chemistry. For the last year he had been experimenting with the newly discovered purple crystal called *iode,* and had recently written a paper expressing the belief that it might have some useful medical applications. "You're saying Thornton shared Chittenden's interest in electricity?"

"I overheard a conversation that seemed to indicate that," answered Children.

There was nothing unusual in members of the Royal Institution asking each other about their work, no matter if it was in a different field of interest. Men of science were by nature curious.

"And now that you've made me think about it, there were elements to it that in retrospect seem a bit disturbing. They were speaking—rather animatedly, I might add—about vital forces, and how electricity might affect the Spark of Life . . . ideas that could be construed as dangerous, especially to a curious young man." Children paused. "Mind you, I'm not suggesting anything is wrong with the theoretical discussion of outlandish ideas. That's how we explore and learn. But given your earlier questions, I thought you might wish to know."

"Thank you," murmured the earl. "As you say, it's likely nothing, but I appreciate your passing it on to me."

CHAPTER 12

The *tick-tick* of the mantel clock seemed to echo the doleful tones of a funeral dirge.

"Perhaps . . ." *Tick-tick.* ". . . that's because my life as I know it is dead," muttered Charlotte as she pulled at her bodice, then tucked a stray lock of hair behind her ear. "Or about to be."

The midmorning sun had filled the parlor with a cheery light, but she was too preoccupied with her fidgeting to notice. *Tick-tick.* She folded and unfolded the single sheet of paper in her hands until the crease was sharp as a knife blade. It took the loud rap of the door knocker to jar her out of her brooding.

The sound was followed by the low exchange of pleasantries as McClellan answered the summons, and then steps in the corridor.

Charlotte sucked in a ragged breath. "Thank you for coming, Wrexford," she intoned, steeling her spine as the earl entered the room. "May I offer you some refreshments?"

He took off his hat and ran a hand through his hair. "Thank you, but no." A look of bemusement tugged at his lips, but she didn't miss the shadow of concern in his eyes. "From the urgency of your note, I sense this meeting isn't meant as an impromptu tea party."

"Correct." She crossed and then recrossed her ankles.

His brows rose ever so slightly.

Damnation. Shilly-shallying wasn't going to make things any easier.

"I wish to ask your advice on something. But first, you need to read this." Charlotte held out the paper without further ado.

Wrexford carefully unfolded it and took his time in perusing the contents.

Her heart began to thump against her ribs.

He slowly raised his gaze and fixed her with a questioning look.

"Do you think I'm doing the right thing?" she said.

Instead of answering, Wrexford moved to the diamond-paned windows and turned to stare out at the quiet street.

Tick-tick.

Charlotte fisted her hands to keep them from shaking. His back was to her, and all she could see of him was an imposing black silhouette, limned in a halo of fluttery light.

Not an encouraging sight.

She must have released a sigh, for he looked around.

"Go ahead and speak your mind, Wrexford," she urged. "Whatever you're thinking, it will be far less upsetting than this . . . this disapproving silence."

"You are misinterpreting my reticence, Mrs. Sloane. What you've asked is impossible to articulate in a simple answer." The earl shifted. "It matters not a whit what I think. The heart of the question is, what do *you* think?"

It wasn't the reply she had expected—or wanted. Wrexford rarely pulled his punches.

"And here I was hoping for you to impose your usual cold logic to a problem, and parse through all the variables to arrive at the correct solution," responded Charlotte, though her attempt at wry humor sounded a little flat. "Instead, you have chosen a most inopportune moment to refrain from expressing your opinion."

"You wish for logic?" Wrexford shifted again, but the refraction of light through the windowpanes still made it impossible to read his face. "Fine. Then let us analyze the benefits and drawbacks of doing what you propose."

He approached and, after pushing the facing armchair a tad closer to hers, took a seat. His knees were nearly touching hers. And yet, the closeness was somehow comforting.

"Before we begin, shall I fetch paper and pencil to make one of our usual lists?" he drawled after placing her letter on the side table.

Charlotte shook her head. "Let's get on with it." If her old life was about to give up the ghost, she would rather it be done with a swift thrust of the knife, rather than from myriad tiny cuts.

"Very well." The earl steepled his fingers. "Let's start with the benefits. Why do you wish to reveal yourself as Lady Charlotte Sophia Anna Mallory Sloane and reenter the world of the beau monde?"

"Because it's the only way I have a chance to prove Nicky is innocent."

"How so?" he pressed. "You're more skilled than most Bow Street Runners in ferreting out information. Your network of informants has access to most every secret that swirls through London."

"But not all of them," replied Charlotte. "Believe me, I've made inquiries with every possible source who might prove helpful. I'm convinced the answers I need can only be found within the highest circles of Society, and even then, they must be extracted by careful questioning."

"You don't trust that I can do that? And Sheffield as well?"

"To a point, sir. But if critical secrets lie with a lady—and we have good reason to think that may be the case—then only I can get them. You admitted as much yesterday."

"Very well," he conceded. "That's one reason. Any other?"

Charlotte pinched at a crease in her skirts.

"There would, of course, be a number of ancillary benefits," he went on, when she didn't answer. "Balls, supper soirees, concerts, drawing rooms, teas . . ." A pause. "Reconciliation with your family, and with it, a likely change in your financial situation. I doubt you would ever have to work again."

Charlotte stared at him in shock, too stunned to react.

Wrexford stared back with unblinking calm.

It took several long moments for her wits to begin working. "How can you think . . ." she sputtered. "All those things have nothing—*nothing*—to do with the decision!"

"Nonetheless, they must be listed. Cause and effect is a scientific principle," he said calmly. "You *did* ask me to apply cold logic to the question."

Her body suddenly felt as if it had turned to ice. "Very well."

"Now, as to drawbacks . . ." He hesitated. "You may make all these changes in your life, and in the end, it will come to naught. You won't find any proof of your cousin's innocence and he will go to the gallows."

Not trusting her voice, Charlotte nodded in confirmation.

Wrexford's gaze turned searching. Probing, piercing to the very depth of her marrow. She looked down at her lap, despite knowing there was nowhere to hide.

"Can you live with that, Mrs. Sloane?" he asked softly. "For it seems to me, that's the only question you should be asking."

"There's one other, and it's even more important," she murmured. "Can I live with myself if I *don't* try?"

He let out a resigned huff. "Well, that was a simple problem to solve."

"I'm sorry, Wrexford. I know you think me—"

"Passionately principled and unflinchingly loyal. To a maddening degree," he cut in. "Do I wish I could change your mind? Yes, because I would rather have you take your time and make this momentous decision based on your own heart, not be forced into it by the needs of someone else."

His mouth quirked. "But I know better than to argue with you on this."

She leaned forward and placed a hand on his knee. "Thank you."

His fingers twined with hers. The connection, however small and fleeting, helped make her feel less alone in facing the challenges that lay ahead.

But the earl, as was his wont, was quick to shake off any show of sentiment. Of late, he had been acting even more detached. Charlotte supposed she could hardly blame him. Still, she couldn't help wishing . . .

"Since you are determined to do this, let us look at the practicalities." Wrexford picked up the letter. "How are you acquainted with the Dowager Countess of Peake?" The elderly lady had a reputation in the highest circles of Society for being a feisty, fire-breathing dragon. "And, more to the point, why ask her for help in being reintroduced to Society?"

"She's my great-aunt by marriage," replied Charlotte. "Of all the adults in my high-in-the-instep family, she was the only one who seemed to understand me." The sudden memories of long-ago laughter brought a tiny smile to her lips. "She possessed a sharp tongue and a sly sense of humor, which, as you can imagine, appealed to someone as unconventional as I was."

The smile gave way to a grimace. "But perhaps that's changed."

"It hasn't," said Wrexford. "Lady Peake is known throughout Society as a Holy Terror."

Charlotte felt a lump form in her throat. If the dowager—

"Which makes her the perfect choice," added the earl with an amused chuckle. "Heaven help anyone who stands in her way when she decides on a course. She is a Force of Nature unto herself."

"Assuming she agrees to help me."

"*Faber est suae quisque fortunae,*" murmured Wrexford. Every man is the artisan of his own fortune.

"There are times when you have more faith in me than I have in myself," she replied.

"That's what friends are for, Mrs. Sloane." He set the sheet of paper on her lap. "Go ahead and send the letter."

Charlotte refolded it with great care.

"Shall we move on to our murder investigation?" said the earl. "I met with Sir Kelvin Hollister last night. Westmorly didn't make an appearance, but I'll track him down. His relationship with Chittenden appears to be more complicated than mere gaming debts."

"So Hollister was helpful?"

"More than he meant to be," came the cryptic reply. Wrexford went on to explain about the encounter, including the fact that DeVere was Lady Julianna Aldrich's guardian. "He was able to slip away before I finished with him, but I intend to question him again. I have the sense he's holding something back."

Repressing a shudder, she thought over what he had just said. "Why would he and Cedric have subjected themselves to such awful dangers?"

"As DeVere said, young men do stupid things. Danger seems to bring out the worst impulses in them. Be it to win a dare, or to prove themselves as devil-may-care as their friends, or simply to spit in the face of Death for the thrill of it, they find it sends fire bubbling through their blood."

"Surely, you were never so foolish."

Wrexford quirked a grimace. "I was likely worse. But I was also lucky."

Would that some of his luck would rub off on her, reflected Charlotte. She had a feeling she was going to need it during the coming weeks.

Forcing her thoughts back to the matter at hand, she said, "You mentioned a dare. Perhaps they were competing in some test of mettle to determine who would win the hand of the lady they both fancied?"

"A modern-day equivalent of knights locked in a trial by combat?"

"Put that way, it does sound rather absurd," conceded Charlotte. "But no more so than any of the other explanations we've considered."

"Let us see what Hollister has to say next time I see him." The earl rose. "I've received permission for another meeting with Locke at first light tomorrow. The choice is yours on whether to come. But the fact is, I may be able to wrest more out of him if you're not present."

As it was the last time, the offer to beg off was tempting. The mere thought of Newgate—the stink, the screams, the air of utter hopelessness—made her skin crawl. And yet it would be cowardly to do so and leave Nicky to rot in such misery.

"I must come," she said.

He nodded grimly. "I expected no less. But if you really wish to help him, you should come prepared to do more than hold his hand and tell him fairie tales about truth always prevailing in the end. Try to think of some way to poke a stick in his arse. The clock is ticking, and my sense is, Locke is still holding something back."

CHAPTER 13

The stench and shrieks within Newgate seemed to grow worse with every visit. Keeping her head down, Charlotte stayed close on Wrexford's heels as he followed their gaoler escort through the winding stone corridors. Thank God the blackness hid the filth beneath their boots. If only it could deaden the pitiful cries coming from the cells. Even at this ungodly early hour—she had climbed into the earl's carriage just after dawn— the prison pulsed with desperation.

The primal misery of the place was like an iron fist, threatening to squeeze the air from her lungs.

At last, the gaoler halted. A lock released with the rattle and groan of rusty metal and then the door clanged shut behind them.

Charlotte let out a silent breath, and steeled her nerves for the coming confrontation. During the ride to Newgate, Wrexford had given her a terse explanation of his meeting with Hollister. He had seemed tired and snappish, his temper dangerously frayed. She sensed he was in no mood for self-pity and prevarications.

Which didn't bode well for her cousin. But they needed more than mumbled half-truths if they were to save his neck.

Locke was awake, and sitting at the small table set in the center of the cell. Charlotte was gratified to see that he had shaved and was wearing a clean shirt. Looking around, she saw that the earl's purse had provided more amenities—blankets, clothing, a hamper of decent food, and even a few bottles of brandy and wine. Hardly luxurious, but a world of difference from the terror of bare stone and starvation.

"Thank you for your generosity, Lord Wrexford—" began Locke.

"Stubble the pleasantries," snapped the earl. "Now that you scrubbed off the initial stink of terror, I expect to get more than irrational blatherings from you." He pulled a stool over to the table and took a seat facing the prisoner.

Charlotte was too jumpy to join them. She moved a few steps to her left, where the lamplight allowed her a better look at Locke's face.

"I've told you what I know—"

"The devil you have." The earl smacked a fist to the tabletop. "Decide now—do you wish to live, Mr. Locke? Or are you happy to dance the hangman's jig as the rope slowly strangles the life out of you?"

"Nicky," began Charlotte.

"Let him answer for himself, Mrs. Sloane."

She fell silent. Never had Wrexford's expression looked so grim.

To Locke, he added, "Your cousin is about to sacrifice everything she holds dear in life in order to try to save your miserable neck. You had better prove to me that you are worth it at this meeting, or, by God, I won't let her do it."

To his credit, Locke faced the earl's wrath without flinching. "I don't blame you for thinking the worst of me, sir. I've given you no reason to think otherwise." He turned his gaze to Charlotte and she saw his eyes were no longer glazed with confusion. "I'd rather die than see you hurt in any way, Charley. If I can't save myself by my own wits, then so be it."

"Then, bloody hell, show you have some," growled the earl.

"Let's all try to use our heads," interjected Charlotte. "Stop bellowing at him, Wrexford, and start asking him your questions."

He shot her a scowl, but thankfully the murderous fury had softened from his features. "Very well, but warn your dear Nicky that my patience is perilously close to snapping."

"I daresay he's aware of that."

Wrexford shifted, his boots scraping against the stone. "Westmorly—tell me more about Westmorly, Locke. Beginning with *your* gambling debts to him."

"We played occasionally at a gaming hell in St. Giles— Lucifer's Lair," answered her cousin without hesitation. "As did some of the other members of the Eos Society. I'm a decent card player, but I had a run of bad luck one night, and Westmorly won more than I should have wagered, given the amount of brandy I had imbibed. But as I told you, the amount wasn't more than I could afford."

"Cedric knew about your losses?" asked Charlotte.

"That's what puzzles me—I have no idea how. Or why." Before Wrexford could comment, Locke added, "I wasn't misleading you, Lord Wrexford. I don't care what your witnesses say they saw, my brother and Westmorly were *not* on good terms. Granted, the breach was a recent one, and while I don't know the exact reasons, I recall Cedric muttering something about the fellow being a yellow-livered snitch."

"And you've no idea what that means?"

"No." Locke blew out his breath. "Have you asked Hollister? As I told you, whatever bad blood had arisen between Cedric and Westmorly, for a time the three of them were spending time together experimenting with electricity."

"I intend to question Hollister again. Despite his avowal, I think he's not telling me everything."

"His explanation of the romantic rivalry may not have been truthful," said Charlotte. To Nicholas, she explained, "He told the earl that Lady Julianna had chosen him over Cedric because she felt they connected on a spiritual plane."

"He's a bloody liar," said Nicholas. "Cedric was entranced by Lady Julianna, and from what I saw of them together, she felt the same way." A pause. "Though to be honest, I found her intensity a little frightening. It . . . well . . . it worried me."

That a twin might resent anyone interfering with that special bond of blood was understandable, mused Charlotte. Which was all the more reason why she needed to be able to talk to Lady Julianna herself.

The earl's unhappy expression indicated he knew what she was thinking. "As I said, I'll question Hollister again."

She didn't envy Hollister the experience.

"And I'm also anxious to have a chat with Westmorly," continued Wrexford. "I asked Sheffield to delve a little deeper into the fellow's affairs, so perhaps he's already uncovered something useful."

The earl then turned his attention back to Locke. "Now, let's talk about some of the gentlemen scholars at the Institution who have been serving as mentors to the Eos Society—starting with Justinian DeVere."

Locke appeared puzzled. "Mr. DeVere? I don't know what to tell you, sir, save that he encouraged us to express our opinions on the various lectures we heard, and was very patient in answering questions and providing further guidance on what books might be of interest."

"It was DeVere who first spoke to your group about electricity, wasn't it?" asked Wrexford.

"Yes."

"And he talked about von Humboldt's experiments on his own body?"

"Yes," confirmed Locke. "Along with mention of Aldini experiments and Galvani's work in medical electricity—that is, electrical current and the human body. At the end of his lecture, he provided a list of scientific readings on the subject."

Charlotte frowned. She had heard of Aldini and Galvani, but it was her impression that their ideas were on the cusp of quackery.

"At our next meeting," continued Locke, "Cedric raised a number of questions about Galvanism, which DeVere answered in great detail—and proceeded to explain why he thought both theories, while intriguing in the abstract, were fundamentally flawed."

"So DeVere didn't encourage further experimentation with medical electricity?" asked Wrexford.

"On the contrary, sir. As we were all leaving the study room, I heard him advise Cedric that it was a waste of time and intellect to delve any deeper into readings on Galvani."

The earl fingered his chin, and took a moment to consider what he had just heard. "What about Lord Thornton?"

Locke appeared nonplussed. "You mean the marquess?" He pursed his lips. "He gave a lecture to us several weeks ago, but to be honest, I don't recall the subject matter—though I'm certain it wasn't electricity. To my knowledge, Cedric wasn't acquainted with him."

"John Children says otherwise," replied Wrexford.

Charlotte watched her cousin lift his shoulders in a helpless shrug. "Then he knows more than I do, milord." A pause. "I swear it."

She believed him. He seemed to have shaken off the fuzzy-witted lethargy of the previous visits and now understood that his life depended on finding the real murderer.

The *clack-clack* of the gaoler's hobnailed boots announced their visit was nearly over.

"You must think more about Westmorly and Thornton," she counseled as the steps grew louder. "Anything you heard or saw of their interactions with Cedric, no matter how insignificant it might seem to you, might be a clue we can follow."

"I—I shall try, Charley."

Keys jangled, sending a shiver down her spine. The lock released.

Wrexford turned and left the cell without a further word, forcing her to hurry after him.

She wanted to think they were making progress, but the reptilian blackness of the corridor seemed to wrap around her like a serpent and squeeze such optimism from her bones.

They needed more than hope. They needed proof.

Lost in thought, Wrexford was unaware of Charlotte's fidgeting until a jarring bump of the carriage wheels drew him back from his brooding. He watched her twitch at her cap and then her coat before beginning to pick at the loose threads of her cuff.

"Is something on your mind, Mrs. Sloane?" he inquired. "Or is it just that your clothing is now crawling with lice?"

"That's not humorous, sir."

"It wasn't meant to be. Newgate is a cesspit of pestilence—and that's only one of the many dangers that lurk within its walls." Dressed in urchin clothing, she looked smaller and more vulnerable than usual. "You're taking your life into your hands every time you go there."

"Then just imagine how Nicky feels, trapped within its terrors and with no hope of escape until I can find a way to prove him innocent," replied Charlotte.

"*We,*" corrected Wrexford. "Until *we* find a find way to prove him innocent."

Her expression softened, betraying a flicker of uncertainty. "My sense is, you don't really believe he's innocent. So why are you helping me?"

"You know why." He met her gaze and held it for a moment. "Because we are friends, Charlotte."

She jumped at the intimacy.

He hadn't called her by her given name since the strange interlude after solving their last murder investigation, when in the heat of the moment . . .

Neither of them had made mention of the kiss since it had happened.

Perhaps because neither of them wished to admit what it might mean.

"Friendship doesn't mean you have to put your life in danger," said Charlotte. "Yet again."

"Have a care what you say. For you know, I will throw it back in your face at the first opportunity." He smiled. "After all, what's sauce for the goose is sauce for the gander."

"Impossible man," she muttered under her breath.

"Yes, well, we're two birds of a feather."

Charlotte shifted uncomfortably on the seat. "I'm grateful for your tolerance of my quirks, Wrexford. I . . ." She hesitated. "I haven't yet sent the letter to Lady Peake. I know you think me impulsive, but on occasion, I *do* take time to think over the ramifications before I act."

"Have you changed your mind?" The earl knew it was a decision fraught with complexities.

"No." She sighed. "Perhaps, as you counseled, the wiser decision would be to wait until I feel ready. God knows, it would certainly be the easier one. But I think I would eventually have to make the step, if only to give the boys more opportunities in life. So there's no point in delaying the moment, especially as I may be able to help Nicky."

"Spoken from both the heart and the head," murmured Wrexford. "I find no fault with such reasoning."

He waited, but got no reply.

"So, what is it that's bothering you?"

Her gaze remained glued to her lap. "I must tell the boys, of course, and McClellan. And Sheffield and Henning."

"I think it's right that they hear it from you before it becomes public knowledge," he agreed.

"I . . . you . . . that is . . ."

Her very un-Charlotte-like dithering might have been amusing, had the subject matter not been so serious.

He remained silent.

"I would like for you to be there, too—that is, if you don't mind," she said in a rush.

The request took him by surprise. "No, I don't mind," Wrexford answered, suddenly aware of an odd little spurt of warmth inside his chest. To cover his reaction, he added, "Just don't ever ask me to escort you to Almack's. Not even for friendship will I don knee breeches and white silk stockings."

"No Almack's," agreed Charlotte. "Are the lemonade and cakes they serve there really so wretched? And is Lady Jersey really so loquacious?"

"Silence well deserves her sobriquet," he said dryly. The Countess of Jersey, one of the patronesses of the exclusive assembly rooms and a leader of the *ton*, was called 'Silence' behind her back because she was notorious for her endless talking. "Don't tell me you never disguised yourself as a servant and sneaked in for a look. Your drawings have it down to perfection."

"I've contrived to see it empty," she replied. "But however unlikely, I didn't wish to take the chance of being recognized."

The earl leaned back against the squabs. "I daresay you'll soon have a chance of seeing it in all its hideous splendor. Lady Peake is a great favorite of Lady Jersey, and I'm sure she'll be intent on introducing you to all the eligible gentlemen of the *ton*. It is, after all, the premier marriage mart in London for those of pedigree and title."

"Marriage?" Her face screwed into an expression of horror. "God perish the thought!"

"I hadn't realized you were so opposed to the idea of a leg shackle," he said dryly.

"Oh, for pity's sake, Wrexford. What aristocratic gentleman in his right mind would want me as a wife?"

"There are some fellows with an open mind about the intellect and abilities of a lady." Watching her eyes, he was struck once again by what a luminous intelligence rippled beneath the sea-blue hue. "Granted, they're not as thick as fleas on a stray mongrel, but they do exist."

Charlotte looked away. "Now you're truly making my skin crawl. Even if what you say is true, you're forgetting my own feelings about life within a gilded cage."

Wrexford glanced out the carriage window. The recent revelations about her past life were still very fresh in his mind, but they had yet to delve into them in any detail, or what the future might hold for her. With her emotions already in a tangle, this didn't seem the right moment to begin.

"We're getting close to your neighborhood," he observed. "I assume you'll want to slip out when we turn down one of the side streets."

She gave a curt nod.

The wheels clattered over the cobblestones, the rough-edged sounds giving voice to the war of emotions playing across her face.

As the carriage drew to a halt, Charlotte slid across the seat and took hold of the door latch.

Her hand, so sure and steady when holding her satirical pen, betrayed a tiny tremor.

"Have you plans for the evening?" she asked abruptly.

"I had thought to begin making inquiries into Westmorly and his activities," answered the earl.

"Might you consider delaying that until tomorrow? I would

like to reveal my secret to the boys and our friends tonight. Now that I've made up my mind, there seems little reason to wait."

"Of course."

"The usual hour, and the usual means of entrance," she murmured. "Now more than ever, I have a reputation to protect." Raven and Hawk had constructed a hidden entrance into her small back garden from the back alleyway, which allowed clandestine comings and goings to proceed under the cloak of darkness.

"I'll alert Sheffield to be there," said Wrexford.

"And I shall send the boys this morning with a note for Henning." Charlotte clicked the door open. And yet, her fingers kept hold of the latch. "I'm terrified, Wrexford."

"Understandably so," replied the earl.

She gave a wry grimace. "Oh, fie. You're supposed to snarl one of your usual sarcastic comments, so I can feel angry rather than cowardly."

"You're the bravest person I know." Wrexford paused. "So, bloody hell, stop your self-indulgent sniveling . . ." He flicked out his foot and booted the door open. "And go do what's needed to be done."

Charlotte drew in a harsh breath.

"I always hated Hamlet," he added. "All that blathering and whinging."

The door slammed in his face, but not before her laugh slipped through the crack.

CHAPTER 14

"You need to eat, m'lady," chided Raven through a mouthful of mashed turnips. "It's important to keep up your strength."

Hawk elbowed his brother. "Don't talk wiv your mouth full," he whispered as he reached across the table to spear a slice of roast capon from the serving platter.

Out of the mouths of babes. They were, of course, not babes any longer, thought Charlotte, observing the boys through lowered lashes. How quickly they were growing. It seemed like just yesterday that she and her late husband had found them curled in the unlocked entryway of their tiny residence, two scrawny little weasels—

"Would you have preferred fish instead of fowl?" inquired McClellan.

"My apologies." She set her fork down. "I fear my earlier visit to Newgate has robbed me of my appetite."

"You still think the cove is innocent?" asked Raven.

"Yes," replied Charlotte. "But, as of yet, neither Wrexford nor I have found any proof of it."

"You'll catch the culprit," announced Hawk. "No villain is a match for you and His Lordship."

She wished she felt as sanguine. "I owe you an apology, sweeting. I haven't forgotten my promise to take you to Kew Gardens, but the investigation has raised some unexpected matters that must be dealt with. We shall go soon."

"Ha—I know there must be something afoot," interjected Raven. "Otherwise you wouldn't be calling for a council of war tonight."

The boy was too clever by half. "Yes," conceded Charlotte. "There are important matters to discuss. So be quick about finishing your supper and getting to work on your lessons for Mr. Linsley. If they aren't done by the time the others arrive, you'll have to miss the meeting."

Eyes widening, Hawk crammed another bite of capon into his mouth before hastily rising and scurrying for the stairs.

Raven wasn't in quite such a rush. He buttered a piece of bread before getting to his feet and raising his eyes to meet hers.

It was unnerving how well he had learned to mimic the earl's scowling stare. She forced herself not to blink.

"Are you finally going to tell us what's been gnawing at your gut?"

"If you wish for the answer, I suggest you fly up to your aerie and finish your mathematics assignment."

An angry flush rose to Raven's cheeks.

McClellan cleared her throat in warning. He ignored it.

"Be damned with mathematics!"

Charlotte bit her lip. "I was under the impression you enjoyed helping Mr. Tyler and Lord Wrexford with their laboratory calculations."

The boy's scowl wavered, but only for an instant. "Yeah, I do. But it ain't—it isn't—worth letting you face whatever trouble you're in without us there to help."

Tears prickled at the corners of her eyes. "I'm not in trouble, sweeting. I've simply been . . ." Raven and Hawk had been very wary about moving from her old residence. Things had worked out very well. However, their lives would undergo yet another transformation, along with hers. She wasn't at all sure of how they would react.

"I've simply been contemplating another change."

Raven stiffened. "Are Hawk and I going to have to leave?"

His voice was flat, but the ripple of uncertainty in his gaze had Charlotte out of her chair in a flash.

"Never." She gathered him in a fierce hug and held on for dear life, no matter that he was far more reserved than his brother and shied away from physical endearments. "We are a family."

The boy was still mostly bones and sharp angles, and yet she felt his muscles uncoil.

"Blood may not tie us together, but love does. And that's an even stronger bond."

He made a dismissive sound, but didn't try to pull away. "Naw, it's the jam tarts we would miss," he drawled—again in perfect imitation of Wrexford.

"I shall see you have your fill tomorrow." She ruffled his hair. "That is, assuming you finish your lessons."

Rolling his eyes, Raven wriggled free. "What change—"

"To your aerie," she said. "*Now.*"

He made another face, but Charlotte saw he was smiling as he turned for the stairs.

McClellan was gathering the plates from the table. "Change, eh? Perhaps it is I who will be asked to go," she murmured.

"And leave me without jam tarts? Heaven forfend."

A chuckle rose over the clink of cutlery. "The lads seem very fond of my Dundee cakes as well."

"So am I," replied Charlotte as she began helping to clear the table. "The cuisine in this house has improved markedly since you arrived. So I do hope you have no plans of moving on."

"None whatsoever." McClellan carried the dishes to the tiny scullery by the pantry. "The position suits me."

"Even though this is a rather eccentric household?" she asked.

The maid set a hand on her hip. "I hope *that* isn't going to change."

A rattle of the back door saved Charlotte from having to reply. She heard it open and close, followed by the brusque *stomp-stomp* of mud being shaken from boots.

A moment later, Wrexford appeared in the kitchen and shrugged out of his overcoat.

"Tyler allowed you out dressed in that?" McClellan raised her brows. "His standards must be slipping."

The earl added his shapeless hat to the pile of rumpled wool. "Much as it pains your cousin's sensibilities, there are times when it's best not to flaunt my lordly finery."

"Thank you for coming, milord," interjected Charlotte. Her nerves were too taut for bantering. "The others have not yet arrived. Would you care for some tea while we wait for them in the parlor?"

Wrexford extracted a bottle from the fold of the overcoat and placed it on the table. "I took the liberty of bringing a bottle of Scottish malt. I imagine Henning—along with the rest of us—will need something stronger than tea before the evening is over."

Curiosity lit in McClellan's eyes, but she turned back to clearing away the remains of supper. "You two go on. I shall bring a tray with glasses and the spirits in a moment."

Wrexford followed Charlotte, noting her rigid gait and the steel-stiff set of her shoulders. Her trepidation was understandable. Snakes may shed their skin often, but in his experience, most people found the process of stripping off one persona and assuming another profoundly daunting.

And here she was attempting to do it for the second time.

"Try to relax," he murmured as she assumed an awkward

perch on the edge of the sofa. "You are among friends. We'll be here to help you navigate through all the shoals and eddies that lie ahead."

She managed a shaky exhale and allowed herself to sink back against the pillows. "I'm very grateful for—"

"Love doesn't require gratitude," he said.

The lamplight caught the crosscurrents of emotion as her eyes widened in shock. *Love* was a word that was rarely said aloud by either of them.

"In a close-knit friendship, such as ties our little band together, it's understood that we're all here to help each other."

Charlotte looked momentarily bereft of speech.

A good thing, he decided, as she might be tempted to ring a peal over his head when he showed her what was in his coat pocket.

Ah, well—in for a penny, in for a pound.

Parchment crackled as Wrexford took a seat in the facing armchair and withdrew a packet tied with a wide black ribbon. "With that in mind," he continued, "I thought that these might prove useful to have."

Her gaze turned wary.

"They won't bite."

"And yet, something tells me I'm not going to be happy having them in my hands."

"Take them, Mrs. Sloane. We'll discuss their contents in a moment, but be assured, you'll find them invaluable at some point."

Charlotte reluctantly took them. After a brief hesitation, she untied the ribbon and slowly unfolded them, setting off a scarlet wink of official wax seals.

It took her several long moments to read them over. When she looked up, her expression was . . .

Impossible to fathom, decided the earl. He waited for her to speak.

"In the name of all that's unholy, how did you manage to get these?"

"I deal with several very skilled legal practitioners for my estate matters. I've always found their expertise and experience to be exemplary."

"B-But Wrexford . . ." Her hands tightened on the documents. "These are patently false."

"They are impeccably official," he corrected. "Anyone seeking to corroborate them will find everything in order."

"Ye gods." Closing her eyes, Charlotte expelled a harried exhale.

"Come, Mrs. Sloane. In this case, pragmatism must assuage any twitches of tender conscience. At some point, you may be asked uncomfortable questions about the boys. These documents show you and your husband took on official guardianship of Master Thomas Ravenwood Sloane and Master Alexander Hawksley Sloane during their infancy."

"But . . ." She read over the ornate script a second time. "But Anthony had no such gentry relatives in County Durham."

"He does now," replied Wrexford calmly.

Charlotte looked to be struggling for an answer.

"It's all in the best interest of the lads," he murmured.

"I know that. And I'm grate—" Another sigh. "That is, it's extraordinarily kind of you to have anticipated what problems might lie ahead." She smoothed a palm over the thick parchment. "I confess, I've been worrying about how to deal with this. It's the first question that will be asked by my relatives."

"And now you have a perfectly good answer." Wrexford allowed a small smile. "Put the documents away in a safe place. If anyone ever demands proof of your relationship to the boys, it's there in all its bureaucratic glory."

She looked up. "Thank you, Wrexford."

"You are most welcome." He sat back. "I'll have a private word with the Weasels and explain the importance of understanding the facts contained in the documents, and the need to repeat them unerringly whenever asked."

"Yes, but you know Raven can be . . ." She bit her lip. "He can be stubborn about these things."

"You may leave Raven to me," replied Wrexford.

At last, a smile from her. "In this case, I shall gladly do so."

"Then it's settled."

"Yes." Charlotte carefully smoothed a crease from her skirts. "Now, if only the rest of the evening proceeds without a wrinkle."

"Well, well, what have we here?" As he entered the parlor, Henning eyed the bottle of Scottish malt on the sideboard and promptly went over to pour himself a glass. His habitual untidiness seemed even more pronounced—bristly jaw, hair sticking up in spiky tufts, a dark smear of some unpleasant substance on his coat.

Charlotte, who had just returned from fetching the boys, also noted the lines of fatigue beneath his scowl. It looked as though it had been a very bad day at his clinic for the poor.

"*Slàinte.*" The surgeon took a quick swallow and looked to her. "Spirits usually signify a solemn occasion. Has someone died?"

Wrexford shifted in his chair. "Stubble the humor and take a seat, Baz. Mrs. Sloane will explain once—"

"What's this—another dead body?" quipped Sheffield as McClellan escorted him into the parlor.

"In a manner of speaking," replied Charlotte. She had taken pains to rehearse a formal speech, but given her audience and their unpredictable sense of humor, she realized improvising was probably a wiser choice.

"I shall explain what that means once everyone is settled." She looked at McClellan, whose expression—like those of the others—was alight with curiosity. "I'd like for you to stay as well."

The maid quickly slid into the spot next to Charlotte, while Sheffield hurried to join Henning on the settee. Raven and Hawk were sitting cross-legged on the carpet at Wrexford's feet. A low word from him stilled their fidgeting.

An expectant silence gripped the room.

Charlotte made herself take a breath. "We've investigated murders before—"

"And done a damnably good job at solving them," piped up Henning.

"Kindly refrain from interruptions," snapped the earl.

The surgeon gave an apologetic shrug and took another slurp of spirits.

"As I was saying, we've investigated murders before, but never one with such a personal connection as this latest Bloody Butcher crime."

Sheffield frowned.

"The victim, Lord Chittenden, was one of my closest childhood friends." Charlotte darted a look around at her six companions. *Friendship.* Despite her fears and worries, she felt a smile quiver at the corners of her mouth. Friendship came in all sorts of unexpected guises. Which perhaps made it that much more profound. A special camaraderie bound them together . . .

Shaking off the momentary musing, she steadied herself for the moment of final revelation.

"He was also . . . my cousin."

Suddenly everyone was speaking at once.

Henning swore as he jerked up from his slouch and sloshed the amber whisky from his glass into his lap.

"That would mean . . ." exclaimed Sheffield overriding the surgeon's oath.

"Is m'lady *really* m'lady?" demanded Raven as Hawk mumbled in confusion.

"Quiet!" commanded Wrexford.

The cacophony instantly ceased.

Charlotte swallowed a nervous laugh. "Thank you, milord."

He nodded and signaled her to continue.

"I'd prefer to avoid sounding like a melodramatic novel and simply recount the facts," she began.

A glint of amusement lit in the earl's eyes, which oddly enough helped settle her jumpy nerves.

"So the facts are these—I was born Charlotte Sophia Anna Mallory, the only daughter of the Earl of Wolcott. Even as a child, I chafed against the rigid rules governing a lady's behavior. I was constantly rebelling . . ." She looked to Raven and Hawk, who were listening intently. "Which infuriated my parents. It made life very difficult for all of us. The more they sought to force me to conform, the more I was determined not to allow my spirit to be crushed. However gilded, I simply couldn't bear to live within a cage."

Am I sounding too maudlin? Charlotte paused for a moment and quirked a grimace. "Quite likely, many of their chidings were deserved. We're never quite as wise as we think we are at that age."

Henning's muffled chuckle was echoed by a small cough from McClellan.

"Wise or not, at age seventeen, I made the impetuous decision to elope with Anthony Sloane, a young man of modest birth who was my drawing teacher. We shared a love of art and an adventurous spirit, which led us to flee to Italy. And for a time, we were very happy in Rome." She looked at her lap, remembering the clarity of the sunlight on the ancient marble ruins. "But Anthony found it hard to maintain an optimistic outlook. When the success he thought he deserved didn't come quickly, he became discouraged."

Her voice faltered as Charlotte thought of her late husband's struggles with his inner demons. Guilt pinched at her heart.

Had she done enough to help him? There had been times when his surrender to self-pity had exasperated her and she hadn't been as supportive as she would have liked.

"We returned to London, and then I eventually became acquainted with all of you." She lifted her shoulders. "That's really all there is to tell about the past. What really matters is the present and the immediate future. You see, I've come to the conclusion that in order to have any chance of proving Nicholas Locke—who is also my cousin—innocent, I must be able to move freely within the highest circles of Society. And to do so, I must come out of the shadows, so to speak, and gain entrée to the *ton.*"

"Let us help," said Sheffield without hesitation. "My grandmother is rather influential, and as she's very fond of me—Lord only knows why—I'm sure I can enlist her aid. And Wrex, of course, has some clout." A grin. "Despite his awful reputation."

Charlotte swallowed a lump in her throat.

"What about your own family?" asked Henning.

"They disowned me long ago. But, thankfully, my brother Wynton, the present earl, also inherited my late father's dislike of London, so by the time he hears of my reappearance, the murder investigation will be over." One way or another.

Sheffield's face pinched in concern. "Are you not aware . . ." He cleared his throat. "I'm very sorry to be the bearer of bad news, but your brother Wynton was thrown from his horse during a fox hunt two years ago and broke his neck."

Her hands knotted together. But try as she might, Charlotte couldn't muster any real grief.

"I'm very sorry," repeated Sheffield, his gaze full of sympathy.

"I wasn't aware of his death—as you know, I don't pay much heed to the social world of the beau monde," murmured Wrexford. "I'm sorry, too."

"Don't be. We were not close." Wynton had been a stiff, pompous prig. His first few letters to her had been cruel and spiteful—she sensed he had taken great glee in telling her how he had convinced their father to expunge her name from the family Bible. She had soon stopped reading them.

"Drink this." McClellan returned from the sideboard with a glass of whisky.

"I'm not in a state of shock," she murmured.

"Drink," ordered Wrexford.

Charlotte quaffed a quick swallow, and to her surprise, the fiery heat sent a welcome warmth spiraling through her core. "If Wynton is dead, that would mean—"

"Your brother Hartley is now the earl," confirmed Sheffield.

Hartley. Dare she hope . . .

Charlotte took another sip. Whatever Hartley's opinion of his wayward sister, it couldn't possibly be any worse than that of Wynton.

It was Wrexford, ever the paragon of dispassionate logic, who broke the awkward silence. "Those complications will all be sorted out later. At present, we need to stay focused on the task at hand. Mrs. Sloane—or rather, Lady Charlotte, as we all must now call her—"

"You see, Mr. Sheffield, there *is* a dead body," she interrupted with a shaky laugh. "My old self has now stuck its spoon in the wall." Much as she wished to protest, she knew the earl was right. A highborn lady who married a commoner retained the right to be called a lady if she so chose. To have any chance of success among the *ton,* she must now become Lady Charlotte Sloane.

"Lady Charlotte." Sheffield inclined a graceful bow.

She shuddered, suddenly feeling as if her ribs were twisting into a steel cage around her heart.

"There's no need for histrionics, milady," countered the earl.

"With a modicum of discretion and some adroit maneuvering, we should be able to guard your most important secrets."

"That will depend a great deal on Lady Peake, and how tolerant she is willing to be," replied Charlotte, finally giving voice to the fear that had been tormenting her for the past few days. Could she find a way to be two different people? Giving up A. J. Quill would be like having her very soul ripped from her being.

"Yes, it will," agreed Wrexford. "But my sense is, the Dragon will greatly enjoy breathing a little fire on the backsides of the pompous prigs of the *ton.*"

She swallowed the last mouthful of whisky and let it burn down her throat before replying. "We shall soon find out."

The earl regarded her for a long moment.

Charlotte dropped her gaze. *Damn his eyes for making me feel so naked.*

Turning to the others, Wrexford announced, "Now that we've finished with the revelations, it seemed to me that there's nothing more to be accomplished this evening. I suggest we all leave Lady Charlotte in peace for the time being." He rose. "Weasels, accompany Henning and Sheffield to the garden exit and make sure they slip away unseen."

Raven hesitated for an instant, then nudged his brother. "I s'pose we better. Without us, they'll likely make a muck of it."

As the men trooped out of the parlor, McClellan got to her feet and collected the empty glasses. "I'll tidy up in the kitchen," she murmured.

The door clicked shut behind her, leaving Charlotte alone with the earl.

She still didn't look up, afraid of revealing what a fraud she was. All her brave talk about being willing to face the consequences was naught but hot breath and bravado. At this moment, she would have given anything to be plain Charlotte Sloane—a Nobody—again.

"Stop feeling sorry for yourself," said Wrexford as he moved to the sideboard and splashed the last of the whisky into a glass. "You thrive on challenges. This one will be no worse than those that have come before."

The coolness of his voice nettled. "That is oh-so easy for you to say. You're not having your life blown to flinders."

Candlelight caught in the swirling amber spirits, sending shadows skittering over his face as he lifted the glass to his lips. "As I recall, you used those exact words to describe your elopement." A quick swallow. "Without a smidgeon of regret, I might add."

"Stop being the Voice of Reason," she muttered. "It's quite annoying when you insist on being so infuriatingly logical."

He laughed.

"I won't give up my pen," she added. "If I have to disappear— yet again—I will do so after Nicky's situation is resolved. London is a large city. I'll find someplace within its neighborhoods where I can slip back into anonymity."

"Of course, that can be done, if you so choose," he answered, "but I don't think it will be necessary. These days, there are more Bluestockings within the *ton* than you might think—ladies who prefer intellectual pursuits rather than the superficial swirl of tea and gossip. If you choose to attend salons that cater to intellectual discussions rather than the endless circle of balls and soirees, Society with quickly deem you an eccentric—or, more politely, an Original—and promptly lose interest in you. Especially when the next scandal or juicy bit of gossip rears its ugly head."

Wrexford gave another swirl of his glass. "And as you know well, there is *always* a new scandal or bit of gossip to make people forget about last week's news."

"So you're saying that even within the *ton*, it's possible to live hidden in the shadows?"

"Yes. They're simply silkier and scented with a more pleasant perfume than the ones in your past."

She blew out her breath, only to have it end in a grudging chuckle. "Thank God for your biting cynicism. Without it, I'm not sure I'd have the nerve to take the next step."

"You'll find a way," said the earl.

"*Aut inveniam viam aut faciam,*" she murmured. I will either find a way or make one.

For a long moment, Wrexford appeared distracted by a ripple of light in his whisky. He then quaffed the dregs and set his glass down beside the empty bottle. "Have you arranged a meeting with Lady Peake?"

"Not yet. I sent my letter this afternoon suggesting we meet for a stroll in Green Park and am awaiting a response." Charlotte grimaced. "A neutral location seems wise in case . . . in case things don't go well."

"You could always employ a spot of blackmail if the dowager proves difficult," drawled Wrexford.

Charlotte let out a dismissive snort. "And just what sort of power do you imagine I have over her?"

"A. J. Quill," he answered. "Tell her you're acquainted with the artist and a refusal to help you will result in a highly unflattering series on her quarrel with the Duchess of Berryhill."

"First of all, I would never stoop to such pettiness—it would be unethical to use my art for personal reasons," retorted Charlotte.

"Yes, but she doesn't know that."

"And secondly," said Charlotte, ignoring his quip, "since you are always so pragmatic, allow me to point out that to my knowledge, there *is* no quarrel between her and the duchess."

His lips twitched. "*Everyone* has a quarrel with the duchess. She's a sharp-tongued, dull-witted battle-axe."

Charlotte pressed her fingertips to her temples. "Go away, Wrexford," she muttered, unsure of whether she was about to laugh or cry. "My head is beginning to ache."

"Very well. Good night, Lady Charlotte." As he moved for the door, he paused to smooth an errant curl back from her brow. A fleeting caress, so quickly done that perhaps she had merely imagined it.

And yet, as Charlotte watched his dark-on-dark silhouette meld into the shadows, its warmth seemed to linger.

CHAPTER 15

Charlotte stared down at the pristine piece of paper, its crisp folds sealed with a scented wafer of rose-colored wax. The faint perfume—a sudden reminder of long-ago sunshine and laughter—tickled her nostrils as she set aside her marketing basket and made herself pick it up from the tray on the side table.

Dare she hope her memory hadn't deceived her? Aunt Alison had always stood out as a bold splash of color amid the unremitting greyness of the rest of her family. An unconventional intellect, an iron will, a tart sense of humor, a sly delight in refusing to fit the pattern card of propriety . . . Charlotte knew that even her stiff-rumped, autocratic father was intimidated by the dowager.

With good reason. Alison didn't suffer fools gladly.

But people changed, she reminded herself. Her own seventeen-year-old self felt as strange and distant as the Man in the Moon.

"Aren't you going to open it?"

Charlotte looked up to find Raven eyeing her intently. But before she could answer, Hawk burst in from the garden, a large glass jar covered with a scrap of gauze clutched in his grimy hands.

"Look, look, I captured a monarch butterfly!" His face—what little could be seen of it through the crust of mud—beamed in pride as he held up his prize.

"A very handsome specimen," admired Charlotte.

"I'm going to draw it," announced Hawk proudly. "And then let it go."

She made a mental note to pay a visit to Hatchard's bookstore and purchase more illustrated volumes on flora and fauna. "An excellent plan. But I suggest you rinse your hands before picking up your sketchbook and pencils—you wouldn't want an errant speck of dirt to alter the accuracy of your art."

"Insects and slugs are disgusting," muttered Raven with a mock shudder as his brother pelted off for the stairs.

"We all have our passions," she murmured. "Be gentle in your teasing. He values your good opinion, and it's important to be supportive of what sparks his imagination."

Raven's grimace softened to a ghost of a grin. "He's very good at drawing, isn't he?"

"Yes, extremely good. More than that, he's very observant and possesses an excellent eye for detail."

Alas, so did Raven, for the boy's gaze immediately went back to the letter in her hand.

"Aren't you going to open it?" he repeated. "It looks like it's from your great-aunt."

Charlotte reluctantly cracked the seal and unfolded the paper.

"Well?"

She knew Raven was heading to his weekly mathematics session with Wrexford's valet. "When you arrive at His Lordship's town house, kindly ask him if I might have use of his unmarked carriage later today." A second glance at the dowager's distinctive script. "I need it to call here at a quarter hour past two."

Concern clouded his eyes. "Are you afraid?"

"I'm terrified." Charlotte forced a smile. "But battles are rarely won without facing one's fears."

"What will you do if The Dragon refuses to help?"

Her heart gave a clench at the note of uncertainty in his voice. The weight of their worries shouldn't be falling on his bony shoulders. "I shall simply find another way to help my cousin." Charlotte ruffled his hair. "Now run along. You mustn't be late for Mr. Tyler."

Raven scuffed his boots, and then suddenly put his arms around her waist and pulled her into a fierce hug.

Before she could react, he was out the door, leaving naught but the whisper of rippling air in his wake.

"*Men.*" Though Charlotte conceded she was hardly one to judge. It wasn't as if she wore her own emotions stitched like gaudy-colored ribbons to the cleavage of her bodice for all to see.

After putting away her purchases in the kitchen pantry, she headed up to her bedchamber. The sound of her steps on the landing drew McClellan from sweeping the floor of Charlotte's workroom. "Did Lady Peake agree to a meeting?"

"Yes." Charlotte closed her eyes for an instant. "And soon, so I must be quick about changing into yet another disguise," she added with an edge of sarcasm. "That of an oh-so proper lady."

McClellan followed Charlotte into her bedchamber. "Sit," she ordered as she moved to the armoire. "Which gown would you like?"

The options were extremely limited. Yet another part of her life that would have to change. Participating in the beau monde's frivolous social swirl required an obscene amount of frills and furbelows.

"It doesn't matter," she replied a little testily. "I leave it for you to choose."

McClellan didn't hesitate. "The slate blue. It's reserved, yet elegant, and it accentuates the color of your eyes."

"Accentuating the color of my eyes is the *least* of my concerns," muttered Charlotte as she stripped off her work gown.

"It shouldn't be," counseled McClellan, handing over a more elaborate corset. "Since you're intent on stepping onto a new battlefield, you must learn to wield a new set of weapons."

"Touché," she conceded. The observation was true, but it didn't make her mood any less prickly as she began lacing herself into the silk and whalebone.

With her maid's help, she rushed through the rest of her toilette and headed back down to the street, where the earl's carriage was waiting.

Charlotte settled into her seat and fisted her hands in her skirts.

Maintaining a tactful silence, McClellan took a place on the facing bench. A rap on the trap signaled for the coachman to get under way.

"Forgive my black humor," she said over the iron-shod clatter of hooves and wheels.

"Change isn't easy," replied her maid. "But one adapts quicker than one might think."

McClellan's cool pragmatism helped settle her jumpy nerves. Leaning back, Charlotte drew a deep breath and sought to compose her thoughts for the coming confrontation. Having faced the prospect of violent death from bullets, blades, and fiery explosives over the past year, she knew that a simple conversation shouldn't have her insides quaking like aspic. And yet . . .

All too soon, the carriage arrived at the entrance of Green Park. Offering up a silent plea for Lady Luck to look favorably on a fellow female, Charlotte steeled her spine and descended to the pavement. McClellan dutifully trailed along behind her, maintaining the correct distance expected of a lady's maid.

She took a moment to survey the surroundings. The rendezvous with her relative had been set for one of the footpaths that threaded through the copse of trees skirting St. James's Palace. To her relief, there were few people in the park at this hour, save for a handful of nursemaids and their young charges playing in the grass near the dairy stall. After smoothing the strings of her bonnet into place, Charlotte set off down Queen's Walk and soon found herself within the welcome shelter of the trees.

She came to a halt in a patch of shade and drew a steadying breath.

A breeze ruffled through the leaves overhead and she was suddenly acutely aware of the flickering patterns of sun and shadow on the gravel beneath her feet. *Light and dark, so clearly defined.* And yet her life seemed to move through a far more subtle play of nebulous greys.

Her musings were suddenly interrupted by a voice from the past.

"My dear Charlotte! Is that really you?"

"Wrex!" Sheffield shouldered his way into the earl's workroom. "Wrex!"

"No need to bellow." The earl looked up from his laboratory ledger. "I'm here, not in Timbuktu."

"Ah, thank God you've risen from your slumber." Wincing as a shaft of sunlight from the mullioned windows cut across his face, Sheffield ran a hand through his hair. "Why the devil is there no food in the breakfast room?"

"Because certain of my friends are like a plague of locusts. Cook has been ordered to lock up the larders, lest they be stripped bare."

"Your butler is far more sympathetic. He's promised to bring me coffee and a crust of bread."

"Is there something urgent?" demanded the earl. "Aside from your growling stomach."

"It would serve you right if I didn't tell you," said his friend primly. "However, my loyalty to Mrs. Slo—that is, Lady Charlotte—compels me to overlook your less-than-hospitable welcome."

"Kit," warned Wrexford as he put down his pen.

"Yes, yes." Sheffield dropped his posturing. "I made the rounds of the gaming hells in Southwark after last night's gathering, hoping to learn a little more about Westmorly." He paused as the earl's butler carried in a tray with a steaming pot of coffee and a cold collation of meat and cheese. "Bless you, Riche."

Holding back his impatience, the earl allowed his friend to take a bite of cheddar before prodding, "*And?*"

"And I uncovered something that may have relevance to our investigation," answered Sheffield. "Two of the porters at Lucifer's Lair were gossiping about a private exchange they overheard several nights ago. Apparently, Jameson Mansfield—the new Earl of Woodbridge, as his father recently passed away—confronted Westmorly and accused him of cheating at cards. He said he wouldn't make it public if Westmorly stopped playing at all the establishments frequented by the *ton.*"

Wrexford frowned. There was no greater sin against the gentlemanly code of honor than to cheat at cards. Those caught at it were usually publicly called out and ostracized from Polite Society. "I wonder why Woodbridge let him off so easily?"

"As do I." Sheffield wolfed down another big bite of meat and cheese. "He's currently at home—I checked with the coachman in the mews. The family town house is just off Hanover Square."

"Well done, Kit. I suggest we pay him a visit." He eyed the still-full tray. "Now, if you please."

After taking a long swallow of coffee, his friend let out a wordless grumble. "Very well. But you owe me a decent supper."

Charlotte should have remembered that her great-aunt always arrived early for any appointment.

The Dowager Marchioness of Peake still cut a magnificent figure. Tall and willowy, with coiffed curls that gleamed like polished silver from beneath her jaunty plumed shako, she was approaching with surprising agility, given the ebony cane clasped in her gloved hand. Age hadn't dimmed her beauty. The regal, fine-boned features of her face drew the eye with their classical symmetry, and while her ivory skin betrayed the wrinkling of time, a lively intelligence glittered in her grey eyes.

Skirts swirling, feather bobbing, she lifted her stick in an imperious salute.

"It *is* you, and grown even more striking than I remember."

Charlotte felt as if the gimlet gaze were cutting through the layers of fabric right down to bare skin. The dowager had always possessed the ability to see through any artifice.

"I feel like I'm seeing a ghost suddenly come to life." The cane gave another waggle. "You have a great deal of explaining to do, my dear."

"It's lovely to see you, Aunt Alison," murmured Charlotte as she brushed a light kiss to the dowager's cheek. "And, yes, I shall endeavor to answer for my misdeeds."

Alison took hold of Charlotte's arm. "Come, let us walk." A wave of her cane indicated a fork in the footpath leading down to the adjoining meadow of St. James's Park. "There is a bench close by that affords a very pleasant view over the lake."

Crunch-crunch. The sound of their steps on the gravel filled the silence as they made their way out of the shade and seated themselves in the sunshine.

The dowager fluffed her skirts and then carefully angled her cane across her lap.

Charlotte felt her throat constrict. The soft kidskin gloves, a lovely smoke-green hue that matched the elegant walking dress, didn't quite disguise how frail her great-aunt's hands had become.

"Italy," said Alison without preamble. "I heard you and your drawing master had hared off to Italy." Her gaze was on the lake, not Charlotte. "Why didn't you write to me?"

"Because I feared ..." Charlotte shifted. *How to explain?* "I feared I had disappointed you. Not just in disgracing the family name, but because you encouraged me to think and to explore." She swallowed hard. "And then I went ahead and, against all common sense, chose to ruin my future."

Alison finally turned to face her. "Do you regret it?"

"No," she answered without hesitation. "Though that's too simple an answer. I am sorry beyond words for the pain I caused you, and all my family. But for me to live as more than a pasteboard cutout, I needed to escape from the gilded cage and spread my own wings." Charlotte made a wry face. "No matter where I ended up."

"Hmmph."

The sound—was it a snort or a sigh?—was too faint to interpret. She waited, watching the dowager's hand tighten on the handle of her cane.

"Tell me about your life," said Alison. "Was Italy all that you dreamed it would be?"

It took longer to tell than Charlotte had expected. She had prepared a story—one as truthful as she could make it—but the dowager kept interrupting with questions. Charlotte answered them as honestly as she could.

Thank God Wrexford's foresight allowed her to explain about the boys.

"So you are a widow, with two wards," murmured Alison when Charlotte had come to the end of her story. "How do you support yourself?"

"Anthony made a living painting portraits, once we returned to England. Through his connections, I found work using my skill at art to do illustrations of fashion and Society."

"Like the ones shown in *Ackermann's Repository?*"

"Yes, similar to those." It wasn't precisely a lie, just a bending of the truth.

"I see." Another question looked to be hovering on her lips, but Alison appeared to change her mind. "So now that we've covered the past, let us speak of the present—and the future."

Though the plume of the dowager's shako was dancing in the breeze, casting her face in flickering patterns of dark and light, Charlotte saw Alison's gaze turn searching.

"Why the sudden desire to reenter Society? From what you've told me, I have the distinct impression that you value your independence even more fiercely than you did as a girl."

"I must think of the boys," she responded. "My entrée into the beau monde will open up opportunities that I can't currently offer to them."

The dowager nodded sagely. "It will also open up opportunities for you." She cleared her throat with a brusque cough. "Including to remarry, if you so choose."

"I assure you that is *not* why I am here," murmured Charlotte.

Alison fixed her with a searching stare, but didn't press the question. Instead, she said, "I'm often accused of possessing a devious mind, so I can't help but wonder if this has anything to do with Cedric's murder and Nicholas's imprisonment for the crime. I know you were close to them."

Charlotte sensed that all hope for her plan hinged on how she answered. "Your mind," she said carefully, "has always been a source of inspiration to me. It's from you that I learned to ask difficult questions, to challenge myself to look beyond the comfortable confines of my world."

Amusement quivered at the corners of the dowager's mouth. "That wasn't an answer to my question."

Charlotte smiled. "No, it wasn't. And I daresay I'm not going to give you the one you want." Shifting position on the slatted seat, she reached out and uncurled the dowager's fingers from the cane. The fragile warmth of them tingled against her palm. "You're right—I'm hopelessly independent and I doubt I shall ever change. In addition, I have secrets that I'm not yet ready to share. Life has taught me to err on caution."

The dowager's expression tightened, but the cane remained untouched in her lap. Which Charlotte decided to take as a good sign.

"And so, although I have no right to ask it, I'm hoping you'll agree to help me without demanding to know all the reasons why. At least for now."

"Hmmph." This time the dowager did reach for her cane. "Come, let us walk again. My old bones become stiff if I sit for too long."

Charlotte helped her to rise. She saw movement in the shade of the nearby trees as McClellan and the dowager's maid made ready to follow.

"It's a cursed nuisance to grow old and feeble," grumbled Alison. "But I suppose I'm fortunate my wits haven't ossified along with my knees."

She said nothing, deciding to place her faith in the fact that the dowager had always preferred plain speaking to platitudes.

Progress was slow at first. Alison was a trifle unsteady on the loose stones, and Charlotte steadied several stumbles.

On reaching the crest of the gentle hill, where the path turned level, the dowager regained her stride. "Have you any other acquaintances within the beau monde?" she asked abruptly. "I seem to recall you were close with that young jackanapes who became Lord Sterling."

"Jeremy," answered Charlotte. "Yes, he and I are friends, and we see each other occasionally."

"Anyone else?"

"Lord Wrexford," she answered. "He and I are also ... friendly."

"*Wrexford?*" The dowager's brows shot up. "How did you come to meet the earl?"

"Through my late husband," she replied. "I'm also acquainted with his friend Mr. Sheffield."

Alison seemed satisfied with the explanation. "About Anthony Sloane." The dowager thought for a moment. "You say his relatives were gentry?"

"Yes, but Anthony was of modest birth—"

"Pfft! It's been a decade since your elopement—and even back then, your parents hushed up the details. No one will have the slightest idea as to his background."

"But—"

"There is an art to storytelling, my dear child. The key is to embellish certain details to make them compelling," said Alison as she paused and gave a flourish of her cane to emphasize the point. Turning, she fixed Charlotte with an owlish squint. "But I daresay you know that."

Charlotte maintained a solemn face. "Imagination is important in any creative endeavor."

That drew a bark of laughter. "Life has been sadly flat without you, Charley." A sigh. "The *ton* is filled with pompous prigs and feather-headed widgeons. I swear, I'm sliding into senility from sheer boredom." Taking hold of Charlotte's arm, she turned toward Piccadilly Street, where her carriage was waiting. "A little intrigue and excitement is what keeps the blood pulsing through one's veins. So whatever it is you are up to, I shall be happy to help."

Charlotte covered the dowager's hand with hers and gave a heartfelt squeeze. "Words feel inadequate to express my gratitude to you—for everything. So I shall simply say thank you, Aunt Alison."

"Nonsense," sniffed the dowager, though her cheeks had turned pink. "It is *I* who should be thanking *you*."

They walked on for several strides. "Come around to my town house tomorrow at half past eleven," added Alison, "and we'll begin to plan a strategy for introducing you to Society." Her eyes took on a speculative gleam. "Perhaps if we ruffle enough feathers, we'll merit one of A. J. Quill's drawings."

"Let us try not to have it come to that," she murmured.

The dowager looked a little disappointed; however, her expression quickly brightened as the footpath took them up through the center of the park's meadow. "Yes, but you said you're on friendly terms with the Earl of Wrexford. And you can't deny that wherever *he* goes, trouble seems to follow."

CHAPTER 16

"W rexford. Sheffield." Jameson Mansfield—the new Lord Woodbridge—inclined a polite nod as he entered the side parlor, though a faint crease between his brows betrayed his puzzlement. "I apologize for receiving you in such an informal room, but the servants are making some repairs in the drawing room." A cough. "To what do I owe the pleasure of a visit?"

"A matter of honor," replied the earl.

Woodbridge maintained a rigid smile, but the color drained from his face. "I—I can't imagine what you mean."

"Then allow me to explain," said Sheffield, who quickly recounted what he had heard the previous evening.

"Is what the porters said true?" asked Wrexford.

Woodbridge moved to the tray of crystal decanters on the sideboard and poured himself a brandy. His hands, noted the earl, were shaking. "May I offer you gentlemen some refreshments?"

"I'd prefer an answer," he replied.

Lifting the glass to his lips, Woodbridge took a long swallow. "Yes, it's true."

"Why?" asked Sheffield. "Why let the cad escape without exposing his misdeeds? That goes against the grain of a gentleman's code of honor."

"I—I have my reasons. They are personal, and I don't wish to discuss them."

"Forgive me, but I'm not inclined to accept that as an answer." Wrexford perched a hip on the arm of the sofa. "You see, I've learned that Lord Chittenden settled gaming debts with Westmorly just days before his murder. Which, as surely you can see, raises unsettling questions."

"I know nothing about that!" exclaimed Woodbridge. Despite the coolness of the room, his forehead was now sheened in sweat. "I swear it."

"Be that as it may, your information may help to solve a very heinous crime."

"B-But the newspapers say Chittenden was the victim of his younger brother, who killed him in order to inherit the title."

"Newspapers care about sales more than they care about the truth," replied Wrexford. "So, again I ask you, why did you allow Westmorly to go unmasked as a cheat?"

Woodbridge tugged at his cravat, as if the elegant folds of snowy white linen were a noose tightening around his throat. His answer, when it came, was barely more than a whisper. "I can't tell you that."

"You're the Earl of Woodbridge," pointed out Sheffield. "And Westmorly is a mere mister. Your word would carry more weight than his."

"I . . ."

The drawing room door came open, cutting short his stuttering. Wrexford turned to see a tall, willow-slim lady dressed in indigo silk reclose it and turn the key before moving across the carpet to join a still-gaping Woodbridge.

"Let us drop all prevarication, Jamie. Given the circumstances, I think we owe these gentlemen an honest answer."

She turned to fix the earl and Sheffield with a cool stare. Like her gown, her eyes were a shimmering shade of grey and dark blue. "Please forgive my brother. He *does* have a sense of honor—he's choosing to protect his sister, which is why a venomous snake like Westmorly was able to wriggle free."

"You have certainly piqued my curiosity, Lady . . ."

"Cordelia," croaked Woodbridge. "Lady Cordelia Mansfield."

Lady Cordelia Mansfield. The earl vaguely recognized the name. A spinster and a Bluestocking, Woodbridge's sister was a member of several intellectual societies, where, much to the horror of Polite Society, she dared to challenge the scholarly papers presented by the gentlemen members.

Which might explain, he reflected, why she was rarely seen at any of the fancy balls and soirees of the beau monde.

By the wary expression on Sheffield's face, he, too, was aware of her reputation.

"Perhaps we should all be seated," said Cordelia, after her brother finished stammering through the formal introductions. "There's no reason to be uncomfortable when one is conducting an interrogation."

The earl noted the glint of sardonic amusement in the lady's eyes. His first impression was that she was a far more formidable opponent than her brother . . . assuming she meant to cross swords with him. As he took his place in one of the overstuffed armchairs, he found himself rather hoping she would.

Sheffield sat in the matching chair, while the two siblings moved to the facing sofa.

"Shall I ring for tea?" Again he heard the edge of mockery in her voice.

"Thank you, but as you've gathered, this isn't a social call," he replied. "No need to go through the charade of polite pleasantries, as I'm sure you and your brother would prefer that we are gone from the premises as quickly as possible."

A smile—one that struck him as genuine—curled the corners of Cordelia's lips. "I, too, favor plain speaking, milord. So let us not waste our breath waltzing through spins and evasions. I overheard your questions to Jamie, and the reason why you want a truthful answer."

"Cordelia," murmured Woodbridge. "I beg you to consider your own reputation before you go on."

Her gaze flashed a challenge at Wrexford and Sheffield. "I'm assuming the gentlemen will give their word of honor that what we say here is to be held in strict confidence."

"Of course," answered the earl, and the agreement was quickly seconded by Sheffield.

Her brother slumped back against the pillows in surrender.

"So I'll ask the question again," said Wrexford. "Why did you allow Westmorly to go unmasked as a cheat?"

Woodbridge exhaled through his nose. "Because to make a public accusation, I would have had to explain to others how I knew Westmorly was cheating, and that would have required . . . putting my sister in a deucedly awkward position."

Sheffield choked back a grunt of surprise. "I don't mean to be indelicate, but . . ."

"But a man's life hangs in the balance," interjected Wrexford. "So forgive us, but we'll need to have a more specific answer than that."

"I expected no less," said Cordelia. "Jamie, I think it best to let me tell the story, as I can do it without hemming and hawing." She raised her chin, and Wrexford found himself applauding her sangfroid. "I'm quite used to men thinking me beyond the pale, so it no longer bothers me that I'm thought odd and eccentric."

A pause. "Those are, of course, the most polite of the adjectives."

"Far be it for either of us to judge anyone," quipped Sheffield. "Our own reputations are not exactly lily-white." He gave a wry smile. "But then, I've always thought that lily-white is a rather colorless hue. And color is what makes things interesting."

Cordelia's mouth pinched for an instant. The earl wasn't sure whether she was offended or simply trying to hold back a laugh.

"As Sheffield says, we are merely interested in learning the facts, not making any moral judgments," he murmured. "So, please, go on, Lady Cordelia."

"Very well." She smoothed a crease from her skirts. "I accompanied my brother to Lucifer's Lair several nights ago—dressed as a man, for obvious reasons."

"That isn't an easy masquerade," challenged Wrexford. "It requires more than just masculine clothing. One has to master gestures and movement."

"I've practiced it over the years and have gained some skill in it," came the cool reply. "Before you ask why, it's because you gentlemen reserve so many interesting things, like boxing matches, carriage races, and smoking cheroots, for yourselves. It's most unfair."

"Smoking is vastly overrated," murmured Sheffield. "It leaves a vile taste in your mouth."

Ignoring the comment, Cordelia continued, "And the atmosphere of a gaming hell makes it easier than most venues. The light is dim, the air is hazed with smoke, and the gentlemen's wits are fuzzed with spirits."

The earl acknowledged her point with a small nod. "True."

Sheffield shifted forward in his seat. "Why were you visiting Lucifer's Lair?"

"To play cards, of course."

Wrexford, too, sat up a little straighter.

"Not for the mere devil-may-care thrill of courting danger," added Cordelia. "Since we are being candid with each other, I will explain . . . up to a point." She let her words sink in, before continuing. "My father had made some imprudent investments recently and my brother and I found ourselves hard-pressed to meet certain family financial obligations. So I decided to use my skill at cards to earn the requisite amount."

Cordelia tugged at her skirts again. A sign, decided Wrexford, that despite her cool demeanor, she wasn't quite as composed as she wished to appear. He liked her better for it.

"Skill doesn't always guarantee success, Lady Cordelia."

"I'm well aware of that, milord. But I'm rather good at mathematics—"

"Actually, she's rather brilliant at mathematics," interjected Woodbridge.

Cordelia shrugged off the praise. "I count well, and I seem to have a knack for calculating the odds—"

"How does that work?" demanded Sheffield. He was now on the edge of his seat.

"Ye gods, Kit. I've told you about numbers and probability any number of times," muttered the earl.

"Yes, but you've never explained what you meant," shot back his friend. "I know you think me a brainless fribble, but I would like to make an attempt to understand the concept."

Cordelia looked about to make a tart reply, but then seemed to change her mind and fixed him with an unblinking stare. Her expression was impossible to read. "If you're serious, you're welcome to pay a call here some afternoon. We'll take a deck of cards and I'll show you exactly what I mean." Her chin rose a notch. "That is, if the idea that a lady might actually possess a brain doesn't curdle your innards."

"On the contrary," replied Sheffield without hesitation. "I would welcome an intelligent conversation with a lady, rather than the endless silly simperings on the weather, or whether I prefer to tie my cravat in an Oriental or a *trone d'amour* knot."

Wrexford caught the momentary flicker of surprise in her eyes.

"Mr. Sheffield," said Woodbridge in a tight voice. "Allow me to warn you that my sister isn't an heiress, so any flirtations you have in mind will be wasted efforts."

To the earl's surprise, Sheffield's face suddenly mottled with anger. "My faults are many, Woodbridge. But chasing after a lady simply to snatch her fortune for my own is *not* one of them."

"Can we put aside such distractions for now, Kit?" suggested Wrexford. "I'm sure Lady Cordelia and her brother would prefer not to draw out this conversation any longer than is absolutely necessary."

"Correct," muttered Woodbridge. "Come, Cordelia, explain to them what you saw, so we may be done with this unpleasantness."

"Very well." His sister shifted her gaze from Sheffield and folded her hands in her lap. "I sat down at one of the tables to play vingt-et-un—I have ways of dealing with my feminine hands and voice, but they aren't relevant. Suffice it to say, I began to win. In short order, I had garnered the amount I needed, and a bit more. But it's not considered good form to immediately rise and leave when one has been on a winning streak. So I remained for a bit, intending to lose a modest amount, before quitting the establishment."

"Westmorly then took a seat at the table when one of the other players ran out of blunt," said Woodbridge.

"He drew my attention because he counts well, too," explained Cordelia. "However, in watching him when it came his turn to deal the cards, I observed that he was also giving himself an unfair advantage." A pause. "He's very clever at palming cards."

"I assume you are sure of this," murmured the earl.

Her reply was a withering look.

"So what did you do?" asked Sheffield.

"I lost a few more hands, which suited me fine, and then quit the game. Jamie, who had been standing behind my chair observing the play, followed me to one of the alcoves and I told him what I had seen."

"Couldn't very well let Westmorly get away with fleecing my friends," muttered Woodbridge. "So during a reshuffling of the deck, I told him I needed to speak to him on an urgent matter."

"As they moved off, I retreated deeper into the shadows, intent on going unnoticed," said Cordelia. "I dress in black, and keep my hat drawn low—"

"Most gentlemen don't wear hats in a gaming hell," pointed out Sheffield.

"Jamie always announces that his young cousin has odd superstitions, including wearing a hat for good luck," she replied.

"Clever," conceded the earl. He was about to press Woodbridge on the details of his talk with Westmorly, but Cordelia's next words caused the questions to die in his throat.

"Given your interest in Lord Chittenden's murder, perhaps my hat did bring a stroke of unexpected luck. You see, as I wedged myself into a dark nook, two gamesters stepped into the alcove with their drinks." She shook her head. "Really, you gentlemen are as fond of gossiping as the tabbies of the *ton*."

The earl didn't disagree.

"One of them immediately began to gabble on about having overheard a nasty exchange between Chittenden and Westmorly," continued Cordelia. "He said Westmorly threatened to expose Chittenden's secret if the baron didn't keep quiet about Westmorly's own peccadillo." Her skirts rustled as she shifted. "Then they moved off in search of a fresh bottle of brandy."

"The fellow didn't elaborate on what those secrets might have been?"

She shook her head. "No, and it didn't occur to me as to mention it to Jamie. It could mean nothing—the two gentlemen were quite cup-shot. But given your concerns, I thought you should know."

"Thank you," replied the earl.

"As for my conversation with Westmorly," said Woodbridge, "I told you earlier exactly what I said."

Wrexford fingered his chin in thought. "Has he been seen
gambling since then?"

"I wouldn't know," muttered Woodbridge. "I don't make a
habit of frequenting the gaming hells."

Deciding there was no more to be learned, he rose. "I appreciate your time—and your candor. You may rest assured that
what you've told us will be held in strict confidence."

"I shall see you out." Woodbridge was quick to get to his
feet.

Sheffield, noted the earl, was a fraction slower to follow.

As they reached the door, Wrexford noted a carefully folded
black overcoat sitting atop one of the bookshelves. Poking out
from behind it was a curled brim.

He turned. "By the by, Lady Cordelia, what style of hat do
you wear as your lucky talisman?"

She smiled. "From what I hear, milord, you have no need of
such superstitious fiddle-faddle."

"One never knows."

The lady had a very musical laugh. "If you must know, it's a
Wellington."

He felt himself stiffen. "A Wellington?"

"Yes," replied Cordelia. "The crown is low enough not to
look absurd on a lady's head, and the jaunty curl of the brim
adds a touch of whimsy."

The flesh-and-blood Wellington wasn't noted for his whimsy—
for those who faced his armies on the Peninsula, he was known as
a harbinger of death. But Wrexford kept such thoughts to himself.

"I see," he murmured. "Well, let us hope that it continues to
be a fortunate choice for you."

Abandoning her half-finished drawing with a frustrated
huff, Charlotte moved from her desk to the window and pressed

her forehead to the mist-chilled glass. The last glimmers of dusk had given way to a black velvet sky threaded with ribbons of smoke-dark clouds.

Somewhere in the distance, a low rumbling warned that rain was imminent.

Her flesh suddenly felt cold as ice. The sound seemed to echo her inner turmoil—an irrational reaction, she knew, given that the meeting with her great-aunt had gone so well. And yet, the prospect of gaining entrée to the inner sanctums of the beau monde—the elegant drawing rooms, the glittering ballrooms— filled her with dread.

Polished flatteries, pasteboard smiles. A thin veneer of civility masking jealousy, greed, and the lust for power. All the things that had compelled her to flee in the first place.

"I *won't* become one of them," vowed Charlotte, her breath fogging the windowpane. "I *won't.*" But the words failed to loosen the knot in her gut.

Turning away from the darkness, she went to warm her fingers over the lone candle burning on the side table. Tomorrow . . . tomorrow she would once again don silks and satin to spin through an intricate dance of lies.

"*Lies,*" she whispered, setting the flame to shivering. "Perhaps my life has been so entangled in lies that they've become woven into the fabric of who I am."

Drawing a shaky breath, she blew out the light and hurried from the room. Sleep, she knew, would never come. Her own weak voice would never chase the demons from her head. For that, she needed a more sarcastic snap and snarl.

Be damned with ruffles and lace. Darting into her bedchamber, Charlotte quickly dressed in breeches and boots, then tiptoed down the stairs.

CHAPTER 17

"Bloody hell."

Wrexford balled up the list he had been writing and tossed it into the fire. The paper emitted a sharp hiss and crackled into ash. As he watched the wisps of smoke tease against the brass fender, he muttered another oath.

His gaze moved to the neat rows of chemicals and glassware lining the shelves above the counter of his workroom. He liked order. Science appealed to him because it was based on reason. One could, through careful study and observation, make sense of random chaos, while people and their motivations were a damnable puzzle. Emotions rarely surrendered to common sense.

Frowning, Wrexford slouched back in his chair and steepled his fingers. Could Lady Cordelia Mansfield be a murderess? The Wellington hat was a chilling coincidence. And there was no question that she had the cleverness and the feisty courage for it. As for motive . . . perhaps Chittenden had threatened to expose her masquerade. She and her brother had admitted to financial pressures, and money was often at the root of evil.

And then, there was the very personal nature of the crime.

A lady scorned and betrayed might be tempted to slice off a man's . . .

No, he just couldn't bring himself to believe it. Yes, Cordelia possessed a steely strength, but there was something about her laugh that didn't resonate with murder.

"Ye gods, Charlotte's stubborn insistence on trusting intuition must be rubbing off on me," he muttered.

Mention of Charlotte made his mood turn even darker.

Wrexford rose and began to pace around the room. It worried him that circumstances were forcing her to make such a momentous decision. What if she hated the change? He didn't doubt that she would make good on her threat to disappear. It was, of course, none of his business how she chose to live her life. And yet, she was a friend.

Friend. He felt another twist in his gut. Sheffield had lapsed into a moody silence on leaving the siblings. It was unlike his friend to brood, and as Wrexford paused to stare into the fire, he couldn't help wondering if his own irascible temper had made him blind to the feelings or needs of those around him.

He was always so bloody quick with his sarcasm. Sheffield deserved more than that.

The *chink* of glass against glass drew him out of his thoughts. Tyler pushed through the door, a tray of just-washed beakers and slides in his arms.

"I've laid out the books on Boyle's experiments," announced his valet. "Do you wish to begin—"

"Stubble Boyle," grumbled the earl. He pursed his lips. "Tell me, am I a self-absorbed prig?"

Tyler set down the tray and wiped his hands on the front of his coat. "Pray tell, what's prompted this sudden bout of introspection? You don't usually give a rat's arse about what anyone thinks of you."

The reply only exacerbated his misgivings. "Never mind," he said through his teeth.

Tyler raised his brows. "I take it the investigation isn't going well."

A grunt was the only answer. Turning away from the taunting flames, Wrexford returned to his desk, determined to make another stab at using logic to organize the facts into some sort of coherent order.

Clink-clink.

He looked up to find his valet had poured a glass of spirits and placed it beside the inkwell.

"*Slàinte,*" murmured Tyler, lifting his own drink in salute.

"That," said the earl, "was a *very* expensive bottle of brandy."

Tyler took an appreciative sip. "But of course, milord. Only the best for you."

"Arse," muttered Wrexford through a grudging laugh. The heat of the brandy helped dispel the chill in his belly. But before he could say more, a scuffing on the window ledge drew his attention.

The latch jiggled and released. A gust of damp air snaked into the room, followed by a wet boot.

"Kindly pour me a brandy, too, Mr. Tyler—assuming His Lordship can afford it." Charlotte landed on the floor with a thump, sending up a spray of mud. "It's raining, and colder than a witch's tit out there."

"An interesting metaphor," observed Wrexford. "But one that's best not repeated inside a Mayfair mansion."

She accepted the brandy from Tyler and took a grateful swallow. "You need not remind me that I'll need to keep my tongue under tight rein—as well as the rest of me." Her mouth tightened. "I'll have McClellan tie an extra knot in my corset strings to make sure I don't come undone."

It was said lightly, but Wrexford heard the edge in Charlotte's voice.

"You can still change your mind."

She looked away. The fall of her cap shadowed her eyes as she took another swallow. "*Alea iacta est.*"

"The die is cast," translated the earl. "Nonsense—Fate is always in flux. As an experienced gamester, I assure you that one can always pick up the ivories and throw them again."

Charlotte didn't smile.

Tyler cleared his throat, and after gathering up the empty tray, he quietly left the room.

"Did the meeting with Lady Peake not go well?" inquired Wrexford, once the door clicked shut.

"On the contrary, it turns out she's quite happy to help me. We are meeting tomorrow to begin planning a strategy."

"Then why are you looking so Friday-faced? You've conquered far greater challenges than a crowd of overbred, overfed aristocrats."

Her lips twitched. "I know. But . . ,"

"*But . . .*"

Charlotte chafed the glass between her palms, setting the amber spirits to swirling. In the light of the burning coals, it looked like liquid fire. "But now I'm one of them."

"Is *that* what you're afraid of?" he jeered. "Hell's bells, you're not at all like them."

"That's what I tell myself, but . . ." She took a seat on the edge of his desk and hugged her arms to her chest. "But what if I'm seduced by all the sumptuous splendors?"

"Somehow I have trouble imagining that a lust for lobster patties will be your undoing."

She laughed in spite of herself. "Thank you, Wrexford. I knew I could count on your mockery to chase away my self-pity."

"I'm always happy to play the motley fool."

Her brows notched together. "It seems I'm not the only one feeling unsettled this evening."

Damnation. She could read him too well.

"Have you uncovered something new?"

Wrexford nodded and quickly explained about Woodbridge and his sister, and what he and his friend had learned. "Sheffield is spending the evening trying to learn Westmorly's whereabouts. He's proving a hard man to find." He grimaced. "I fear Kit is out of sorts with me. I . . . I haven't been a good friend to him of late."

"I confess, you gentlemen have very peculiar ways of expressing your camaraderie."

He felt Charlotte studying his face.

"But he knows you see his strengths, though he takes great pains to hide them," she continued. "So whatever friction there is between you at the moment, it's not because either of you doubt the elemental bonds of your friendship."

"Perhaps." He took a long swallow of brandy and then recounted the exchange with Lady Cordelia on calculating the odds on cards.

"She sounds very intriguing."

"I haven't told you the whole of it yet." The earl hesitated. "Logic warns me to be suspicious of coincidences, but on rare occasions, they do happen."

"Don't keep me in suspense, Wrexford."

"It concerns the hat she wears when masquerading as a man," he replied. "It's a Wellington, and she considers it her lucky talisman."

"Surely, you're jesting!"

He shook his head. "I assume you're in no mood for levity. Nor am I."

Neither of them spoke for several moments. The silence seemed to amplify the crackling of the coals.

"Do you think her capable of such a crime?" Charlotte finally asked.

The earl took his time in considering the question. "She reminds me of you," he answered. "She possesses great intelligence, as well as a core of elemental strength, and there's no question that she'll wield both to protect her family. How that might tie in to Chittenden is as yet unknown."

Wrexford let out his breath. "That said, I sensed no guile or malice to her—quite the opposite in fact. But we both know that a thin veneer of civility can mask a soul that is rotten to the core."

Charlotte looked about to speak when her eyes suddenly widened. "Good Lord—Cordelia Mansfield. I now remember why the name strikes me as familiar. As we walked back to her carriage from our meeting in Green Park, Aunt Alison told me about a salon of intellectually minded ladies who, she thinks, may offer me a sanctuary of kindred spirits within the *ton.* Lady Cordelia was one of the members she mentioned."

"She has a reputation as a Bluestocking," he said.

"A lady who isn't afraid to challenge conventional thinking," mused Charlotte. "It seems I've made the right decision to seek entrée into Polite Society. I must now investigate Lady Cordelia, as well as Lady Julianna."

She set her glass aside and turned to stare at the shimmying flames in the hearth.

Wrexford didn't interrupt her brooding. His own thoughts were none too steady. He hated seeing the look of vulnerability lurking in the shadows beneath her lashes.

And yet he wasn't sure how to help. The recent moment of profound connection between them—the fleeting kiss, the murmurs, however oblique, of feelings for each other—now seemed more tenuous. He had drawn back, not wanting to crowd her as she wrestled with all the difficult decisions to make about the future. And she, too, had seemed to put some distance between them.

Perhaps all his sharp edges were beginning to chafe against her sensibilities—

The sound of hurried steps in the corridor suddenly intruded on his thoughts. He looked up just as Sheffield flung open the door.

"Westmorly is a damnably difficult fellow to track down," announced his friend. "But I've located his current lodging. He's taken room at a small hotel just off Russell Square." Spotting Charlotte, he gave a nod. "Good evening, milady," he added, politely ignoring the fact that she was dressed in the grubby togs of an urchin.

"Mr. Sheffield," ackowledged Charlotte as she uncrossed her booted legs and slid down from her perch on his desk.

Wrexford glance at the mantel clock. "Given the hour, we may find him at home."

"Unless he's gambling at one of the less salubrious spots in Town," said Sheffield.

"I'm willling to take a chance on that." He rose. "If you'll excuse us, Lady Charlotte—"

Her eyes darkened. "I'll play the lady within the mansions of Mayfair, Wrexford. But don't think I mean to surrender my independence outside of the gilded cage." She tugged at the brim of her hat. "I'm coming with you."

Charlotte watched a scowl take hold of his features. "It might be useful for me to look around the area," she added quickly. "Perhaps one of the street sweeps has noticed Westmorly's nocturnal movements and whether he's accompanied by any companions."

A glimmer of understanding flashed in the earl's eyes. She released a silent breath, grateful that he grasped how much it chafed her to feel helpless while he and the others were pursuing promising leads.

"That makes some sense," he allowed. "Come, we'll go through the mews and take my carriage as far as Montague Place."

The ride passed with little conversation. Sheffield was unnaturally silent, noted Charlotte, as she watched him from beneath the brim of her hat. He looked pensive rather than angry. But given her own unsettled state of mind, she didn't dare hazard a guess as to why.

Shadows flitted around them as they descended from the carriage. Most of the windows of the houses lining the narrow street were dark, and the few widely spaced streetlights cast naught but a weak aureole of light. Sheffield led the way, cutting through a back alley and approaching a squat grey granite building through the small swath of unpruned garden that sat at its rear.

"Westmorly has a set of rooms on the top floor," he whispered, pointing up at a pair of dormer windows set in the slate tiling of the lower slope.

It looked black as Hades behind the mullioned glass.

"It looks like he's either out or asleep." Wrexford moved to the scullery door. Pulling a thin metal probe from his boot, he made short work of opening the lock.

Charlotte followed him and Sheffield inside. "I should come with you. If he's in, I'll simply slink away," she explained. "If he's not, it's important that I have a look around. My eyes see things that yours don't."

The earl didn't argue.

"The main stairs are this way," indicated Sheffield. "There's no one on duty at the front desk at this hour. The residents all have keys, so they can come and go during the evening."

A single sconce was burning in the corridor, its lone flame doing little to lighten the gloom. It was quiet, thought Charlotte, cocking an ear and listening for the sounds of movement on the floors above. *Too quiet.* She felt a prickling at the back of her neck.

The reception area was deserted. Wrexford paused only long enough to pick up a candlestick and strike a spark to the wick. Cupping the flame, he started up the treads, taking them two at a time.

As Charlotte reached the next landing, she heard a scrabbling behind one of the closed doors and a bolt being thrown into place.

Up they climbed, the darkness wrapping around them like a shroud. The air turned thick and seemed to stick in her lungs.

On reaching the top floor, Sheffield wordlessly pointed to the door on the left.

Wrexford fisted his gloved hand and knocked.

The echo died away, leaving the landing quiet as a crypt.

He rapped again, and waited, impatiently shifting his weight from foot to foot. On getting no response, he tried the latch.

The door swung open.

Raising the candle, he crossed into the darkness. After several steps, Charlotte heard him halt and swear a low oath.

She smelled it, too—a mix of burnt gunpowder and the coppery scent of fresh-spilled blood.

Wrexford had found a lamp on the side table. Glass and metal rattled as he hurriedly coaxed a flame to life. The flare of light skittered across his cheekbones, deepening the hollows beneath his eyes.

Darting forward, Charlotte followed her nose to one of the side chambers, and pushed the door open.

"Ye gods," Sheffield hissed through his teeth as he came up behind her.

The lamp's glow had not yet penetrated the darkness, but a blade of moonlight cut through the windowpanes, illuminating the grisly scene at the writing desk. A man—his head half blown away by the force of a pistol shot—was slumped back in a slat-back wooden chair. Blood and bits of brain spattered his coat and shirtfront. The weapon, still grasped in his lifeless hand, had fallen—

She caught Wrexford's sleeve as he started to push past her. "A moment, sir," she said. "Let me study the details a little longer before we do anything to disturb the scene."

He went very still. "What do you see?"

Charlotte didn't answer. Her gaze moved slowly over the floorboards and the worn carpet covering half the room. "Angle the light there." A curt wave indicated an area by the fringed side closest to them.

Crouching down, she took another long moment to examine the fibers. "I've seen enough. You may go closer now."

Wrexford, to his credit, didn't press her for an explanation. Moving lightly, he paced a methodical circle around the dead man, pausing every few steps to make an observation. Only then did he approach the desk.

"There's a note," he said, looking down at the single sheet of paper on the blotter. "*I can't live with the shame of my actions any longer,*" he read aloud. "*Forgive me.*"

Sheffield swallowed hard as the lamplight flickered over the ruined face, then averted his eyes from the corpse.

"If you're going to be sick," murmured Charlotte, noting that he had gone a little green around the gills, "kindly step out to the entrance foyer."

"No, no, I won't embarrass myself," came the choked reply.

"There's no shame in a visceral reaction to violent death." She moved closer, studying the gruesome patterns of blood and brains.

"Do you think . . ." Sheffield made himelf look at the dead man. "Is it possible he's confessing to a more serious crime than cheating?"

"The words," said Charlotte, "are conveniently cryptic."

The earl exhaled a low grunt. "Your mind is as devious as mine."

"W-What do you mean?" asked his friend.

The wind gusted, pelting rain against the window glass.

Avoiding the blood dripping from the desktop onto the carpet, Wrexford squatted down and made a close inspection of the weapon. Charlotte picked her way close to the corpse, forcing aside emotion to see the tableau as a puzzle.

And something wasn't fitting together.

She waited until Wrexford straightened before asking him to hold the lamp closer to the dead man's chest. Picking up the letter opener from the top of the blotter, she shifted one side of the unbuttoned coat open a fraction wider, revealing more of the shirtfront.

The earl leaned in closer. "How the devil did you see that?"

"I merely suspected something of the sort."

He shook his head and muttered something under his breath about unholy magic.

"It's logic, not magic, Wrexford," countered Charlotte. "Look at the blood on his shirt. It's saturated around the left breast, and yet it's the right part of his head that's blown away." She straightened. "When you analyze the spray of blood and fragments from that wound, it's clear they couldn't have caused that much volume."

"Then what did?" asked Sheffield. He shuffled forward, curiosity overcoming his squeamishness.

Charlotte touched the tip of the letter opener to a tiny tear in the linen. "A narrow blade pierced the heart. My guess is, that was the cause of death, for by the amount of blood, his vital organ was still pumping."

"Much as I'd like to argue, I think you're right," muttered Wrexford. "The hand shows no sign of power residue. Who-ever this is, he didn't fire the shot that spattered his brains to Kingdom Come."

Sheffield hitched in a breath. "So you're saying this wasn't self-murder."

"No." She carefully set down the letter opener and looked to the earl. "Cedric was killed by a single stab to the heart. Can you arrange for Henning to examine the body? He might be able to tell whether the same weapon was used for both crimes."

Wrexford nodded. "Kit, take the carriage and go to Bow

Street. Leave word for Griffin to come here as soon as possible. Then head to Henning's surgery and bring him back here."

"Of course."

"Lady Charlotte and I need to look over a few other things—" The earl's words were suddenly cut off by the sound of thumping on the stairs and agitated voices coming from the landing.

Charlotte darted to the entranceway and ducked behind the door as it flung open.

A burly man burst in, followed by two companions brandishing cudgels and lanterns.

"Well, well," drawled Griffin, skidding to a halt.

Charlotte cringed and tugged her hat lower. She and the Runner had encountered each other on several occasions during the past murder investigations, and she knew very well that his lumbering movements and untidy clothing disguised a very sharp mind. So far, he hadn't discerned that the ragged urchin he knew as Phoenix was not . . .

"Another dead gentleman?" added the Runner. "Why does it not surprise me to find you here, milord?"

"Because you realize what a kindhearted fellow I am," replied Wrexford. "Count yourself fortunate, for when it comes to the twisted minds of the *ton*, you know that you need my help in unraveling the truth."

"It looks to me like self-murder," said Griffin. "One of the other residents alerted the watchman, and reported hearing naught but a single shot fired."

"It's meant to look that way," replied the earl. "But come, I have something interesting to show you."

As the three men trooped toward the desk, Sheffield shifted his stance, blocking the view of the door.

Charlotte seized the moment to slip out of the room.

Griffin whirled around just in time to catch a flutter in the shadows. "Was that Phoenix?" he demanded. "Damnation—call him back!"

"For what reason?" inquired the earl.

"To offer him a position at Bow Street," growled the Runner, after casting an unhappy look at his men. "It seems the grubby little street rat is always two steps ahead of us! How the devil does he know what evil is lurking in every nook and cranny of London?"

Ha! thought Charlotte as she turned for the stairs. At present, she was simply praying that her feet didn't get hopelessly tangled in all the half-truths and deceptions demanded by her chosen path.

"Never mind Phoenix," came Wrexford's reply. "If you want answers to this particular crime, I suggest you send one of your men to fetch a mortuary cart and take the body to Henning's surgery."

CHAPTER 18

"How can you eat broiled kidneys?" Tyler gave a mock shudder as he entered the breakfast room. "Henning's clothing is noxious enough to rob a fellow of his appetite, but had I watched him wield his scalpels in the wee hours of the morning..." Another grimace. "I'd be eating bread and water for the next week."

Wrexford poured himself another cup of coffee. "I think better on a full stomach."

"A good thing, as this latest murder looks to be a devilishly difficult one to solve." Tyler took a seat at the table and plucked a fresh-baked sultana muffin from the platter of pastries. "You've identified the victim?"

"It's Westmorly," confirmed the earl. He and his valet had briefly discussed the new turn of events earlier that morning. "Griffin just sent word that his men brought one of the porters from the Royal Institution to the surgery, and the man identified what was left of the face."

"Has Henning any further thoughts on whether the murder weapon might be the same as the one used on Lord Chittenden?"

"It's impossible to say. The blade is too slim, and the surface too smooth to have left any distinctive marks. What he can say is that the method and the angle of the thrust were very similar."

"So," replied his valet, "you're assuming it's the work of the same dastard."

Wrexford stared down at the sin-dark dregs in his cup. "That's the logical line of reasoning."

Tyler raised his brows. "And that bothers you?"

"In this case, perhaps." Something was niggling at the edges of his consciousness, though he couldn't put a finger on what it was. "I need to make some more inquiries at the Institution concerning Westmorly's activities. Griffin has agreed for now to tell the newspapers it was suicide, so as not to alert the murderer to the fact that his ruse was spotted."

"Ah—speaking of inquiries, I've made a bit of headway with the fragments of snuff."

"Indeed?" The earl had already started to rise, but reluctantly resumed his seat. Though he had little faith that the spiced tobacco would yield anything useful, it would be churlish not to listen.

"It was the lad who sparked an idea," explained Tyler. "He pointed out that if the microscope had a greater magnification, we would have a better chance of isolating the various ingredients. That got me to thinking . . ." The valet paused to take a bite of his muffin. "I purchased a more powerful lens, and we built a wire scaffolding that allowed it to augment the instrument's other lenses."

Wrexford was now paying full attention. "And?"

A smile. "And it allowed us to identify bits of cinnamon bark as one of the ingredients. We also noted some fragments that have a distinctive red speckling. I suspect they are some sort of spice, so I've an appointment later today with a botanist at the Royal Society who specializes in the field."

"Well done." Knowing the exact ingredients of the snuff mixture would make inquiries among the tobacconists of London a far less daunting task. Not that he expected it to matter.

"As I said, it's Raven who deserves much of the credit. It was an obvious solution, but sometimes it takes seeing a problem in a new light to spot a way to solve it. He's a clever rascal." Tyler popped the rest of the muffin into his mouth before rising with a long-suffering sigh. "Alas, I had better go see if those disgusting stains can be removed from your waistcoat before heading off for my meeting."

Wrexford pushed back his plate. "I, too, have some people I wish to speak with at the Royal Institution." Children's information concerning Lord Thornton might lead to naught, but he couldn't overlook it.

"Is there any other task for me to undertake when I'm done with the botanist?"

"Actually, there is. I'd like for you to make the rounds of the taverns that cater to the servants of Mayfair." He pulled out a handful of coins from his pocket and placed them on the table. "Be generous with tankards of ale, and see what you can learn about Woodbridge and his spinster sister."

"You think they may somehow fit in to the murder of Lady Charlotte's cousin?"

"I've not yet formed an opinion," he answered. "Let's just say it's a possibility that ought not be overlooked."

He hadn't mentioned it to Charlotte, as he wasn't quite sure whether it was just a figment of his imagination . . . but as he had first leaned in close to Westmorly's corpse, he could have sworn that he caught a faint whiff of a lady's perfume.

Charlotte untied the strings of her bonnet and set it on the side table, though a part of her wanted to hurl it into the flames of the fire blazing in her workroom hearth.

Muttering an oath, she sat at her desk and took her head in

her hands. Things were moving at a dizzying pace. *Dear God in heaven*—tomorrow she was to make a round of morning calls with Alison, followed by an evening meeting of Lady Thirkell's philosophical salon. More engagements were scrawled on the notepaper in her reticule. And then, all too soon . . .

"I thought you might like some tea," announced McClellan as she entered the room, bearing a tray with a steaming pot and a plate of ginger biscuits.

"Ah, yes—Pip, pip. The English panacea for whatever ails you."

"I took the liberty of bringing a measure of whisky to fortify the brew." McClellan busied herself with mixing two cups. "We Scots know that the English aren't always in the right."

Charlotte gratefully accepted the concoction and took a sip. "Thank you."

The maid merely nodded and let a companionable silence settle over the room.

Another sip, and the mellow warmth began to spread through her limbs. "It could be worse," murmured Charlotte. "I could be heading for the gibbet at Tyburn rather than a round of cakes and gossip with the grande dames of Mayfair."

"Perhaps you should stop thinking of this transformation as the death of your old self," counseled McClellan. "The essence of who you are isn't changing a whit. You're merely taking on new plumage." She paused. "After all, one of your street monikers is Phoenix, a bird who rises from the ashes with bold, beautiful new feathers with which to fly into the future."

Charlotte stared at her palette of watercolors and suddenly felt a smile stealing across her lips.

"I'm not telling you anything you don't know," the maid went on. "You've undergone transformations before."

"If I'm to wear new plumage," she quipped, "at least I will be draped in the latest styles." One of her longtime informants was Madame Françoise—née Franzenelli—a clever, streetwise

Italian who had established herself as London's most exclusive modiste.

"I paid a visit to Franny after my meeting with Aunt Alison. She's kindly agreed to deliver several of her creations—including a ball gown—by tomorrow morning."

"I take it the dowager has begun to put her plans in motion."

"Yes."

A whirling dervish would be an accurate way to describe the dowager.

"And oddly enough, she seems to have taken the challenge to heart," answered Charlotte with a rueful grimace. "We are visiting the crème de la crème of Society tomorrow, and then—likely all too soon—she intends to have me accompany her to a grand ball."

McClellan pursed her lips. "Do you perchance know how to waltz?"

She shook her head.

"Well, you had better start learning. There's a pianoforte in Wrexford's music room. Tyler and I shall expect you and the boys to come round tonight after dark for a first lesson."

"The boys—"

"The boys should begin learning some social graces," replied the maid. "And we'll need them as practice partners."

"But—"

"Would you rather make a cake of yourself when Wrexford or Lord Sterling leads you out on the dance floor?" challenged McClellan.

Charlotte froze, the protest dying on her lips as she imagined the musicians striking up the first lilting notes—and the feeling of her slippers being glued to the parquet.

"Very well. We'll be there."

Wrexford gazed out of the arched windows of the Royal Institution's study room as he thought over what he had learned from his queries. A clearer picture of Westmorly in life had emerged. Which only raised more questions about his death.

A frustrated sigh fogged the glass.

Word of the death had already spread through the halls of the Institution. The reaction among the members had been shock, but little sympathy. Benjamin Westmorly wasn't well liked. Everyone seemed to agree that he was extremely bright and excelled at scientific reasoning and mathematics. But he was also seen as an ambitious toadeater, someone who was always looking to insinuate himself into the inner circle of those who looked to be influential in Society.

The earl watched the fancy carriages with their matched horses and liveried tigers wheeling along the street below. He had also learned that Westmorly had apparently acquired a taste for the finer things in life, along with his Oxford education. And yet, his family finances were modest at best. Rumors of large debts had floated around the clubs shortly after his arrival in London. But from what Wrexford had just gathered, those whispers had soon disappeared.

A clever fellow could make cheating and blackmail over personal secrets very profitable, mused the earl. Until he chose the wrong person to diddle.

The question was who.

Turning away from the view of Albemarle Street, Wrexford made his way through the archway and out into the corridor. An even more elemental question was whether Westmorly's murder was indeed connected to Chittenden, or a simple but sordid act of revenge.

The idea of coincidence went against his belief in scientific order. Most things could be explained by logic . . .

And yet the more pieces he gathered to the puzzle, the harder it was to see how any of them fit together.

Just ahead was the grand marble staircase leading down to the main entrance. Looking up, Wrexford slowed his steps, and then suddenly turned on his heel and headed back into the bowels of the building. Several turns and another set of stairs brought him up to the floor housing the laboratories of the senior members. Thornton's space, he knew, was halfway down the central corridor—

As he turned the corner, a door came open.

On instinct, he halted and ducked back into the side hall.

"Come, come, Thornton, we must hurry or we'll be late for the meeting," came a querulous voice.

"Hold your water, Fitz. Let me just gather my papers . . ."

Wrexford waited a moment before sneaking a peek. Thornton emerged, a portfolio case in one hand and a set of keys in the other. A harried jiggling drew the door shut and the earl heard the *snick* of a lock.

"Let us hope that Lexington doesn't prose on for hours," grumbled Thornton as he and his colleague set off in the opposite direction.

Gentlemen do not spy on other gentlemen. But in this case, be damned with the code of honor, thought Wrexford, reaching for the steel probe he always carried in his boot.

Given that a life was at stake, Thornton would likely forgive the transgression . . . assuming he ever learned about it.

And assuming he had nothing to hide.

It was only a matter of moments before the earl was inside the laboratory with the door relocked. The windows were shuttered, but a lamp had been left burning, its wick turned down low.

Holding himself very still, Wrexford made a careful survey of the surroundings before touching anything. How a man worked often revealed much about him.

Creativity is rarely tidy, he thought wryly as he ran his gaze over the bookshelves and work counters. The chemicals were all arranged in meticulous order and the precision instruments were spotless. However, books, laboratory notebooks, and piles of paper lay in apparent helter-pelter disarray around the room. The scene reminded him of his own workroom—though Tyler did his best to keep the clutter under control.

Starting at the nearest corner, Wrexford slowly circled the room, taking in the beakers filled with colored fluids, the microscope, the spirit lamps, the array of tweezers and scalpels . . .

Nothing appeared out of the ordinary.

Moving on to the large desk near the shuttered windows, he crouched down and began a methodical search of the drawers—bills, correspondence, folders containing scientific papers published by various societies around the country. Hardly the stuff to stir any suspicions.

Rising, he returned to the work counters and thumbed through several of the laboratory ledgers. They, too, appeared perfectly in order.

Satisfied, the earl turned and took a step toward the door. The movement stirred the air, and out of the corner of his eye, he saw a flutter of fabric within a shadowed recess in the far corner of the room. Wrexford hesitated, but curiosity got the better of him. He went over to investigate what lay beneath the canvas covering.

A cabinet. And a padlock was looped through the sturdy iron hasp.

Snick-snick.

Wrexford eased the door open. It took a moment for his eyes to adjust to the gloom within, but the contents slowly came into focus.

"Bloody hell," muttered the earl as he found himself staring at a voltaic pile and a coil of thick copper wire.

Blinking, he sat back on his haunches. On the lower shelf were two leather-bound books stacked atop one another. Next to them was a metal box. Light glinted off the gold-stamped titles as he gingerly lifted the books from the cabinet.

De Viribus Electricitatis in Motu Musculari Commentarius, Luigi Galvani's treatise on animal electricity, was the top volume. And beneath it was *De L'électricité Animale à la Stimulation Cérébrale Chez L'homme,* Giovanni Aldini's explorations on the same subject.

Wrexford swore again. Galvani's theory on animal electric fluid had stirred a great controversy at the turn of the century with Alessandro Volta, who had offered a more scientific explanation for why a dead frog's legs could be made to twitch. Most rational men of science now sided with Volta, but Galvani's nephew, Giovanni Aldini, had continued his uncle's work . . . espousing even more unsettling theories.

Placing the books back on the shelf, the earl withdrew the box and balanced it on his thighs. A foreboding tingled against his palms as a foul smell swirled up to clog his nostrils.

Shallowing his breathing, Wrexford undid the latch and raised the cover . . . then snapped it shut with an unholy oath.

The remains of a heart—it looked to be that of a large rat—lay on a piece of bloodstained paper, several wires still attached to the putrefying flesh.

He waited for his pulse to steady before placing the box back on the shelf exactly as he had found it. After relocking the cabinet, he smoothed the canvas back in place. His first impulse was to escape from the noxious hellhole as quickly as possible, but he forced himself to double-check that no signs of his search were evident.

After what felt like an eon, he stepped out into the corridor and reset the door lock. Flushing the lingering foulness from his lungs with several deep inhales, Wrexford hurried to one of the back stairwells and exited from the rear of the building.

But rather than return to his town house, he flagged down a hackney and barked an order for it to head east.

"M'lady, m'lady!" The sound of Hawk's excited voice floated down from his aerie as Charlotte passed through the entrance foyer.

Smiling, she set down her marketing basket and began to

undo her bonnet. No doubt the boys, who had been at their lessons earlier, were anxious to hear a report on her first foray into Polite Society. However, they would likely find her visit to Alison's residence—and all the endless recounting of the rules to be followed—rather boring.

Save for a description of the cakes. The dowager served divine pastries to go along with her expensive tea.

"M'lady!" Another breathless shout as the boy skidded to a halt at the foot of the stairs.

"Ye heavens!" teased Charlotte. "I merely traveled to South Audley Street, not the exotic ends of the earth." Granted Mayfair *was* another world, but they would all have to become more familiar with its customs and inhabitants. "Shall we—"

"Look! Look!" Hawk had a piece of paper clutched in his grimy fist and was waving it in the air.

"He's right," said Raven, who had followed his brother. "You need to take a peep."

Letting the strings of her bonnet slip through her fingers, Charlotte hurried across the rag rug and plucked the paper from his fingers.

It was a pencil drawing—

"Alice . . . her friends . . . a toff . . ." Hawk was tripping over his tongue in his haste to explain.

She took him by the arm. "Come, let us sit in the parlor. You can catch your breath and then start at the beginning."

Raven fell in step behind them. It must be important news, she decided, for he refrained from any good-natured needling of his brother.

Ignoring the muck embedded on the seat of Hawk's pants, Charlotte sat down and patted a place on the sofa beside her. "Now tell me about this." On closer inspection, she saw it was a sketch of a coat.

"It's *him*!" replied Hawk.

"The man who murdered your cousin," clarified Raven.

Charlotte's fingers tightened on the paper. "How—"

"Alice!" explained Hawk. "Alice sent word that she remembered something else about the man in the hat. So we went to see her . . ." A guilty flush colored his face. "That is, after our lessons with Mr. Linsley."

Likely much abbreviated, but she didn't have the heart to scold them.

"Tell her what Alice said," urged Raven.

Hawk drew in another gulp of air. "Alice and her friends got to thinking more about the night. One of 'em recalled the hat—she, too, saw the flash of something shiny on the band—and remembered the cove wore a dark coat with just a single shoulder cape."

Charlotte was studying the sketch. A caped coat wasn't unusual, though the more popular style was for two capes. And this particular one seemed distinctive. "What is this?" she asked, pointing to the edge of the cape.

"Alice is very good at details," said Raven. "She said she knew this was important to you, so she made herself picture the moment—"

"And she thinks there was a band of braid trimming the shoulder cape," cut in Hawk. "It fluttered in the wind as he passed by, and she said the moonlight caught on the texture—it wasn't quite the same as the smooth wool, and the color was dark, but not quite as dark as the rest of the coat."

Charlotte tried to hold her excitement in check. The detail—if it were true—could be vital. But was the girl's memory accurate, or was it merely wishful thinking? Experience had taught her that the passage of time often played tricks with one's memory.

She looked up at Hawk's expectant face. "This could be invaluable information, but we mustn't let our hopes soar too high."

"Oiy." Raven nodded sagely. To his brother, he added, "Alice might have been mistaken."

"She was sure of it," insisted Hawk.

"Every detail helps," assured Charlotte. "And I know Alice has a keen eye." She carefully refolded the sketch. "Thanks to both of you, the picture of our quarry is taking shape on paper."

Now they just had to find the flesh-and-blood dastard to match it.

That, however, would have to wait. As soon as darkness descended over the city, the world of silks and satins must take precedence over sleuthing.

CHAPTER 19

"What do I know of Aldini and Vitalism?" Henning looked up from the bubbling cauldron on his worktable and took a moment to wipe his spectacles on a rag. A draft from the ill-fitting window swirled the rising steam, leaving a mizzle of droplets on his unshaven cheeks. "Surely, *that* man's theories aren't coming back to life again here in England?"

"God only knows what wild ideas are lurking deep in the shadows," responded Wrexford as he tossed his hat on the surgeon's desk and unbuttoned his coat. "Ready to crawl out if someone shines a light their way."

"It sounds like you've shoved your hand up some dark crevasse," said the surgeon, "and come away with a nasty bite."

"You could say that." Hooking his boot around a stool, he drew it up to the table and took a seat. "I paid a visit to the Royal Institution and learned a little more about Westmorly, though nothing that might provide a clue as to who killed him. My sense is, he had made a number of enemies through his blackmailing. Any of them could have wished him dead."

"A thoroughly dirty dish," agreed Henning.

"From what Locke has told me, Westmorly knew some dirty secret about Chittenden and was extorting money to keep quiet about it. But—"

"But I can't see him as Chittenden's murderer," interrupted Henning. "First of all, why would a blackmailer kill the goose who lays the golden egg?"

"There's that," conceded the earl.

"More important, the knife thrusts that killed both men were done by a skilled hand. Someone knew what he—"

"Or she," interrupted Wrexford.

"A woman scorned, taking her revenge by murdering the handsome young Tulips of the *ton*?" Henning made a rude sound. "You've been reading too many of Ann Radcliffe's novels."

"Give me a better plot. For it feels as if I'm getting nowhere in trying to work out a scenario for what was going on within the Eos Society." The earl braced his elbows on the scarred wood. "However, perhaps I've stumbled upon a new lead. Getting back to my question about Aldini and Vitalism . . ."

Wrexford explained about his grotesque discovery in Thornton's laboratory. "I confess, I've paid little attention to such ideas. But as you're a medical man, I wondered whether you've done any reading in the field."

"I have," confirmed the surgeon. "Beginning with the discoveries of Galvani and Volta, and their invention of a device that could create electrical current—"

"The voltaic pile," said Wrexford.

"Correct, laddie. Galvani may be mocked by many as a mere dancing master of dead frogs, but he did apply scientific thinking to his experiments. The fact that electricity could affect a body led him to theorize there existed what he called a 'nervous-electric fluid.' He believed illnesses might be caused by blockages of the fluid. And that led him to speculate that electricity might be a powerful force for good."

Henning cracked his knuckles before continuing. "The

voltaic pile generated great excitement within the medical world, as many wondered whether it could effect wondrous cures. Fix palsied limbs, bring new vitality to the old—"

"Raise the dead," muttered the earl.

"Yes, well, Galvani's ideas were taken to the extreme by his nephew, Aldini. You remember what a spectacle he created over the George Foster affair."

The earl shook his head. "I was out of the country at the time, traveling with my brother in a remote part of Ireland."

"You missed nothing but a regrettable farce." Henning made a face. "Aldini had made himself the darling of London with his demonstrations of making dead frogs twitch. He then claimed his process could bring a man back to life. He got his chance when a man named George Foster was convicted of murder, sentenced to be hanged, and then given over for dissection. Aldini got permission to perform his experiment on the condemned man's corpse."

Wrexford grimaced, but said nothing.

"Foster was hung at the gallows of Newgate, and his body was immediately taken to the Royal College of Surgeons, where an audience eagerly awaited the momentous event. Aldini had attached a set of conducting rods to his voltaic pile and pressed them to Foster's head, caused the jaw to start quivering and the left eye to fly open."

This time, the earl couldn't hold back an oath.

"It gets more revolting," said Henning. "He then inserted the rod up poor Foster's . . ." A cough. "The fellow's legs kicked up, his arm raised, and his back arched in a bow."

"But he didn't get up and walk away."

"Nor did he punch Aldini in the nose," quipped Henning. "Indeed, after that, the public's interest in the experiment died down, and after further experiments, Aldini conceded that he didn't have the power to make a dead heart start beating."

The earl shifted. "So the idea of reanimating the dead went to its own grave?"

"No, there are others who keep searching for the secret of Life. I take it, you haven't heard of Karl August Weinhold, a German who claims he's brought animals back from the dead."

"Surely, you jest."

"Unfortunately not. His experiments involved dissecting a cat and replacing its spine with a miniature voltaic pile constructed of zinc and copper. Touching the reconstructed animal with a connecting rod from a larger pile supposedly reanimated its heart and made it dance for several minutes."

"Ye gods. Surely, no sensible person believes in such blatant quackery," muttered Wrexford.

Henning looked thoughtful. "I happen to agree with you. However, we both know it's important to be open-minded on such seemingly quackish subjects. One has only to look at the history of science, and how something that is thought to be absurdly impossible in one era becomes routine in another," pointed out the surgeon. "There is so much we don't know about the human body, and so much we don't know about electricity." He shrugged. "With the new developments regarding the trough battery, a more powerful variation of the voltaic pile, men of science will have far more current with which to experiment. Who is to say what the limits are?"

"I am the first to agree that science holds infinite mysteries that rational exploration can unlock." Frowning, Wrexford lapsed into silence for several long moments. "You know my heretical views on most subjects. But tell me, do you truly believe that a man can be raised from the dead?"

Henning let out a cynical laugh. "It has happened once before. Or so the Holy Scriptures tell us." A pause. "Though there's no mention of thunderbolts . . . is there?"

"Careful, Baz. You are treading dangerously close to blasphemy."

"Blasphemy is likely the least of my sins," retorted the surgeon. "I'm resigned to roasting in hell for Eternity. Assuming, of course, that such a fiery pit exists somewhere in this universe."

The earl grimaced and rose.

"If it will be of any help, I'll do some further reading about Vitalism," offered Henning. "As I said, the concept of an animal electricity—a vital force, as yet beyond our understanding, that is elemental to life—is not completely mad. There are some very rational men of science on the Continent who believe it exists."

"What's happening here isn't rational," replied Wrexford. "Young men obsessed to the point of experimenting on their own bodies, murder, mutilation . . ." He let out his breath. "Evil is at play here, Baz. And we must find a way to stop it."

A look of grim acknowledgment chased the cynicism from the surgeon's face. "I agree. Let me ask around about Lord Thornton. I have a few friends at the Royal College of Surgeons who might know of any clandestine work being done on Vitalism."

"Do it quickly." Feeling bone-weary and unsettled by the day, Wrexford turned to take his leave. "One of the other things I heard this afternoon was that a trial date has been set for Nicholas Locke. I haven't had a chance to tell Lady Charlotte yet, but we haven't much time."

"Stop squirming, Weasels," commanded Tyler, adding a brusque *tap-tap* of his baton on the pianoforte to punctuate his words. "It's important that we help Lady Charlotte prepare for her first ball—and to do that, you'll need to act like gentlemen."

The boys immediately ceased their horseplay and stood at attention. Charlotte would have smiled at their solemn faces and clean—relatively clean—clothing if her own nerves weren't stretched so taut.

"That's better," murmured the valet. "Now I'm going to demonstrate the basic steps of the waltz when McClellan plays the tune." He gave a nod to the maid. "It's a basic one-two-three rhythm. Watch my feet for a bit, and then we'll practice together."

One-two-three, one-two-three . . . Charlotte studied his steps, but after a few moments, she found her focus straying. In her previous visits to the earl's town house, she had never been outside the confines of his workroom, and curiosity drew her gaze up from the parquet floor. The furnishings of the music room were obviously expensive, but they had an understated elegance. The colors were muted and the polished woods wore a graceful patina of age. Not a glint of gold leaf or ornate silver assaulted the eye.

More than that, there was an air of well-used comfort to the space. She had the sense that it was designed for living rather than as a showcase to impress visitors. The chairs and sofa looked invitingly rumpled, and the paintings on the walls seemed very personal choices.

A shiver of intimate awareness tickled down Charlotte's spine as she spotted a portrait on the far wall of a lovely, dark-haired young lady with two young boys playing at her feet.

Could it be . . .

Tyler's brusque *tap-tap* jarred her back to the present moment. "Lady Charlotte, now that you've observed the steps, let us try it together," he said. "Weasels, pay strict attention, as I shall then ask each of you to serve as milady's dancing partner while I follow along and make any corrections."

Shaking off her musings, she quickly moved to join him. The carpet had been rolled up, allowing ample room for dancing.

"Raise your hand and place it against mine, like so," he said, demonstrating what he meant. "And then, I shall place my other hand at the small of your back."

She felt a light pressure as Tyler drew her a touch closer and she suddenly understood why the dance was considered risqué by the high sticklers in Society. No wonder girls fresh from the schoolroom weren't permitted such liberties.

"Mac, you may begin the music, but keep to a sedate tempo for now," he counseled. "And now, milady, be ready to start on the count of three . . ."

In no mood for conversation, Wrexford let himself into his town house through the back tradesmen's entrance to avoid encountering any of the servants. After making his way to the kitchen and lighting a candle, he shrugged out of his overcoat and let his hat drop atop the damp wool. Despite the warmth of the banked stove, the chill of the late-night rain seemed intent on seeping into his bones.

Perhaps, he thought, his prickly mood would yield to the heat of Scottish whisky. It would at least dull the edges.

What lay at the heart of his disquiet was not something he cared to contemplate right now.

The flickering flame lit the way through the silent shadows as he climbed the stairs and headed for his workroom. But when he was halfway down the corridor, a peal of laughter pieced the stillness.

Wrexford stopped and cocked an ear. Was his imagination playing tricks on him, or was that really the sound of a pianoforte coming from the music room?

"What the devil . . ." Puzzled, he reversed direction and went to investigate.

A flutter of light danced through the half-open door, along with more hilarity. Quickening his steps, the earl leaned a shoulder to the fluted molding and took a peek inside.

"No, no, *no*, Master Alexander Hawksley!" chided Tyler, tapping his baton to Hawk's scrawny shoulders. "You must stand up straight, and keep your arm in a graceful arch—like so!" He demonstrated the position, much to the chortling amusement of Raven. "Lady Charlotte cannot perform properly if her gentleman partner is shirking his duties."

"Sorry," intoned the boy, trying mightily to add an inch or two to his height.

"That's better," said Tyler, flashing a wink to Charlotte.

She was dressed in her urchin garb, noted Wrexford, save that she had removed her boots and was wearing satin dancing slippers. It should have looked ridiculously absurd . . .

And yet it didn't.

As his gaze took in the sight of her willowy body, its curves and long-legged grace accentuated by the snug-fitting boy's breeches and stockings, he felt his breath catch in his throat.

"Mac, you may start the music again," called Tyler.

A laugh quivering on her lips, Charlotte followed Hawk's lead through an awkward turn—

And then froze in midstep as she spotted him.

"M-Milord!" she stammered, her expression pinching in embarrassment.

"I'm learning to be a proper gentleman," exclaimed Hawk proudly. But as his brother made a very rude sound, he responded with a word that would have singed Satan's ears.

"It appears we have a bit of polishing to do," drawled Wrexford.

"M-My apologies for this invasion of your privacy," continued Charlotte. "I can explain—"

"It was my idea," said McClellan as she rose from her seat at the pianoforte. "It occurred to me that Lady Charlotte had never learned the waltz, and Tyler and I didn't wish for her to be put in an awkward position at her first ball."

"So we decided to give her a lesson and some practice," added Tyler. "And given her coming entrée into Polite Society, it seemed a good idea to include the Weasels." He waggled his brows at them. "We wouldn't want the little beasts to behave like savages when they are introduced to the dowager."

Raven mimed a hideous face, but the earl saw him dart a concerned look at Charlotte. "Oiy, we'll try not to disgrace ourselves."

"I think we've practiced our lessons enough for one night. Come, gather your coats, Weasels"—Charlotte still looked ill at ease—"let us leave His Lordship in peace."

"Not so fast." Wrexford stepped into the room. "There is an old adage that says 'practice makes perfect.'"

She made a face. "Since when have you taken to spouting platitudes?"

He laughed. Charlotte somehow always managed to tease him out of a black humor. "It's a truism, as well as a platitude. And since your first foray into a Mayfair ballroom will be here sooner than you might like, I daresay one more spin across the dance floor can do no harm."

"But—"

Wrexford silenced her protest by taking her hand. "Relax," he murmured, feeling a tingling current of warmth melt through his own tension and fatigue. "Just follow my lead."

All of a sudden, Charlotte was aware of a pulsing against her palm. *Electricity*—the word flashed to mind, and for an instant, the thought of Cedric, and his frightening experiments, sent a shiver through her core. But no, she quickly realized, this was a positive force, its heat helping to dispel her doubts and fears.

Looking up, she met Wrexford's eyes. A warmth was there too, pooled within their smoke-green hue. It softened the austere angles of his face and—

As they passed under the chandelier, Charlotte saw the lines of worry etched around his mouth. She tightened her hand, which strangely enough drew a smile to his lips.

"Have I sprouted purple spots or grown a set of horns?" he inquired.

"Sorry, I was simply thinking . . ."

He spun her through an intricate turn. "About what?"

About how much I like dancing with you.

"About the fact that I've actually never attended a ball before," she answered. "I eloped before I was of age to make my come-out in Society." A sigh slipped out. "If you must know, I'm worried that I'm going to make a cake of myself."

Another spin, another turn. "You dance exceedingly well," replied Wrexford.

Charlotte wasn't at all sure how her feet were moving so effortlessly across the floor. "That's because I'm with you." She made a wry face. "With a stranger, I'll probably be so nervous that I'll trip on my skirts and fall flat on my . . . derriere."

"So promise me the first dance."

"But—"

"Clearly, it's the logical solution," he reasoned. "I'll make rude remarks about the other guests, and in raking me over the coals for my cynicism, you'll forget about letting your nerves tie you in knots."

She smiled. "I may always count on you for a rational solution to any problem."

A glint of amusement lit in his eyes. "Unlike you, I have no imagination." Drawing her a touch closer, Wrexford twirled through another figure of the dance. "So my mind must plod along in a straight line."

Feeling a bit breathless, Charlotte needed a moment to still her thudding heart. "Straight lines are boring. And you, sir, are never boring."

That drew a chuckle. "I can guess what adjective you would find most fitting."

She let a moment dance by, savoring the feel of his body moving in harmony with hers. "I doubt it."

"Oh?" He raised his brows. "Nonetheless, I shall try. Let's start with *aggravating*? *Annoying*? *Arrogant*—"

"Are you going in alphabetical order? Or—"

Charlotte stopped short, all at once aware that the music had ceased. Looking around, she saw Tyler and McClellan were watching them with bemusement, while Raven and Hawk were trying to hold back their chortles.

"It appears that Lady Charlotte has mastered the waltz's footwork," said the valet after clearing his throat with a cough. "I see no need for further practice this evening."

"Aye," agreed McClellan. "Shall we retire to the kitchen for some refreshments?"

"Jam tarts?" said both boys in hopeful unison.

"Perhaps." A pause. "There may even be a package of Cook's ginger biscuits to take home."

As the pelter of footsteps echoed down the corridor, Wrexford waved for McClellan and Tyler to follow the boys. "You go on. I need to have a word with Lady Charlotte."

So she hadn't been wrong about his troubled mien when first he had entered the room. "What have you discovered?" she demanded, though her insides clenched in fear at what the answer would be.

His expression turned bleak. "Nothing good."

"Nicky—"

"Locke is fine, though a date for the trial has been set." The earl frowned. "And it's even sooner than I expected."

"Dear God. That means . . ." Charlotte looked away to the far windows, where shadows dipped and darted through the midnight gloom. "That means we haven't much time to prove him innocent."

Wrexford took her arm. "Come, sit."

Ye gods. That didn't bode well.

"H-Has there been another murder?"

A low rumble seemed to catch in his throat. "In a sense."

"Wrexford!" Now she was truly alarmed. "You're speaking in riddles."

The earl took a seat on the sofa and drew her down beside

him before he responded. "That's because I'm having trouble making any rational assessment of it." Leaning back, he ran a hand through his hair. "The only creature to lose its life was a rat—at least I am guessing it was a rat . . ."

Charlotte listened in growing horror as he went on to describe the macabre discovery in Thornton's laboratory, and his subsequent conversation with Henning about Galvani and Aldini.

"That's horrible," she whispered when he finished. "But surely it points the finger of guilt at Lord Thornton."

He shook his head. "You know as well as I do that conjecture is merely spitting into the wind. To convince the authorities, we need proof, and so far, there's not a scrap of evidence tying him to Chittenden's death."

In her heart, she knew he was right. Still, she couldn't help but grasp at straws. "Surely, the hidden voltaic pile and grisly remains of that poor creature hint at nefarious doings."

"Unfortunately, experiments on animals are not uncommon among the gentlemen who belong to the Royal Institution. Curiosity is a trait encouraged by science, and its members often explore ideas outside their own field of expertise. Thornton can simply claim he was interested in testing the principles of medical electricity for himself."

"Then we must find the proof," responded Charlotte. But even to her own ears, the assertion rang hollow.

Wrexford, to his credit, refrained from using his incisive logic to point out how daunting—nay, hopeless—a task it would be. Instead, he gave a small nod. "If the proof is there, we will uncover it."

At that moment, Charlotte wanted to throw her arms around him and hold on very tightly. With her own emotions turning topsy-turvy, she needed his unshakable calm to steady her shaky spirits.

He was watching her intently, and as their eyes met, his expression turned inscrutable.

She quickly looked away, hoping to hide how vulnerable she felt.

Wrexford found her hand and twined his fingers with hers.

The coals crackled in the hearth, raindrops pattered against the window glass, a sheet of music fluttered in a stirring of the air . . . the small, ordinary sounds of everyday moments. And yet they were inexplicably calming.

The worst of her fears slowly subsided.

"Thank you, Wrexford." His simple gesture and companionable silence had somehow been more eloquent than any words. "For not telling me I'm a bloody fool."

A ghost of a smile. "I've too many faults of my own to think of flinging holier-than-thou pontifications at others." He turned his head to stare into the fire. "Besides, there's nothing foolish about trying to move heaven and earth to save a loved one."

Charlotte curled her fingers more tightly around his, suddenly recalling that the earl's younger brother had lost his life on some hardscrabble battlefield during the Peninsular War. He never spoke of the details, but she had a sense that he thought himself partly to blame.

She couldn't imagine how, but it was a private pain, and she had always considered it too intimate to probe.

However, the strange current that had connected them earlier seemed to still be thrumming between them.

"Not a day goes by that I don't think about Thomas, and how I failed to save him." Wrexford shifted, his gaze coming to rest on their entwined hands. "He had been ordered by his regimental commander to lead a detachment of cavalry in reconnoitering a strategic mountain pass. I arrived at his camp from Wellesley's headquarters barely an hour after they had ridden out—and was carrying an urgent dispatch countermanding the order. Our partisan spies had learned that the French had an ambush in place."

He closed his eyes for an instant. "It should have been easy to press on and catch up with the regiment. But a fierce storm blew in from the mountains, with high winds and driving rain. Our party rode as hard as we could, but the guide lost his way . . ."

"Oh, Wrexford," she whispered, pressing the palm of her other hand to his cheek.

" 'The best laid schemes of mice and men . . .' " A very Wrexford-like quip, coolly unemotional. And yet, the anguish in his eyes belied such cynicism.

Charlotte leaned closer, her lips feathering against his. She felt his breath catch and then—

"You had better come quickly if you wish some sweets!" Hawk burst into the room and skidded to a halt. "Raven is fast devouring all the tarts."

The earl pulled back and brushed a crease from his trousers. "Thank you, but Lady Charlotte and I prefer brandy to pastries, Weasel." He rose and moved to the sideboard. "We'll join you in a moment."

As the boy raced back to the kitchen, he filled two glasses and carried them back to the sofa.

"My brother is gone. Let us concentrate on keeping your cousin alive." The chink in his armor had closed. She didn't challenge it. "Tomorrow I shall continue making inquiries about Thornton, and see if I can contrive to meet with him."

"And I," replied Charlotte, "will do all I can to cultivate a friendship with Lady Julianna and Lady Cordelia at the evening soiree."

The earl handed her a brandy. "Between the two of us, may a useful clue come to light."

"A clue." She suddenly straightened. "Thank God you reminded me of what Hawk discovered this afternoon . . ."

"A hat, and now a coat," he mused when her explanation was done. "Assuming that memory and a momentary glance in the dark are accurate, it still doesn't tell us much."

"I suppose not," admitted Charlotte. "But let us not say so to Hawk. He's so very proud of being able to help." She took a sip of her drink. "He's quite skilled at art, you know. And so curious about the natural world around him."

Her brows drew together. "I've neglected to encourage his interests, especially in recent days, and I worry that he might feel cast in his brother's shadow. I've promised to take him to the Royal Botanic Gardens at Kew, and I mean to keep it. Darkness must not squeeze out light . . ."

"A wise philosophy." He raised his glass in quick salute. "To *Lux.*"

"And to *Veritas.*"

"Yes, may Truth not be swallowed in the shadows."

CHAPTER 20

His boots squelching, his hat dripping, Wrexford hurried through the entrance of the Royal Institution.

"Looks like we've had enuff rain this morning te float Noah's Ark, milord," said one of the porters as he helped the earl out of his sodden overcoat.

"Indeed." The damn fellow likely wouldn't sound so cheerful if he were soaked to the skin. "By the by, is Thornton in the building today?"

"Not that I know of, sir. But I was called away for a time to help with moving some crates in the wine cellar."

The earl thought for a moment. "What about DeVere?"

"Oiy. He's been here for some hours."

After a muttered thanks, Wrexford made his way to the reading room, intent on drying his trousers by the blazing fire before heading upstairs to search for the scholar.

DeVere, however, was sitting in one of the deep leather chairs by the hearth, a book of hand-colored botanical prints open in his lap.

"Is gardening among your many interests?" asked the earl,

taking up a position by the brass fender and turning his back to the flames.

DeVere looked up with a faint smile. "My interest in peas is purely scientific. I've been working with green and yellow varieties to see if I can detect patterns about how traits are passed on."

"Interesting." Wrexford looked around. The room was deserted at this hour. "Might I ask you a few questions on a different subject?"

The book fell shut. "Certainly."

The earl shifted the facing chair a little closer to DeVere and took a seat. The man had a high opinion of himself and at times could be a pompous arse. But there was no questioning his intelligence and expertise in a number of scientific disciplines.

"I shall be direct if you don't mind, rather than waste your time or mine in oblique pleasantries," he began. "Has Lord Thornton shown any interest in voltaic piles?"

The scholar took his time before answering. "That depends on what you mean. If you're asking whether I know of his doing any actual experimenting, the answer is no. However, he has, on several occasions, engaged me in lengthy conversations on electrical current and its possibilities."

Wrexford felt a prickling at the back of his neck. "Could you be a little more specific?"

DeVere's mouth thinned for an instant. "I'm not sure that would be helpful. When discussing theories, we all tend to get a little carried away. Imagination can tangle with reality, and we say things we don't really believe."

"I applaud your sense of honor, but in this case, I hope you will be forthright." He gave another glance around the room. "A life may depend on it."

"I see." The scholar sat back and steepled his fingers. "I'm aware of . . . might we say, your interest in solving crimes. Does this have something to do with . . ." He let his question trail off.

Wrexford met the other man's gaze and said nothing.

"I see," repeated DeVere, and then looked away. "How to put this . . ." His fingertips came up to tap at the point of his chin. "Thornton seemed fascinated by Aldini's experiments. He kept pressing me on whether I thought Vitalism was a viable theory, and could it be possible that Aldini had just not discovered the correct way to use electrical current to . . ."

Wrexford edged forward in his chair.

"To reanimate the dead," finished the scholar after a slight hesitation. "But that said, I truly don't think he believes in that fiddle-faddle. Ideas are exciting, and we men of science like to play with them—but in words only. I'm repeating the conversation as accurately as I can, because you asked for complete candor. However, I'll reiterate again that I think he merely got carried away in his theoretical enthusiasm."

"Thank you," responded the earl. "I understand your caveat and agree with your reasoning. Science is indeed all about questioning accepted assumptions, and imagining the unthinkable."

DeVere nodded. "Is there something else?"

"Yes." This was much more delicate. "I understand you're the guardian of Lady Julianna Aldrich."

"Yes." The scholar looked a little unsettled. "What possible connection could this have with your other question?"

"I'm simply trying to get a clearer picture of the Eos Society and its members. I've heard that some of the young gentlemen were acquainted with Lady Julianna and I wondered how that came about?"

"Why, through me, of course," replied the scholar. "I hold frequent soirees for my scientific-minded acquaintances. Some of the members aren't serious scholars and didn't choose to come. But Lord Chittenden, Sir Kelvin Hollister, and Benjamin Westmorly often attended."

"Is Lady Julianna interested in science?"

"Very much so. The fact is, she's brilliant." DeVere paused. "Though others use less flattering words."

"Oh?" The earl raised a brow.

"As you know, intelligence isn't encouraged in the young ladies of the *ton.*"

"You're saying she's a Bluestocking?"

The scholar considered the question. "She's conversant in literature, history, mathematics, and science—she has an inquisitive mind, so I've seen to it that she's had the finest tutors money can hire."

They must be *very* fine, thought Wrexford, seeing as DeVere was rich as Croesus.

"She's also deeply interested in more esoteric subjects, like traditional Indian philosophies and beliefs."

Wrexford frowned. "Do you mean mysticism?"

"Our English words aren't always capable of capturing the nuances of Indian beliefs," answered DeVere carefully.

A beautiful, exotic young lady with an aura of intellectual mystery—no wonder the members of the Eos Society were drawn to her like moths to a flame.

"Julianna is different. It's one of the reasons I invited the Eos Society to my entertainments. If she is to meet a kindred soul who will accept her for who she is, it will likely be a young man interested in science."

Ah, now we're at the heart of the matter, thought the earl, hoping to discern the truth from the lies regarding the romantic entanglements. "Sir Kelvin claims she favored his suit over that of Lord Chittenden. Is that true?"

DeVere let out a light laugh. "I like to think of myself as Lady Julianna's friend and mentor, but do you really think a nineteen-year-old would confide such intimate affairs of the heart to her guardian?"

Wrexford answered with a wry grimace. "Thankfully, I know precious little about nineteen-year-old young ladies and how their minds work." He rose as one of the porters entered the room.

"Mr. DeVere, your ward has arrived, and is waiting in the corridor for you to escort her to the lecture hall."

"Please tell her I'll be there momentarily." To the earl, he added, "She is very much looking forward to Children's lecture on electrical current."

"I imagine it will be very interesting," said Wrexford as the scholar began to gather up his books. "Again, my thanks for your time and candor."

"I wish you luck in . . . whatever conundrum you're looking to solve."

"I shall need it," murmured the earl under his breath. He started to move away and then suddenly thought of one last query.

"Do you know whether Thornton wears a Wellington hat with something shiny attached to its band?"

DeVere looked at him blankly. "I haven't the foggiest notion. Why?"

"It's not important." Wrexford left the room, intent on checking whether Thornton was attending the upcoming lecture.

As he left the room, he passed a young lady chatting with one of the Institution's governors. She was dressed in an elegant walking gown of slate-colored silk with a paisley shawl of finely woven Kashmir wool draped around her shoulders. The muted tones of burgundy and grey accentuated the reddish highlights in her dark mahogany hair.

Lady Julianna Aldrich was bewitchingly beautiful, noted Wrexford. And as their eyes met for an instant, he understood how young men could be entranced by the siren song swirling in those sea-green orbs.

Tie me to the mast.

Laughing at something her companion said, she looked away. He continued up the stairs and into the lecture hall. There was, however, no sign of Thornton, and after waiting for a quarter hour, watching as the seats filled to capacity, he decided to try his luck elsewhere.

Alison gave an owlish squint through her quizzing glass as her butler escorted Charlotte into the drawing room. "Is that another Madame Franchot creation?"

"Why, yes, it is," she answered.

The dowager gave a low snort and patted a spot on the sofa beside her. "Come. Sit. You have many secrets I'm anxious to learn, my dear. But I just might sell my soul to Lucifer to discover how you convinced London's most exclusive dressmaker to fashion your wardrobe."

Charlotte repressed a smile. The dowager's tart sense of humor hadn't diminished over the years. Much as the earlier round of social calls had been terrifying to contemplate, Alison's pithy commentary—whispered sotto voce as the teacups were passed—and unflinching support had made the first foray into London's beau monde go far smoother than she ever imagined possible.

That was, of course, because not only was the dowager a Dragon, she was also impressively accomplished at telling outrageous farididdles. Who would have guessed that such an elderly grande dame could spout such lies?

"I lust after one of her ball gown designs—*L'Ange de Ciel*," continued Alison. "But I've been told I'm on a waiting list that will likely stretch into the next century." A sigh. "No doubt Madame Franchot doesn't want a bag of old bones making her divine creations look less than celestial."

"The story of how I know her is one you shall hear at some point, Aunt Alison," replied Charlotte. "In the meantime, I shall have a word with Franny about the gown." She allowed a small pause. "Have you perchance thought of what fabric might suit?"

"The sky-blue watered silk from Italy," answered the dowager without hesitation.

"A lovely choice," murmured Charlotte.

The reply sparked a glint of amusement in Alison's gaze. "I may be tottering into senility, but I like to think I still have a discerning eye—and not just for color, my dear." She patted Charlotte's arm. "The curious, courageous girl I knew has grown into a strong, principled young lady. I'm very glad you've come back to me."

"As am I." Charlotte clasped the dowager's frail fingers and gave a quick squeeze. "I missed your wisdom and your laughter." A smile. "Most of all, I missed your believing in me more than I believed in myself."

"Nonsense. It seems to me you've done quite well without my counsel." Alison looked away, and covered a sniff with a cough to clear her throat. "You did magnificently in charming the tabbies this morning. But I sense that tonight, you're looking to do more than spout superficial pleasantries."

Charlotte's smile grew more pronounced. The Dragon was still sharp as a battle-axe. "You're correct."

The dowager's expression turned expectant. "Who are you looking to meet?"

"Lady Julianna Aldrich and Lady Cordelia Mansfield," she answered.

"Hmmph." Alison thought for a long moment. "Can you tell me the reasons why?"

"I've learned that Lady Julianna and Cedric had a romantic attachment. I would like to see if some discreet questioning may elicit any helpful information on who might have wished him ill."

Charlotte considered how to answer the rest of the question. "As for Lady Cordelia, I can't reveal why at this moment, but I wish to meet her and make some assessment of her character."

Alison gave a brusque nod. "Well, then, I imagine it would

help to know a little about their backgrounds. And no one knows more than I do about the skeletons in the beau monde's family closets."

"I was hoping as much."

"Then let us get down to brass tacks." The dowager fluffed her skirts. "Lady Julianna grew up in India. She lost her parents during the Second Maratha War when the Chief of Baroda attacked the town in which her family was living. She was the lone survivor, and her father's will designated Justinian DeVere as her guardian."

"DeVere?" Charlotte recalled that Wrexford had mentioned the fact of his guardianship in passing. She hadn't given it much thought as of yet, but any connection to Lady Julianna now seemed important to understand. "Isn't he the nabob who's said to be incredibly wealthy?"

"Yes, he and the gel's father were close friends," explained the dowager. "Apparently, her upbringing was eccentric by English standards. DeVere indulged her intellectual interests. She's very bookish, and interested in all sorts of arcane subjects, which, of course, make the beau monde shudder in horror. However . . ."

Alison's brows rose in a cynical arch. "DeVere has given her a very large dowry, and as we all know, money covers a multitude of sins. I'm sure Cedric wasn't the only gentleman paying court to her."

Charlotte nodded. "So it seems. Sir Kelvin Hollister is said to have ultimately won her regard."

"Sir Kelvin? I find that very hard to fathom," replied the dowager. "I grant you, he possesses a handsome face, but I seem to recall hearing whispers that he's less than a gentleman."

"What do you mean?"

"There were rumors of a very ugly incident during his time at university. I don't know any of the details, but I shall make inquiries if you wish."

"Thank you. That might prove helpful," she murmured. "Is Lady Julianna interested in science?"

"She seems to share DeVere's interest in botany. She attends many of the public lectures at the Royal Institution, and plays hostess to his scientific soirees. I've also heard she cultivates a number of exotic plants in the large conservatory that DeVere had added to his villa."

Alison frowned in thought. "Though at Lady Thirkell's weekly salon, Lady Julianna spends a good deal of the time playing with a very complicated, colorful deck of cards involving numbers and symbols, which she says is based on an ancient Indian system of . . ." The dowager gave a vague wave of her hand. "It was something to the effect of . . . divining the workings of the cosmos."

Puzzled, Charlotte took a moment to consider the odd information. *Colorful cards . . . an arcane philosophy . . .* she was suddenly reminded of something she had seen during her stay in Italy. "Do you mean something like the *Tarocco Piemontese?* My husband and I had friends in Italy who dabbled in cartomancy, the art of divining the future through an elaborate system of illustrated cards."

"I couldn't say," answered Alison. "A number of our members find it fascinating, but it strikes me as fiddle-faddle, so I haven't paid much attention to her explanations."

"How odd," mused Charlotte. "Such mysticism seems at odds with rational thought. Though Wrexford says science often involves imagining the unimaginable."

"I fear I'm too old for my brain to budge from ordinary thinking," quipped the dowager. "Though I daresay you're right." Her expression turned pensive. "Lady Julianna is a strange mix of fire and ice."

"I have the sense you don't like her," said Charlotte.

"She's poised and polished, with faultlessly correct manners," answered Alison. "But her smile doesn't quite reach her eyes."

An interesting observation.

"However, I'm old and opinionated," added the dowager. "So I may be judging her too harshly."

The clock on the mantel chimed, signaling that it was time for them to leave for Lady Thirkell's salon.

"And what is your opinion of Lady Cordelia?" asked Charlotte as she helped her aunt gather her cane and rise from the sofa.

"Her tongue is nearly as sharp as mine," answered Alison dryly. "She's very smart, and doesn't care whether that offends people."

Highly intelligent and highly unconventional. "She sounds like a lady who is unafraid of taking risks."

"I think very little frightens Lady Cordelia," agreed the dowager. "But enough of my nattering. Let us see what your impression is when you meet them."

CHAPTER 21

Fatigued and frustrated, Wrexford entered White's, feeling desperately in need of a brandy. Failure seemed to be dogging his steps—he had made the rounds of every scientific haunt and private club he could think of. But his quarry had proved elusive.

"Why the black face?" Sheffield looked up in alarm as the earl stalked into the reading room. "Is Lady Charlotte—"

"Lady Charlotte is, to my knowledge, drinking tea at Lady Thirkell's salon. I, on the other hand, am in need of a stronger libation." He signaled for the porter to bring a bottle.

"And two glasses," murmured his friend.

Wrexford slouched into the leather armchair next to Sheffield and blew out his breath. "Confound it, I—"

He stopped abruptly on spotting the small table sitting in front of Sheffield's chair. Several piles of playing cards sat atop the dark-grained wood, along with an open book. "What the devil are you doing?"

"Studying the principles of probability." Sheffield didn't meet his gaze. "Lady Cordelia was kind enough to explain some of the basic concepts when I paid a call on her and her brother this afternoon. She also gave me a book on the subject."

The earl raised his brows. "You always complain that reading is boring."

"Perhaps I've changed my mind."

"And perhaps—" Wrexford bit back a sarcastic retort. "My apologies, Kit. I'm in a foul mood." After a glance around showed their only company were two elderly gentlemen sleeping in their chairs near the fire, he lowered his voice and gave a terse explanation of what he had discovered in Thornton's laboratory.

"Ye gods." Sheffield's face tightened in shock.

"I've spent the day trying to have a word with him," continued the earl.

"And say what?"

A good question. He made a face. "I merely wanted to have a conversation with him about electricity. DeVere seems to think his passion is merely intellectual, but I wish to decide for myself." Silence settled between them for a moment. "You think that's unwise?"

"You are asking *my* advice?"

"I'm beginning to question my own judgment," admitted the earl. He waited for the porter to set down the brandy and retreat before going on. "I seem to be spinning in naught but circles. So, yes, I would welcome your counsel."

"Very well—then I think it may be a mistake to confront him," answered his friend. "I agree with Lady Charlotte that the finger of guilt points to him. And if that's true, he's a coldly cunning demon, so we can't afford to give any hint that his perfidy has been discovered."

Sheffield edged forward in his chair, ignoring the glass of brandy that the earl had poured for him. "We need to go back to his laboratory and try to find some evidence that will tie him to Chittenden's murder."

"The missing bollock?" muttered Wrexford.

Sheffield winced. "God only knows where *that* is hidden." He shifted uncomfortably. "We can't hope for miracles, but if we can find a thin blade that might have caused the mortal wound . . . or a black silk handkerchief similar to the one found in Locke's rooms . . . or anything that we might argue is suspicious . . . Griffin trusts your instincts. However, he needs some tangible evidence before he can open an official investigation."

"And an investigation, even if it ultimately comes to naught, casts enough of a doubt as to the real killer that it may save Locke from the hangman's noose," mused the earl.

"So, why are we wasting time in chin wagging? Given the hour, I doubt Thornton is working at the Institution."

Wrexford rose. "You're right. Let us go and see if we can trap a fiend with his own ghoulish hubris."

The introductions finally done, Charlotte gratefully accepted a cup of tea from their hostess and moved to take a seat at the far end of the grand parlor, intent on composing her thoughts.

The light from two ornate brass oil lamps on the refreshment table flickered over the members of Lady Thirkell's weekly salon as they helped themselves to the sumptuous array of pastries and biscuits. Names and faces blurred together amid the swirls of color. The babble of unfamiliar voices tangled with feminine laughter.

Charlotte drew a steadying breath. And yet, despite being a stranger among a circle of close-knit friends, she had a sense that with time, she might come to feel at home among these ladies.

She spotted Alison, half hidden by an ancient marble statue of Athena, conversing with a trio of other elegantly attired silver-haired matrons. Next to them were two middle-aged ladies who looked considerably more eccentric.

Good heavens—is one of them wearing a Chinese robe embroidered with dancing dragons?

The dowager caught her eye and gave a mock grimace before turning back to her friends. Repressing a smile, Charlotte shifted her gaze and began a careful study of her surroundings. The muted wallpaper and draperies, done in soft shades of cream and taupe, created a neutral backdrop for an eclectic array of decorative objects. Stone antiquities rubbed shoulders with Renaissance bronzes; delicate Meissen china sat atop a lacquered tea chest from China . . . an ornate Louis XIV candelabra flanked a sun-bleached conch shell . . . The effect should have been hideous.

But it wasn't at all. All the items felt carefully chosen, and arranged to please the owner rather than impress visitors. Charlotte wished she had her pen and paints at hand so she could attempt to capture the unique vitality of the room on paper.

Lady Thirkell must be an exceedingly interesting individual—

"We are quite informal here. I hope that doesn't shock you."

A deep-noted voice jarred Charlotte from her thoughts. It reminded her of cool water running over smooth rocks. Unfeminine, perhaps, but not unpleasing. She looked up.

"Forgive me for startling you. Your great-aunt suggested that I introduce myself to you, seeing as you're new to our little gathering." The lady held out her hand, an unusually strong and direct gesture for a female. Her face held the same boldness— her nose was a trifle too prominent, her cheekbones too slanted, her mouth too wide to fit the pattern card of delicate feminine beauty. And yet she seemed to be comfortable in her own skin.

"I'm Cordelia Mansfield—Lady Cordelia, if you wish to be proper."

A pause. "Though I find propriety vastly overrated."

Charlotte accepted Cordelia's hand. "You'll get no argument from me on that."

A smile tugged at the corners of Cordelia's mouth. "I'm not sure whether to be disappointed or delighted."

A lady who made no bones about challenging convention, noted Charlotte.

"I'm Charlotte Sloane—Lady Charlotte," she continued, taking care to match her new acquaintance's ironic tone.

Cordelia eyed her thoughtfully before asking, "Lady Peake mentioned that you're newly arrived in London. From where have you come?"

"Italy. My late husband was an artist and found Rome a place of great inspiration."

"Are you interested in ancient Rome?"

"I've studied Latin and have read the classics," she answered. "But my interest is primarily in art, not history. I, too, paint."

"That's a ladylike skill I've never managed to master. I'm all thumbs when it comes to drawing—I can't for the life of me make a straight line."

"Art is rarely about straight lines," murmured Charlotte.

"Indeed?" Cordelia's expression altered, though the play of light and shadow made it hard to read. "Then what do you think it's about?"

She knew she was being tested. "For me, it's all about how you see the world around you. I enjoy observing things carefully and trying to discern all the subtle nuances."

Before Cordelia could respond, Charlotte decided to toss out her own challenge. "Aunt Alison mentioned your name and said you have a gift for mathematics. For me, adding and subtracting seem more of a chore than an interesting pursuit."

"Oh, numbers are far more creative than that," replied Cordelia. "One can make them do all sorts of fascinating things." A pause. "Things that explain the mysteries of the universe."

Charlotte suddenly felt as if a finger were tickling at the nape of her neck. "I see I have much to learn from among those who attend this salon. Have you a mystery in particular that interests you?"

"Must I choose just one? Hmm, let me think . . ."

But their tête-à-tête was interrupted as a hail from their hostess rose from the hum of conversation near the bank of windows. "Lady Cordelia, you must come and explain Pythagoras and his theory of mathematics and music!"

"If you will excuse me, Lady Charlotte . . ."

"But of course."

Cordelia gathered her skirts, but hesitated for a heartbeat. "I do look forward to continuing our conversation."

And our verbal feints and parries, thought Charlotte as she watched Cordelia move away to join the others. No question the lady had a rapier-sharp tongue and a spine of steel. But whether that ought to be held as a mark against her remained to be seen.

"So, I see you've met Lady Cordelia." Alison settled into the chair next to her and took a sip of her ratafia punch. "I'm curious as to your impression."

"She seems fond of testing the mettle of those she meets."

The dowager chuckled. "I think it is her way of separating the wheat from the chaff, so to speak. She doesn't suffer fools gladly."

"Then I imagine she's more at home here than she is in any other Mayfair drawing room," replied Charlotte, her gaze still on Cordelia.

Alison set aside her glass and regripped her cane. "I believe Lady Julianna is in one of the side salons. Shall I introduce you?"

A mizzling rain had begun to fall. As Wrexford and Sheffield crossed Piccadilly Street, their steps stirred serpentine swirls of fog. The earl led the way up Albemarle Street and around to the rear of the Royal Institution, where a special patron's portal allowed entrance at all hours to those select few who possessed a key.

Being a generous benefactor, he was one of them. The lock clicked open. Ignoring the candlesticks on the side table, he touched Sheffield's arm and made a gesture for him to head to the side stairwell.

"We'll strike a light once we're inside Thornton's laboratory," he whispered as he started to feel his way up the treads.

They climbed in silence, the gloom adding an air of foreboding to the darkness. On reaching the next landing, Wrexford eased the door open a crack. The corridor was wreathed in shadows, the only light a faint glimmer coming from a distant wall sconce at the other end of the building. He was just about to proceed when the furtive scuff of steps caused him to freeze.

Someone was coming.

He waited. A pinprick of fire—a candle flame—appeared from the adjoining corridor, casting wildly dancing flickers of light and dark across the wall.

Closer, closer. Through the slivered opening, Wrexford could make a figure wearing a caped coat . . .

And a Wellington hat.

Thump-thump. The dowager edged around the weathered fragment of a classical Doric column topped with a potted fern. "Ah, there you are, Lady Julianna." The fronds rustled. "I wish for you to meet my great-niece, who has recently taken up residence in London. The two of you share some common interests."

"Oh?" Julianna responded with a polite smile. "And what might those be, Lady Peake?"

Alison tipped the silver knob of her cane at the elaborate-colored pasteboard cards arrayed on the low table. "Art, for one thing. As for the others . . ." She gave a vague wave. "I shall leave you to discover that for yourselves. I'm growing fatigued and wish to sit with the other old fossils and catch up on all the latest *on dits.*"

"Your great-aunt is quite an Original," murmured Julianna as the dowager stomped away.

"She most certainly doesn't conform to convention," replied Charlotte.

"I daresay none of us who attend these salons do, Miss . . ."

"Lady Charlotte Sloane." Charlotte leaned in for a closer look at the cards. "These are quite remarkable. The line work is exquisitely drawn, and the coloring is quite unusual. It's rare to see nuances that are so subtle, yet so sophisticated."

Julianna cocked her head. "Most people don't appreciate nuance or subtlety."

"Perhaps because it's harder to understand."

The heiress's laugh was softly musical. "Indeed, things that are out of the ordinary require extra effort to comprehend." Without looking down, Julianna gathered the cards and reshuffled them, her fingers moving with quicksilver grace. "But in my experience, it proves worthwhile."

An interesting observation.

"Pray, have we other common interests, aside from art, Lady Charlotte?" went on the heiress.

"The late Lord Chittenden," replied Charlotte.

The flesh seemed to tighten over Julianna's face, making her cheekbones look sharp as knife blades. "You knew His Lordship?"

"Intimately." The word was deliberately chosen to see what reaction it would draw. The spasm of emotion was gone in an instant, but it told Charlotte what she wanted to know. Julianna wasn't quite so cynical as she wished to appear.

"We were cousins, and the very best of friends during our childhood," she explained, taking a seat in the *chinoise*-style chair facing the heiress. "Though the connection grew more tenuous after my late husband and I moved to Italy. He was a very talented painter, and I, too, dabbled in art."

Nuances and subtlety. With a tiny alteration here, a small omission there, Alison had cobbled together a story that didn't stray far from the truth. And yet it painted a far different picture of Charlotte's marriage to Anthony Sloane.

"My parents didn't approve of the fact that I had married a mere mister," she added. "They thought I could have looked higher."

A flicker of understanding stirred in Julianna's gaze. "But that would have demanded that you sacrifice your passions." A card turned faceup, then another. "I believe there will come a day when those of our sex shall have control over their own destiny."

Charlotte regarded the pair of numbers. Each one was intertwined with a series of arcane geometric symbols. "Let us hope such things are written in the cards."

"You would be surprised at what the *Maya-Moksha* can tell us."

"Indeed?" It was Charlotte's turn to toss out a challenge. "Is that what the game is called? Tell me more about it."

"It's not a game, it's a philosophy," replied Julianna. "And it would take far longer than an evening to convey even a rudimentary understanding of its systems. You see, along with learning the traditional English skills deemed acceptable for a lady, I studied Indian philosophy with a savant for a number of years. I like expanding my understanding of the worlds outside of our own. We learn by challenging our preconceptions."

Charlotte could understand how Cedric would have found Julianna bewitchingly seductive. Beneath the demure façade of a beau monde belle was a spark of rare fire.

"I have a very enlightened guardian and am quite fortunate that he's always had an open mind on what is, and is not, proper for a lady."

"So it would seem." Charlotte touched a fingertip to the numeral 6. "Are these cards related to the *Tarocchi*?"

"No, no." The heiress gave an enigmatic smile. "It's not about fortune-telling. The system is based on numbers . . . a way the natural order of the universe can predict certain . . . relationships."

"How?" pressed Charlotte.

"As I said, that's not so simple to explain. One must grasp the conceptual framework." Julianna drew in a slow breath. "Cedric was making great headway. It grieves me to think about . . ." She looked away, not before Charlotte saw the glimmer of tears in her eyes.

"Cedric and I shared many secrets during our childhood," pressed Charlotte. "I should like very much to understand this . . . in homage to his memory."

Julianna bowed her head and appeared to lapse into deep thought. After several moments, she looked up. "Do you like challenges, Lady Charlotte?"

"I wouldn't have seen the splendors of Rome . . ."

Or have caused the Prince Regent to take to his bed for a week because of my scathing caricature of him in a corset.

". . . if I was afraid of embracing them," answered Charlotte.

In response, Julianna took up a small notebook and pencil from the table. For a short interval, there was no sound between them, save for the soft *scratch-scratch* of the graphite. The heiress then tore out two pages and passed them over.

"Very well, then. Here's a momentous event I've discerned from the physical and metaphysical elements of the system. It will happen in the near future. But to work out what it is won't be easy. You'll have to study the science of the cards."

Charlotte had a feeling that Wrexford would use a far less complimentary word than *science*. Nonetheless, she carefully folded the papers.

"And here is a book on the subject." The heiress pulled a slim leather-bound volume from the reticule sitting beside her chair, then gathered her cards and placed them in a pasteboard box. "Along with a deck of *Maya-Moksha* numbers."

"Surely, you don't wish to give away your magnificent cards," protested Charlotte. "They must be irreplaceable."

"I have many other decks of equal beauty," replied the heiress. "It would give me great pleasure to know that Cedric's childhood friend—someone bound to him by both sentiment and blood—will enjoy learning their secrets."

"Thank you. That's quite gracious of you." As Charlotte shifted slightly to settle the gift in her lap, she saw a stirring within the shadows of the foyer connecting the side salons.

A flutter of smoky amethyst silk.

How long had Cordelia Mansfield been eavesdropping? And why?

"Cedric was very special to me," murmured Julianna. "It's hard to believe that his brother could have murdered him in such a horrible fashion. They seemed . . . very close." A heartbeat of silence. "But then, who knows what evil lurks in the hearts of those we think we know best?"

"I don't believe Nicholas killed Cedric," replied Charlotte.

"But the newspapers say the evidence . . ." The heiress's eyes widened. "Who else could it be?"

"I don't know. But . . ." Charlotte's hands tightened on the book and box of cards. "But I hope that the truth will come out and justice will prevail."

Seeing the lady in the dragon robe approaching with an armful of books, Charlotte quickly rose and added, "I mustn't keep you from your friends, so I'll take my leave now. However, I look forward to furthering our acquaintance."

"As do I."

Their gazes met and held for a moment before Charlotte turned and moved off in search of her great-aunt, suddenly feeling a pressing need to return to the solitude of her own house and parse over all that she had heard.

"I see you met the Enchantress of Numbers," murmured Cordelia as Charlotte moved into the foyer connecting the side salon and the grand parlor.

"Yes." Charlotte pretended not to notice the edge of sarcasm in her voice. "You two seem to share a keen interest in mathematics."

"Actually, I would say her interest in numbers is metaphysical, not mathematical."

"And yet earlier you told me that mathematics could reveal the mysteries of the universe," replied Charlotte.

"When applied rationally and its formulas proved through logic and empirical observation, mathematics can indeed be revelatory."

"You don't believe that numbers can tell us anything about the future?" she pressed.

Cordelia's brows gave a mocking twitch. "On the contrary—I can predict a number of future events with absolute certainty. For example, I can calculate the arc of the moon through the night sky and tell you where it will be an hour from now. Or create an equation based on weight, trajectory, and force that will pinpoint when and where a cannonball will land."

She made a face. "But will numbers tell me the fate of nations or in what year the Day of Judgment shall fall?" Her gaze darted to the book and box. "Let's just say I'm skeptical."

"Skepticism is important in scientific inquiry," replied Charlotte. "Or so Lord Wrexford says."

"You're acquainted with Wrexford?"

"I am," said Charlotte, but chose not to elaborate.

Cordelia opened her mouth to speak, then seemed to think better of it and made a show of patting back a tiny yawn. "If you'll excuse, I'm feeling a trifle fatigued, so I think I shall seek out our hostess and take my leave."

From somewhere in the room came the sharp *cawk-cawk* of Lady Thirkell's pet parrot.

"Enjoy your parlor games," added Cordelia, spearing another look at Julianna's gifts. "Who knows? Perhaps you'll discover something interesting."

CHAPTER 22

The earl held his breath as Thornton passed by the stairwell. For an instant, the candle flame flitted over his rain-spattered face, catching the wild light in his eyes as he darted a nervous glance over his shoulder.

And then his visage was once again swallowed by the darkness.

Picking up his pace, the marquess continued down the corridor, the flapping of his coat adding to the blur of light and dark patterns skittering through the gloom. To Wrexford's surprise, he didn't stop at the entrance to his own laboratory, but kept going and darted into the adjoining corridor.

"What's happening?" whispered Sheffield as the sound of the steps faded away.

"It's Thornton," replied the earl. "He's heading to the back of the building." He eased the door open. "Whatever mischief he's up to, let us catch him in the act. Stay close."

Drawing the pistol from his pocket, Wrexford set off in pursuit.

Hugging close to the wall, they followed Thornton into the

side corridor. The darkness seemed to squeeze the air from the narrow space. The earl shallowed his breathing, the thud of his heart sounding unnaturally loud in the stifling silence.

Another turn and he spotted a flare of light up ahead. He halted and felt Sheffield brush up against his back. Thornton had set his candle down on the floor and was crouched down by a door, working with a steel probe to open the lock.

Wrexford took a moment to gauge the distance, then gave a quick tap to Sheffield's sleeve. They covered the distance swiftly, and reached their quarry just as a soft *snick* sounded and the door released.

Thornton picked up the light and placed a palm on the paneled wood—

Grabbing the marquess's collar, Wrexford shoved him inside as Sheffield drew the door closed behind them.

"W-What the devil," sputtered Thornton, then fell silent as the snout of the pistol jammed up against his throat. The candle had gone out, leaving them shrouded in blackness.

"*Devil* is an apt word," muttered Wrexford as he swung his prisoner around and pushed him up against the near wall. "Find a lamp and light it, Kit. And then let us have Lord Thornton explain to us why he just broke into Justinian DeVere's laboratory."

Glass rattled against metal, flint struck steel, igniting a soft hiss as a wick burst into flame.

The oily glow illuminated Thornton's face. It was pale as death.

"Go to hell," said the marquess through clenched teeth. "I've got nothing to say to you, Wrexford." He inhaled through his nose. "Save for the fact that I'm surprised at your perfidy. I would have thought you possessed more honor and more intelligence than to be conspiring with a madman on such despicable experiments."

Wrexford frowned in consternation . . . and then chuffed a

quick laugh. "A clever ploy to play the innocent—but, clearly, you're a diabolically clever fellow. However, I know what evil you're up to, so don't bother trying to gammon us."

Sheffield picked up a scalpel from the work counter and waggled it to punctuate the warning. "The only words we want to hear from you are a confession as to why you murdered Lord Chittenden and Benjamin Westmorly."

It was Thornton's turn to look nonplussed. "*I?* A murderer?" He lifted his chin, unflinching as the pistol's barrel dug deeper into his flesh.

Wrexford could feel the jumpy pulsing of the fellow's blood against the steel.

"It's you who are mad," continued the marquess. "Let us not waste our breath in whatever word games you are playing. Go ahead—pull the trigger and be done with it. I may have failed to bring you miscreants to justice, but someone eventually will."

"Another eloquent avowal. However . . ." Wrexford reached out slowly and took the hat from Thornton's head. "You made a crucial mistake by wearing such a distinctive head covering to the scenes of the Bloody Butcher murders. We've found witnesses who have described it." As he angled the hat to the lamp, light winked off the silver button on the band.

"Bloody hell—that isn't my hat!" sputtered Thornton. "I hung my hat and my coat in the private cloakroom of my corridor earlier today. When I went to fetch them this evening, someone had taken mine—by mistake, I assumed, as this one was hung on the peg. But as it was raining, I took it."

A grimace spasmed over his face. "The damnable thing doesn't even fit—it's too small!"

If Thornton was putting on an act, thought the earl, he ought to take up a career on the stage. He handed the hat to Sheffield. "Put it on him, Kit, and let us see if he's telling the truth."

Sheffield did as requested, taking great care to test how it sat on the marquess's brow. "It does appear to be the wrong size."

Still, Wrexford remained wary. The dastard they were chasing was diabolically cunning. "If you're not the murderer, why were you breaking into DeVere's laboratory?"

"Because," shot back the marquess, "I'm trying to piece together what evil is afoot here in the Institution, and I have good reason to believe the heart of it lies with DeVere's protégés . . ."

"Go on," said Wrexford, seeing that Thornton hesitated.

"That is, the three young leaders of the Eos Society—Chittenden, Westmorly, and Hollister. I thought I might find some clue among DeVere's work as to what dark mischief they were doing." Another pause. "And as you know, two of them are dead. Surely, that in itself should stir suspicions."

"Indeed, it does," said the earl. "But given *your* recent actions, those suspicions fall squarely on you at this moment. You'll have to give more than vague innuendoes and an ill-fitting hat to convince us of your innocence."

A flush darkened Thornton's cheekbones. "Then listen carefully and judge for yourself." He hitched in a breath. "Might you kindly remove your weapon from my windpipe?"

Wrexford allowed a sliver of space. "Be quick with your tongue. I'm not known for my patience."

"For the past year, DeVere has held frequent soirees for the scientific community," began Thornton. "He's an excellent host—the suppers are superb and the company is always interesting, so I frequently attended them. It quickly became apparent that he paid particular attention to the three young men and saw to it that they were included in the inner circle of influential guests. They, of course, were flattered, and I had the sense that they looked up to him as a mentor."

The marquess hesitated. "After several weeks, DeVere began inviting them to stay, after the other guests took their leave, for a private scientific salon within a salon." He smoothed his lapel. "His ward, Lady Julianna Aldrich, also took part in the discussions. She's apparently quite knowledgeable in a variety of subjects and could hold her own."

"Yes, DeVere described her to me as brilliant," said Wrexford. "She's also beautiful. And young men being young men, I would guess that the desire to impress the lady added an extra edge to the gatherings."

"Much as we like to think otherwise, mankind is, for the most part, ruled by its most primitive urges," observed the marquess dryly. "I was told the competition for her regard turned . . . fierce."

Ah, here we are finally coming to the crux of the matter, thought Wrexford. "Told by whom?"

With a whisper of wool, Thornton shifted his shoulders against the plaster wall. "Chittenden. He came to me several weeks ago, seeking my counsel, and—"

"Why you?" interrupted the earl.

"Chittenden had attended my lecture on *iode,* an element recently discovered by Davy and Gay-Lussac that may have medical uses. Afterward, he approached me with some queries, and I invited him to discuss them over a brandy at White's." A shrug. "I liked him. He was friendly and well-spoken, as well as intelligent and inquisitive. After that, we met on occasion to talk about science." Thornton shook his head. "As to why he came to me for counsel, I couldn't tell you. I suppose he trusted my judgment."

Wrexford considered the unvarnished answer. It struck him as truthful. "I see. So, on what pressing matter did he wish your advice?"

Thornton pursed his lips. "If I knew the exact answer to that, I might have an idea of why he's dead."

A low growl rumbled in Sheffield's throat. The scalpel rose a notch. "As His Lordship said, we're in no mood for playing games."

"Nor am I," countered the marquess angrily. "This is a deadly serious matter. Not only am I concerned about the lives of bright young men, but I'm also gravely worried about the reputation of the Royal Institution—and science in this country— if scientific knowledge is being used for Evil."

Thornton slowly raised a hand—the pistol was still within a hairsbreadth of his throat—and ran his fingers through his hair. "All I can tell you is that Chittenden came to me a week before his death in a state of great mental agitation. He was clearly confused—even fearful—about something, and asked some very pointed questions about the morality of scientific experiments, and how far one should push the boundaries. I tried to get him to confide exactly what he was talking about. But he wouldn't."

The marquess paused to draw in a measured breath. "I did get him to promise to think about confiding whatever dreadful secret it was. However . . ."

"However, someone murdered him before he could do so," finished Wrexford. He slid his pistol back into his pocket. "You suspect that the young men were repeating the electrical experiments of Galvani and Aldini on living—or recently living— creatures."

Thornton's eyes widened. "How did you guess—"

"Never mind that now," said the earl. "But I surmise that's why the voltaic pile and animal remains were in your laboratory."

The earl's words caused a spasm of surprise to flit over Thornton's face, and then he nodded. "Yes, I was trying to understand just what they were looking for." A tiny muscle in his jaw twitched. "And the conclusion I came to makes my blood run cold."

Charlotte took a seat at her worktable and placed a blank sheet of drawing paper next to her palette. It was late and she was exhausted, but her mind was spinning with too many thoughts for sleep to come. Picking up her pen, she dipped it into the inkwell and . . . simply stared at the pristine white surface.

For all the twists and turns the murder investigation had taken, the truth had remained maddeningly elusive. Try as she might, she simply couldn't picture how all the clues fit together.

Charlotte closed her eyes for an instant. "Do I dare use my art to try to smoke out the murderer?"

A provocative headline might stir up enough questions among the public and government to prod the murderer into making a fatal mistake. And she could envision the perfect one: THERE'S AN ELECTRICITY CRACKLING THROUGH THE HALLOWED HALLS OF THE ROYAL INSTITUTION AS NEW QUESTIONS SWIRL AROUND THE MURDER OF LORD CHITTENDEN!

By the grace of God, the strategy had worked in the past, but it was a dangerous move, one that could do great harm if her intuition was wrong. Science was still looked on by many with great suspicion—a witch's brew of frightening theories and incomprehensible experiments that challenged the familiar beliefs of the past.

Wrexford would not thank her for throwing oil on the fires of fear that burned deep in the hearts of conventional thinkers.

Choices, choices.

It was one thing to be willing to sacrifice her own future in the battle to save Nicholas from the gallows. But did she have a moral right to blacken the reputation of London's most august scientific institution by making scandalous innuendoes?

Backing off from the idea—at least for the moment—Charlotte wiped her pen clean and retreated to a safer subject for the drawing she owed to Mr. Fores. A hint that her cousin had an alibi for the night of the murder might provoke public opinion to wonder whether the evidence was strong enough for the judges at the Old Bailey to convict him. It was the sort of titillating speculation to set all of London's tongues to wagging, from the stinking slums to the glittering mansions—

"Oiy, you ought te be sleeping."

Raven's chiding drew her out of her brooding. She looked around to see him standing in the doorway. "So should you."

He cocked a saucy grin. "Me 'n Hawk ain't fancy ladies who need hours abed and a jar of Olympian Dew to preserve the delicate bloom of our complexions."

She laughed in spite of her troubled mood. Several weeks ago, she had done a satire on the sudden popularity of highly dubious—and highly expensive—facial potions that had taken hold with the ladies of the beau monde. "No, your secret is mud, which is likely as effective as Olympian Dew's fiddle-faddle. Perhaps we should take to selling 'La Boue de St. Giles' and become rich as Croesus."

"You're not supposed to say *ain't*," counseled Hawk as he moved out from behind his brother. "It ain't proper English."

Raven made a rude sound.

Ignoring the teasing, Hawk hurried to where Charlotte was seated, a plume of steam fuzzing his face as he held up her favorite mug. "We thought you might like some tea."

Her throat tightened on seeing the uncertainty in Hawk's eyes. With the murder and the topsy-turvy changes in her own life, she felt a stab of guilt over how little attention she had paid to the boys lately.

Charlotte took the mug from his hands and set it on the tabletop. "Thank you," she murmured as she enfolded him in a fierce hug. "Forgive me. I . . . haven't been myself lately." Perhaps because she was struggling to sort out just who Lady Charlotte Sloane was.

"S'all right," said Raven as he shuffled over to her worktable. "We know you're worried about your cousin."

"And yer wery busy being a fancy lady," piped up Hawk. His pronunciation tended to lapse when he was worried about something.

"To the devil with being a fancy lady," she replied, ruffling his hair. "I must on occasion wrap myself in silks and satins, but I promise you, that will never change who I am . . ." She blinked back a tear. "Or what is most precious to me."

Raven was watching her intently. "You ain't gonna faint again, are ye?" It was said lightly, but she could tell that for all his nonchalance, he, too, was looking for reassurance that their cobbled-together family was not in danger of breaking apart.

"Watch your tongue, Weasel," she retorted, choosing to mimic Wrexford's caustic chiding of the boys. "And stop mangling the King's English, or no jam tarts for a week."

They exchanged horrified grimaces, but their eyes lit with laughter.

Charlotte kept her arms around Hawk, savoring his warmth and all the familiar little knobs and juts of his skinny body. All too soon, he would too big to cuddle in her lap.

Shifting his stance, Raven picked up one of her pencils and twirled it between his fingers. "You should show her the drawing you did today," he said to his brother. "Mr. Linsley was very impressed, m'lady."

"I would very much like to see it!" she exclaimed.

Hawk pulled a small notebook from his pocket—she had recently purchased it for him, along with several miniature sticks of artist's graphite—and shyly thumbed through the pages. "It's just a plain gillyflower that I saw in Covent Garden Market on the way to our lessons. I had to rush so I wouldn't be late."

Finding the sketch, he flattened the spine and handed her the book.

"Why, it's . . ." Charlotte's voice trailed off. The lines were quickly drawn and yet they deftly captured the exuberant curls of the petals and delicate arch of the spikey leaves.

"It's magnificent," she murmured. "You've made it come to life."

The praise brought a flush of pink to his cheeks.

Choices, choices. In that instant, Charlotte snapped the book closed, her mind made up. Yes, the dark shadow of Death was taunting them at every turn—but that was all the more reason to celebrate the bright flickers of Life.

"Come morning, I shall make arrangements for us to visit the Royal Botanic Gardens at Kew for the day after tomorrow, so you can see the exotic specimen collection brought back to Britain by Sir Joseph Banks."

"The Botanic Gardens!" Hawk's eyes widened and a note of wonder fluttered in his voice.

"Yes. And we'll have McClellan pack a picnic and accompany us." She turned to Raven. "Will you come along, too?"

He shook his head. "The new lenses for His Lordship's microscopes will be arriving from Holland that day, and Mr. Tyler said I could assist him with polishing them. And we expect to get the results back on the snuff sample he took to the botanist at the Royal Society. So he might need my help in preparing the slides, if he needs to have another look at it."

Mention of the snuff reminded her of the exotic cards and the book explaining how to work with them, which she had received from Lady Julianna. Given Raven's skill with mathematics, she had considered showing them to him. But after reading the first few pages, Charlotte had decided against it. Had it merely been about numbers, she would have seen no harm in it. However, she found its logic . . . impenetrable.

Raven, for all his cleverness and knowledge of life's grim realities, was still a child. Perhaps she was simply being naïve, but she wished to shield him from its talk of Good versus Evil, and the elemental struggle between them to rule the universe.

"That sounds very important," she replied. "It appears you are finding the work with Mr. Tyler interesting."

"Yeah, I am." For Raven, that was a rare show of his feelings.

Yet another debt of thanks she owed to Wrexford. For a man who claimed to have no tender sensibilities, he had quickly recognized the boy's curiosity and taken pains to encourage it.

"I can take your drawing to Mr. Fores when you're done," offered Raven. "I promised to assist Mr. Tyler in making an inventory of the chemicals, first thing in the morning."

"But it will be hours before he is ready for you."

He grinned. "Oiy, but I'm teaching the bootboy how to play dice, and after that, Cook will feed me a very nice breakfast."

The boys, she knew, were friendly with all the servants who worked for the earl.

"And then I can tidy up the laboratory and check over the monthly entry in the accounting ledger for any errors until he comes." A pause. "Mr. Tyler sometimes makes mistakes in his addition and subtraction. But I fix them before His Lordship reviews the numbers."

Charlotte held back a smile. "That's very loyal of you."

"Lord Wrexford says loyalty to friends and family is very important."

"He's right." Charlotte regarded their faces, aware that she couldn't imagine her life without them. Swallowing the lump in her throat, she looked back to her drawing. "You two scamper up to your aerie while I finish my work. Tomorrow promises to be a busy day."

CHAPTER 23

"I don't understand," said Sheffield, breaking the heavy silence. "Granted, you two are far more knowledgeable about science than I am, but I seem to recall that both Aldini and Galvani ultimately acknowledged that they were wrong about electricity having the power to bring the dead back to life."

"They did," agreed Wrexford. "However, the history of science shows us that many things that were thought impossible in the past prove to be valid concepts when modern techniques and discoveries are applied to them."

Thornton nodded. "The allure of making momentous breakthroughs is what drives many of us who are fascinated by science. There is so much we don't know."

Sheffield made a face. "And perhaps some of it is best left that way."

"Perhaps," said Wrexford. "But it's rather like Pandora's box—we have opened the lid on scientific inquiry, and it cannot be stuffed back into a dark hole simply because some of the results frighten us."

He looked to Thornton. "You mentioned that something made your blood run cold. What is it that spooked you?"

"It's merely a suspicion, based on a few things Chittenden let drop in his agitated ramblings," replied the marquess. "But I think they were working on developing a more potent electrolyte—"

"What the devil is an *electrolyte*?" interrupted Sheffield.

"It's a conductor, Kit," explained the earl. "In the case of the voltaic pile, it's a liquid solution that creates a chemical reaction, allowing the electrical charge to flow."

Sheffield still looked baffled, but Thornton gave a grim nod. "I have no idea what the electrolyte might be—or even if I'm right. However, I was hoping I might find some answers here."

"Then let us conduct a thorough search." Wrexford found another lamp. "But carefully, so as not to leave any evidence that we were here." He lit the wick and turned up the flame. "You didn't worry that DeVere might be working late?"

"No," answered Thornton. "I learned he has a supper engagement at Richmond House with the director of the Royal Botanic Gardens this evening, and plans to stay out at Kew for the next day or two."

"Still, we ought to be quick about it." The earl was already crouched down in front of the nearest storage cabinet.

Thornton moved to the work counter and its array of canisters and chemicals, but Sheffield hesitated.

"I'm happy to help, but I fear I might overlook some important clue because I have no idea what it means."

"Take a seat at DeVere's desk and have a look through the drawers," said Wrexford, knowing his friend had an observant eye. "Let us know if you see anything that doesn't have to do with botany."

With the marquess's hat still in hand, Sheffield did as he was told. Setting it down on the blotter, he went to work.

The lamplight pooled over a stack of shallow pasteboard boxes as Wrexford opened the cabinet doors. Next to them were four oversized books, piled atop one another. A look at the gold-stamped title of the top one showed it was a portfolio of botanical etchings from the seventeenth century. He shifted the others to check on their contents.

All artwork.

The boxes proved to hold naught but carefully labeled packets of seeds.

Ye gods—were there really that many different species of the Asteraceae *family?*

The earl shut the doors and moved on to the next storage cabinet. Hearing a low grunt from Thornton, he assumed the marquess wasn't having any better luck.

DeVere appeared to be a man of meticulous habits. These shelves were as orderly as the previous ones. Wrexford continued to search carefully, but he couldn't shake the sense that he was missing something.

He didn't doubt Thornton's story. However outlandish, it had the ring of truth.

And yet . . .

He finished with the last pile of papers and sat back on his haunches. "I have been thinking . . . two of the three men involved in the experiments are dead. Perhaps Hollister can now be convinced to tell us everything. He seemed a rather spineless fellow to me when we had a little chat."

"Spineless?" Thornton shook his head. "My impression is quite the contrary. Yes, he's capable of playing the obsequious toadeater when it behooves him. But I've watched him over the last few months, and at heart, he strikes me as a coldly calculating bastard." His brows drew together. "Indeed, I'd be tempted to believe he might have murdered the other two if I could think of a compelling motive."

"Immortality?" suggested Sheffield. "The fame of making a historic discovery and having your name known by countless generations to come." His face looked unnaturally pale as he leaned closer to the glass-globed flame.

"Or the actual power to defeat death, if one controlled the dark, dreadful secret of reanimation."

Shadows seemed to stir and slither like serpents through the darkness just outside the lamplight.

"God perish the thought," intoned Thornton.

"Let us keep looking," muttered Wrexford, shaking off the sudden tickling sensation at the nape of his neck. "Whatever unholy force is at play, we need to find a way to stop it."

Blowing out his breath, Thornton shifted his attention to the shelves above DeVere's collection of microscopes and magnifying glasses. Metal rattled as he began to search through a set of brass boxes.

Sheffield returned to riffling through the desk drawers.

Feeling a little shaken, Wrexford opened yet another cabinet. From the very start of this investigation, his usual sense of dispassionate logic seemed to have been turned topsy-turvy. He didn't really wish to analyze the reasons why.

But I must.

Emotion had no place in objective reasoning. But concern for Charlotte and the upheavals she was facing were perhaps clouding his judgment . . .

He finished sorting through a pile of papers and carefully put them back in place.

Or was it a far more visceral feeling than mere concern? Unflinching honesty—with himself, as well as with others—was something in which he took pride. And honesty compelled him to admit that his heart was in danger of overruling his head—

"This may be nothing . . ."

Sheffield's voice drew him from his thoughts.

"But you did say to speak up if I found something unrelated to botany." His friend held up several coils of copper wire.

"They are different widths, and there are tags hanging from the string wrapping with odd notations that make no sense to me."

Thornton hurried over to examine them. After several long moments, he looked up at Wrexford. "Copper is the wire of choice for a voltaic pile. The writing looks to be some sort of mathematical notation. A private system, perhaps?"

The earl rose and joined the others at the desk. "I'm not an expert in botany, but I can't think of any purpose for which these might be used."

"Nor I," replied Thornton.

"They were well hidden between several folders at the bottom of a drawer," offered Sheffield.

"The type of electrical experiments we're looking for require a goodly amount of space," said Wrexford. "There's no sign that anything like that has taken place here."

"No," intoned Thornton. "But having been a frequent guest in DeVere's villa, I know that he has a large, well-equipped laboratory there. And given that the young men of the Eos Society spent time there . . ." His words trailed off, leaving the unspoken thought thrumming in the stillness.

"Are you suggesting—" began Sheffield.

"That we break into DeVere's home and have a look around?" finished the earl. He raised a brow at Thornton.

"There's a back entrance located close to the laboratory for the delivery of supplies. And the laboratory itself is located in a separate wing, well away from the living quarters. It should be easy to enter and leave the premises without anyone being the wiser," said the marquess. "Especially as DeVere is spending the night in Kew."

"We would have to move fast," observed Sheffield.

Thornton picked up the mystery hat. "What say you, Wrexford?"

The earl cupped a hand over the lamp's glass chimney and

blew out the flame. "Let's be off. Given what's at stake, I think a clandestine visit to DeVere's villa is in order."

The drawing was done and sent off with Raven, but despite the lateness of the hour, Charlotte still felt too on edge for sleep to come. There was much to think about . . .

If only the whirling-dervish bits and bobs would come together to form some sort of coherent picture.

Heaving a sigh of frustration, she took out Lady Julianna's colored cards, along with the numerical riddle and accompanying book, and spread them out on her worktable for another look. Wrexford would, she knew, dismiss them as habble-gabble nonsense, so it was pointless to broach the subject with him.

She could well imagine his huffs and snarls as he ridiculed the mystical system.

And somehow that made her smile.

Wrexford. A man of such maddening contradictions and conundrums.

"Which makes us birds of a feather," she whispered. The fire in the hearth had burned down to embers, and yet the thought warmed the chill from her bones. His friendship was comforting . . .

Though there were times in the wee hours of the morning—those solitary moments of lying in bed wrapped in naught but the night's black velvet darkness and her own wayward imaginings—when she let herself dream of a more intimate connection. Of how his flesh would feel against hers . . .

"Madness," she chided. "Utter madness."

Especially as Wrexford seemed to have retreated into himself of late. She could only guess at the reasons. Perhaps he was embarrassed by his show of vulnerability at the end of their last investigation, when the heat of the moment had sparked him to voice sentiments that he now regretted.

The threat of imminent death did strange things to the mind. Charlotte looked out the window, watching the ghostly skeins of fog twine with the wind-ruffled ivy leaves.

There were still interludes where the special bond felt undeniable. Together they had moved through the figures of the waltz with perfect harmony. And in talking afterward of loss and regret, the simple act of holding hands had seemed to connect them in ways that defied words.

But for most of the time, Wrexford appeared intent on holding himself aloof. Perhaps it had become a habit. Or perhaps he didn't wish for anyone to touch his heart.

Another smile tugged at her lip. An impossibility, as he claimed he didn't have one. That was another thing she appreciated about the earl—he could laugh at himself. Few men could.

After a moment, she simply shook her head. Whatever confusions clouded their relationship, they were friends. And for that, she was profoundly grateful . . .

Forcing her attention back to the matter at hand, Charlotte picked up one of the cards and subjected the intricate design to a more thorough scrutiny. The drawing was superbly rendered, and yet it didn't strike an inner chord. But then, art was subjective. To Lady Julianna, the twirling lines and subtle colors spoke to the heart.

She set the card aside and took a long look at the seemingly endless procession of number and spaces on the pages of Julianna's puzzle.

"I might as well try and read Sanskrit," she muttered. It was hopeless. She hadn't a snowball's chance in hell of deciphering the message . . . and Wrexford would likely just toss it in the fire.

However, she did know someone who might be up to the challenge. Come morning, she would see whether her hunch was correct.

*   *   *

"It seems DeVere has installed the latest-model German puzzle lock," muttered Wrexford as he shifted his position beside the outer door to the villa and gave another jiggle of his metal probe.

"Is that a problem?" asked Sheffield.

"No." Another jiggle, and then a smile as the mechanism released with a well-oiled *snick*. "It just requires a little coaxing."

"Follow me." Thornton edged past the earl and eased open the door. "And move lightly. The corridor floor is flagged in stone as DeVere moves a great deal of plantings and soil in and out of the laboratory."

There were no lights burning anywhere in this wing of the sprawling residence, but the marquess led the way without hesitation. However, at the end of the short corridor, he was forced to stop. "This door is locked, too."

"DeVere seems awfully concerned with preserving his privacy," murmured Wrexford as he felt around for the keyhole. The portal itself, he noted, was reinforced with thick bands of iron.

"You know how secretive scholars can be in general. And if he's up to something nefarious ..." Thornton shifted nervously as a floorboard creaked close by. "I don't mean to rush you, but the servants will be rising before long, and I'd like not to have to explain my presence here to a Bow Street magistrate."

"Voilà," said the earl, and gestured for his companions to enter.

Once the draperies were drawn, they lit lamps and without wasting words set to searching the space. Wrexford headed to the trestle tables by the windows, where containers of potting soil were filled with sprouting seedlings.

All looked in order.

Frowning, he slowly turned in a slow circle, making a careful survey of the room. Everything about the laboratory—the books, the beakers, the watering cans—confirmed it as a place of serious botanical research. There was no sign of a voltaic pile, nor any of the accouterments necessary to perform the grim experiments the young men had been performing on themselves.

For an instant, he wondered whether Thornton was part of a conspiracy to misdirect his investigation and make him look like a bloody fool.

But a low oath from the marquess as he hurriedly closed a drawer and moved on quelled the suspicion.

"It *has* to be here," added Thornton. The lamplight showed his face had gone taut, and beads of sweat were forming on his brow. "I just *know* it does."

"We haven't finished looking," said the earl. However, he had a sinking feeling that they weren't going to find anything incriminating.

Charlotte would likely tease him unmercifully for saying so, but the space had no aura of evil to it. Which meant—

"Come have a look at this." Sheffield's urgent whisper cut short his musing.

Wrexford edged around to where his friend was crouched down in a narrow alcove beside a long, narrow terra-cotta planter. The lamplight played over a half dozen slender beanstalks of varying heights.

Each was fastened to a wooden support stake with several twists of copper wire—a thin gauge was used for the smallest plants progressing to a thicker gauge for the tallest.

"Damnation," muttered Thornton as his gaze fell on the wires. "Damn, damn, damn."

"This explains the coils of copper," murmured Sheffield. "It would appear our surmise about DeVere was wrong."

Which meant, thought Wrexford, that the evil had to be elsewhere. But at that moment, he hadn't a clue as to where to start looking.

The clock was ticking . . . He clenched his hands, feeling his gut knot in guilt at having failed Charlotte.

And time was slipping through his helpless fingers, like so many mockingly elusive grains of sand.

CHAPTER 24

A small cough snapped Charlotte's meandering thoughts back into focus. She blinked and set down her pen, realizing that her drawing paper was covered with naught but mindless doodles.

"His Lordship is here," added McClellan from the doorway. "And wonders if he might have a word with you."

"Yes, yes, of course." She grabbed a rag from her paint box and scrubbed at spatters of black ink on her fingers. "I'll be there in a moment." A glance at the mantel clock showed it was later in the morning than she had thought.

Tick-tick. Charlotte quelled the impulse to grab it and hurl it out the window. Pique would not uncoil the hangman's knot, but still, she found her hands were shaking.

Drawing a steadying breath, she gathered up Lady Julianna's items and headed for the stairs.

Wrexford was standing by the windows with his back to the door, the broad bulk of his shoulders blocking much of the sunlight. His hair was in dire need of trimming, she noted. How odd that the tiny details seemed to take on such clarity in times of crisis.

He turned as she entered the room. Shadows darkened the hollows beneath his eyes, and his mouth was thinned in a grim line.

Charlotte felt her heart lurch and thud up against her ribs. "I take it there's bad news?"

"I was wrong about Thornton. He's not involved in anything evil—quite the opposite in fact." He explained about the encounter at the Royal Institution, and their clandestine visit to DeVere's villa.

When the earl was done, she merely nodded, unable to summon anything to say. All hope for Nicholas seemed to be slipping away.

"I'm sorry. You asked for my help, and all I've done is spin in circles."

Charlotte had never heard such a note of defeat in his voice. "Ye gods, you mustn't say such a thing, Wrexford! I—I had no right to ask you to undertake such an impossible task. You could have—you *should* have—told me to go to the devil, and yet you didn't." She drew in a measured breath. "Without you, I would have given up long ago."

"I would do anything for you," he said softly.

Her heart lurched again, but it was more of a flutter than a thud.

"Would you?" Charlotte set down the book and box of cards. "Then please . . ." She moved a step closer and reached up to press her palm to his cheek. "Don't be so hard on yourself. I can't bear to see you trapped in such shadows."

Surprise flickered in his eyes, then quickly gave way to some other emotion.

The warmth of his skin pulsed against her hand, and all the sharp-edged angles of his face seemed to soften. A tiny smile quivered at the corners of his mouth.

At that instant, all the mental wrestling with what they were and weren't to each other suddenly melted away. She stood on tiptoes . . . and felt the feathery intake of his breath against her lips as she leaned closer—

"I thought you might like some tea." McClellan shouldered through the half-closed door and stopped short. "I took the liberty of adding a bottle of Scottish malt to the tray, milord," she added dryly, "as you looked like you might be in need of stronger sustenance."

"Thank you," said Wrexford, drawing back a step.

"I'll just set it down here on the table." McClellan caught Charlotte's eye and lifted an apologetic shrug. "If you need anything else, I'll be in the kitchen."

"Thank you," echoed Charlotte, unsure whether to laugh or cry. A fitting reaction, she decided, taking a seat on the sofa. Emotions were never simple when it came to the earl.

He waited until the maid was gone before joining her. "Much as I'm tempted to gulp down the whole bloody bottle, I had better keep a clear head."

"Wrexford—"

Her breath caught in her throat as the earl brushed a quick kiss to her brow and slouched back against the pillows. "You need not worry," he murmured. "The moment of weakness has passed."

A cryptic statement, if ever there was one.

However, another quick smile seemed to say far more. "Let us concentrate on the matter at hand. Other things can be unraveled later," he added. "All is not lost for Locke. For one thing, your drawing is already stirring questions as to the evidence—"

"I know I have no right to use my influence for personal reason," she began, only to halt as the earl made a rude sound.

"Truth isn't merely personal," he continued. "It's fundamental to the rights of everyone, so stubble any misgivings. You did the right thing."

She felt a knot loosen in her gut.

"And even more important, Thornton confirmed my belief that Hollister may not be as innocent as he claims. I plan on pursuing that lead when I leave here."

"You're right, of course," said Charlotte quickly. "We must think . . ." She suddenly frowned. "Something bothers me about the hat. If it doesn't belong to Thornton, then how did it get there?"

"That's another lead to pursue. Woodbridge frequently attends lectures at the Institution—and Children, one of our leading scientific lights, was speaking yesterday afternoon," he replied. "As you've so sagely pointed out in the past, women are as clever and ruthless as men. So we mustn't overlook his sister as a suspect. Perhaps she was spooked by my questions about the hat, and decided to cast suspicions on someone else."

"You may leave Lady Cordelia to me. I have a good excuse to pay her a visit this afternoon."

His brows rose in question.

Ignoring the tea tray, Charlotte picked up the book and box of cards. "I, too, have a report to make on the activities of last night. And do hear me out before you make any rude remarks," she said, before proceeding with a quick account of her conversations with Lady Cordelia and Lady Julianna.

The earl kept his teeth clenched until she had finished. "I shall refrain from sullying your delicate ears with my true sentiments on such metaphysical habble-gabble. Let's just say you were right to suppose my advice would be to toss the lot of it into the fire."

"I understand your skepticism, sir. And I don't disagree. But as I said, it gives me a reason to visit Lady Cordelia," replied Charlotte. "It can do no harm, and if perchance her expertise in mathematics can make any sense of this—" She held up the papers given to her by Lady Julianna. "Then some good may come of it."

Wrexford uttered something unintelligible. She didn't bother asking him to repeat it.

"I haven't said anything to Raven about this," added Charlotte. "He's still just a child, and sees enough of humanity's darker side without being exposed to philosophies that might be . . . unsettling."

"In that, at least, we are in full agreement."

Seizing the opportunity to change the subject, she asked, "What about Hollister? Have you any idea on how to manage a meeting with him?"

"As it happens, he resides at the Albany Hotel—just one floor above Locke's rooms," answered Wrexford. "I should have seen that connection sooner. But be assured that I intend to pry out whatever secrets he's hiding when next we speak."

We all have secrets, thought Charlotte. That didn't mean Hollister's would help save Nicholas. But she told herself not to lose hope.

"If he has any information that may stay the hangman's hand, I'm sure you will find it."

His jaw tightened for an instant—her platitude didn't fool him in the least.

"I will do my best."

"That is all we can ask of ourselves." Another bromide, but it was all she could summon. But as he nodded and turned to take his leave, Charlotte suddenly recalled a happier topic. "Before you go, I have one last matter to discuss. I promised Hawk that I would take him to see Sir Joseph Banks's exotic botanical collection at the Royal Botanic Gardens. Would you mind if we make use of your unmarked carriage and undercoachman first thing tomorrow morning for the visit?"

"The carriage is always at your command," responded Wrexford. "Raven doesn't wish to accompany you?"

"He would rather stay and help Mr. Tyler in your laboratory—but only if it meets with your approval. You must feel free to say something if his presence is a distraction."

"On the contrary. He's a very bright lad, and is proving to be a very able assistant." The earl paused for thought. "Indeed, he appears quite curious about science, and it seems to me that advanced lessons might be in order. They would, of course, require an additional tutor, as Mr. Linsley doesn't have the necessary expertise." His expression turned tentative. "I would hope that we won't have to brangle over financial arrangements—"

"No," she interrupted. "As you pointed out last time, friendship shouldn't be measured in guineas and pence."

"Excellent, then I will go ahead and find the appropriate person and make the arrangements."

"Thank you, Wrexford." Charlotte smiled. *For making even the darkest moments seem a bit brighter.*

The shadows in his eyes lightened ever so slightly. He nodded—no other words were necessary. They understood each other perfectly.

As the door clicked shut behind him, she turned her attention back to the items on the tea table. The plume of steam from the pot had faded away, but the swirl of colors on the cards reminded her of the challenges ahead.

Nulla tenaci invia est via. For the tenacious, no road is impassable.

Lost in thought, Wrexford entered his workroom and took a seat at his desk, intent on reading the book on Aldini's work that he had just purchased on his way home. It was too early to seek out Hollister, and perhaps more information on Vitalism would help—

The *clink* of glass drew him from his musing.

"Sorry," murmured Raven, quickly finishing his adjustments to the microscope as the earl looked up. "I needed to set up a stronger lens, but we haven't quite perfected the cradle."

"No need to apologize, lad," replied the earl gruffly.

"I should say not," called Tyler, who emerged a moment later from one of the supply alcoves. "Remember, it was Master

Raven's ingenious idea to add an auxiliary lens for greater magnification." He carefully inserted a set of thin glass slides into the microscope.

Wrexford rose and went to have a closer look. "What are you examining?"

"The sample of snuff you had me take to the Royal Society," answered Tyler, a note of excitement shading his voice. "Mr. Sachem has identified all the elements of the mixture. The bitter almonds and cloves are fairly common additions to the tobacco. But the last ingredient isn't—it's *Curcuma longa,* of the *Zingiberaceae* family."

The earl frowned. "Is that of any help?"

"Perhaps." Tyler was already looking through the eyepiece. "I wanted to have another look at it myself before going and making inquiries among my tobacconist friends. They may have heard of who might be using it."

The valet gave a grunt. "With the new lens I can see it's quite a distinctive orange color."

"*Curcuma longa,*" said Raven slowly. "Of the *Zing . . . Zingeribera—*"

"*Zingiberaceae* family," repeated Tyler. "All living organisms have a scientific name based on a system devised by a fellow named Carolus Linnaeus, lad. That's because there are many different local names for flora and fauna, so the system allows scholars from around the world to speak a common language."

"Ye mean every weed and flower has a fancy name?"

"Aye," replied the valet. "As do animals, reptiles, fish, and insects. It's all based on common traits and . . . well, it's a bit complicated to explain, but I'm happy to do so if you're interested."

Raven made a face. "Sounds like a mouthful of gibberish to me. But Hawk would likely find it fascinating."

"I imagine he would," said the earl, making a mental note to buy an illustrated book of common English plants with their Latin names for the boy.

"Come, help me put away the snuff," said Tyler, after a last look through the microscope, "and let us ready the things we'll need for polishing the new lenses when they arrive . . ."

Preoccupied with his own scientific inquiries, Wrexford brought his attention back to the book on electricity. There were still several hours to go before he could set out in search of his quarry.

And after reading the first few pages, Wrexford felt Hollister had better have answers for a great many questions.

CHAPTER 25

"This way, milady." The butler escorted Charlotte past a closed set of double doors—from the muted sound of masculine voices echoing against the oak, she guessed it was the drawing room—and down a corridor leading to the back of the house. Shadows flickered over the dark wainscoting. Only one of the wall sconces was lit, but the weak light was enough to see the patterned runner underfoot had seen better days.

Up ahead was a half-open door. As they approached, she heard the murmur of voices and then a light laugh.

Damnation. It appeared that Cordelia was not alone. Somehow, she would have to improvise . . .

"Lady Charlotte—what a pleasant surprise." Cordelia rose from the sofa. "I was just telling Mr. Sheffield how much I enjoyed making your acquaintance."

Talk about surprises.

Sheffield rose as well. A deck of playing cards and a pile of facedown discards were set on the low table in front of them, along with a notebook and pencil. "Lady Charlotte," he said, his eyes not quite meeting hers.

"Apparently, the two of you know each other," continued Cordelia, after indicating that Charlotte should take a seat in the facing armchair.

"Yes," she replied. Her gaze lingered on the arrangement of cards.

An amused chuckle slipped from Cordelia's lips. "Are you interested in games of chance, Lady Charlotte? Mr. Sheffield has asked me to explain the mathematics of probability to him and how to calculate the odds of risk and reward. We're making headway . . ." She paused as they resumed their seats. "You are welcome to join in the lesson, if you wish."

"Many things in life require that we gamble on the outcome." Charlotte looked up. "Those choices are challenging enough. So, no, I don't find card games particularly alluring."

Cordelia eyed her thoughtfully. "A very interesting answer."

"And a wise one." Sheffield shifted uncomfortably. "I ought to give up playing, as I clearly have no head for understanding the nuances of how to make good decisions."

"Nonsense," snapped Cordelia, turning her gimlet gaze on him. "You have a very sharp mind, and you grasp concepts quite easily."

Sheffield blinked.

"Is there a reason why you wish to portray yourself as a buffle-brained widgeon to others?"

Charlotte bit back a smile at the odd look that spread across her friend's face. It mingled shock and . . . something she couldn't quite define.

"I—I . . ."

Ignoring his stammer, Cordelia turned over a fresh card from the deck. "For example, you now hold an eight. So recall the cards that have already been dealt and tell me whether you would take another card in this game of vingt-et-un."

He thought for a moment. "No."

"Why?"

To Charlotte's surprise, he answered with a crisp mathematical analysis.

"You see!" said Cordelia with a note of triumph. For an instant, her features seemed to soften. "You're not an idiot."

"Er . . ." Sheffield cleared his throat with an embarrassed cough. "Only because you explain things very well."

An awkward silence stretched on for several long moments as Cordelia reshuffled the cards. "Forgive me, Lady Charlotte— I've neglected to offer you some refreshments." She made a rueful face. "I'm not often called upon to exercise my ladylike graces."

"That suits me perfectly well, as I've no desire to drink and engage in superficial conversation," replied Charlotte. "In fact, I'd rather stay on the subject of mathematics."

"Indeed?"

"Yes, the reason I've come is to ask your help in solving a puzzle involving numbers."

A flare of interest lit in Cordelia's hazel eyes, and for an instant, her dark lashes seemed aglitter with a spark of gold.

"Lady Julianna presented me with a conundrum the other night—a challenge, if you will," continued Charlotte. "However, my mathematical skills are no match for its complexity."

"She enjoys weaving intricate games within games. So, yes, her puzzles tend to be arcane," responded Cordelia. "Why do you care about solving it?"

"Because my cousin was recently murdered—quite luridly, as you've no doubt read in all the newspapers," she answered, deciding not to mince words. "Lady Julianna seemed to hint that the answer to the puzzle might shed some light on the crime. So, however unlikely, I feel I can't ignore the possibility."

"As I said, Lady Julianna likes to play games," murmured Cordelia. She took a moment to turn over several cards.

The queen of hearts. The ace of spades. The three of clubs.

And do you like playing games, too, Lady Cordelia? wondered Charlotte as she smoothed out a crease in her skirts. If the cards were meant as some esoteric warning to frighten her off, it was a wasted effort.

Cordelia leaned back against the pillows. "I had thought the evidence against your other cousin was considered irrefutably damning. But I saw that gadfly A. J. Quill's latest drawing raised some questions as to his guilt. I take it you agree?"

"There are enough questions that I'm not yet ready to believe him capable of the crime."

"I agree," interjected Sheffield. "The evidence is all circumstantial. And no witness has come forward to place Locke at the scene of the murder."

"Well, it would certainly be a miscarriage of justice to send the wrong man to the gallows." Cordelia hesitated, a frown flitting over her face. And then she abruptly held out her hand. "Let me have a look at the puzzle."

Charlotte handed over the package containing all the material.

The papers unfolded with a whispery crackle.

Drawing in a deep breath, Sheffield stood up and went to stand by the bank of windows overlooking the walled garden.

With a quick flick of her hand, Cordelia brushed the playing cards to one side of the table and laid out a selection of the fanciful numerical cards.

"Hmmph." After subjecting them to a careful scrutiny, she opened the book and turned her attention to a back-and-forth study of the handwritten numbers and the printed pages.

Charlotte rose, too, and went to have a look at the series of watercolor sketches hung by the bookcases. They were seascapes, rendered with a deft hand and a keen eye for the nuanced colors of the ocean at dawn.

But it wasn't the artistic merit that had her heartbeat kicking up a notch. She had suddenly recalled Wrexford's recounting of his meeting with Cordelia and her brother—*a side parlor . . . a bookcase by a doorway . . . a hat and coat tucked on the top shelf . . .*

She moved slowly down the line of paintings, trying to keep her breathing steady. Sheffield, she noted, had shifted slightly and was watching her out of the corner of his eye.

Thump-thump. Giving the last watercolor a cursory glance, Charlotte then edged around the jut of the bookcase and cast her gaze on shelves of leather-bound volumes.

From the sofa came the rustle of silk and the flutter of turning pages.

Higher, higher—she raised her eyes upward. And there it was—the top shelf, shrouded in shadows.

Still, it was clear there was no folded coat.

And no hat.

She moved back a step for a better angle, just to be sure—

"Ye gods, surely you aren't thinking . . ." Sheffield's voice was barely a whisper, but it felt like a daggerpoint pricking between her shoulder blades.

Charlotte spun around with a start.

"The hat—why are you and Wrex so bloody interested in a hat? I recall now that he asked Lady Cordelia about what type of hat she wore when disguised as a man. And last night, he thought Thornton guilty because of what he had perched on his head."

"Because," answered Charlotte, "Raven and Hawk have learned that someone wearing a Wellington hat was seen at both the Bloody Butcher murders and in the gardens of Kensington Palace at the time of Cedric's death."

"That may be, but you're wrong to think Lady Cordelia can be guilty." Sheffield gave a wry smile. "You've often told Wrex that one must trust intuition, as well as logic."

Charlotte saw Cordelia look up from the book and papers.

"And so I feel compelled to speak out," he went on, raising

his voice. "I'm certain—beyond a shadow of a doubt—that the villain we seek is elsewhere."

Cordelia arched her brows, looking more amused than rattled. "I beg your pardon?"

"It's not here," said Charlotte, ignoring the question.

Sheffield didn't flinch. "Nonetheless, I stand by the feeling in my gut."

She felt the air leach from her lungs. Sheffield had proven he possessed excellent instincts. But Nicholas's life was hanging in the balance. If an error in judgment was to wrap a noose around his neck, she would rather it be hers . . .

The sudden scuff of steps crossing the carpet interrupted her thoughts.

A hinge creaked as a cabinet door came open. "Are you perchance looking for this?" Cordelia held up a gentleman's hat.

It was, saw Charlotte, a Wellington.

"I'm usually more careful than to leave my disguise lying out in plain sight, but I was distracted on the night I returned from the gaming hell, as Jamie and I were arguing over whether he had done the right thing in letting Westmorly slither away without making his perfidy known to his peers." Cordelia shrugged. "And so Lord Wrexford noticed my hat and coat on the shelf."

"You would have chosen to denounce Westmorly?" asked Charlotte.

"Granted, I consider many of Society's rules absurd and unfair, especially for those of our sex," came the answer. "But adhering to a code of honor is not one of them." Cordelia assessed Sheffield with a challenging stare. "By the by, you are a *very* odd fellow. Not many gentlemen would choose to support a stranger over a friend."

"I, too, believe in a code of honor. I don't think you're guilty."

Her brows quirked. "Guilty of what?"

The air seemed to thrum with an unseen current. Strangely enough, Charlotte felt the vibrations loosened the tightness in her chest.

Alea iacta est. The die is cast. Or rather, the cards had been dealt. She must gather her wits and play what Fate had tossed her way.

"Since truth and honor go hand in hand," she said, breaking the electric silence between the other two, "let us not waste our breath in cat-and-mouse conversations. Did you kill Lord Chittenden, Lady Cordelia?"

If Cordelia was shocked by the question, she hid it well and answered calmly, "I did not."

"What about Benjamin Westmorly?"

A hesitation, and then a curt laugh. "Had the thought occurred to me, I might have been tempted. But, no, again I must assert my innocence." Cordelia frowned. "Wait—I thought the newspapers reported it as self-murder, triggered by despair over the fact that his cheating at cards was about to be made public."

"It was made to look like that," replied Charlotte. "The authorities are keeping the truth a secret so as not to alert the killer that the ruse didn't work."

"And how, may I ask, do you know that?" asked Cordelia.

"I have my sources."

"Which include me," interjected Sheffield. "Wrexford and I discovered the body . . ." A quick glance at Charlotte. "Along with another friend, whose identity I'm not at liberty to reveal."

"Hmmph." Looking pensive, Cordelia returned to her seat on the sofa. "My own eccentricities appear to have drawn me into a circle of equally unorthodox individuals." Her lips twitched. "Tell me, is Lady Peake also a sleuth?"

"She would be extremely good at it," murmured Charlotte.

"A frightening thought."

Their eyes met and they both smiled.

Sheffield cleared his throat with a cough. Or perhaps it was a chuckle. "Indeed. You ladies have *no* idea how terrifying it is for us gentlemen to encounter a female who uses her head for anything other than a perch for her bonnet."

"But my Wellington looks so very fetching," murmured Cordelia. She was still holding the hat, and with a flourish, she put it on and pulled the brim down to a jaunty angle.

Charlotte was suddenly aware that the tiny hairs at the back of her neck were standing on end.

No, no, no . . .

"Very fetching," she agreed, taking great care to mask her reaction.

Sheffield, however, must have noted something in her face, for his eyes flickered in question.

Charlotte pretended not to see it. "It's an excellent choice for a lady. It's tall enough to hide the upswept knot of feminine tresses, but not so towering as to draw attention to the more delicate contours of a female face."

"Precisely," said Cordelia. "I see you do have an artist's perception for detail. It must prove very useful in sleuthing."

A casual shrug. "The devil is in the details," she said, catching the glint of a silver ornament. "Indeed, I see yours has a nice decorative touch on the grosgrain band."

"All of the hats made by Tobias and Company have such a button." Cordelia took off her Wellington and set it aside. "Speaking of details . . ." She looked down at the exotic Indian cards. "You think I may be able to help you learn where Lucifer is lurking by solving this puzzle?"

"Yes." Charlotte let a moment of silence slide by. It now seemed a pointless exercise, but she didn't wish to reveal her thoughts. "That is, if you're willing."

"You've probably guessed that I like challenges." Cordelia gathered up the cards. "If it were merely mathematics, I would feel confident of success. But the arcane instructions on how to interpret the numbers make it a far more complex problem. Nonetheless, I will set to work on it and see what I can do."

"Thank you." Anxious to take her leave, Charlotte inclined a nod. "As time is of the essence, we should leave you in peace."

Sheffield looked about to protest, then appeared to change his mind. He inclined a graceful bow, and echoed Charlotte's sentiments. "Yes, we're very grateful for your help, Lady Cordelia. Given time is of the essence, I shall forgo the rest of my lesson and leave you to work on it."

"Save your thanks until I actually accomplish something," she said dryly as she rang a bell to summon the butler. "I can't make any promises."

"Whether or not the conundrum is solved, it's exceedingly open-minded of you to trust in virtual strangers," he replied.

Charlotte didn't miss the undertone of reproach directed at her.

Their escort appeared in the doorway, and led the way back to the entrance foyer, where McClellan, playing the role of a proper lady's maid, was waiting. Once outside, Charlotte accepted Sheffield's arm with a silent oath. She could feel the tension radiating beneath the well-tailored wool, and a sidelong glance showed his usual nonchalant smile had thinned to a grim line.

Opening the door to the waiting carriage, he helped her and McClellan up the rungs, then climbed in after them.

She winced as it slammed shut with a tad more force than necessary.

"Damnation—you're wrong, Lady Charlotte!"

"Please unclench your fists, Mr. Sheffield," said McClellan as she primly smoothed at her skirts. "Or I may be forced to bloody your nose."

Looking abashed, he slumped back against the squabs. "Forgive me. I . . . I can't quite explain it, but I . . ."

"You feel passionately about defending someone whom you consider a friend," finished Charlotte.

"I do?" The carriage hit a rut, the lamp's lurching flame illuminating his face as it went through a series of odd little contortions. "I'm too frivolous to have deep feelings . . . but perhaps you're right." Sheffield shook his head in confusion. "I like her. More than that, I admire her. Here I am, always whinging and feeling sorry for myself because of my ill luck in being born a younger son. And yet, a female's lot in life, however highborn, is far more difficult than mine. Like you, Lady Cordelia has the courage and strength to be true to herself. She makes me want . . ." He blew out a harried breath. "She makes me want to be better than I think I can be."

Charlotte's heart clenched. She knew all too well the feeling of seeing only the best in someone, rather than the complex reality of how personal strengths could weave together with weaknesses—and create fatal flaws. Her late husband . . .

"You're a far better man than you think you are, Kit Sheffield," she said.

His eyes widened in surprise.

"Aye," murmured McClellan. "A very bonny one."

"You're unflinchingly loyal, compassionate, honorable—and strong," went on Charlotte. "Your friends know that, even if you don't."

"Thank you for that." He looked away for a moment. "Lud knows, you're a far better judge of people than I am. But in this case, I'm certain you're mistaken."

"I like Lady Cordelia, too. Very much so, in fact. But that doesn't mean she's innocent. A cunning killer must possess courage and strength. Not to speak of the ability to hide a core of evil beneath a façade of normalcy."

"*Why?*" he demanded. "Tell me why you think she is guilty."

Charlotte drew in a heavy breath. "As I said, Hawk and Raven have been asking around about all the Bloody Butcher murders. And they've discovered that someone wearing a Wellington hat with a silver ornament was spotted at all three of the murder scenes."

"Ye gods—that's not much to go on," he protested, though his voice had a certain hollow ring to it. "How many Wellington hats, with some sort of decoration on the band, do you think there are in London?"

"Quite a lot," she answered. "However, I'm quite certain the number worn by a lady in the dead of night is very, very small."

Sheffield's face fell. "H-How can you possibly be sure that it was a lady wearing the hat? Was a face seen?" A note of defiance had crept back into his voice. "And if so, why hasn't Griffin—"

"Please let me finish." She hated what she had to say next. "You're right—I can't be entirely certain. But Alice-the-Eel-Girl saw someone in Kensington Gardens at the time of Cedric's murder. The person was walking quickly along the footpath close to where she was curled up for the night, and in passing, an overhanging tree branch, dislodged the hat—just enough that the person had to reach up and reset it."

He frowned in confusion. "But—"

"Allow me to explain, Mr. Sheffield," she said gently. "You know I'm good at seeing the small details. I dress as a man on occasion, so I'm intimately familiar with how I must put on a gentleman's hat, in order to hide my coiled hair." Charlotte pantomimed a motion. "It must go on from back to front, like so."

"She's right, sir. Front to back would knock the pins loose," agreed McClellan. "And besides, it's a natural reflex for a lady. That's how a bonnet goes on."

"You saw how Lady Cordelia put on her Wellington just now," pressed Charlotte. "It was a natural movement. She did it without thinking."

Sheffield looked as if he had been punched in the gut. "And you're saying that . . ."

"That Alice observed exactly the same movement," she finished. "And of all our little band of urchins, Alice is the most careful and sharp-eyed."

"But . . . but someone replaced Thornton's hat with a Wellington. It had to have been—"

"As we just agreed," interrupted Charlotte, "there are a great many of them in London. That switch seems to have been an honest mistake."

For an instant, a look of raw pain flickered through Sheffield's lashes. But he quickly blinked it away.

"I'm so sorry," whispered Charlotte. "I'll need to find proof. But I fear it will be there."

He looked away for a moment, casting his face in shadows, before he responded with a shrug. "Perhaps Wrex is right—perhaps it best to think the worst of people, so that way you are never disappointed."

Wrexford slipped into the reception room and quickly took up a position behind an arrangement of potted palms. The crowd from the lecture hall was fast filing into the space, the clink of champagne glasses punctuating the rising hum of animated voices.

The visiting Italian scholar's presentation on his latest experiments with electricity was sparking a great deal of comment.

Peering through the leafy fronds, the earl began a close scrutiny of the faces. Hollister hadn't been in his rooms at the Albany Hotel, but the earl had managed to learn that he was slated to be part of the evening's activities as a member of Sir Joseph Banks's party.

It seemed unlikely that a toadeater like Hollister would risk offending such an illustrious personage as Banks . . .

Sure enough, Wrexford spotted his quarry entering from one of the side salons in the company of Sir Joseph.

Moving out from the knife-edged shadows, he began to work his way through the crowd. Hollister paused by the refreshment table, then was blocked from view by the swaying plumage of the Duchess of Wright's massive turban as she swept in to take a glass of punch.

"Damnation," he muttered, trying to squeeze around a group of gentlemen engaged in a heated debate about the lecture. The duchess had moved on, but where the devil was Hollister?

"Language, Wrexford," came a whispered warning, punctuated by the rap of an ebony cane against his shin. "Have a care, sir, or you might make some elderly crone swoon from shock."

"But not you, Lady Peake," he replied, darting another quick look around the room. "You are made of sterner stuff."

Alison chuckled. "Yes, fire, brimstone, and reptile scales— I know what you young people call me."

"It's meant as a compliment. Unlike so many of your pasteboard peers, you have spark and color."

"Hmmph. It seems the gossipmongers are wrong," she replied dryly. "You can be quite charming when you choose to be."

Wrexford caught a glimpse of Hollister at the far end of the room. Their eyes met for an instant through the swirl of colored silks and dark evening coats, and then Hollister spun around on his heel and hurried through the archway leading out to the side set of stairs.

The earl bit back a second oath. Pursuit was useless. Even without the dowager blocking his path, he had no hope of catching up with his quarry.

"Take my arm, Wrexford, and escort me over there." Alison waved her cane at a spot behind one of the large marble plinths. "I wish to have a private word with you."

Quelling his frustration, he did as he was asked.

"That's better. Now"—Alison studied his face for a moment—"is something amiss?"

His gaze darted once again to the archway. "Nothing that need concern you."

"Don't patronize me, young man," she retorted. "I'm quite aware that Charlotte is up to something havey-cavey. And I fear she may be putting herself in danger." A sniff. "She's always been too brave and too principled for her own good."

"I'm more than aware of that," he said tersely. "Leave Lady Charlotte to me."

"Is that so?" Alison fixed him with an owlish squint. "And what, may I ask, are your intentions regarding my grand-niece?"

"My intentions, Lady Peake, are to see that your stubborn, maddening, willful grandniece doesn't come to grief," he muttered. The dowager's mention of danger had his innards coiling in a knot. "To which end, I really must take my leave. Forgive me for not explaining why."

Her frail fingers clutched his sleeve. "What can I do to help?" she demanded.

"Leave this battle to me, Lady Peake." Wrexford covered her hand with his. "Let us each fight to our strengths. There will be other wars to wage in the coming weeks . . ."

Assuming I can keep Charlotte from charging in where angels should fear to tread. So far, she had refrained from taking terrible risks. But worry and frustration were making her desperate.

"Balls, soirees, morning calls—she will need a clever general to help her maneuver through the world of Polite Society," he continued. "There will be enemies lurking behind the glittering smiles and polished manners, looking to attack, simply because they will scent blood and take pleasure in trying to cause hurt."

Alison squared her shoulders. "Ha—let them try! The battlefield of the beau monde is one with which I'm intimately familiar. Anyone who seeks to hurt her will have to cross verbal swords with me. And they'll quickly find my blade slicing off their tongues."

"Heaven help the fool who dares throw down the gauntlet."
A smile ghosted over his lips. "However, for now—"

"Yes, yes—for now, you must go," she urged, releasing her
hold.

He gave a gruff nod and turned for the entranceway.

A *tap-tap* of the ebony cane touched his boot. "I shall count
on you to keep her out of trouble."

CHAPTER 26

"Slow down, sweetening," Charlotte cautioned as she and McClellan climbed down from the carriage and followed Hawk through the entrance to the Royal Botanic Gardens. The clouds had cleared during the ride from Town and the dew-damp foliage was sparkling with the morning sunlight. "You mustn't run along the paths."

"Ha! I can barely walk!" Hawk made a pained face. "What wiv the stiff collar, the tight coat, and all these cursed buttons and furbelows, I feel like a trussed pig."

"But you look like a little gentleman," replied McClellan in a voice that held a note of warning. "Rather than a heathen savage."

Charlotte suppressed a smile. She had recently purchased fancy new clothing for both boys in preparation for their first forays into Polite Society. But she wasn't quite sure how the maid had managed to get Hawk dressed in his finery.

Bribery, no doubt. There was likely a platter of fresh-baked jam tarts waiting at home.

"McClellan is right. You look very handsome," she murmured. By some miracle, his face was still clean, and his hair untangled. However, the vast array of plantings and thick bed of dark earth didn't bode well for that lasting long.

The thought of such mayhem helped lift her spirits.

On waking, she had promised herself to set aside all worries for a few hours. Now, seeing the look of wonder on Hawk's face as his gaze fell on one spectacular specimen after another, she didn't regret it. No word had come from Wrexford the previous evening, and she assumed he had made no progress in finding Hollister. As for her own discovery about Cordelia . . . it could wait until evening.

"Here is a guide to the gardens"—Charlotte reached into her reticule for the leather-bound volume she had ordered from Hatchards—"along with some sketchbooks. Come, let us make some drawings of the plants that capture your fancy . . ."

The sunlight soon warmed the chill from the morning air. Bees buzzed through the colorful flowers, and a gentle breeze ruffled the foliage, perfuming the air with the sweet essence of a world in bloom.

Closing her eyes, Charlotte took a moment to breathe in deeply and listen to the *scratch-scratch* of Hawk's pencil adding to the symphony of garden sounds. This had been a good idea. Life must be celebrated, no matter that Death was stalking through the shadows.

"Look, look!" he exclaimed, holding up a page for her to see.

"It's wonderful," she replied, determined to keep the specter of dread at bay. After admiring the drawing, she pointed to another intriguing specimen up ahead. "Shall we move on and see if we can capture that one on paper?"

For the next few hours, they made their way through the winding pathways, taking delight in the profusion of colors and textures. On reaching the famous pagoda designed by William Chambers in the previous century, they found a bench and McClellan spread out their picnic. All around them, monarch butterflies flitted through the gold-flecked light, bright dots of orange and black against the ever-changing shades of green.

It's an idyllic place, thought Charlotte as Hawk's happy chattering rose above the ruffling of the long grasses. The boys needed to broaden their horizons with trips to the countryside.

A laugh from McClellan drew her back to the moment. Hawk had set off in chase of a squirrel, only to take a tumble as his foot snagged in a bramble.

"I would have caught it, if I hadn't been wearing such cursedly stiff shoes," he grumbled on his return.

Charlotte dusted the dirt from his shoulders. "Oh, come, gentlemanly dress is a small price to pay for such a magical place, is it not?"

He grinned. "Yeah, I s'ppose so."

"Then do try not to destroy your coat," drawled McClellan as he gobbled down a chicken leg and wiped his fingers on his sleeve. "At least, not until the carriage ride home."

Smiling, Charlotte shaded her eyes and spotted a flash of sunlight through the trees. "Ah, there is the hothouse where Sir Joseph's original specimen collection is housed. Shall we take a stroll to view them, once we're finished with our picnic?"

Wrexford was jarred from his brooding by the thump of a boot against his workroom door. It was followed by an oath as the latch sprung open and Sheffield stalked in.

"You must be ill," drawled the earl, seeing his friend's hands were empty. "It's the hour of the midday meal, and yet you've purloined no food or drink from my larders."

Sheffield didn't respond with a quip—a sign that something was seriously amiss. Instead, he went to stand by the hearth, his back to the room, and braced his hands on the marble mantel.

The silence felt louder than the cracking of the coals. It sent a frisson of alarm skittering down Wrexford's spine.

"What's wrong?" he asked.

Sheffield turned, his expression bleak. "Be damned with what she believes the evidence says—in this case, I think Lady Charlotte is bloody wrong."

He stiffened. "About what?"

"You haven't heard?" Surprise flickered in his friend's eyes.

"Lady Charlotte arranged several days ago to take Hawk on a visit to the Royal Botanic Gardens this morning. They departed by carriage at an early hour and aren't expected back until the end of the day," answered Wrexford. "I imagine she intends to tell me whatever she's discovered then." He shifted in his chair. "However, I'd rather hear it from you now."

Sheffield drew a heavy breath and proceeded to explain about the meeting with Lady Cordelia, and Charlotte's shocking observation. "A gesture, glimpsed for an instant, in the dead of night, by a child!" he finished, unable to hold back a grimace. "It seems far too thin a thread to use as a hangman's noose."

"Alice has proven herself to be a very accurate observer," pointed out the earl. "She's not prone to fantasy."

Sheffield had the grace to flush. "I wasn't implying she's making things up. Just that she might be . . . mistaken."

Wrexford sensed that he must tread carefully. "That's possible. But we both know Lady Charlotte is not prone to jumping to conclusions. She cares deeply about justice, and would never want to accuse the wrong person." He hesitated, aware that the wrong words might injure their friendship. "I doubt she is basing her assessment solely on the gesture. Lady Cordelia does possess a Wellington hat, and has admitted to masquerading as a man."

"I simply can't believe she's capable of cold-blooded murder. You met her. Do you?"

How to answer?

"Would that I had the godlike powers to discern what lies in the deepest, darkest recesses of the heart, Kit. However admirable a person may appear, I fear we can never know what demons lurk within."

Sheffield's shoulders slumped. "I know what you say is reasonable. Just as I know what you say about Lady Charlotte is true, and that I should listen to my head, and not my heart." He huffed a self-mocking laugh. "Ye gods, unrepentant rogues like us aren't supposed to have hearts."

Wrexford rose and went to pour two measures of Scottish malt from the decanter on the sideboard.

"They are," muttered his friend, "cursedly painful encumbrances."

"So they are." The earl handed his friend a glass, the brusque movement sending shards of fire-gold light skittering over the far wall. "But we must be able to feel pain, if we are to be able to feel joy."

Sheffield watched the patterns flash and die away as he drew in a mouthful of whisky and swallowed. "I never thought I'd hear *you* wax poetic about sentiment."

Women seem to be addling our wits.

"There are others who do it far more skillfully than I," he replied. "Such as, 'The course of true love never did run smooth.'"

"Or quote from Shakespeare's *A Midsummer Night's Dream.*"

Wrexford allowed a faint smile. "I never thought I'd hear *you* correctly identify the Bard."

"A lucky guess," murmured his friend through another mouthful of malt.

The momentary glimmer of Sheffield-like humor in his friend's eyes was reassuring. In response, he cocked his glass in salute. "To us rogues, and all our many faults."

They finished their drinks in companionable silence. Wrexford welcomed the mellow fire of the whisky as it seemed to chase away some of the darkness of his own thoughts. A glance at Sheffield showed the tension was melting from his features.

Still, the worry that he hadn't been as good a friend as he

should have been prickled at his conscience. "If Lady Cordelia is innocent," he said, "we will—"

"Milord!" Tyler shouldered his way through the door. "The fellow I set to watching the Albany Hotel has just sent word that Hollister has returned to his rooms. If you hurry, you can catch him there."

A kiss of warm, moist air caressed her cheeks as Charlotte clicked open the brass-mullioned glass door and stepped inside the large hothouse. Brick walkways meandered through long rows of raised beds filled with plantings. Around the perimeter, a selection of potted trees in all shapes and sizes created an exotic jungle-like feeling. Shadows flickered through the leaves, punctuating the steady *drip-drip* of unseen water.

She heard a sound of wonder catch in Hawk's throat. She felt it, too. It was as if they had suddenly been transported to another world.

"Do be careful, sweeting. You heard the attendant—we mustn't touch anything," she reminded as he bent low to examine a cluster of magenta-striped leaves. "And watch your step when we move through the potted trees . . ."

She stopped short on seeing a flutter of movement through the foliage. A gentleman came around the corner of the walkway, head bent in study of the papers in his hands. He looked up over the top of his gold-rimmed spectacles as Charlotte cleared her throat, a look of mild surprise on his patrician face.

"I do hope we aren't intruding, sir," she added quickly. "The attendant did say we were permitted to enter and have a look at the specimens collected by Sir Joseph Banks."

"Yes, yes, they are open to the public, though I don't usually see visitors here at this hour," he replied.

She smiled and gestured to Hawk—who thankfully hadn't yet covered his new clothing in muck. "My ward was so excited about the visit that he was up before dawn."

"Ah—it's always a pleasure to see a young man interested in botany." The gentleman turned his gaze on Hawk, his silvery brows arching as he spotted the two books and pencil in the boy's hand. "Are you taking notes, lad?"

"I'm making some drawings, sir," answered Hawk.

"Indeed? Might I have a look?"

Hawk looked uncertain, but Charlotte gave him an encouraging nod.

"Why, these are quite good," murmured the gentleman, after studying several of the sketches. "Are you familiar with the drawings of Franz Bauer?"

"N-No, sir."

"Oh, you must see some of his work. He's a master of botanical art, and worked closely here at the Royal Botanic Gardens with Sir Joseph some years ago. There's a cabinet close by that contains a selection of his work."

He paused as a clerk hurried in with a sheaf of papers. "Your pardon, Mr. DeVere, but I just wanted to confirm that I may send your article to the Royal Society for its upcoming journal."

DeVere. Charlotte felt her breath catch in her throat.

"Yes, yes, all is in order," replied DeVere with a brusque wave. As the man scurried away, he turned back to Hawk. "Come, I'll show you, and I can point out some of the most exotic specimens in the collection along the way." He looked to Charlotte. "Assuming that is agreeable to you?"

"Why, how very kind of you, sir," answered Charlotte, deciding to make no mention of her name or her acquaintance with his ward. "That would be lovely."

"Excellent." He placed a hand on Hawk's shoulder. "This way."

Charlotte fell in step behind them, followed by McClellan, who dutifully maintained a respectful distance.

DeVere stopped by a raised planting bed enclosed in glass and began to identify the specimens to a wide-eyed Hawk. As he explained their history and significance, she found her mind wandering.

Despite her resolve to put all thoughts of investigation aside for this interlude, the unexpected encounter with DeVere was an all-too-sharp reminder of the conundrums within conundrums threatening her cousin.

And her friends.

Moving to the bank of brass-framed glass windows, Charlotte stared out at the idyllic scene. How could everything look so calm and peaceful when her world felt as if it was on the verge of smashing to flinders?

Her brooding deepened as she considered her last conversation with Sheffield. She was unhappy at having disillusioned him. *Damnation*—she liked Cordelia, too, but it was impossible to ignore how the facts added up.

What were the odds that there were *two* women venturing out disguised as gentlemen?

Or rather, *three* women. A wry grimace pulled at Charlotte's mouth. Though dressed in her usual urchin's rags, she would never be mistaken for a gentleman.

She sighed, her breath momentarily fogging the glass. In truth, such masquerades probably happened far more often than people realized. There were so many interesting places and events forbidden to women—prizefights, taverns, university lectures . . . the list was endless. It was only natural that any female with a sense of curiosity and adventure would chafe against such restrictions. And those with a devil-may-care courage, to go along with their imagination, had likely dared to take the risk.

After all, it was now known that women disguised as Jack Tars had fought in the gun crews at the Battle of Trafalgar . . .

A shuffling on the bricks drew her back to the present moment. "Now, if you come this way, lad, we'll have a look at Bauer's art. I assure you, it's magnificent."

Charlotte made herself stay focused for the rest of the tour. It wasn't hard, as the drawings were indeed spectacular. She preferred the nuances of the human face, but Bauer managed to create an aura of individuality to each of his plants.

Hawk's murmurs of admiration and shy questions earned a look of approval from DeVere. "You have a keen eye and an impressive knowledge for a lad of your age." To Charlotte, he said, "It seems you've engaged an excellent tutor."

"The young man is recently down from Oxford and came highly recommended."

"Excellent." DeVere nodded and turned back to Hawk. "You have the talent to be a very good botanical artist, lad. But you must continue to work diligently at your studies." He reached into the cabinet and took out a book. "As inspiration, allow me to present you with a copy of *Delineations of Exotick Plants Cultivated in the Royal Garden at Kew*—a special compendium of Bauer's illustrations."

Hawk's eyes widened in wonder. He quickly wiped his hands on the front of his jacket before accepting the gift.

She winced, wondering how he had managed to acquire the sticky substance now streaked on the fabric.

"T-Thank you, sir."

"You've been more than generous already." Charlotte started to rummage in her reticule. "Please allow me to purchase the book—"

"Nonsense," he replied, dismissing her protest. "You may repay me by encouraging your ward to pursue an interest in science."

It may only have been a reflection from the glass, but his eyes seemed to take on a brighter glitter. "There are so many momentous discoveries waiting to be made, but we need minds of bold imagination and fearless curiosity."

An eloquent speech. And yet it raised a pebbling of gooseflesh on her arms.

"You are too kind," she murmured, deciding not to argue.

He responded with a graceful flourish. "It has been my pleasure. However, I must now excuse myself, as I have a meeting with the head superintendent in Kew Palace."

After another round of pleasantries, DeVere turned away and followed the walkway to a staff outbuilding attached to the rear of the hothouse. Through the tall windows of the hothouse, Charlotte watched him cross the lawns and disappear behind a copse of trees.

The rattle of buckets interrupted her thoughts. Two gardeners were approaching with a barrow loaded with water and tools for tending the plantings.

"Come, we must allow the men to do their work," she murmured.

"Wait!" protested Hawk, taking her hand and tugging her back toward the section of the hothouse that held the special collection. "You must have a look at one of the rare specimens. It's wery, wery interesting."

Charlotte noticed the lapse in his pronunciation, which only occurred when he was agitated. Feeling a stab of guilt over her earlier inattention, she dutifully followed along.

"See?" he said, pointing a finger at one of the terra-cotta pots lining the walkway.

"Yes, very nice," murmured Charlotte, though she was a little surprised that it had captured his fancy. The sword-shaped leaves and center stalk of small white flowers were rather ordinary. Still, she made a show of admiring it until the *clank-clank* of the barrow came closer.

"Come along, sweeting," she said, and this time he didn't argue.

Once outside, the shadows suddenly grew deeper, and a look up at the sky showed ominous grey clouds scudding in from the west.

"Perhaps it would be best to return home," murmured Charlotte. Seeing the troubled look on Hawk's face, she ruffled his hair. "Don't fret. We shall return again soon."

The book clasped to chest, he remained strangely silent on the walk back to the waiting carriage. It wasn't until the door clicked shut and the wheels began to bump over the road that he released a pent-up breath.

"Is something amiss—" she began.

"*Curcuma longa,*" said Hawk, his voice taut with excitement. "The plant I showed you is a *Curcuma longa,* of the Zin . . . *Zingiberaceae* family. Mr. DeVere said it's a wery rare plant, and that the Royal Botanic Gardens here at Kew have the only specimen in England."

Charlotte shook her head in puzzlement.

"The snuff!" he exclaimed. "Raven told me that Mr. Tyler received word from the botanical expert, who identified the mysterious ingredient in the snuff you found at the murder scene."

Ye gods . . .

"I thought it best to keep mum until we were alone. But"—Hawk flashed a triumphant smile—"but it's *Curcuma longa!*"

CHAPTER 27

"The bloody dastard is proving slippery as an eel," muttered Wrexford as he finished a quick check of Hollister's rooms. "It looks like he's wriggled through our fingers again."

"Wherever he's gone, it appears he was in a hurry," observed Sheffield as he looked around at the half-open bureau drawers and items of clothing scattered on the floor of the bedchamber. "Perhaps because of your interrogation, he sensed the noose drawing tighter around his neck and is fleeing the country."

The earl heard the hopeful note in his friend's voice. "Perhaps, Kit. But don't let your hopes take wing quite yet." He slid the lock pick back in his boot. "However, now that we are here in his private quarters, let us make a thorough search of the place."

"If there's a shred of evidence here as to his guilt, I vow I shall find it."

It took the better part of an hour, but a grunt of triumph finally slipped from Sheffield's lips.

Wrexford hurried into the dressing room, where his friend was crouched down beside a small trunk. A pile of dirty linen was strewn around his feet, but several books were in his hands.

"Have a look at this!"

He took the top one, which was cracked open to a spread of illustrations. They depicted the hideous experiment Aldini had done on the newly dead body of George Foster, the criminal hung at Newgate.

"Look at the handwritten notes in the margin," urged Sheffield.

A quick read showed them to be notations on why Aldini had failed to reanimate the dead man and what changes in the procedure would likely result in success.

"The other book is on Galvani's experiments. Surely, if we take these to Griffin, he can go arrest Hollister."

Wrexford hated having to throw water on his friend's fire. "Even if this turns out to be Hollister's handwriting, it's not proof of any wrongdoing. He can claim it's merely scientific speculation."

"Do *you* believe that?" asked Sheffield.

"No," he answered. "When you put it together with the other circumstantial evidence, I think it's clear Hollister is involved in something terrible. But we need to know exactly what."

"Then let us find him and get the truth out of him," Sheffield's expression turned hard as stone. "No matter if it means shoving a hand down his gullet, and pulling out his vital organs, one by one."

"You are sure?" whispered Charlotte.

"Oiy," answered Hawk. "Raven had Mr. Tyler write it down, cuz he thought I'd like te see what a mouthful the scientific names are. The expert from the Royal Society says it only grows in a certain area of northern India."

Charlotte felt another chill take hold of her flesh and turned to McClellan. "Wrexford found no incriminating evidence in either of DeVere's two laboratories." She hesitated as she looked at Hawk, but then recalled that both boys already knew all the sordid details about the investigation. "But that doesn't mean there isn't some hidden place, filled with the ghastly electrical implements designed to reanimate the dead."

She made a wry face. "Though I confess, that sounds like a scene from one of Ann Radcliffe's horrid novels."

"Would that all this was naught but mere fiction," said McClellan. "But your cousin is dead and Evil is still afoot in the streets of London."

Charlotte nodded, grateful for the maid's unflappable aura of calm, and took a moment to think. "Hawk, as soon as we arrive home, you and your brother must go and let Wrexford know what we've discovered," she said. A glance out the window showed the landscape was passing with agonizing slowness. "We need to have a council of war."

"Oiy!" Grimacing, he tugged at the collar of his new shirt and grumbled, "If I weren't dressed like a bloody street fiddler's monkey, I could jump outta the carriage sooner."

"Language, young man," warned McClellan. "Or would you rather I wash your mouth with soap rather than stuff it with sweets?"

Forcing her innards to unclench, Charlotte allowed a smile, and then turned the talk to the morning activities, and all the marvelous sights they had seen. It was a long ride back to Town, and the darkness of Death mustn't be allowed to overshadow all else.

Hawk laughed at something McClellan said and she felt a lump rise in her throat. The boys were growing so quickly and developing their own interests. She wanted with all her heart to give them good guidance and encouragement.

And love. But that went without saying.

Nothing mattered more than love. It gave one the strength to face any adversity.

"Look, look, m'lady!" Hawk was paging through the book of Bauer's art and suddenly held up a page. "He's drawn a bug on one of the leaves!"

"It's marvelous, isn't it?" She patted the seat beside her. "Come, shall we look at it together . . ."

His lively chatter and the exquisite colors and details of the art made the journey pass more quickly than she thought possible. The carriage clattered to a halt and the three of them hurried into her house.

"I'll go fetch Raven," called Hawk, flinging off his jacket as he raced for the stairs, "and we'll fly to alert His Lordship."

"Would you care for some tea?" asked McClellan as Charlotte removed her bonnet and shrugged off her cloak.

"Thank you, but no." What she desperately needed was some solitude in which to think.

"Well, then . . ." The maid picked up Hawk's jacket, her brows rising as she surveyed the streak on its front. "I'll be in the kitchen if you need me. This may require some witchcraft to remove."

"Thank you," repeated Charlotte, but her mind was already spinning, spinning, spinning . . .

Once seated at her desk, she set a fresh sheet of paper on her blotter. *Is it possible the trail leads back to DeVere?* Wrexford had searched carefully for any incriminating evidence and had found nothing.

And yet . . .

Her pencil moved over the paper, sketching in the sword-shaped plant at its center and a series of lines and arrows radiating out to the confusion of clues—*grains of snuff, a slender knife, a voltaic pile, a Wellington hat, the shadowy outline of a figure.* Something had to tie them all together.

She just had to see it.

"Sir Kelvin Hollister?" The grizzled porter at Boodle's scratched at his chin. "Aye, he was here earlier, milord, closeted in one o' the private rooms with a gent I didn't recognize. But you've just missed him."

Wrexford cursed. He and Sheffield had spent the last few hours searching through Mayfair, trying to catch up with their quarry. It appeared they were getting closer. But not close enough.

He took out his purse and gave it a discreet shake. "Any idea what other haunts he favors in Town?"

The porter's eyes widened at the muted clink of gold against gold. "You could try the Golden Cockerel in St. Giles, milord." He looked around before adding, "I've heard murmurs here in the club that it's known as a place where a gentleman who needs a hidey-hole can take refuge."

Wrexford passed over several guineas. "Let's be off, Kit. If we hurry, perhaps we can finally run him to ground."

"His Lordship ain't—isn't—at home," announced Hawk in a rush as he pushed open the door to her workroom. "Mr. Tyler says he and Mr. Sheffield went off to confront Sir Kelvin Hollister, and they've been gone fer hours."

Repressing an oath, Charlotte looked down at her scribbles. Hollister was another maddening thread in her tangled sketch. His connection with her slain cousin was through science . . .

And through Lady Julianna Aldrich.

She suddenly felt a prickling between her shoulder blades.

"Raven stayed with Mr. Tyler," continued Hawk, "so he can come tell you when His Lordship returns." He edged closer to her desk, watching her intently. "You want for me to run any other errands?"

"No, there's nothing for us to do but wait," she answered.

His gaze shifted to the drawing paper. "What's that?"

"Just random doodles," replied Charlotte, still contemplating the crisscrossing squiggles and arrows. "They sometimes help me think."

Think.

All at once, the idea that had been lurking at the edge of her consciousness snapped into sharp focus.

He craned his neck. "Why—"

"I fear I'm too exhausted to contemplate any more questions tonight," she cut in. "It's been a very long day. We should both get some sleep."

Hawk's eyes betrayed a tiny flicker, but he reluctantly lifted his shoulders in a shrug. "Oiy, I s'ppose so."

Charlotte pulled him close and pressed a kiss to his tangled curls. "Rest easy, sweeting. Because of you, we are gathering more and more clues that may lead us to the killer."

"We'll find him, m'lady."

From the lips of a child to the ears of the Almighty. Charlotte prayed that would be so. Time was slipping away. Nicholas's trial was scheduled to begin in two days.

She forced a smile. "Of course, we will—if only for Mr. Tyler's sake. Lord Wrexford gets *very* ill-tempered when logic refuses to unravel a conundrum."

Hawk's expression remained solemn. "Raven says he gets angry because he doesn't like to disappoint you."

Her throat seized. Charlotte looked away, unable to muster any reply. The earl's feelings weren't a subject she dared contemplate right now. Life and Death. Hope and Fear. They were too entangled, too confusing. For now, all her thoughts must be on Nicholas and keeping him from the gallows.

"If *you* don't wish to disappoint me," she said lightly, "you'll fly up to your aerie without further argument."

He hesitated, then backed away and slipped out into the shadows.

Charlotte waited, listening for the creaks of the steps leading up to the attic. Satisfied, she extinguished the lamp and moved into the corridor.

A whispery snore from within McClellan's bedchamber assured her that the maid was sleeping soundly. A few swift strides brought her to her own room, where she quickly undressed in the dark. *Moleskin pants, threadbare coat, floppy cap*—it took only a few moments for Charlotte to transform herself into a grubby street urchin.

After hiding the last errant wisps of hair under her cap, she tucked her boots under her arm and crept down to the kitchen, where a careful flick released the back door's lock.

"Wrexford will have no cause for complaint," she murmured as the night breeze tickled against her cheeks. The leaves rustled. A twig snapped. "In and out . . ." Quickening her pace, Charlotte crossed through the garden to the back wall. "I'm simply going to take a quick look to see if my hunch is right."

Wrexford rapped on the trap of the hackney. "Stop—we'll get out here."

"It's late and I'm thirsty," groused Sheffield as he climbed down to the street. "Why are we walking the rest of the way to your town house?"

"Because," growled the earl, "I need to think." The trip to St. Giles had been a wild-goose chase.

"And you can't do that sitting by the hearth with a glass of good Scottish malt in hand?"

"Stubble the whinging. It's only a short way." And moving his limbs might jog loose some forgotten clue. At the moment, he couldn't think of what else to do.

Sheffield fell in step beside him, maintaining a tactful silence.

It was late, and Mayfair was sinking into slumber, the night sounds muffled by the swirls of fog ghosting in from the river. At the next turn, Wrexford cut through a narrow alleyway that led to Bruton Street and the north end of Berkeley Square. He paused at the far end, and then drew back into the shadows as he spotted a lone figure approaching.

As he shifted to check the other direction, he heard his friend draw in a sharp breath.

Wrexford fixed him with a questioning frown.

Sheffield waited for the figure to pass. A glimmer of moonlight showed his face had turned unnaturally pale. "It's Lady Cordelia—"

"Sssshhh." He didn't wait to hear more. Taking his friend's arm, he pulled him close. "Let us move quickly and quietly. When I give the signal, we'll take her by surprise. It's about time we get some bloody answers."

A grim nod was Sheffield's only response.

Easing out of the opening, the earl set off with a wraithlike stealth, hugging close to the buildings, where the muddled shadows hid their movements. Closer, closer—Lady Cordelia was making pursuit easy, he observed. Though she kept up a rapid pace, she never bothered to check on her surroundings, or whether anyone was following her.

A mistake. But perhaps she had grown overconfident in her cleverness.

The gap between them was closing. In another few strides, she would be within arm's length. Wrexford hesitated, however, as she hurried through a turn and headed toward Berkeley Square.

What the devil is she up to?

Cordelia crossed the street and darted into the dark-hued foliage of the square's central gardens. The earl waited a moment, then signaled for Sheffield to follow. It was dark beneath the tall plane trees, with only a scattering of starlight filtering through the leaves. Keeping to the grassy verge, he followed the soft *crunch-crunch* of her steps on the graveled footpath. She paused at a gap in the bushes and appeared to be surveying the town houses straight ahead.

One of which was his.

Wrexford crept closer. The breeze stirred the shoulder capes of her coat just as he grabbed her around the waist and clapped a hand over her mouth.

Cordelia tried to scream, but he tightened his grip, muffling all but a tiny squeak.

Jerking her off her feet, he pivoted and retreated into the gloom, ignoring her thrashing punches and kicks. Twisting her around to face him, he thrust her up against a tree with enough force to knock the breath from her lungs.

Fear sparked for an instant in her eyes, though she continued to struggle.

Good. Perhaps the shock of staring Death in the face will help loosen her tongue.

Sheffield had come up beside him. He caught one of her flailing fists and leaned in close. "Hold your fire! We need to talk."

Surprise spasmed over her face as recognition dawned. Slumping back, she went very still.

Keeping her pinned against the tree trunk, Wrexford lifted his palm from her mouth.

"T-Thank God," she stuttered. "I feared that I might not be able to gain access to your town house."

"Why?" he demanded. "So you could murder me in my bed?"

"Stop terrorizing her, Wrex," snapped his friend, "and let her explain."

Charlotte hitched in a shaky breath. "Good heavens, you really think *I* might be the Bloody Butcher and Lord Chittenden's murderer?"

"You clearly possess the audacious cleverness and steely nerve," replied the earl.

"*Men.*" She huffed a grim snort. "Just because I'm a female who dares challenge convention, that doesn't mean I'm the Devil Incarnate."

Wrexford suddenly felt a little ashamed of himself. He lifted his forearm away from her chest and bent down to pick up her fallen hat. "Our suspicions are based on facts, not prejudice. We have evidence that says the Bloody Butcher wears a Wellington hat."

"So do a great many other people in London," she replied. "And like all but one of them, I'm innocent of those ghastly crimes."

"So you say," murmured Wrexford.

"Let us see if she's carrying a weapon," responded Sheffield. "Would that put your doubts to rest?"

He arched a questioning brow. "Lady Cordelia?"

"You are welcome to do so."

Sheffield cleared his throat. "Forgive me, but this will require me to lay hands—"

"At this point, it's rather absurd to stand on propriety, sir." She fixed the earl with a challenging stare. "However, I suggest that Lord Wrexford conduct the search, so he's satisfied nothing has been missed."

"Very well." The earl crouched down and began with her boots. She stood with unflinching sangfroid as he worked his way upward. After patting down her shoulders, he allowed a grudging smile. "It appears I owe you an apology—"

"To the devil with my sensibilities. I didn't come here for apologies," replied Cordelia. "I think your friend Lady Charlotte may be in grave danger."

CHAPTER 28

The pale Portland stone rose out of a sea of silvery mist. Two towers flanked the imposing façade of the grand villa, their crenellated battlements standing in stark silhouette against the black velvet sky.

Charlotte paused in the copse of oaks bordering the rear lawns, taking a moment to get her bearings. Justinian DeVere didn't lack in imagination or money, she observed. Having received permission from the Prince Regent to build a personal enclave in the Marylebone Park, he had commissioned the renowned architect John Nash to design the main residence. The result was a fanciful blend of East and West.

A smile tugged at her lips. Indeed, she recalled having done a satirical drawing on its exotic excesses when the structure was first completed. But seen in the mizzled moonlight, it had an undeniable grandeur that made the tiny hairs on the back of her neck stand on end.

Repressing a shiver, Charlotte moved through the trees to the west side of the villa, looking for the grand conservatory attached to the main wing. A wink of starry light from the peaked glass caught her eye, and she hurried across the gardens. A glance up showed no lights in the villa windows. She had heard that DeVere was due to spend yet another night at Kew Palace, so the servants had likely retired early.

Cocking an ear, Charlotte listened for any sounds of life. Satisfied, she found the outer door used by the barrows and let herself in.

A moist warmth immediately enveloped her. The lush perfume of the blooms—floral sweetness mingling with an earthier spice—was a little overpowering. After a small shake to clear her head, she slowly made her way through the towering rows of potted trees, seeking the section of the conservatory that held the smaller specimens.

The glass roof allowed enough light to navigate the narrow walkways between the plantings. Shadows flitted over raised beds and terra-cotta urns, their leafy shapes strangely distorted by the ever-shifting darkness. A steady *drip-drip* punctuated the rustling of the nearby palm fronds. The sounds should have been soothing, but her nerves were too on edge.

Charlotte stopped and made herself look around. Was there a logic to the layout? Scientific nomenclature would be lost on her, but—

She let out a sigh of relief on spotting the neatly lettered signs—in plain English—framed in brass and attached to each of the raised beds. The arrangement appeared to be geographical, and she quickly found her way to the section marked *India.* It was divided into subsections of neat squares. One by one, Charlotte carefully examined the contents.

As she moved to the end of the bed, a telltale flicker of yellow and white caught her eye.

"*Eureka,*" she murmured. She leaned low over the specimen, just to be sure it was—

And suddenly felt the kiss of cold steel against the back of her neck.

"Don't move." A metallic *click* signaled the cock of a pistol's hammer.

Charlotte cursed herself for being so careless. The water sounds had masked the scuff of approaching steps.

"Now, why, I wonder, would a street urchin break into a hothouse?"

"I wuz only lookin' fer food," she answered in the rough-cut slur of the slums, hoping her captor would take pity on a child and let her go.

"Oh, I think not." The gun barrel dug in harder against her flesh. "You spoke just a moment ago in Greek. Which begs the question—who are you?"

Damnation.

"Turn around," ordered Lady Julianna. "And do it very slowly. I assure you, I'm quite skilled with a pistol, and would have no compunction about pulling the trigger."

Charlotte closed her eyes for an instant, aware that she had allowed her hard-won street skills to lose their edge. Her life was changing, and her concerns had become more complex—mere survival had given way to thoughts of a future for the boys, the demands of retaking her place in Society, her relationship with Wrexford . . .

But all that was moot if she didn't quickly gather her wits and find a way to dodge disaster.

Keeping her head bowed, she did as she was told.

A dainty finger flicked out and tipped up the brim of her floppy hat.

Gritting her teeth, Charlotte rued her carelessness. She had skipped her usual ritual of blackening her face with dirt, as this was to have been a simple in-and-out. She buried her chin in the fold of her coat, hoping against hope—

But to no avail.

Julianna plucked off the cap and tossed it aside. Charlotte heard a sharp intake of breath. "Lady Charlotte?"

Silence stretched for the space of a heartbeat.

"I can explain," she murmured, her mind racing to cobble together a credible story.

"Please do." It was said pleasantly, but the pistol was still aimed at her heart.

"I was trying to puzzle out your riddle," began Charlotte. "I didn't wish to admit defeat, and so . . . and so I decided to try to sneak a surreptitious look at your family library, in hope of finding a clue." She picked at a thread on her cuff. "The door to the conservatory seemed the best choice. However, it's so magnificent in here, I fear I became distracted."

"We are kindred souls, you and I," replied Julianna. "You have imagination and daring. And you're a very good liar." A pause. "But not quite good enough."

Charlotte remained silent.

"You wish me to believe you're examining our *Curcuma longa*—one of the rarest specimens we possess—simply by chance?"

She shrugged. "Life is full of inexplicable coincidences."

Julianna let out a peal of laughter. "Indeed. And then again, at times the cosmos aligns in exquisitely beautiful harmony."

The odd comment left Charlotte a little off balance. "Oh?"

A gleam came to her captor's eyes. "Here I was trying to figure out a way to coax you into visiting me. And then, as if by magic, you appear."

"But why—" began Charlotte, only to be interrupted by the tattoo of footsteps on the flagged walkway.

"Julianna! We must pack our bags and flee." A voice cut through the foliage, rough with urgency. "Things have gotten out of hand!"

DeVere's ward shifted slightly, her free hand sliding into the folds of her skirts as a gentleman rounded the bend.

"I fear—" Hollister skidded to a stop on seeing she wasn't alone. "W-What the devil is going on here?"

"Dear Cedric's cousin has come to pay me a visit," answered Julianna. "It seems she's exceedingly clever and has somehow come to have an inkling of the truth."

His face went ashen. "All the more reason to leave the country! Lord Wrexford is also on our trail."

Charlotte heard the note of rising panic in his voice. No wonder the villain's trail had been so devilishly difficult to untangle. The two of them had been working together.

But in what way?

"I'll find some rope," continued Hollister. "We can bind and gag her. By the time she's discovered, we'll be well on our way to the Continent."

"Leave now? Just when we're on the cusp of mankind's greatest discovery?" replied Julianna. "Oh, I think not."

"Surely, you must see reason," he pleaded. "This madness must stop!"

"Madness?"

Hollister's face was sheened in sweat. "W-What I meant was . . ." He wet his lips. "We can begin again, in a place where we'll be under less scrutiny with our experiments. Perhaps India, where life is not held so dear, or . . ."

Shifting her stance, Charlotte darted a look around, gauging her chances of bolting. They were, she decided, grim. The raised beds and jumble of terra-cotta pots made the narrow walkway—blocked in both directions by the conspirators—the only avenue of escape.

A soft laugh from Julianna cut short Hollister's stuttering. "You're right, my love. It's time to begin anew."

His shoulders slumped in relief.

"Come, give me a kiss to celebrate a glittering future."

Smiling, he started forward.

In the same instant, Charlotte caught the gleam of steel, moving quick as a cobra. "No!" she cried.

Too late.

The blade pierced his chest with lethal accuracy, thrusting up and in between his ribs.

Charlotte watched in horror as a look of mild surprise widened his eyes for a heartbeat, before he went limp and slumped into his murderer's arms.

Julianna spun away and, with a graceful flick of her wrist, freed her knife as she pushed Hollister away, allowing his corpse to topple onto the walkway.

"A man of little imagination or courage." The pistol in her other hand was once again aimed at Charlotte's heart. "But he served his purpose." In the gloom, her eyes seemed to spark with fire. "As will you."

Ye gods—she is truly stark raving mad. Charlotte swallowed a spurt of panic and made herself concentrate on how to survive.

"And just what is my part in your grand plan?" she asked.

Julianna's smile was chilling in its utter lack of emotion. It sent fear slithering down Charlotte's spine. "You'll see soon enough." She gestured with her pistol. "This way."

Charlotte slowly turned. *Think, think!* Her eye for detail allowed her to summon a picture of the way she had come. The collection of potted tree specimens afforded the best opportunity for escape, she decided. The tangle of trunks and fronds might cause even a crack shot to miss.

Clouds drifted in to cover the moon, deepening the gloom within the glass conservatory. *Darkness is my friend,* Charlotte told herself, seeking to steady her emotions. The thought of friendship—nay, the thought of love—crackled through her body like a jolt of electricity. *Be damned with fear.* She had too much to live for. The boys growing to manhood . . .

And Wrexford. Whatever confusions tangled their relationship, she was not ready to give it up.

The kiss of steel shoved up against her back. "Move."

Charlotte took a step, only to see a spectral silhouette take shape from the shadows.

"Ju-Ju, my dear." A mournful sigh followed as Justinian De-Vere cast a look at Hollister's crumpled body and shook his head. "This can't go on."

"I know, I know, and there will be no need," she replied in a honeyed voice. "We're almost there. Tonight it will happen, and then our momentous discovery will make the world deem all the sacrifices worthwhile."

"Mr. DeVere," murmured Charlotte. "Please, you must make her see reason."

"*Reason!*" repeated Julianna. "What do you know of *reason*, limited as you are by conventional thinking? Like your cousin, your mind is incapable of understanding the divine workings of the cosmos."

"Mr. DeVere." Charlotte fixed him with a steady stare. "Surely, you don't wish to see any more lives lost in this experiment."

He drew in a deep breath. "Julianna—"

"The secret is now in our hands, I swear it!" declared his ward. "We've worked so hard for this, and now we're so close. The new electrolyte has proved successful. And with this one last element . . ." She touched a hand to Charlotte's coiled hair. "Imagine the accolades when we succeed at transcending to a new plane of knowledge and unleashing the power of eternal life."

Her voice had a macabre note of persuasiveness to it. Madness could make hell sound like heaven. "You've agreed with me on this, Justinian—Western thinking is so very limited. In India, the idea of reincarnation has been understood for centuries. We're simply discovering a different form of it. Think of it—bringing back corporeal life for the people we love."

Charlotte suddenly understood how an unspeakable horror had kindled the obsession behind her twisted thinking . . . a young girl witnessing the murder of her parents . . . the sense of unbearable loss.

But that did not forgive—

"Just one more sacrifice, that's all," she crooned. "And then you'll be one of the most famous men of science in history, immortal in the annals of great thinkers."

"Just one more?" repeated DeVere.

Ye gods, he was as deranged as she was, realized Charlotte.

"One more," promised Julianna.

"Mr. DeVere—"

But he had already turned his back to her and disappeared into the darkness.

The pistol's snout dug in between Charlotte's shoulder blades. "Move!"

"Danger!" exclaimed Sheffield. "Have you found something in the puzzle Lady Charlotte brought to you?"

Cordelia shook her head. "No, I can't begin to make sense of all that mystical habble-gabble. It's something far simpler—the bloody hat!"

She made a wry face. "I suddenly recalled that I've seen a Wellington hat in Lady Julianna's private study. As you know, I've often attended the scientific soirees at the DeVere villa, and one evening I took a wrong turn on my way to the ladies' withdrawing room and came upon her gathering some books to take back to the drawing room. She was quick to leave the room and close the door—locking it, I might add. But I did catch a glimpse of the hat and a dark overcoat."

"Did the overcoat perchance have one shoulder cape trimmed in braid?"

"Why, yes. I believe it did. Is that important?"

Before Wrexford could respond, a hackney came careening into the square, shaking and shuddering like a bat flying out of hell.

He started to reach for his pistol as the door flung open.

Damnation. On seeing a small figure dart down from the cab, he pushed through the bushes. "Over here, lad."

Hawk spun around, terror writ plain on his face. "Oiy, oiy—ye got te come quickly!"

The earl raced across the cobbles, Sheffield and Cordelia right on his heels.

"M'lady . . . m'lady," gasped the boy.

"Steady, steady." Wrexford seized him, only to realize his own hands were shaking. "What's wrong?"

"M'lady's in trouble!" Hawk managed to explain about following Charlotte to DeVere's villa and what he had seen through the glass windows of the conservatory.

"Hoy, there," called the driver. "The imp promised some fancy toff wud pay me double the fare fer making the trip quick-like."

Wrexford dug out his purse and flung it at the man. "You'll have a second one of these if you get us back to Marylebone Park even faster." To Hawk, he added, "Fetch Raven and Tyler. Then go find Griffin and bring him to DeVere's villa as quickly as you can."

Sheffield was already climbing into the hackney.

"No need for you to come along," said Wrexford as Cordelia placed a booted foot on the rung.

"The villa is a labyrinth," she replied. "But I think I know where to look for Lady Julianna."

"Then up you go. And let us pray you're right."

The soft *swish-swish* of the leaves indicated that the grove of potted trees lay just around the bend. Charlotte coiled her muscles, ready to—

Julianna fisted a hand in her collar and jammed the pistol up against her skull. "A clever thought. I, too, would have chosen this place to try an escape. However, as you see, your mind is no match for mine."

They marched through the greenery in silence, and several

more turns brought them to the door leading into the villa. The latch clicked open and then fell shut behind them.

Inside, the opulent furnishings and expensive artwork spoke loudly of wealth and taste. The whisper of madness could only be heard in the sound of their footsteps crossing the thick Axminster carpets.

Anger clenched in Charlotte's chest. Let her captor think she would go meekly, like a lamb being led to slaughter. Hubris could be a two-edged sword.

Julianna paused just long enough to pick up one of the oil lamps from a side table, then shoved her forward. "Keep moving."

At the end of a long teak-paneled corridor, Charlotte was ordered to shift a sixteenth-century tapestry wall hanging. Behind it was a matching door, barely perceptible amid the decorative flutings.

At Julianna's touch, it swung open noiselessly. A finger of lamplight showed a spiral staircase made of pale stone, winding down, down . . .

Drawing a deep breath, Charlotte plunged into the gloom.

CHAPTER 29

Wrexford paused under a stately oak to get his bearings. Up ahead, at the end of a wide graveled drive, was the villa's main entrance with its flanking towers, and on either side a fanciful sprawl of exotic architecture made up the two large wings that receded into the muddled darkness. The east one, he knew, held DeVere's laboratory, a place that had held no hint of malfeasance on his first search. He was quite sure he hadn't missed anything.

Which meant the evil was hidden elsewhere.

"Hawk said Lady Charlotte entered the conservatory through a door facing the rear gardens," whispered Sheffield, interrupting the earl's thoughts.

"Lady Julianna will have taken her to a more private place," he answered, trying not to let his imagination run wild . . . *a serpentine coil of copper wire, hissing and sparking with red-gold fire . . . the bubbling of the electrolyte . . . the smell of singed flesh . . .*

"I've an idea of where," offered Cordelia. "DeVere's private quarters and laboratory are in the east wing, while Lady Julianna inhabits the west wing. There's a section at the rear that visitors are not permitted to enter. She says it's because her experiments with plants are very sensitive to temperature and light." A pause. "Which has always struck me as strange, as she never talks about botany and there are no books on the subject in her private library."

An astute observation.

"It made me curious," continued Cordelia. "So one evening, when I noticed her heading into the forbidden corridor, I decided to follow. I saw her pass through a door hidden in the wood paneling of a corridor—"

"What's the quickest route to the spot?" demanded Wrexford.

She thought for a moment. "I would say through the door of her music room, which opens onto an Indian tea terrace. But I don't think it's possible to get in that way. It's equipped with a very formidable-looking lock. I suppose we could try—"

"Show me to the terrace," he ordered.

Cordelia didn't waste any time with words. She simply turned and moved off through the trees.

Charlotte winced as the muddled shadows gave way to a bright, blinding burst of flames.

" 'Let there be light,' " said Julianna, extinguishing the taper she had used to ignite the three oversized Argand lamps.

A quick look around the room they had just entered showed it was a well-equipped laboratory fashioned from polished steel, white tile, and varnished wood. Gleaming brass instruments sat on the spotless counters, reflecting an abstract beauty . . .

If only it hadn't been twisted by an unstable mind.

"Isn't it divine?" said Julianna.

Charlotte turned. "You think yourself the Almighty?"

A shrug. "An archaic concept. There are powerful forces beyond the understanding of ordinary minds—and ordinary mortals. When I prove that death can be transcended, all the old beliefs will give way to a new world."

"So have thought countless charlatans and lunatics in the past"—she was growing heartily sick of her captor's cat-in-the-cream-pot smile—"until their quackeries crumbled into dust."

Anger flared in Julianna's eyes, but it was chased away by a nasty laugh as she gave an airy wave at the far corner of the laboratory. "We shall soon see who is right and who is wrong."

On spotting the massive, coffin-like wooden box, bristling with the assembly of metal plates and copper wires, Charlotte felt her innards give a sickening lurch. It was a trough battery—the most powerful type of voltaic pile. Placing the metal disks and pads side by side within a waterproofed box, rather than stacking them upright, where the weight would squeeze the electrolyte solution out of the assembly, allowed it to generate a frighteningly strong current of electricity.

Adding to the horror, it was sitting on a table next to a padded table with leather restraining straps.

"Strip off your shirt and breeches, and put this on." Julianna held out a simple knee-length linen chemise, with a row of buttons that allowed it to open in the front.

"M-May I keep on my boots?"

"If you like."

Steady, steady—she must find a way to keep her captor talking. Like Raven and Hawk, Charlotte carried a knife in her boot. A moment of distraction was all that was needed. But she wouldn't get a second chance.

"If I'm to be sacrificed to your unique genius," said Charlotte as she began to change her clothing, "might I at least hear how you figured out your momentous discovery?" In her experience, hubris loved an audience. "After all, Galvani and Aldini, the leading scientific minds in the field of electricity, came to the conclusion that reanimation of the dead was not possible."

Julianna made a rude sound. "That's because their ideas on the subject were flawed. They failed to understand the missing element."

"Oh?" Charlotte was aware of needing to choose her words with care. She must dance along the razor's edge between needling and flattering, provoking just enough emotion... "You mean to say you are smarter than they are?"

"Precisely. You see, I understood that the secret to reanimation was that mere metal and chemicals weren't enough to raise the dead. The surge of electricity also needed to be powered by some essence of Life."

Charlotte's blood turned cold. "You mean you had to add some sort of human fluid to the electrolyte?"

A beatific smile. "Yes."

"And so began the Bloody Butcher murders?" she said.

"Tsk, tsk, such a hysterical moniker," responded Julianna. "It's quite simple when you think about it. I realized that one had to use like-to-like—a dead body needs a human essence, along with the electrical stimulus, in order to bring it back to life."

Perhaps there was a mad sort of logic to the idea. But no abstract concept could change the fact that her captor's experiments were nothing more than cold-blooded murder.

"And thus you began killing random victims?"

"I merely chose the victims and watched as Sir Kelvin did the actual blade work," said Julianna. "Until he lost his nerve."

"Is that why you killed him?"

"As you saw, he had become a liability. He was too weak, and prone to panic." A frown momentarily pinched between Julianna's brows. "And he nearly ruined things by being too loose-lipped around one of his friends."

"You mean Westmorly?" Charlotte sought to fit in another piece of the puzzle. "Was he, too, part of your secret cabal?"

"That sneak and cheat? No, I knew from the start he could never be trusted. But Sir Kelvin was careless and let slip some comments that gave his friend the opportunity for blackmail."

"So you killed him, too?"

"Like most men, Westmorly was susceptible to feminine wiles. I sent a note asking for a late-night meeting, saying I would do anything to ensure his silence. He was more than happy to agree."

"But you didn't take a body part because that would have given away that it wasn't self-murder." Charlotte took grim satisfaction in adding, "Bow Street knows it wasn't. You weren't as clever as you thought."

Julianna looked unconcerned. "It hardly matters now. And as for body parts, I didn't need any more. Through trial and error, I came to realize that your cousins must hold the ultimate solution. But, alas, Sir Kelvin became too squeamish when confronted with the need to sacrifice Cedric for the Higher Good. So I had to do it myself."

Charlotte fisted her hands to quell the urge to throttle the sickening smile from Julianna's face.

"Dear me, I see I've upset you. Like dear Cedric, you appear to possess a too-tender conscience." Julianna brushed a lock of loosened hair from her cheek. "I expect that from females, but he disappointed me. His passion for science should have allowed him to see beyond the silly strictures of conventional morality. But, no, he balked at taking a few lives for the good of humanity." A shadow seemed to darken her gaze, but it passed in an instant. "In life, he refused to cross over to a higher plane of intelligence. In death, however, he'll have the chance to be part of mankind's greatest miracle."

Much as Charlotte dreaded hearing the answer, she made herself ask the question. She must gather all the facts, in order to make sure Nicholas was exonerated of his brother's murder.

For I will survive, she vowed. *And see that justice prevails.*

"So it was you who killed Cedric. But . . ." Charlotte drew a shaky breath. "But why the terrible mutilation?"

"Oh, come—surely, the answer is obvious. The body part I chose contains the very essence of life. Added to the new electrolyte I've formulated, it will create a supremely powerful conductor." Julianna punctuated her words with a tiny wave of the pistol.

Charlotte caught the note of rising excitement in her voice.

"But the transcendent moment in all this came when I realized that using *blood relatives* would supply the last missing piece to the puzzle. And with Cedric and Nicholas, I had the special gift of twins!" her captor went on. "With all due modesty, my plan for how to arrange it all was quite ingenious. Sir Kelvin planted the evidence to make sure Nicholas was arrested for the crime. A death sentence would have been certain, and steps were already being taken to bribe the executioner to turn over the still-warm body."

"Ghoul," rasped Charlotte, unable to contain her disgust.

"Call me names now, but the world will soon recognize my brilliance. I regret that Cedric had to die, but sacrifices must be made to achieve greatness." Julianna's expression looked very faraway, as if she were in a trance. "When Wrexford and you started asking unwelcome questions, I feared you might ruin my plans. But then, I realized that *you* were the ultimate gift from the cosmos. A woman relative was even better than a fraternal twin. Think on it—an electrical current carrying the male essence of life to a fecund female . . ."

Charlotte saw her captor dart a glance at the padded table and the full force of what Julianna intended struck home.

"This time, it *cannot* fail."

Oh, yes, it can. And will.

A smile once again curled on her captor's lips. "Did you not decipher the puzzle I created for you? In it, I revealed that the cards had predicted this was your destiny."

"I didn't bother reading past the first few pages of your habble-gabble book and scribbled numbers," she answered. "I don't believe we're in thrall to some mystical force. I think we have the power to create our own destiny."

"Enough talking." Eyes narrowing in irritation, Julianna gestured with the pistol. "Move to the other side of the room and let us begin."

Though her heart was thumping against her ribs, Charlotte felt a strange calm come over her.

Love. Love for those she held dear was more than a match for madness, she told herself.

"I assure you, I'll make the process of death painless," continued her captor. "I've prepared a potion that will simply put you to sleep. But don't worry, you'll soon come back to life."

And pigs will sprout spun-sugar wings and fly to the moon.

Allowing her shoulders to slump, Charlotte turned and slowly crossed the tiles. She needed to get a little closer . . .

"Stop here."

A surreptitious glance around showed that Julianna had paused to adjust the workings of the trough battery with one hand, the aim of her weapon angling askew as her attention momentarily shifted to releasing a lever—

Charlotte spun around and smacked the pistol from her captor's hand.

With an angry hiss, Julianna grabbed up a long metal conducting rod attached to a length of copper wire and gave a menacing swing, trying to force Charlotte back against the padded table.

Sparks flew from its tip as she danced back. The air crackled as one of the tiny embers caused a flame to lick up from the linen of her chemise. Ducking low, Charlotte managed to bat out the fire and draw her knife just as Julianna came at her again.

*   *   *

Cordelia came to a halt. "Up ahead, we must pass through an archway and into a small picture gallery. At the other end is an opening, which leads into a wood-paneled corridor. At the first turn, there's a door built into the decorative fluting of the wall."

Wrexford could just make out a darker shape within the gloom. "You two wait here."

"Wrex—" began Sheffield.

"Competent as Lady Cordelia appears, she'll be a distraction if things turn violent. And we can't leave her alone. This cursed place is too dangerous."

His friend didn't argue. "Godspeed," he murmured.

The earl was already moving. The archway door was ajar, and he eased through the crack. A small domed skylight allowed in a glimmer of light, just enough to illuminate the figure standing still as a statue in the center of the gallery.

"I thought you might show up," intoned Justinian DeVere. "I'm sorry it's come to this." He pursed his lips. "Julianna is brilliant, you know. Absolutely brilliant."

"She's a vicious, deranged murderess," responded Wrexford.

"You don't understand. The murder of her parents was a grave shock at an early age. As a result, she suffers from certain unfortunate impulses. But these things often accompany genius. The result will be worth—"

"Don't you dare seek to justify what you've allowed." The earl made to move by him. "Get out of my way."

DeVere caught his arm. "It's too late, I'm afraid. I regret what's happened, but we both know that scientific discovery requires sacrifices. I will make arrangements after tonight to have Julianna confined in a private facility . . ."

Wrexford heard a tiny *snick* as the other man pulled his hand from his pocket. Pivoting, he smashed his elbow into DeVere's ribs just as the scholar pulled the trigger of his pocket pistol, causing the bullet to shatter one of the priceless Oriental vases.

"Wrex!" Sheffield burst into the room, his own weapon at the ready.

"Take charge of this miscreant," called the earl, shoving De-Vere to the floor and breaking into a run.

Backing away, Julianna set aside the rod and snatched up a deadly-looking scalpel from the table of tools beside the trough battery. "You wish to cross blades with me? So be it—you need to die one way or another. I became quite skilled with a knife in India, as I studied anatomy as part of my scientific training." She glided forward. "So I'll take pleasure in sliding my sharpened steel into your heart for trying to stand in the way of Progress."

The silvery point flicked back and forth, like the forked tongue of a serpent seeking to scent its prey.

"You are welcome to try." Charlotte dropped to a wary crouch and shifted her grip on the hilt. She was no stranger to wielding a knife in self-defense. There had been occasions when she had been forced to ward off footpads. Once or twice, she had even drawn blood.

But never had the clashes been a fight to the death.

"I suggest you surrender," counseled Julianna. "Poison will be far more pleasant."

Charlotte slid a step to her left so as not to be trapped against a metal cabinet.

Flick-flick. The scalpel continued its sinuous probing.

"Because I *will* kill you. I *must.*" Her rising voice had a manic trill. "You see, the cards have predicted that I possess special powers and am destined for greatness."

Julianna was beyond madness, thought Charlotte, keeping her feet moving. Beyond humanity. She must find a way to use that to her advantage. In a battle of steel against steel, her adversary held the edge.

Think! What would Wrexford—the master of dispassionate logic—counsel?

Charlotte glanced around the laboratory. The earl would tell her to use her strengths—see all the little details, and then use her imagination to do the unexpected.

A faint hissing from the trough battery drew her attention . . . And all at once, an idea came to mind.

Edging back, she wove a careful retreat through the worktables and storage carts.

Julianna seemed in no hurry to end the cat-and-mouse pursuit. She came on slowly, with a predator's stalking step. "Surrender to Fate. It's no use trying to evade your destiny."

In answer, Charlotte slid through a gap between tables and grabbed up a large beaker filled with the electrolyte solution used to power the trough battery. A snap of her wrist sent its contents flying through the air.

Julianna let out a grunt as the liquid hit her in the face, splashing over her hair and the bodice of her gown. And then she laughed. "That's merely the excess fluid. It does nothing to stop my plan."

At the same moment, Charlotte spotted what she was looking for—a cut-crystal bottle capped with a silver stopper, sitting on a stone slab next to the voltaic pile.

Dear Cedric. She darted forward. *I won't allow you to be desecrated yet again.*

"*No!*" A cart toppled in a cacophony of shattering glass and thumping metal as Julianna realized what Charlotte intended to do and began a mad dash toward the trough battery. "*No!*"

But Charlotte was quicker. Dropping her knife, she snatched up the bottle and hurled it to the tiled floor. It exploded into a spray of shards and silvery droplets.

"You'll not use Cedric or me for your vile experiments!" she called. "His essence is gone and your devil-cursed dream is dead, as well it should be." Beside her, the metal conducting rod was vibrating against the stone slab, a gentle humming at odds with the terrible power coursing through it. "It's over. Now is the time to surrender to reason."

Her face contorting in fury, Julianna let out a wordless snarl. Her scalpel shot up, a lethal flash cutting through the lamplight as she suddenly threw herself forward.

In the same instant, Charlotte grabbed the rod's leather grip and raised it as a defensive shield.

Metal clashed against metal.

As if punched by an unseen hand, Julianna was flung back. Her body hung suspended in midair for an instant, steam spiraling up from her burnt hand. And then, hair dancing on end, she crumpled to the floor.

Hands shaking, Charlotte dropped the smoking rod. The reek of singed flesh clogged her nostrils as a deathly silence settled over the room.

Is it really over?

Swallowing against the burn of bile rising in her throat, she managed to shuffle over to where Julianna lay spread-eagle on her back, eyes wide open, mouth frozen in an O of shock.

"May God have mercy on you—for you'll get none from me." Indeed, Charlotte found that she felt nothing. No relief, no sense of triumph, just an overpowering numbness in every fiber of her being.

Suddenly too spent to remain on her feet, she took a seat on the overturned cart. The lamplight seemed to fade in and out, as if struggling to keep darkness at bay. Hugging her arms to her chest, Charlotte closed her eyes and allowed the swirling shadows to wrap her in oblivion.

CHAPTER 30

The silence was terrifying.

Wrexford pressed his ear to the closed door, praying to any god who would listen for a hint of Charlotte's voice. A whisper, a sigh—anything. His throat was suddenly so tight, he could barely breathe. He couldn't imagine his world without her.

Swallowing his fear, the earl cocked his pistol and eased the latch open.

The lamp flames—two white-hot spots of gold, unwavering within their glass globes—blazed with a blinding intensity. It took an instant for his eyes to adjust. Then his gaze was drawn down to the pooling light on the floor.

Crumpled silk . . . a slender ankle . . .

His heart stopped dead. And yet, somehow, he managed another step. And then another.

Relief slammed into his chest, releasing his pent-up breath in a rush of air. *Mahogany-colored hair*—not Charlotte's. As he crouched down, the acrid scent of burnt flesh filled his nostrils. He looked away from the ugly burn on Julianna's hand to the porcelain perfection of her face, looking so peaceful in death's repose.

A beauty that was only skin deep.

After taking a moment to close her eyelids over her sightless orbs, Wrexford rose, hoping against hope . . .

"Charlotte?"

No answer.

His boots crunched over broken glass. "Charlotte?"

Through the tangle of light and shadows, he spotted a flutter of movement. Charlotte was seated amidst the shadowed wreckage, head bowed, arms crossed and clenched tightly around her chest, as if holding herself together.

She didn't look up at his approach.

He slowly leaned down and touched his fingertips to her cheek. Her skin felt cold as ice.

"I'm here, sweeting. Come back to me."

A whisper of air—the first stirring of life. Wrexford dared to take it as a good sign. He shrugged out of his coat and wrapped it around her shoulders. Beneath his palms, he felt a shiver spasm through her body.

After brushing a kiss to her brow, he lifted her up and drew her close.

Thump-thump. The erratic thud of her pulse shuddered through the layers of wool and linen as their bodies fitted together.

"Charlotte."

At last, a reaction. The earl felt her hands slide up the slope of his shoulders and clasp at the back of his neck.

Thump-thump. They stood together, still and silent, as her heartbeat slowly steadied.

"Oh, Wrexford," whispered Charlotte, her fingers twining in his hair. "Thank you . . . Thank you for being . . . for being you." Her breath fluttered against his cheek. "A beacon of light in the unbearable darkness."

"When you're not facing them alone, things are never quite as black as they seem," he murmured.

Charlotte looked up, her lips quivering in a ghost of a smile before she made herself look at Julianna's lifeless body. "I cannot regret that she's dead." A swallow caught for an instant in her throat. "But no matter that a venomous evil was coursing through her veins, I didn't mean to . . ." She shuddered. "Lady Julianna came at me with a scalpel. I grabbed up the rod attached to the trough battery to warn her off. But she slashed out at me and hit . . ." It took a moment for her to go on. "You were a soldier. D-Did you ever kill—"

"More than once," he replied. "It's a profoundly wrenching experience, even when the act is done to save innocent lives. I thank God that it never became easier. But I also felt no guilt in doing what had to be done to defend right from wrong."

The color was returning to her cheeks. He hugged her closer, aware of how all his own sharp edges seemed to soften against her. "Come, let us sit." Wrexford perched himself on the fallen cart and settled her on his lap. Be it an hour or an eternity, he would keep her in his arms for however long she needed for the shock to subside.

Charlotte buried her cheek in the rumpled linen of his shirt, reveling in the warmth and the earthy scent of bay rum and male musk.

Wrexford. Somehow, all the little details—his shape, his textures, the rhythm of his breath going in and out of his lungs— had become so intimately familiar. It was almost as if he had become part of her being.

The thought was comforting beyond words.

Closing her eyes, she let herself drift away . . .

She wasn't sure how long she was lost in such reveries, but the sound of footsteps suddenly wrenched her back to the present.

"Wrex?" It was Sheffield's voice, she realized.

"Is . . . Is she hurt?"

"Just a little shaken," replied the earl.

"Thank God," uttered Sheffield. He came closer and ran a hand through his disheveled hair. "You gave us all quite a fright, Lady Charlotte."

She looked up. "I'm so sorry—I didn't mean to." A wry grimace tugged at her lips. " 'The best laid plans schemes of mice and men' . . . Speaking of which, how did you know where I was?"

"A Weasel," answered Wrexford. "Luckily for us, they are far cleverer creatures than mice."

"Hawk—"

"He sensed you were straying into danger," interjected the earl, "and followed you here. When he saw a light appear in the upper windows of the villa just after you entered the conservatory, he thought it best to come inform me."

"Apparently, he and his brother fought tooth and claw to come along with Griffin and his men," added Sheffield. "But Tyler convinced them that it might endanger your secret."

"Griffin is here?" she asked.

"He and his men just arrived and are dealing with DeVere," answered Sheffield. To the earl, he added, "In the commotion, I was able to spirit Lady Cordelia out of the villa. She insisted she was perfectly capable of finding a hackney, garbed as she was in men's clothing." He drew a breath. "And we both agreed you might need me."

"What was Lady Cordelia doing here—" began Charlotte, and then fell silent on hearing the clatter of hobnailed boots on the stone stairs.

A long shadow fell across the room.

"Hmmph!"

Charlotte winced as heavy steps scraped across the tiles.

"More dead bodies, milord?" drawled Griffin. "I've discovered Sir Kelvin Hollister's corpse in the conservatory. And now this."

"Be grateful for the courage of Lady Julianna's kidnap victim, else there would have been more."

"Indeed." The Runner turned from his examination of Lady Julianna and fixed Charlotte with a gimlet gaze. "Might someone explain to me what the devil is going on here?"

"It's a long story and will have to wait until tomorrow," shot back Wrexford. "Lady Charlotte is in a state of shock. I need to escort her home as soon as possible."

"It was Lady Julianna who stabbed Sir Kelvin," offered Charlotte, feeling the Runner deserved the skeletal facts. "They were behind the Bloody Butcher murders, but apparently they had a falling-out when Sir Kelvin lost his nerve about killing Lord Chittenden. She performed the grisly deed on her own, and then she murdered Westmorly when he tried to blackmail them over some incriminating evidence that he had overheard from Sir Kelvin. He, too, had to die because she feared he was about to crack under interrogation and ruin their momentous plan."

"*What* plan?" demanded the Runner.

"You'll have all the gory details in the morning," interrupted the earl. Before the Runner could form another question, he added, "Trust me, Griffin. I shall make you look good to your superiors."

The Runner considered the request. "Very well." Another glance at Charlotte. "I'll agree to wait—but only if you promise to meet me for breakfast at the Hanged Man before the magistrate makes his appearance at Bow Street."

"And buy you enough shirred eggs, fried beefsteak, and broiled kidneys to sicken an ox," muttered the earl.

Griffin's mouth quirked at the corners. "But of course. A man in my position can't live on patience alone."

"I—and my purse—will be there," said the earl as he helped Charlotte to her feet.

She didn't need to pretend her legs were wobbly as aspic.

"Now, if you'll excuse us . . ."

The Runner stepped aside to allow them to leave.

"This case gets more curious by the minute," he growled to Sheffield, once they were alone. "Who is Lady Charlotte? And how is she involved in all this?"

"It's a mystery to me," answered Sheffield with a straight face. "I believe she's a relative of Lady Peake and the late Lord Chittenden, but I really can't say any more than that."

"Hmmph." Griffin stared into the murky stairwell. "You've no idea why she's wearing men's boots?"

"Was she?" Sheffield assumed a look of surprise. "I'm sure Wrexford will have an explanation."

The Runner's eyes narrowed. "I suppose you also didn't notice that she's the same height and build as Phoenix, that elusive imp who seems to know about every bloody crime in Town before it's happened."

Sheffield rolled his eyes. "Are you suggesting an aristocratic lady dresses as an urchin and possesses the eyes and ears to learn all the hidden secrets of London?" He made a face. "Ha, ha, ha—why, that's absurd."

Griffin let out a low belch. "Yes, isn't it?"

"Come, aren't we wasting time with wild speculations?" murmured the earl's friend. "Shouldn't we be hauling DeVere's worthless carcass to Newgate? He knew his ward was guilty of murder."

The mention of DeVere diverted the Runner's attention from Charlotte. "Unless His Lordship has proof of DeVere's involvement in the murders, he will likely escape any prosecution."

"But he knew," protested Sheffield. "He told us as much."

Griffin's expression hardened. "That may be. However, to me, he claims he had no idea that his ward was engaged in anything but serious scientific research."

"The man's lying through his teeth."

"I don't doubt it. But without evidence to the contrary, there's nothing we can do."

"But that's bloody unfair," exclaimed Sheffield. "Four people are dead because of his spineless silence. And a fifth was perilously close to shuffling off her mortal coil."

"Aye, but much of life isn't fair, Mr. Sheffield," pointed out the Runner. He looked around and blew out his breath. "You and His Lordship, along with your various shadowy friends, have achieved no small measure of justice—Locke will be exonerated, the murderers have met with a suitable punishment for their crimes." He paused. "It may seem imperfect, but sometimes, despite our best efforts, we must be satisfied with that."

For a moment, Charlotte felt herself drifting away again. The hackney—Wrexford had somehow found a conveyance, though she couldn't remember how—was jolting over the cobbles and the darkness seemed alive, tugging at her consciousness with mist-chilled fingers . . .

The earl shifted and his shoulder pressed up against hers, the solid warmth of him bringing her back from the void.

Still, the oddest thoughts seemed to be spinning like whirling dervishes inside her head. "Tell me, Wrexford," she murmured. "Do you think it's possible to bring the dead back to life?"

He took his time in replying. "Science is all about seeking rational answers to the mysteries of Life. That does not mean they exist."

A very Wrexford-like answer, coolly dispassionate, brilliantly analytical.

But then, he surprised her by going on. "And perhaps that's for the best. Uncertainty challenges us. It keeps us from becoming too complacent." He drew in a breath. "If we knew we would live forever, I can't help but wonder whether it would rob us of our essential humanity. That our existence is finite allows us to feel emotions—joy and sorrow, loss and redemption . . ." His breath seemed to catch in his throat. "And, most important, love."

Charlotte leaned into him. It was strange, she mused, how his hard muscles and chiseled contours had come to feel so comfortable. A steadying presence, when her own equilibrium turned a little shaky.

"But love doesn't fit into a clockwork universe that runs with unerring precision," she pointed out. "It wreaks havoc with order and logic."

A chuffed laugh. "I suppose I'm learning from you that the unexpected or unpredictable adds a certain dash of color to the dull metallic turning of gears and levers."

"Now you are sounding like an artist, not a man of science."

"We've talked about this before—perhaps the two aren't mutually exclusive."

Charlotte curled closer to him, and slid her hand down to find his. Their fingers curled together.

"I hope not, because love . . ." She drew in a breath. "Love transcends all philosophical abstractions about Existence. This terrible ordeal has reminded me that Life— no matter the jumble of good and bad, of hope and fear—is so very precious."

"Indeed. Perhaps because life and love are inextricably intertwined." Starlight winked through the tiny window, tangling with the shadows. "You took on dauntingly difficult challenges because of love." A pause. "All of those who care about you did as well— the Weasels, Lady Peake, Sheffield, Henning, McClellan, Tyler . . ."

"And you?"

He tightened his hold, sending a rush of welcome warmth pulsing against her palm. "And me," he agreed. "Most definitely me."

"Are you saying—"

Wrexford silenced her with a gossamer touch of his lips. "There's time enough for talk later, when your emotions are on a more even keel," he murmured. "For now, let's simply celebrate that we're alive at this very moment, with the past behind us and the future lying ahead . . ." A smile quirked at the corners of his mouth. "Filled with all manner of surprises to bewitch and bedevil us."

CHAPTER 31

A celebration of Life. Wrexford smoothed the knot of his cravat into place and patted down the creases in his coat—

"Did I just see you taking an interest in your sartorial splendor?" Tyler came into the earl's dressing room with a pair of freshly pressed shirts in his arms. "I think I may swoon from shock."

"Feel free to do so," he retorted. "Then you may pick yourself—and your sarcastic tongue—off the floor and seek another position."

"Ha," sniffed the valet. "You wouldn't dare—for I'd take my secret recipe for boot polish with me."

"You're lucky I'm very fond of my Hessians."

Tyler eyed the earl's tasseled boots with a critical squint. "Do try not to muck them up. The shine is perfect."

Wrexford made a rude sound and went back to adjusting his cuff.

"Are you going somewhere special?"

"Nicholas Locke was released from Newgate last night. Lady Peake is having a small celebration at her town house."

"There is," murmured Tyler, "much to celebrate."

"Indeed, there is." Wrexford picked up his hat. After allowing a small smile, he descended the stairs and made the short walk from Berkeley Square to the dowager's residence.

Sheffield was already there, along with Lady Cordelia—who had a deck of cards fanned out on the tea table and was in the middle of explaining a rather advanced concept of mathematical probability.

His friend looked up. "We'll join you in a moment," he mumbled, before returning his attention to the cards. "I just need to grasp this one last point . . ."

Even more amusing was the sight of the Weasels standing beside the dowager. With their pristine clothing, carefully combed hair, and scrubbed faces, the earl barely recognized them.

"Ye gods—the little beasts look almost human," he observed.

"Yes, I know," said Charlotte as she broke away from her cousin to come greet him. "It's a miracle that I got them here without some noxious substance sticking to various parts of their anatomy."

"Miracles do happen," he quipped. Henning was also standing by the dowager; and for once, he didn't look as though he had just been dragged through a thicket of gorse.

Lady Peake laughed at something the boys said and offered them more sweets.

"I feel that I've been blessed with more than my share of miracles," replied Charlotte, flashing a happy look at Locke.

Her smile nearly took his breath away. Given the recent ordeal, her resilience was remarkable. But then, Charlotte drew her strength from principle and passion, not hubris and greed.

Wrexford tried to read in her eyes what she was thinking. But the quicksilver ripples were impossible to fathom.

She watched Locke respond to a summons from the dowager to come join her circle before abruptly changing the subject. "I haven't had the chance to properly thank you for everything, Wrexford." They hadn't seen each other since the awful events of two nights ago. "My wits were rather fuzzed on the ride home from DeVere's villa. I . . . I fear I was rambling and not making any sense."

Is she regretting the mention of love?

"Understandably so." Keeping his tone light, he offered her his arm. "Shall we fetch some champagne? A toast to the triumph of Good over Evil seems in order before we move on to more murky subjects."

Shadows tangled with contradictions—was that how he saw their relationship? They had gone to stand in a quiet spot by the mullioned windows, and though a gold-tinged glow illuminated its every chiseled plane and hollow, his face remained a cipher.

"To Light winning out over Darkness," said the earl, lifting his glass in salute.

Repressing a sigh, Charlotte took a sip, making herself savor the sweet effervescence of the wine and the sparkle of sunlight winking off the cut-crystal goblet. "Only because of you and your logic."

"No, only because of you and your determination to hope against hope." A flicker seemed to stir beneath his dark lashes. "You wouldn't give up."

Charlotte made a wry face. "Yes, well, you know how stubborn I am."

"And courageous and compassionate," he said softly.

"I . . . I couldn't have done it alone."

"You didn't have to."

His words stirred even more uncertainties. "Only because . . . only because you felt obliged by a sense of gentlemanly honor to help."

"I didn't do it because I felt an obligation, Lady Charlotte."

"And yet . . ." Confusion caught in her throat. She knew the word *love* had been mentioned during the ride home. However, their emotions had been overset. And given his puzzling detachment over the past few weeks, she assumed he had come to regret showing any chink in his armor.

"And yet the truth is, I've no right to keep tangling you in my problems," she went on. "God knows, I've turned your orderly world upside down."

"Strangely enough, I find that tumbling arse over brainbox is rather exhilarating."

"But . . ." Charlotte stopped. Was that a gleam of laughter in his eyes?

"The truth is," went on Wrexford. "Given all the worries weighing on you in recent weeks—your revelations about your past, your cousin's murder, your momentous decision to reach out to your family—I felt it unfair to press for any discussion of personal feelings."

"I . . . I thought perhaps you wished to distance yourself from me and my havey-cavey household," said Charlotte in a small voice.

He suddenly looked a little vulnerable. "And I thought perhaps you wished for me to do so."

"I feared . . . I don't know exactly what I feared." She hesitated. "I'm a coward about a great many things."

Wrexford touched her cheek and a crackle of sparks shot through her body. "You're the bravest person I know."

"Ha! All too soon, I must face my first ball, a prospect that is even more frightening than blades, bullets, and . . ." She drew a shuddering breath. "And that terrifying force we call electricity."

"Power can be used for good, as well as evil. I sense that in the right hands, electricity will be a positive force," said Wrexford. "But for now, let us deal with the next few steps in front of us."

"Seeing how many missteps I made in this investigation,"

replied Charlotte, "I had better have another practice session on the waltz with Tyler and McClellan if I am to avoid making a complete cake of myself."

He took her hand. "Remember, you promised the first dance to me, so be assured I'll steady any stumbles."

Her heart fluttered and kissed up against her ribs. For the longest time, she had told herself that strength could only come from within. That might have been true in the past, but not any longer.

"Knowing I'll have your support is more comforting than you can possibly imagine."

"Then it's settled. When the time comes, we shall dance your first waltz together—"

A loud *thump* interrupted him as the dowager rapped her cane on the floor. "Hear, hear, everyone. Let us come together for a toast."

"And then . . ." Wrexford turned and drew her toward the gathering circle of family and friends.

"And then," he murmured, "who knows where the spins and twirls will take us?"

AUTHOR'S NOTE

An author gets amazingly lucky when history proves to be stranger than fiction! A key to the plot in this book is an obsession with bringing the dead back to life through the power of electrical current. And while that idea may seem merely the stuff of science fiction—Mary Shelley's *Frankenstein* is, of course, the iconic example of imagining that sort of scientific discovery—Shelley's plot wasn't a mere flight of fancy.

In 1802, Alexander Volta invented the voltaic pile, an early type of battery that generated electricity through chemistry. The discovery ignited great excitement throughout the scientific world, as it was thought that this new, wondrous force would hold unimaginable possibilities for changing the world. (And, of course, it did! Today we can't imagine a world without electricity, and all the myriad ways we've harnessed it to do our bidding.)

However, in Regency times, the idea that the current generated by voltaic piles could reanimate the dead was the focus of serious study. When early experiments showed that the legs of dead frogs could be made to move when current was attached to them, it sparked all sorts of speculation. Men of science like Luigi Galvani and Giovanni Aldini were sure that the secret was there—they just had to find it! There were all sorts of debates about "life forces," which went on well into Victorian times, and the race to be the first one to change life as we know it did indeed become an obsession to some. So, alas, the gruesome experiments performed on cadavers that are described in the pages of the story are all taken from actual history!

Galvani, Aldini, and Volta are all real historical figures, and I've used various aspects of their work to shape my plot. I also mention real-life luminaries of the London scientific community of the day, including Humphry Davy and John Children, as well as the famous Royal Institution—whose present-day administrators were exceedingly gracious about my committing mayhem within its august walls when I paid them a visit during a recent research trip to London. However, my villains, and the madness behind their idea of how to reanimate the dead, are purely fictional.

On a lighter note, Kensington Palace, a lovely redbrick royal residence set in Kensington Gardens adjacent to Hyde Park, did host many scientific soirees during the Regency era. The royal Duke of Sussex (a title now held by Prince Harry), one of King George III's younger sons, was very interested in science and often hosted gatherings in his apartments there. And as described in the book, he was very fond of birds and allowed his flock to fly around the residence! You can read more about the history of Kensington Palace under the "Diversions" tab on my website (www.andreapenrose.com), along with other fun highlights of Regency history.

As I've said in the Author's Notes of my previous books, one of the reasons I love writing in the Regency era is because it's considered the birth of the modern world. In every aspect of society—science, politics, social conventions, art, music, literature—radical new ideas were clashing with the thinking of the past. The world was changing at a rapid-fire pace, and that was both exhilarating and frightening. So, in many ways, it's a mirror of our own times, especially as new technology—and discoveries such as how to generate electricity—was one of the elemental forces driving change.

For those of you interested in reading more about the Regency era, *The Birth of the Modern: World Society 1815-1830* by Paul Johnson gives a wonderful overview of the world and how it was changing during the early 1800s. And for those who wish to read more on the electrical experiments to reanimate the dead, a fascinating book is *Raising the Dead: The Men Who Created Frankenstein* by Andy Dougan. —*Andrea Penrose*

ACKNOWLEDGMENTS

Writing entails much solitary effort, which makes me even more grateful for all the wonderful people who help bring a book from that first faint glimmer of an idea to the printed (and digital) page.

Many thanks go to my wonderful agent, Kevan Lyon, for her guidance and encouragement in navigating the ever-changing waters of modern publishing. And I'm incredibly grateful to my fabulous editor, Wendy McCurdy, whose suggestions and counsel always make me a better writer.

I'm also sending heartfelt shout-outs to special friends . . .

To "Professor Plotto," whose astounding breadth of knowledge—from the esoteric to the sublime—is a source of constant inspiration . . .

To my amazing blog group, The Word Wenches—Joanna Bourne, Nicola Cornick, Anne Gracie, Susanna Kearsley, Susan King, Mary Jo Putney, and Patricia Rice—who are always there with a cyber crying towel and a virtual slug of single malt scotch! I'm extraordinarily lucky to have such wonderful brainstorming partners and beta readers. But most of all, I'm extraordinarily lucky to have such wonderful friends . . .

To Lauren Willig, for our Yale Club cookie talks . . . to the Saybrook Fellowship, whose collective creativity and scholarship are constant reminders that books and ideas make the world a brighter place . . .

And lastly, hugs to all the PR, production, and art staff at Kensington Books. You guys are the best!